The Proper Order of Seasons

a novel

KIMBERLY BAKER JACOVICH

<u>For If They Fall</u>

"The entire story has been such a wondrous adventure of love, prejudice, faith, history, fear and trust – and consummate writing skill. You have created a story that will last, in my heart for a long time." Luvnheath

"…this long and absorbing story … was monumental in its scope. In places, it was harrowing to read, your description of Maria's madness was stark and chilling, a fine piece of writing." Nlindabrit

"I was drawn to this story from the opening chapter, and the biblical quote with which it began ~ It hooked me immediately and what followed has, in my opinion, been a masterpiece in writing. The prose and the story were compelling and it quickly became a must read. It has been a most remarkable read." JV

"Congratulations on completing this tale. … truly remarkable writing and depth." Tamsin1

"I am sorry to see this wonderful story come to an end. Your prose was marvelous. It takes a very fine words craftsman to make words read so aesthetically pleasing – so lyrical … Like another writer who I read about recently who when he was on his game, his prose was "always rhythmically on beat…" That's a real gift. It was "Too Brief a Treat" as far as I'm concerned. You reminded us that in a world filled with sadness and suffering, dreariness and depression, there is always hope, faith and redemption." Pat Maynor (Layla)

"Your writing is phenomenal." Lurker

"I was in both heaven and awe with your skill at using the written word. The story was great, but was a short second to your ability to write. You are a true artist." HOW2

"I have truly enjoyed this tale from beginning to end. You are certainly one of my all-time favorite authors. This story was magnificent..." bonniech

"...a wonderfully written story – true to itself from beginning to end. Your concluding paragraphs in your epilogue moved me to tears. (A feat which is not commonplace.) Oh, to write so eloquently! You have a gift with words." Sue

Before the Wind

"I just finished reading Before the Wind and I loved it. It's very rare to come across something so well-researched and thoughtfully written. Even more rare to find each character brought to vivid life ... You seem to have a deep understanding... Amazing scenes that are all the more powerful for the restraint you used. Really beautiful work. Before the Wind had the feeling like it came right out the center of you, like you wouldn't have been able to stop it even if you tried. I can't remember who said something along the lines of 'Write about your passions because it will show', but I think it's great advice and obvious in your work." Eileen trueenough

To See You Again

"Your story is really great; and your writing magnificent. It is also a breath of fresh air. You write really well. Really, really well." "This was really great ... a gem. Sparkling like a perfect sapphire in a bed of new fallen snow. You really do have the gift." Kit Prate, author of *Sharpshooter*

"You are bringing this [story] to a close with the same brilliance with which it began. I am awed." Lacy

"You have a great talent and I'd love to see more of your work." Rhonda Bonderson

"This was a wonderfully told story from go to whoa; very heartfelt and emotional." Helen Cooper

"Great story, beautifully written with very well-developed characters. I eagerly waited for each chapter which speaks highly of the writer." Patricia Limbrick

"I had to tell you how marvelous I think your story, "To See You Again", is – savoring the last chapters. It has some keen psychological insights and great writing." Starlit Drifter Julia

"Your writing is very good and deals with complex events and emotions. You have a great talent." Susan Wilburn

Cover Art: Sunlight and Shadow by Julian Onderdonk
1910 oil on canvas Public Domain

ACKNOWLEDGMENTS

To all those who have offered kind words over the years
~I remember & thank each of you.

The author acknowledges the following books: George Bird Grinnell, *The Cheyenne Indians,* University of Nebraska Press, Bison Book Edition, 1972; William A. Fletcher, *Rebel Private: Front and Rear,* Meridian, an imprint of Dutton Signet, a division of Penguin Books USA Inc., 1997; Randolph B. Marcy, Captain, U.S. Army, *The Prairie Traveler,* Perigee Books, The Berkley Publishing Group, a division of Penguin Putnam, Inc., 1994

*The Volunteer or It Is My Country's Call by Harry MacCarthy, 1861   *The Raven by Edgar Allen Poe, 1845

For
My husband Paul,
My son Taylor Evan &
My daughter Mackenna Jane, with all my love.

And for my grandfather, William Joseph Conroy,
the original storyteller.

To everything there is a season,
A time for every purpose under heaven:

A time to be born
and a time to die;
A time to plant,
and a time to pluck that which is planted;
A time to kill,
and a time to heal;
A time to break down,
and a time to build up;
A time to weep,
and a time to laugh;
A time to mourn,
and a time to dance;
A time to cast away stones,
and a time to gather stones together;
A time to embrace,
and a time to refrain from embracing;
A time to get,
and a time to lose;
A time to keep,
and a time to cast away;
A time to rend,
and a time to sew;
A time to keep silence,
and a time to speak;
A time to love,
and a time to hate;
A time of war,
and a time of peace.

Ecclesiastes 3:1-8

CONTENTS

BOOK ONE

prologue.

He walked alone with her bundled in his best blanket, the horse stepping lightly beside him. He had found a stand of trees close by a clear running stream. She would be pleased with his choice, but he feared for water haunts that might carry her away. She, of course, would laugh at his superstitions. She had taught him well the white man's ways, their language, their laws, and their practice of ciphering. He learned quickly, and she had said he was very clever. It had pleased him due to her pleasure from it. He stopped the horse and lifted her from its back, finding the grandest and prettiest of the trees. It was difficult work, but he had finally positioned her just right in a cradling bough as a baby in its mother's arms. He began to wail and undo the plait of his long hair, sawing through a handful with his knife. His son had been left where he had been killed, covered with a buffalo robe, allowing coyote and wolf, bear and eagle to scatter him over the land. In his anguished heart, he felt deep loneliness stir and his one thought that renewed him was this: a son for a son.

Nathaniel

He rode on, outracing winter. It was December, mayhap his birthday. Another upon him with little ado, near to seven months after Lee's surrender and Johnston and Sherman's armistice. Without consent, he had left then with another, traveling westerly to Alexandria, locating a federal headquarters to register and obtain parole, but soon parted ways when told Texans were not welcome due to horse stealing claims.

At the war's onset when dreams still sprung up from him, he with much ritual tracked and numbered his days, etching in his mind the pleasant imaginings of his homecoming. But when receipt of a soiled and tatty missive arrived, carrying word his heart and mind spurned, home was no longer of import.

It was after Gettysburg when the letter had reached him, nearly eight months delayed, and he'd sat himself beneath the full shade of a rhododendron bush, grown taller than a man, to read it. Too long without word from home, his hands palsied, eyes straining at his brother James' cramped script. As he read, the life left him, never to be recovered. He held an epistle of falsehoods in his grip, utter lies, and he denied it as a nonbeliever denying holy scripture.

He now took out that selfsame letter from his coat pocket, his long fingers running along its ragged edge. No need to open it, the words never forgotten, a dirge in his mind:

With pen in trembling hand this morning, the 15ᵗʰ of October in the year of Our Lord 1862, I send word of the Deaths of your Wife and Daughter. Nearing the stroke of Midnight, Jane McPherson Keegan commenced to breathe no longer and shortly thereafter, the babe, Molly followed, taken by the Fever that has darkened our doorstep and that of our neighbor's. Gone home to rest in God's Heavenly Kingdom. Be assured there will be a proper and fitting Christian Burial.

Five years gone and still incomprehensible to him. He'd damned himself for not having felt the loss. Certain, at the precise moment of their passing, his heart would have ruptured. After months roaming the Paha Sapa*, he had not yet healed, but he at last decided it was time. So, nigh to six years later, he urged his mount southward traversing pine forests and switchbacks, grass prairies and mountain paths.

He wore a Confederate gray slouch-brimmed hat and a red flannel shirt, sutler-bought on a whim, remembering it to be her favorite color. All else was made by his own hand, buffalo skin leggings, leather breeches, a deerskin coat and moccasins of deer elk. His long hair, the color of chicory, was tied back at the nape with leather cording. He kept his face clean-shaven. His blue eyes were war-hardened, fierce with loss. The horse he rode was true and strong, and never faltered under the heavy load of six beaver traps, a blanket roll, an extra pair of moccasins,

---

*The Black Hills

a butcher knife, a hatchet, and a wooden box for beaver bait. He held his carbine in his hand, resting it lightly on the saddlebow.

He moved over the loose shale and on past scrub juniper and pine, riding the horse like liquid, with only the muted thud of unshod hooves and creaking tack. The day turned warmer, the cold morning rains over midway into the foothills, the sky cloudless and blue. But it would soon be dark, the sunlight snuffed out like thumb and forefinger to a candle's flame.

He remembered his boyhood days with affection, but his current state turned the memories gloomy, certain the weaving of his life would remain fraught and fated. In the flyblown world so recently weathered, he believed even the strongest of men would have fallen to madness or mindless violence. And the questions again dogged him as the winds wailed, hearing Jane.

What insidious choice had been made to have led him here? Now alone, wretched, a heart in despair, losing the ones most dear to him, spilling from his cupped hands, through his fingers, water through a sieve.

The family that remained would be his saving grace, bringing him some comfort to think this true. He slowed his horse to a stop and pulled out a pocket watch from his vest, shifting loyalty oath papers aside. He pushed down on the winding stem, opening it, and ran the ball of his thumb over a lock of blonde hair secured there. He whispered: "Deo Vindice*." Closing the lid and returning it to his pocket, he rode on.

---

* God will vindicate Motto of Confederacy

Burnet County, Texas
January 1866

John

Crouched on his heels on the barn roof's spine, John Keegan regarded the approaching stranger on horseback with his quick bottle-green eyes. As if to warn him off, he stood to full height, long-boned and well-muscled. The wool coat he wore was buttoned up to his chin and his wide-brimmed hat was pulled low against the winter winds, covering long, light hair. When he squinted a bit, he saw something familiar in the way the man held himself as he rode.

Against his will, John felt hope growing, though mindful the outcome would be the same. He shook his head and bit his bottom lip, tasting blood, surprised at the pinch of tears. A bitter lesson learned that no good came from dwelling on things that couldn't be changed, so he promptly broke off from it. He folded himself back into a crouch, grabbed the hammer from his work belt, and commenced with his labor.

Near to a quarter hour later, the rider came into the courtyard. John watched with growing curiosity. Joseph, his father, a tall man with close-cropped light hair and similar eye coloring to his own, watched the rider as well from the large porch of the white clapboard house. A Connecticut Yankee, born and bred, he had come to Texas in 1840, just after the Texas Revolution, settling the family in the sweeping lands of

22

Robertson's Colony, becoming Burnet County in 1852, with its bountiful prairie grasses, timber and rich soil.

His father would often tell tales of the journey and how he had always longed to travel to far off places, dreaming of the West at a time when many were not so willing to risk their *hair* for land. Although, his father declared, it was their mother, Mary O'Brien Keegan, who had been the most persuasive, pushing him to act as she packed up their belongings at nearly the moment she had first heard him speak of Sterling Robertson and Moses Austin's land grants, and he barely time to entertain the notion. John's father and mother with his older brother James in tow, made their way to Texas soon after with more gumption than sense.

With the War between the States' end, Texas was again being settled, making the old Cheyenne, Two Crows, who squatted their land unopposed, greatly uneasy. But his older brother James, had been jubilant, no doubt, due to the arrival of the Federal Colonel Thomas Langford and his daughter, Isabel, comely and of the appropriate age.

John tried to catch his father's eye, but saw that the stranger on horseback held his father's attention. He couldn't stop from thinking his father saw something familiar in the rider, too. *But then again, why would he?* From John's vantage on the rooftop, the man looked more like a lost soldier, one of the many casualties of war than anyone his family would be acquainted.

Just then the sun broke through a layer of clouds and shone down on the man on horseback, lighting him up like a saint on one of his mother's holy cards. To John's thinking, the man didn't look quite so grand, but there was something about him, something different from all the other drifters passing through to God knows where.

Joseph

A few minutes later, the rider drew up to the porch and stopped. Without invite, he swung his leg over the saddle and its trappings. Joseph Keegan watched from the top step while the man walked the horse to the yard rail and looped the reins around it. He couldn't see the face beneath the broad hat brim. The man held a new Sharps Carbine in his hand, an 1865 model absent of bayonet lugs.

"State your business, stranger," he said.

"I've come home, Pa."

Joseph was stunned by those words, his anger flaring. *Liar! My son is dead,* he nearly shouted, but instead found himself saying, "Show me your face. I can't make you out."

The man lifted his hand to his hat, letting it slide down his back, the buckskin hat strings catching at his throat. "I've come home."

Joseph's eyes widened, his eyebrows lifting. "Nathaniel?" he whispered and then hurried down the stairs. Exuberant now, calling out to his son, "Nathaniel! My God, boy, we thought you'd gone to your eternal rest."

Joseph heaved the smaller man up and into his muscular arms, smothering him into his broad chest. He set him down and moved his son to arms' length and examined him, not trusting what he saw there. He touched his fingers to Nathaniel's cheek, wet with tears. Joseph grabbed up the boy again, running his hand over the dark head of hair, his own tears unconcealed.

When he found his voice, Joseph grinned and said, "Just wait until your Mama sees you. She'll be over the moon."

He took Nathaniel by the arm, speaking as he led him up the steps. "After Jane and Molly's passing, your Ma's not been the same. Not hearing from you, thinking the worst, well, there's no easy way to say it but straight out: Your mama took ill."

Joseph was quiet a moment, seeing the sadness come to the boy's eyes, so much like his mother's. He gave a pat to Nathaniel's flagging shoulder, and with a grin, said, "Now don't look so down in the mouth, son. Being here, coming home, well, I think that's just about the best medicine for her." His throat constricted, his voice cracking, saying, "For all of us."

John

The wide legs of John's pants flapped in the wind, the brim of his hat blown up straight. It was an unusual cold snap, but without a doubt a good blow was coming. John hadn't moved, watching the two men with interest. He was puzzled when his father held the rawboned drifter to him.

Snapping to, he skittered down the roof to a lower overhang and then

25

to the ladder propped against it. The only one who could move quicker than he, far lither, was Nathaniel. His brother was of a slighter, slender frame, wiry and fluid, able to climb trees and rock face easier than any creature birthed to it. With his mind on Nathaniel, he jumped down from the ladder at the third rung, impatient to get to the house.

He'd given his brother a year to write them, a year to send some word, to just come home. He'd seen many veterans of the war, so hideously maimed only those who loved them stomach enough to hold them in their gaze. He pitied them and was glad it wasn't him and then cursed bitterly for his cowardice, his judgments, and rational or not, he thought because of this Nathaniel was lost to them. It was obvious to John that God was punishing his family because of him.

Still believing this, he couldn't help but turn his eyes away when Tom Porter came to visit, a good friend to him before the war. His face was grotesquely misshapen from where a minie ball had struck, making it hard for John to look upon him. Tom seemed not to notice and remained in good spirits, explaining to John, all the while revealing his hideous grin, that ugly was better than dead. He told John that he'd been so scared so many times he'd wished he'd never signed up with Hood's Brigade what with him being only fifteen at the time and the Confederate Congress's conscription law of 1862 only applying to those 18 to 45 years of age.

John knew about the law. His father had used it against him so many times he finally gave up on enlisting. It certainly wasn't about the Confederate cause as his family were all Unionists, though unspoken.

But it had been about finding Nathaniel to make sure he was safe, which made him laugh aloud at the notion of his brother ever needing his help. There wasn't a better shot or woodsman than Nathaniel, coming by it naturally, but also owed to Two Crows' tutelage.

Of course, he could have signed up anyway, but his father and James together had been a force too strong for him. John still wondered how James managed not to be conscripted. He supposed it was because of those headaches James suffered. When they struck, he would crawl away and hole-up in his room for days like a sick and sightless animal. John could accept this, but he couldn't shake the sight of James giving money to a county official at the start of the war. It had come down to those who owned a certain number of slaves or could pay $300 or more avoided conscription. Most couldn't and took to calling themselves Common Men. He didn't give it much thought back then, being young and not yet knowing the nefarious ways of men. Besides which, his father had gained sizable political influence and James with him and because of this John had been certain his father would've done whatever he could to keep Nathaniel from the fray.

But Nathaniel had left without a word to anyone. Even his wife, Jane, had been given a bad shock, left with only the receding warmth of the bed where her husband had lain and a letter on his pillow. In those parts of the letter she'd been willing to share, Nathaniel claimed it to be his duty as a Texan and Keegan.

After hearing that, John hardly kept a civil tongue in his head whenever he spoke to James. He couldn't shake the feeling that somehow it was all his brother's doing. It should have been James, the eldest of the sons, who'd set off to war. His father was stoic, remaining silent on the matter. Much of his time was given to reassuring their mother and Jane the war would soon be over and Nathaniel would be home before Christmas.

It never worked out like his father had said, though, what with the years passing by and Jane and Molly dead, Nathaniel the same. A hard shudder ran through John and he felt his eyes fill. He swallowed and breathed in the cold air, settling himself, grateful at how good he'd become at harnessing his feelings, now a man full-grown.

Nathaniel

Nathaniel hadn't spoken since entering the home. Overwhelmed and fatigued, he could hear his father's voice as though from a distance. He lifted his head, turning his eyes away from the fire burning in the kitchen's sizeable hearth and looked around the room.

His father came up beside him, embracing him again. Nathaniel trembled at the touch. He could only think to blame it on the war and his own personal exile, no longer at ease with such intimate affection. Even so, he did allow his father to take off his coat, the hat left where it hung down his back, the carbine still gripped in his hand.

"Come see your mama."

He looked at his father and nodded. After a long beat, he finally spoke. "Reckon I'll give her a fright."

His father seemed to consider this for a moment. "It'll be a shock for sure, but it'll be a good one."

With each step moving him closer to his mother's bedroom, Nathaniel grew more subdued. He wasn't sure what to expect, blaming himself for his mother's ill health.

For a long time, he'd kept his own company, which now made it difficult for him to speak. There was a great deal whirling through his mind, but he lacked the natural way of conversing. His silence didn't seem to disturb his father, perhaps remembering him to be the quiet sort.

At the bedroom door, his father stopped before entering and peered at him. "You don't look well," he said, putting a hand to Nathaniel's shoulder. "Best be ready for your mama to do a whole lot of fussing."

Nathaniel smiled and nodded. His hands shook and his legs felt leaden, too heavy to move forward. He watched as the door swung open and saw the remembered wallpaper replete with tiny pink roses, the floral rows interrupted by family oil portraits.

He saw his mother in one standing alongside an ornate wood chair where his grandmother sat, a handsome woman, but stony-faced. His grandfather stood behind his mother, eyes bright and his hand resting upon her shoulder in a tender gesture. His mother had loved her father, his grandfather, greatly. He had died unexpectedly, a man still in his early years with tremendous wealth. His death had left his mother broken-hearted and under the full care of his grandmother, a woman whom his mother described as spiteful and mad as a hatter. At seventeen, she had run away with his father, eloping, against his grandmother's wishes, wanting her to marry a man of wealth and privilege.

Years ago, she had told Nathaniel this and many other stories of her life as a young girl in Manhattan and the happier days of summering in Nyack near the Hudson River when her father had still lived. It was not a place he ever wished to see, but he had loved the time spent with her.

"Come in. Come in, boy," his father said, coaxing him into the room.

Nathaniel turned his eyes away from the portraits hanging on the wall. He glanced over at the bed where his mother was sleeping. She wore her hair in a long plait, grayer than he recalled. Her face was as pale as watered milk, but still quite beautiful.

His father stood next to him and took him by the elbow, moving him toward the bed. Nathaniel stopped and waited by a tall bureau in the shadows, leaning his Sharps against it. He watched his father walk over to the bed.

"Mary," his father whispered, his words still reaching Nathaniel. He touched her shoulder and sat on the bed. "Mary, Mary, darling ..."

His mother opened her eyes and smiled. "Joseph," she said.

His father smiled at her and reached out, running a hand across the crown of her head. "I have something to tell you, something that will make you very happy."

She looked at him, her listless eyes seeming to brighten. "What is it, Joseph?" she asked.

He grinned and squeezed her hand. "Our boy's come home, Mother.

Our boy's come home."

His mother immediately searched the room. Her eyes stilled when she spotted him in the shadows, as he tugged at a loose thread of a doily. She sat up and held her arms open to him. "Nathaniel. Come here to me."

Nathaniel could see she was crying and went over to her, letting her embrace him. He lowered himself onto the bed, his father quickly sidestepping away, allowing him room. The sudden press of the man's hand was cool against his neck. He turned to his father, seeing him dab at his eyes with a kerchief.

Nathaniel looked back to his mother, staggered by her joy. He watched her as she studied his face. Then she reached out and touched his cheek and he started at the contact, from the coolness of her fingers. Gradually he relaxed as she stroked his hair, tucking the loose strands behind his ears.

"I've come home," he said in a low voice.

At that she drew him to her and held him close for a very long time. Exhausted, his head dropped to her shoulder, his eyes closing. The room was warm, her arms comforting, and his mind drifted. Foggy-headed, he began to mumble as if he were talking in his sleep, in a dream. He worked to rouse, desperate to shush himself from speaking, hiding away his sorrow, his heart rent years ago. He felt his mother release her hold and, blear-eyed, watched while she moved around him on the bed, dropping her bare feet to the floor. She stood and turned to him.

"You're not well," she said. "I want you to get in this bed right now."

31

Nathaniel shook his head. A cough started from deep inside him and he swallowed, subduing it. He shivered. "No, Ma'am. I can't do that."

"You can, and you will."

He mustered the energy to stand, shocked by his weakness. He shook his head. "Haven't had a proper bath in some time."

"Nonsense," his mother said. Without waiting, her hands began to work the buttons of his shirt, pulling his arms free from the sleeves.

He allowed her this, his father suddenly by her side, helping her. Through it all, he distanced himself from their efficient and at times intrusive handling, removing his clothing to his drawers. Exhaustion left him muddled, insubstantial.

At last they were finished, and Nathaniel lay on the bed while his mother covered him with a quilt. His eyes immediately closed, and he was very near to sleeping. But before he fell asleep, he realized for the first time in years, he was not afraid.

John

Although John had been anxious to find out who the stranger was, he took the time to put his father's old carpenter tools away in the barn. After completing the task, he strode forward looking only to the house, but spun his lanky form around at the sound of approaching horses.

From the porch steps, he watched as a group of men on horseback rode into the courtyard. Most were dressed in the skins of animals, and all were blackened by blood. Scalps strung on strips of leather were long before counted and divided among them. Though none were schooled, each, John was certain, understood well the ways of currency.

They were in Colonel Thomas Langford's employ. The former Union colonel paid them well to take care of the Indian problem, but he refused to pay the hundred-dollar bounty each scalp could bring them. Langford, a doctor before the war and four years through it, found the whole thing barbaric, distasteful, and turned a blind eye to the scalping. With cattle and horses stolen by the thousands, well over a half-decade, and again during the war when Comanche and Comanchero found the Federal Army to be a willing buyer of Texas stock and with the Rangers gone off to fight, folks had little choice, but to take matters into their own hands.

His father understood this, sympathized with them, desperate himself to end the raids and deadly attacks still occurring. Though he refused to pay these evil men who looked out at the world through predacious eyes.

Near to a dozen well-armed men came toward him and brought their mounts to a standstill some distance from the porch. Before John could call out to his father, the man was right beside him and his older brother James to his left, just then coming from the stable. None had any weaponry, only the courage of those who had staked claim to a land.

His father nudged him back and John found himself looking from behind the broad shoulder-tops of his brother and father. He quickly side-stepped to the right several paces, but stayed a foot back.

His father called out, "You're in trespass, Caden."

John looked hard at the man his father addressed. He was squat, quite short in stature. His brown hair was greased-grimed and stuck heavy and slick to his forehead. His eyes were gray like cold steel flint. The brim of his hat was misshapen, and John would have laughed if it weren't for the look in the man's eyes.

Caden held his father's gaze a long beat. His father was not afraid, but John felt fear growing in himself. His breath came short and quick, his heart beating a fierce tempo in his chest. He felt the sudden dampness of sweat on his palms and under his arms. His bowels clenched, aching him.

The round little man grinned. "You can take it up with the Colonel if you're a mind to. Our job is to track down and, if we see fit, kill all those thievin' savages. The committee's behind us and not a one of them's got a problem with us being on their land. Fact is they've welcomed us with open arms. I can't figure you out, Keegan, can't figure you at all, seeing you've been hit as hard as all the others. How many head of cattle and horses been lost to you just this past year alone?"

As John watched, he sensed his father wasn't having any of it, and choosing not to be drawn in, merely shrugged his impressive shoulders. It suddenly occurred to John that Jake Caden had not once unhorsed when near his father or for that matter, his brother James. He could only attribute it to the man's size, knowing he'd look the fool measuring only mid-chest to them. With this budding realization, John felt less afraid.

Caden was irritable, looking out into the distance for a time. "No matter," he said. "We're here on business. We been following an unshod pony, tracks led us here." A lift of his chin. "That black looks like the one I caught glimpse of with my glass."

John shuffled his feet and looked at his father. The men were mute, waiting. His father said nothing. Caden laughed and leisurely rested a hand on the pommel, reins loose in his fingers.

He said, "Folks been sayin' you 'n yours hold a kindness toward them that would take your hair whilst cleaving you from stem to stern. Hear tell one's living right here like he's family. Now that ain't right, Keegan, and if'n you've got another one about, we can't abide that. Ain't lookin' to cause trouble. Just hand 'im over and we'll be on our way."

John held his breath a minute and waited, wondering about the man his father had brought into their home. His right hand fisted for want of his Spencer. He looked to his left and studied his brother who was at first staring hard at the side of his father's face and then at the black gelding with its indisputable tells of Indian. The muscle in James' jaw pulsed and John saw plainly on the man's face the warring within him.

35

James had a strong hatred for Indians and John was uncertain what James would do. His brother had gone up against their father too many times to count. With Nathaniel gone, James had little opposition, their father too busy tending to their mother's ills. *Melancholia*, his father had called it.

It'd been difficult for John to watch his mother's decline, slowly fading away, hardly eating, sleeping too much. Those times when she wasn't, she'd taken to sitting on the porch in the same high-back rocker staring down the wide dirt track, waiting. The melancholia had come on his mother, little by little, after Jane and the babe had died. At times, he could still hear her cries, the sound of it coming back to him, stirring up in him, especially in his dreams. Over and over, she had called out the names of the dead in a terrible, shrill voice.

He'd been grateful when she had finally quit. He avoided his mother ever since as best he could. Ashamed of her, but mostly ashamed of himself, and believing there was nothing that could mark him a coward more.

His father suddenly stepped forward and gave a strong shake of his head. "It's my concern who lives on my land, Mr. Caden. Hear me well, you've tracked the wrong man. It's my son you've been following, just now come home to us after years fighting this terrible and cruel war. Too many years gone and exhausted to the marrow of him. He's been to hell and by the Lord's great mercy has found his way out. I'll not have you trouble him. Mark my words, Mr. Caden, you cause harm to what's mine and I *will* kill you."

36

At that John heard above him the sound of a window shoved up and a familiar voice, though deeper, raspier than he remembered, call out. "All of you men leave this land and don't come back. I've no fear of killing you."

There was angry grumbling and one of the men raised his gun and began to fire up at the window. John jumped at the sound. He started forward, but found he couldn't move, his father's firm grip on his shoulder holding him in place. James' face showed his bewilderment. The same look he wore ever since their father spoke of his son coming home. John's heart raced at the thought, thrilled, but then was instantly terrified Nathaniel would be killed. A cruel God to render such an outcome to one who'd survived all hardships of war. He felt hot tears and he looked at his father. He could see fear and anger keen in the man's eyes.

"Pa?" At first said quietly, but then he heard himself yelling, "PA!"

Without looking up at the window, John heard one report and the man who'd been shooting fell from his horse, the back of his head gone. The scalp hunters, at first laughing, were stunned to see it, and none stirred. In that moment, John chanced to move, his head bent around to see over the porch-roof. At an awkward angle, he stole a glance at the upstairs window. His breath caught to see his beloved brother, coal black hair falling over the carbine, a cheek resting against the stock as intimate as a lover. The fingers gentle, the touch quick, like he remembered. Another report, another man down who'd risked raising his gun and drawing bead on his brother.

John turned and saw his father was headed to the front door, somehow able to reach his rifle. *Was that his mother he saw through the door's dark screen?* He had little time to think about it.

Above them, Nathaniel shouted, "It'll be you next." John gazed upon the bunch and saw that the men knew exactly who Nathaniel meant. He was certain himself the black eye of the muzzle bore was aimed direct and unforgiving on Jake Caden. Nathaniel called out again, "Get off this land."

Two men lay on the ground, one on his back with no face to speak of, the other face-down, brain matter oozing from his blown-open skull. Caden glanced down at the dead men and then squinted up at the window for a time, his face knotted in anger. He wheeled his horse around without saying a word. A moment later, he stopped short and turned his head to look again up at the window. He gave an unamused grin and traced a finger across his throat. Once turned around, the band of men left in an unhurried trot, a tight circle around the little man, at least having the good sense to remove their dead.

John looked to his father, the man's eyes hot upon Caden's back. He spoke aloud as if the man could hear him, a heated growl. "Just try it ya bastard," he said. "Just try it."

John shivered at the tone, clearly not an empty threat, seeing his father for the first time as a man capable of dark and terrible things.

Nathaniel

Nathaniel lay shivering on the floor beneath the window, his cotton string half-drawers damp with sweat. He shifted and lifted his head to get a look at the wound in his arm. The blood pooled underneath him, darkening the floorboards. He lowered his head down, his mind vacant, his vision graying. His lips quirked up, a chevron of a smile, remembering his surprise at the give of his legs, his bones growing soft. At the time, he'd been intent on the fleshy one, he recognized as the leader. He had been gesturing at Nathaniel with such vigor, running a finger across his throat. It had meant to intimidate, but it was of no import to Nathaniel, having been in the bowels of hell and, by God's good grace, surviving.

He cursed, bringing on a bout of fierce coughing. His arm throbbed and the wind tore at the curtains, feeling the sharp cold bite of it against his chilled skin. Too weak to move, he closed his eyes, his mind drifting.

The odor of blood was getting stronger and he gagged, bringing up bile and haunts. He worked to fix his mind on something else, but the more he struggled against it, the quicker it came upon him. He could not stop the turn and fall of his brain.

"No!" he shouted to the empty room. He tried to push up from the floor but had no strength. *Damn it to hell!* He could feel tears cold on his face. *Libera nos a malo...deliver us from evil.*

The wind chilled him, the smell of blood rank. He could no longer hold it back, trundling forward like a storm.

He was back there again, as real to him as that day in the autumn of eighteen hundred and sixty-three. That September morning had been cold when the boys of the 5th Texas were ordered again on the march. They roused slowly, gathering their rifles, canteens, blankets and haversacks, joking and grumbling all the while. Once on the move, the singing commenced first low and soft, and then gradually blooming into a stirring version of "The Bonnie Blue Flag." For miles, they sang out, paying no heed to the order to keep quiet. Soon, however, their march turned silent, as it was the practice that the closer to battle the men kept their own council, summoning courage, making peace with God, convincing themselves not to run every step taken forward, perhaps, to their death. Most held steady, trudged on, faces affectless, accepting.

When the 5th Texas arrived at the battle, it was in full-swing. Orders were shouted out to get down and stay flat. From Nathaniel's position, he could hear the rattle and hiss of carbine balls coming straight off their very own front, too close for his liking. Then suddenly there was shouting all around him to fix bayonet, to charge, and he found himself pressing on into it.

In Nathaniel's mind, it felt like no time at all, when the Yankees had begun to retreat, high tailing it toward a worm rail fence where most had started their charge. A deadly mistake on their part, as all of them seemed determined to escape at the same time. They pushed and shoved against each other, only to jam up at the rail. The boys continued shooting at them, but Nathaniel chose not to partake, likening it to a turkey shoot with all but the prize.

At least, it would be a simple task to find their pards, all right there one on top of the other.

He had walked too many godless battlefields with lantern high, calling out the names of boys he'd come to love, hearing the far-off calls of others doing the same.

How many times?

"Too many," he said, answering his own question aloud, though he could barely hear his voice above the din. *Well, good for them,* he thought to himself, as he moved toward a farmhouse close to the worm rail fence. He wondered about the family who might still be inside the house as hell exploded around them. To think of his Janie or mother in the middle of such horror only served to make him sick at heart and stir his loneliness.

He lifted his head up and looked through the window, the panes still intact, though the walls were riddled with holes. There was no movement inside the house, though in his mind he could see the family tucked in their beds, sleeping, peaceful and unaware, knowing it to be untrue.

A sudden shot close to his head brought him around and back into it. He got off a few of his own from his position and then moved forward. He found cover and began to reload his rifle, biting the paper from the cartridge. He poured the powder down the bore and was about to ready his ramrod when he felt a sharp burning alongside his head.

He raised his hand to it slowly like in a dream, his fingers coming back wet. He looked down and blood ran into his eyes, blinding him.

Dizziness overcame him, and he knelt on the ground, retching up the meager breakfast he had that morning. He wiped at his mouth and then his eyes to clear away the blood. He stood up and staggered over to a large tree.

There between the broad tree roots an enemy soldier sat hunkered down and leaning forward over his crossed legs. He was young and close to death. When the boy straightened to look at him, Nathaniel could see he was keeping a tight grip on his intestines.

This one had just forgotten to die, Nathaniel reasoned and shoved him aside, nearly toppling him over a large root. Setting the boy to rights, Nathaniel then took the boy's spot up against the trunk. On a different day, he would have been ashamed and it did him no good to hear the dying boy's whimpering. Nathaniel shushed him when he heard shouting in the distance, straining to make sense of it. The order to charge did ring out clearly, but in no shape to fight, he gave himself permission to break ranks, a ridiculous notion to have in the light of the chaos. With his back pressed against the trunk, he began to shimmy himself up, feeling the scrape of bark through his threadbare coat. He gathered his footing and then without further glance or fuss to the boy, set off to find the nearest field infirmary.

At the rear, he entered the first tent he saw and searched around for an empty spot to lay down, wanting to be far away from the wretchedness. He snatched up some rags from a rickety table and eventually found a place to settle. He pulled together some straw for a bed and dropped to the ground. Closing his eyes, he put the dirty scrap on his wound. By then the side of his face was blooming with pain, his head weighted. In his misery, he thought about the young boy by the tree and his heart clamped shut.

He was penitent and started to pray, but the prayer was gibberish to his ears. The pain in his head was severe and sleep pulled at him. Though nearly done in, it was impossible to doze as the clamor of the wounded and dying woke him at every turn. At some point in the middle of it all, a surgeon, muddled from chloroform, treated his wound. The surgeon spoke only once, telling Nathaniel that those not submitting to amputation would quickly see their flesh corrupted, mormal.

And with that, Nathaniel's visions shifted to another time and place when he'd suffered a rifle shot to the foot. He'd shouted himself hoarse refusing amputation, making things clear with the point and press of his skinning knife. He hardly slept for fear of waking to a missing limb. But he'd been fortunate, his foot saved and intact, though he carried a prominent limp for well over a year, and still most days ached without mercy.

Everything came back to him amid bleeding out on a floor of his boyhood home, though outright gratified not to be nearing his end in some blood-soaked field. With that, his vision grayed, his brain teemed and ebbed no longer of use. In the distance, he heard the thumping of boot steps. The sound drawing closer as the door swung open. Nathaniel lifted his head a beat, groaned, and then fell unconscious.

Mary

They'd hoped against fever, but Mary saw it raging in her boy without need to lay hand upon him. His breathing was a wet rattle, his teeth chattering, his coughing nonstop. He fought the blankets, shoving them off at every turn. She couldn't deny the severity of his illness. The arm wound only added to it.

Another time she would have prayed for him with surety of faith, easily putting his life in the hands of God. But she no longer prayed, believing herself a fool to think she'd ever had God's ear. She often wondered if it had been after baby Jacob's death when the breach had begun. She was certain it had to have been a moment of such great and tragic influence to bring it to ruin in her. It wasn't that she disbelieved in God; she merely turned her back on Him as she felt He had on her.

With the return of her son, her spirits improved quickly. Always thin, she felt enlivened rather than weakened from her long months of meager eating. She was surprised to find her body immediately craving certain foods: potatoes baked hot and steaming with sweet butter within its rind, corn and carrot and lamb, all the tastes vivid in her.

She'd gotten dressed quickly, her mind on preparing him supper, a feast, hungry to take back her kitchen. But once more, God was cruel, like a trickster, giving her hope, kindling her belief, and she almost letting Him in again. She had offered a brief acknowledgment, Praise Lord, but to no purpose, turning away from her afresh.

By his bedside, her appetite damped the first time he vomited on himself while she was redressing his wound. She hadn't been prepared, not alert to the signs, maternal instincts lost or never carried. She felt herself wanting at every turn. He'd flinched terribly at the blistering burn of it on his open wound. He'd retched and strained against her, vomiting until his stomach was only an empty sac.

In his delirium, the screams and ravings tore at her heart, his howls of grief. She watched her son trapped in dark violence just as she imagined him throughout the pregnancy. Her sweet boy, her Nathaniel, when mere embryo, had grown for months within her with every beat of her tormented heart, trapped in the turmoil of the womb, ignorant of his begetting, *demonic and fierce*.

Suddenly her mind fragmented in brief and frightening images: unexpected light eyes, long black plait, a blooded, stolen cavalry jacket, epaulets of gold braiding on the shoulders. A child, her boy, caught up at his neck, his nearly white hair, bright as the sun, a swipe of a knife blade, gouts of blood, and then warbling, screaming, wild, raging, hurtling afar o'er heaven and earth, a mother's reckoning.

He came upon her then, the smell of him strong in her nostrils, choking her, bear grease and sweat, the sharp smell of hatred. Thrown down hard, her back struck ground, her breath gone out of her in a rush. One word over and over screamed in the pan of her brain, "Jesus, Jesus, Jesus." Her body collapsing, her legs spread and then pierced to the earth with a pain ferocious and unbearable.

She came back from that hellish moment of remembering, uncertain of the world around her. She sat motionlessly for a long time, her fingers

45

locked tight in her lap, tears and sweat on her face. She couldn't bear up to it. Not again.

From the bed, she could hear him moaning. She studied her child, his sufferings, and she nearly called out God's name for the sake of her son. Her fear for him was overpowering. She watched as his nightmares were vivid and cruel upon him, his horrors relived a thousand times. The mind was not able to stand such sorrow, best to slip away, the pain muffled, cowed, no longer remembered or endured. She started then down a familiar path, but stopped when the boy called out for her, plaintive and frightened and utterly lost. She heard herself talking to him, her words soothing, her voice low, her hand touching his face. "Hush now. Your mama's here. Your mama's here.

James

James entered the darkening room and looked over to the bed, surprised to see John curled up next to Nathaniel asleep. The sight of them stirred memories in him of a crude one-room log house and the simple pallet he and Nathaniel had shared up in the loft when they were young boys. He remembered the years of sleeping and waking together side-by-side and the comfort of his younger brother against him when the bad dreams came. He'd loved Nathaniel then more than any other.

What of it? In his mind, he said, *things change*. Even so, it couldn't stop the wave of envy that broke over him while he studied the two in the dimming light, their intimacy unspoiled and easy. Instantly cross when there was a loosening of something in his chest and his footing suddenly gone as a long-forgotten tenderness swelled up in him. Never one for pointless sentiment, it took little time to regain his balance.

A minute later, he walked to the bed and rocked John's shoulder hard a few times, waking him. He watched, amazed to see that John still woke as a child would wake, untroubled and unafraid, coming aware slowly, no flash of fear or threat crossing his fine, young features.

"John, get up," James whispered, his eyes shifting to Nathaniel who for the moment seemed to be sleeping.

It would soon be full dark and while John clumsily worked himself free of the coverings, James lit the bedside candle-lamps. The light from the hearth-fire and the two candles was enough to watch his ailing brother from the nearby chair. All would sup and then sleep as it was his turn to keep vigil.

John's voice came in a soft rush over to him. "He slept better me being there."

James looked at him and nodded. "You did right. No need to feel foolish."

John was quiet, rubbing at his eyes. "Curious thing happened when I climbed in next to him. What I could make out of what he was saying, sounded like, don't fret, don't fret. Then he'd pat my arm. Would only quiet down when I'd push up close to him."

James' face was a perfect mask while his heart hammered. Those words, though familiar, were merely a memory from a silent part of his life, an old life no longer his. He moved to the bedside chair and sat. He looked over at Nathaniel who lay on the bed stricken, near-dead. His voice was calm when he spoke. "Looks to be sleeping restful now."

John nodded. "Don't suppose you'd be doing the same for him as me, but it does help."

James heard the anger in his younger brother. It had been the same since Nathaniel had gone to war, the boy blaming him and James knowing he'd the right to it. An ache pinched at his temple and he rubbed at the side of his head. "I've been watching over that boy long before you were born."

John stood next to James, looking down at him where he sat. "I reckon those words are meant to reassure me."

James' head snapped up, his eyes burned. He said, "Take it the way you want." He looked away and then down at his hands. "Go. It's been a hard day for all. Go eat, sleep."

James remained in the chair, body rigid, listening to the sound of his brother's footsteps moving across the floor and then the opening and shutting of the door. A pain distinct, sharp, but this time to the heart. He touched a finger to his chest and said, "Damn."

Two Crows

Two Crows went upstairs and into the bedroom. He moved along the wall and then lowered down to the floor, squatting in the deep shadows. His long arms and slender brown hands rested on his knees, the feel of the worn buckskin soft against his wrists. He watched the boy struggle in his sleep, sweating hard and fighting for breath while the other boy, James, slept in the chair beside the bed.

He saw that the boy's tasoom, spirit, was near to release, soon to walk the hanging road. He continued watching until a slant of light from the moon came through the window and passed over the boy's face. Then from where he hunkered, he stood fluid and effortless, aware he could wait no longer.

Two Crows spoke the boy's name and Nathaniel came awake slowly, swimming up from sleep, his eyes cloudy, confused. He pressed a palm flat against Nathaniel's mouth to keep him from yelling out, not wanting to wake James. When there was a flicker of recognition in the boy's eyes, Two Crows removed his hand. He saw Nathaniel was naked save for his underclothes, so he lifted the blanket from the bed and draped it over the boy's narrow shoulders. They moved together out of the house and into the dark.

Once in the night air, Nathaniel began to shiver hard in Two Crows' grasp, though his face was slick with sweat. He could see Nathaniel's eyes were open, glassy and unseeing, shining with fever. They moved together across the open pasture land of the homestead until they came up on hardwood trees. Crowned by the trees was the Cheyenne's lodge. Two Crows led Nathaniel inside and lowered him down onto the thick buffalo robes with remarkable tenderness.

An owl then called in the deep night and Two Crows sang against it. He crouched down beside Nathaniel who had immediately fallen into a feverish sleep. From the fire, the smoke of the sweet grass rose and coiled. Two Crows caught it and cupped it in his hands like liquid. He began to purify himself and with the lingering scent of the smoke on his palms, he placed them flat on Nathaniel's chest.

He spoke to the boy, even though he was no longer conscious. He said, "Mat to' ho wat. To burn the sweet grass."

He picked up the buffalo-skin rattle and began the holy prayers, his face lifted, his voice plaintive, haunting. He shook the rattle over the bare chest to drive out the bad spirits. The scent of vanilla from the smoldering sweet grass tied to the stem of his pipe was strong in the close air of the lodge. Quiet, he hovered a time over the right side of Nathaniel's rib cage and then lowered down, his mouth open, and began to suck the flesh, drawing out the evil causing the sickness.

He sat up for a time, eyes closed, and then leaned over Nathaniel again. He held his clay-brown hands above the bare torso and then pressed both palms flat on the warm chest. He felt the heart beating, the blood pulsing, the lungs filling with air, all a bit stronger.

Two Crows shifted his body, feeling sore all over, and blew into the fire, bringing it up. Then he settled cross-legged on the ground across from Nathaniel. To his surprise, he felt something on his face, wetness

50

there. He lifted his hand and touched a finger to his cheek, struck by the realization he'd been crying.

James

James was deep in sleep when he startled awake, nearly pitching himself from the chair, at his mother's screams. His right leg had gone dead, no feeling in it at all, and when he stood he felt it begin to collapse under his weight. He caught the chair back with his hand, keeping himself from falling to the floor.

Alarmed, he shouted, "Damn it! You scared the devil out of me!"

It was dark in the room, having blown out the candles hours before, the hearth fire only red coals. He worked to clear away his brain of confusion. It took him only a single moment more to register that the bed was empty and with a hurried glance around the room saw there was no sign of Nathaniel.

"Where the hell is he?" He looked over at his mother. Her screams had stopped, turning into hard-wracked sobs. In between the sobbing she muttered, "My boy, my boy."

This did nothing, but anger James, already feeling the blame and hating the guilt he felt growing there in him. *How was he to know Nathaniel would wander off?* The boy had been out of his head all night, not a moment coherent to be able to navigate himself out the door. Who had the right to cast blame on him for falling asleep? He'd been all day felling trees for the winter's wood, checking the cattle and fence lines.

A full day's work. James' anger was gaining the more he mulled things over.

He walked to his mother's side, the pain of needles starting in his leg as it came alive. He touched her arm in a small gesture of comfort, but then took it away. He watched as she wrung her hands in despair. He shook his head and turned to leave the room. When he got to the doorway, his father and brother, both sleep-tousled and bleary-eyed, were coming from their rooms. James paused there a moment and looked over his shoulder at his mother, memory strong in him.

It had been a month after Nathaniel had left, the day overcast, chilly. She stood in the doorway with the baby in her arms, the jamb supporting her.

"Leave me in peace," Jane shouted to him. "Go now!"

"I brought supplies," James said to her. "I know you've not been to town in some time."

"Go!" Jane went to turn back into the house.

"Take it for the baby, for Molly," he said. "Take it for Nathaniel."

"Don't you dare speak his name, James Keegan!" She spat, shaking in her rage. "Don't you dare speak his name!"

"I love him, too, Jane," he said to her.

"You've got a peculiar way of showing it, James," Jane said. "You send him off to war and you talk of love."

"Weren't just me," James said. "Nathaniel had a say in it."

"But he did it for you, James," she said. "You knew he'd do just about anything for you."

52

"It was his decision, Jane." James shook his head. *"He's a man grown. Why didn't you stop him then?"*

"I never got the chance and you know it!" Jane stood away from the door frame, clutching the baby against her. *"You know full well he left without a word, leaving only a letter and me with no way of telling him my feelings on the matter. And that more than likely your doing as well."*

"Think what you like, Jane Keegan, I can't change your mind. But I'll not have you starving to death because of your hatred toward me. That's my niece you got in your arms, my brother's child and she needs food like her mama needs food. You wouldn't want to harm your child. So take it and curse me all the while you eat. But take it just the same."

"I'll do just that. I'll do just that," Jane said to him. *"Leave it on the porch. I'm going inside out of this chill. When I come back out, I expect you'll be gone."*

James nodded, satisfied. "If that's how you want it. I'll be back next week. Mama's been asking for you. She's not been out of bed for a month, heartsick over Nathaniel."

"I am sorry," she said, *"but that's just one more thing to lay at your feet."*

James came around then to the sound of his mother's sobs. Anger and guilt raked through him, and with spite said, "You haven't voiced it, but I can hear your blame plain enough. Tell John I can use his help looking for *your* boy."

Two Crows

They lost hope. With spring, they moved across plains of blue gama and buffalo grasses, through forest land of post oak, blackjack and hickory, and then over grasslands of bluestem and switch grass and side oats. For weeks, the man and woman went on, and overnight spring was fast approaching summer.

One morning, they rode into a camp, a Conestago pitched along the bank of a small creek. It was quiet, the man certain everyone was dead, spirited away in the night. Pilgrims, his wife had called her people, crossing a great sea of grasses as they had crossed the great waters.

He swung down from the Paint and walked over to her. She was leaning against her pony's neck, fingers gripped its mane. He spoke to her, taking her from the pony. He carried her to the
wagon, lowering her down into its shade. He held her hand tenderly and leaned forward to kiss her. At that moment, he heard the snick of a hammer behind him, and then felt the bite of metal against his neck.

He went still, fixed as stone. "My wife is sick," he said in the white man's tongue.

"She's no Indian," the man behind him said pushing the gun barrel deeper.

"She is my wife."

"Wife? More like your prisoner."

"She is my wife." Long, brown hands dangled loosely from the round

of his knees, thighs and calves tightly coiled. After a moment, he was aware the gun was no longer pressed to his neck. Still in a squat, he turned. Over him towered a tall man with long, lank hair, damp with sweat, sticking to his forehead. His green eyes were wild, haunted, the darkness beneath them black bruises.

Sitting back on his haunches, he said to the man, "You are ill. I have medicines that will help." He stood up while the man thought this over.

"Medicine?"

"Yes, I can help."

The wildness in the pale eyes was replaced with hope. "It's not me that needs healing. My wife and son. My boy… he's dying!"

With a quick nod to the man, he knelt by his wife and finding a blanket put it over her. Her blue eyes opened when he lifted her up to drink from his water skin, and she smiled. He patted her hand and then stood, aware of the muzzle's black bore on him.

The man pointed him to the rear of the wagon and he walked over to it. A distant sound brought his head around and he looked toward the far side of the Conestoga. A dried hide of scalp clacked against the wagon in the wind. Long, limp strands of blue-black hair, dull even in full sunlight, was lashed to the wagon bed like a dark, ragged bird. Glimpsing a familiar amulet, he walked over for a closer look.

"Leave it be." The man grabbed his arm and turned him away from the scalp. Suddenly, the man bent over and began to retch. He watched the huge back bow and convulse with sickness. The man recovered, reaching for a canteen hanging on a stob, took a swig and then rinsed

the water through his mouth, spitting it out in a long stream.

The man turned to him, the rifle gripped in his hands. "I make no apologies for what I've done – only to my God. It was justly deserved."

With nothing to say to the man, he only nodded and walked to the rear of the wagon. When he climbed up and opened the canvas flap of the wagon, the coppery tang of blood was strong to his nose. It hung there in the hot, stale air. He could barely make out the woman and child so he moved closer. Linsey-woolsey had been wrapped around the boy's head. The woman lay next to the boy, her eyes opened, but sightless.

He squatted down beside the boy and unwrapped the cloth. While he worked to remove the bandage from the loose flap of skin, the boy moaned, but didn't awaken. Pulling the cloth free, he saw that the skull showed stark and white where the knife blade had sliced through, a sharp contrast to where the blood had blackened.

The man was there beside him, his voice a whisper.

"Please. Save him."

Two Crows woke from his sleep with foreboding, his ancient heart racing in his chest. His dream had been strong, haunting, and though awake, it took some time to center himself. At last no longer groggy, he pushed up from the bed of skins and robes and looked around the lodge. He froze, breathless, his heart hammering with the realization the boy had gone.

He took up his buffalo robe and draped it over his shoulders and got to his feet. He went to leave the lodge, but before he took a step the

56

younger boy, John, entered and stood in front of him. Two Crows had little time to recover when the boy started to question him in a high, breathy voice, looking at him through ruined eyes.

"Why isn't he here?" The boy's voice wavered. "This was my last hope." He dropped down into a squat, holding his head in his hands. "Son of a bitch!"

Two Crows set his mouth in a tight line. "He was here," he told the boy.

John's head lifted, his face strained with emotion. "What?"

"He was here."

"You let him leave?" The boy's disbelief plain by his tone. "Why would you let him leave?"

"I was not able to keep awake," Two Crows stated.

"Seems to be catchin'," John said. His words were sarcastic, disapproving. "You should've come for someone at the house. Pa's out of his head with worry and Ma's takin' to her bed. You must've seen he was sick." He lowered his voice and said, "I'm scared for him, Two Crows. Pa thinks he's got lung fever, maybe the grippe that took Jane and the baby. He can't die. I won't let him die. Not when he's only just come back to us. I'm never going to let that happen. Son of a bitch!"

"You cannot change what has passed." An inarguable fact, but Two Crows saw the boy did not understand, his eyes livid, his gaze ferocious upon him.

"Shut up! Just shut up with that kind of talk! I got no time for this." A sob came from him then. "Nathaniel thinks the world of you. And here you sit, saying something like that." He turned and left without a glance back.

Two Crows pulled the robe tight around his shoulders. He felt dizzy, his head booming. He sat down hard, his heart heavy with worry. Words came again to him from his dream about another. *Please. Save him.*

Nathaniel

In the soft orange light of the fire, Nathaniel had seen and heard the dead around him to the point of dread and alternate pining. Eventually, they had become corporeal, lessening the fear. When he saw Jane, sitting cross-legged on the robes, he wept. She came near and draped her body over him. To keep her there he wound himself around her, only to find he was on top of the ruins of a corpse, while the wailing of a Cheyenne medicine song filled his ears. He knew then he'd finally gone mad.

His daughter, Molly, appeared to him whenever he slept. It was a frightful visitation. Her black hair was curled into tight ringlets against her fine head the way he remembered it to be, but her blue eyes gleamed oddly. She held out her baby girl fingers to him and he saw past them to her withered limbs, a graveyard child. At the sight, he nearly scraped his face raw, clawing at his eyes. Rather to be blind than to see his child this way. But then he feared the darkness and stared for hours at the fire.

Jane was there again, outside this time, Nathaniel able to see her through the thick skins of the lodge. Her near-white hair was worn in a long braid down her back and she shone as bright and mesmerizing as the moon. She was dancing a Scottish reel around the fire. He watched her bare feet move deftly over the winter grasses, her arms held aloft. She tossed back her head in a full laugh, her steps without pause.

Sometime later, he left the lodge and held court with his wife and daughter in the hip-deep waters of a creek. With the moon waning, and the burning heat in him cooled, he went to the creek bank and stretched out fully on a buffalo robe, feeling the comforting press of them against him. He fell deeply asleep, waking only once, shivering. He tucked the robe under his chin to get warm, faintly aware they were gone. He wondered a moment where they'd gotten to, but before he could reason it out, sleep had claimed him.

When Nathaniel woke, it was still dark. He rose slowly, becoming dizzy as he stood, the robe forgotten by his feet. His legs barely held him, his eyes rolling. He steadied and looked out at the shadowed lands hearing the wing flap of bats and the sound of night creatures. He moved forward, making his way up a familiar hillock. On the other side of it was a white-washed house, a pale ghost in the darkness and over near the grove of oaks a creek cut its way through the earth. It had grown colder, and the wind came at him hard from the north. He shivered, lumbering his way over the dead winter grasses, and then moving along a wagon trace eventually turning onto a dirt path. He shivered again as if in a fit.

Once on the porch of the house, he stepped toward the door and lifted the latch. With a shaking hand, he opened the door, the moonlight slanting over him and into the room. He jumped back when he heard moaning, realizing it was only the wind through the stove's flue-pipe. His heart pulsed in his ear when he saw the daguerreotype of his wife and daughter on a small table. He picked it up, a white doily catching on it. His hands burned as they warmed up and he nearly dropped it. He set it back on the table, portrait side face down.

He looked around the room and then made his way to the bedroom. Once there, he sat on the edge of the bed and leaned back on his elbows, surprised by the bite of pain in his arm. Finding Jane's log cabin quilt at the foot of the bed, he pulled it over himself and immediately passed into sleep.

Later, he woke and looked around the room, knowing it was mid-morning by the heat of the sun on his skin coming from the small bedroom window. He didn't move, listening to the sound of his heart in his ears.

Adjusting memory to suit him, his heart sped up with exhilaration. He waited, listening, certain Jane would be calling out to him. The rational part of his brain spoke of its absurdity to think she was somehow in the kitchen preparing breakfast, but still he did.

He remembered how she would sing while she cooked. Her singing, which she did beautifully, always carried to their bedroom, pausing in the middle of a song to scold him saying all had been ruined because of his dawdling and again he listened, straining to hear her. It would be eggs and fried trout and bread baked fresh and he'd stand in the doorway watching her toil over the cookstove with Molly nearby playing on the deerskin rug.

While he ate, he'd hold Molly on his lap and feed her bits of egg and bread. Jane would already be outside scattering grain to the chickens and he'd watch her through the large south-side window facing the creek and oak grove. He'd study her, watching how the wind caught at the loose strands of her hair and how the sun quickly colored her cheeks. He'd rise then and cross to the window and tap on the glass to get her attention. When she would look at him, he'd point to the bonnet she never wore and because of that her hair was sun-bleached nearly white.

With her face, clear in his mind, he closed his eyes and drifted back to sleep. All things in his head began to run together in succession like stars in a constellation, producing their own perfect and proper order, their place necessary and appropriate in the world: the day of their wedding, the night Molly was born, the large and small moments remembered with great sentiment. It was a deep sleep that came to him, not allowing it to be ruined by all things unbearable.

Isabel

Isabel Langford had found the cottage the previous year and had worked to get it to its former appearance or how she imagined it to have been. She believed tragedy must have befallen those who'd lived there because of the disarray and apparent abandonment. It was Keegan land,

and the river flowing through the parcel was coveted by her father.

Thomas Mitchell Langford had been a well-respected doctor in the East, a highly ranked officer in the Federal Army and was currently trying his hand at horse-breeding. He was the most fair-minded, most kind, and gentle man that Isabel had known. He was also a man of honor and courage. Although the river clearly would open acres of grazing land for him, having the benefit of needed water, he didn't resent Joseph Keegan's flat out refusal to sell. Perhaps it was sentiment fueling the decision on Keegan's part as Isabel remembered the daguerreotype of a woman and child in the small home. There was also a crib and children's toys stuffed in a wooden chest and a beautiful wedding gown found in another. The thought of the family no longer there made her profoundly sad.

She often wondered about the occupants of the house and wanted to ask what had become of them on those occasions when she had gone with her father to the Keegan homestead. But the timing never seemed right, the question insensitive, inappropriate, and more than not she would be prying into things too painful for the family.

On her first visit with the Keegan's, Isabel had liked Mary right from the start. She seemed to be as wanting of female companionship as Isabel, herself. For many years, it had only been Isabel and her father. Her mother had died when she was very young and her father never chose to remarry, although many women made their intent clearly known.

As a young girl, Isabel had boarded and studied at Miss Porter's

School in Farmington, Connecticut. She became interested in the Arts, dance being her first love, although she felt she lacked the long-limbed elegance and delicate grace of a dancer. She viewed them as waif-like, almost ethereal. Her father indulged her and though she very well might have turned out annoying and affected, she was of a different nature, compassionate and generous beyond what others viewed as appropriate or sensible.

At twenty-four, she was unmarried, but was said to be quite lovely with her dark hair, intelligent blue eyes and slender figure. She'd had many suitors, but none she seriously considered marrying, all but one. She hastily tamped down those thoughts. Her father came first, although she did hope to someday find love and eventually marry. It wasn't the success or failure of the ranch that was important to her, but more the reparation of Thomas Langford's health and peace of mind after the terrible burdens of war. Isabel chose to forsake all things for him.

Her decision was easily made as the potential suitors in Texas were dismally few, far different from the social climes she'd known in Connecticut. She did, however, find it refreshing to be away from all the irrelevance and over-indulgence and pomposity of the young men, graduates of Trinity and Yale and Wesleyan, all with unimaginative ambitions and certain to become disgracefully wealthy, arrogant, old fools. She was too intelligent and too self-possessed, and held a deep romanticism, which did surprise her due to a past sorrow, to be stifled in any way. To her good fortune, her father secretly applauded her occasional indignant outbursts during those dull, obligatory dinner parties.

In a land that was sometimes harsh and unfamiliar and at times unbearably lonely, she did find companionship with the two Keegan brothers who were both very handsome and quite gregarious. John was a bit younger, she surmised at least by six years, and tended to stumble over himself whenever she was around, his lovely face holding a schoolboy blush. She found him endearing, quite sweet.

With James, she found it was his initial aloofness that drew her to him, her natural inquisitiveness getting the better of her, wondering why he held himself at a distance from her, though he was always courteous, almost pleasant. After a time, he became much more attentive as he and her father's relationship progressed into a close friendship. Many nights she would find James at the TML Ranch playing chess and talking horses with her father.

Thomas Langford had more than once mentioned that James Keegan would make some young woman a fine husband. Isabel, for the most part, agreed, but there was something not quite right and she'd not allowed herself to become too emotionally involved with him. She told herself it was for his sake, not wanting to hurt him. But in truth, she hesitated merely because of an odd feeling she had every time she was with him. She was being ridiculous, of course. Immediately, she thought of the upcoming spring dance, though several months away. James had asked her to accompany him and she'd accepted the invitation. When she'd told her father, he was practically giddy.

Burnet County was at times wild and lawless, but the dances held in town were civil having rules all had to comply with if they wanted to attend. No guns were allowed and had to be left at the general store. Since Isabel's arrival, she'd gone to several dances with her father. It had been an enjoyable time, even though there had been talk of brutal, lawless men roaming the countryside, as well as, Indians. Her father worried about her wandering too far from the ranch, but she couldn't imagine living her life sequestered, unable to breathe. Her rifle was never forgotten on her rides, and she was quite adept with it. While other young girls were learning household skills, Isabel was hunting grouse with her father, eating over an evening fire in the wilds of Connecticut's Northwest hills.

Isabel sat her horse and watched the quiet house. The cottage had given her a sense of purpose and satisfaction as she scrubbed the floors and washed down the walls, purchasing new floral fabric for the curtains and sewing a tablecloth and slipcovers to match. At times when she sat quietly in the warmth of the afternoon sunlight flowing through the windows, gratifyingly tired, she did feel, in small moments, as if she were prying, interfering in things that shouldn't be disturbed or intruded upon, no matter how well-meaning her intentions.

She imagined the woman and child she'd seen in the daguerreotype sitting on the front porch swing. She saw them there singing and laughing, enjoying the day, enjoying their time together. The man wasn't as clear to her, not having seen any likeness of him, but if a Keegan brother had lived there, he was more than likely tall and fair and quite good-looking. She thought back on her conversations with James, dimly recalling a brief mention of another brother. It was a passing remark and their conversation had gone off in a different direction. She'd forgotten all about it.

She dropped down from the horse and tied the reins around the porch rail. She stood there for a moment and studied the house carefully. She felt something was different. She looked at the river and oak grove, not noticing anything unusual.

Isabel pushed the door open and stepped inside, closing it behind her. Her eyes swept around the room and then focused on the union case holding the daguerreotype lying flat on the pedestal table, the doily on the floor. The hair on her arms rose and she shivered. She thought of her rifle still in its boot and she ran to get it. Usually level-headed, she heard the voice telling her not to go back inside, to leave. However, wanting whomever might be there out, far outweighed her fear, certain the intruder held little sentiment for the dead and their memories.

Her thoughts raced about her mind as quickly as her hands performed the task of preparing her weapon. She moved through the house with the rifle raised. She saw the bedroom door was ajar. Cautiously, she entered the room, her heart pounding inside her chest like a wild thing. She struggled to get air into her lungs.

The morning sun filled the room and there on the bed was a man asleep, light-skinned, but flushed. He was covered by the hand-worked quilt she'd found in the home months ago nearly destroyed by mice. She'd done her best to mend it. Her sewing was adequate, but could hardly compare to the woman who'd made it.

She looked at the man and saw he wore no boots, a scarred bare foot hanging over the side of the bed. He was quite handsome and her eyes were drawn to his hair, its color as dark as lampblack, finding herself lost in its length. There was something about the man, something as old as the land.

She started to call to him, but her throat tightened up and she felt breathless. She moved closer to the bed and lifted the rifle to the man's chest about to give him a poke when she heard her name being called from outside, bringing her up short. Her heart thrummed hard and fast in her chest.

The voice called out again, "Hello the house! Miss Langford, you in there?" She recognized it to be Billy Holmes, an older ranch hand at the TML. She stood still, not daring to look at the man on the bed. In that moment, she'd quickly changed her mind, hoping he remained asleep, not wanting an altercation between the two men. She immediately left the room and made her way through the house and out onto the porch.

"What is it, Mr. Holmes? Is there trouble?"

The cowboy shook his head. "No need to worry. Your Pa asked me to find you and send you on back home."

Isabel rested the rifle across the forearm of her plain wool coat. "My father would only send someone searching for me if there was something wrong. You may as well tell me."

Holmes smiled. "Your father reckoned you wouldn't just come along peaceable. All I can tell you is horses came up missing. Not sure if it's Indians or no-accounts. You ain't seen nothing out of the ordinary on your ride, have you Miss Langford?"

Again, she felt compelled to keep the dark-haired man's presence hidden. She said, "Nothing out of the ordinary that I can recall, Mr. Holmes."

Holmes nodded and looked toward the creek and then the stand of trees. He said, "Well, it's best to err on the side of caution, my Ma always said."

Isabel laughed. "Your mother is very wise, Mr. Holmes."

"That she was, Miss Langford." He thumbed back his hat. "You best come along with me now. There's been talk of Comanche. Ben Thomas's place got hit last week and Hank Lewis's two days ago. Jake Caden and his boys are out huntin'. Should handle the situation just fine."

Isabel looked at him and said, "And how does Mr. Caden plan on handling the situation?"

Holmes didn't seem to notice her irritation. He looked at her. "Any way he can, I reckon."

"My father would never allow needless killing."

"It wasn't just stolen horses." He paused a moment and looked at her hard, seeming to appraise her. He nodded, apparently concluding she wasn't of a fragile nature. He spoke low, "Ben Thomas' wife was killed."

Her breath caught in her throat. Although she tried to be courageous, she found Texas to be a frightening, violent country. Whenever she heard of cruelties, inflicted by man or the land itself, she had to force her thoughts to more pleasant things, sweeter times, or she would break down crying, fearing she'd never stop.

"Are you sure it was the Comanche?"

Billy Holmes was quiet for a bit. He turned his head and spat and then looked at her. "They're sure."

Isabel nodded and walked to her horse. She shoved the rifle in its scabbard and placed her foot into the stirrup. She raised herself easily into the saddle. She didn't dare think what lay ahead for the Comanche or the settlers. She prayed her father would be spared from misfortune and the Indians would be quickly brought to heel.

Her thoughts went to the man sleeping in the cottage, wondering if he might be ill, not having stirred at all. She was certain their voices carried into the house. There was nothing she could do to help him without Holmes finding out about him. It was plain he'd be considered a suspicious character. She could only wish for his safe passage. She sat her horse watching the house until Billy Holmes called her name. She turned away and followed behind the cowboy.

Joseph

Joseph came upon the whitewashed cottage, surprisingly well-kept. A miracle to see it this way, and he could not imagine how it happened. More than four years abandoned, not one of them the heart to go back. But Joseph came back this day with the world alive around him, close to midmorning. He'd an inkling Nathaniel returned to this place, couldn't help himself, but not. Joseph was certain the blame for all things was as bright and sharp as a lightning strike upon the boy.

It was a thing he couldn't quite name, just an ill-defined belief that as a boy Nathaniel decided to bear all sins. Perhaps it was a burden drawn from his violent begetting, predetermined and irrevocable, a need to make amends. He had seen the truth of it when the boy had taken the blame for James' breaches. He'd endured punishment after punishment until Joseph no longer had the heart to use the rod upon him.

He had hoped the boy would get angry and defend himself, to no longer endure what was not his to bear. It went unheeded. After a time, he spoke to Nathaniel plainly, letting the boy know he was aware it was James in the wrong and not him. But still Nathaniel continued to take the punishment as though he was put on God's Good Earth to suffer all things for his brother.

Nathaniel watched over James like a mother her child. Joseph recognized that James' headaches, often rendering him sightless, tore at Nathaniel. He came to understand that taking on James' punishment was Nathaniel's way of caring for his brother. With that, he began disciplining James only after sending Nathaniel away from home on an errand or off to do his chores.

James stood it well, even when Joseph whipped him for not owning up to his wrongdoings as an honorable man should. Through his tears, James nodded and promised to be good and never again take advantage of his younger brother, no matter how easily it could be done. Joseph couldn't quite blame James, the temptation in most boys stronger than conscience. But to him it could only be regarded as a sign of weakness, a breach in the boy, a scar upon him, an imperfection grown more and more worrisome to Joseph over time.

In the earlier years, when Joseph lay in bed at night a voice would speak in his head precisely when sleep was close to settling over him, jerking him awake. What was spoken brought him to tears and he'd shout out into the darkness. Mary never woke from his outbursts and he was grateful, not wanting to explain his fear. The only comfort after his fright was the imagined press of his long dead father's hand upon his shoulder, leaving him with an unspoken promise that all would be well, so strong was his faith in his father to make it so.

As he rode closer to the house, he heard the words again after so many years. They were spoken as if to provoke him, saying: *"There will be blood."*

"Whose?" Joseph questioned aloud. "Whose? Dammit!"

His hands shook, loathing stirring in him. It had been his place to protect Nathaniel, his place as father, telling himself he had, but knowing it was a lie as all of it was from the beginning. War-blown, his

71

boy's heart and soul in shreds because of him, because he was neither protector nor father.

Joseph lifted the latch and stepped into the house, the breath catching in his throat when he looked around the room. He leaned a moment against the jamb, his heart beating like a thin stone skipped across water. A soft cough to settle it, and then closed the door and moved into the room. His hands shook, and he fisted them, bringing them up to his eyes to rub away what he thought could only be some trickery, a dreadful illusion.

His neck prickled, and he spun around, a sense of someone there. Purely imagined, he assured himself, but still not fully certain. The house was cold but didn't hold the dankness of abandoned places. He was almost expecting to see Molly toddle out to him, her sweet baby's mouth in a perfect "O," her tongue working to get out his name: "Papa!" And then there would be her laughter, a joy, boundless. In her, he could almost hold God in his heart again. His throat clenched, his stomach burned, the anger still keen in him.

The next moment shifted to recrimination. There was so much more to be done than to have a good wallow. Endure, move forward as they all must. Nathaniel's coming home attested to this. His son was strong, much stronger than he. His thoughts spoke of failure and he cursed in frustration. He walked along, eyes searching. He had only been in their bedroom once, after the birth of Molly. They had all gathered around to get a look. The baby cleaned and swaddled, a tuft of black hair jutting out from beneath the blanket, the pale skin luminescent in the soft light.

Mary had wept, and Nathaniel had hugged her, his eyes misted, gleaming.

Joseph continued forward, pushing open the bedroom door. Nathaniel was there on the bed, log cabin quilt tucked around him, a bare foot poking out and Joseph sickened by the scars, the child's flesh ruined. He bent over the boy and curved his large palm against Nathaniel's forehead, holding it there. A soft cry sprung from his mouth, he choked, the coolness of tears slick on his skin. His heart broke for the boy, and he hesitated to wake him, a rare thing to find peace.

Nathaniel shifted then, his legs drawn up. He spooned against the blankets pulled loose, a feather pillow. He smiled in his sleep as his fingers curled around flannel and wool. Joseph thought, *dreaming of Jane, no doubt*. He straightened, at a loss, willing to give his life if only that could be enough. But God most certainly would have none of it, better to see them all suffer, to have no one spared.

Joseph felt eyes on him then, watching him, eyes resembling Mary's. The first time seeing this child, he could not deny his love. He was a beautiful boy, a glorious gift, and in that moment, became his own. Joseph moved to the bed. He smiled down at Nathaniel. He was frightened by the boy's cough, the rattle of his lungs. Nathaniel's eyes shut as though suddenly dozing, but then opened, startling Joseph when he spoke, the words unconnected, fevered.

But there was one query, clearly stated and immediately understood, and Joseph's eyes became wet-rimmed, his mouth becoming dry. He couldn't speak for a time, the grief fresh, and then very quietly, he said,

73

"They've passed on."

At that, Joseph took up his son like a child, dismayed by how thin he was, and carried him in his arms to his horse, with only thoughts of home.

Nathaniel

For Nathaniel, the passing days had been of intermittent waking, vivid dreaming, and black nothingness. There had also been voices, although he couldn't remember what had been said. He was weak and muzzy-minded, feeble as an old woman. They had stripped and bathed him, only briefly feeling the humiliation of being unclothed and helpless. The relief from the cool cloth moving across his heated body, and the solace he'd gotten from the gentle hands touching him had been worth any unease. No sooner had the misery of the fever ended when the shivering began, his limbs convulsing. The sharp pull on his wound caused it to throb, keeping him from true sleep. He had dozed in and out until exhaustion had finally claimed him.

He awakened to a storm rolling across the land sounding like the brutal rumblings of a far-off battle. Memories rose in him too hard to hold down. The medicine they had given him still had its hold, making him groggy, his eyelids weighted, though it did nothing to stop the grisly imaginings.

The storm trundled closer and Nathaniel frantically directed his thoughts, reawakening a kinder time: Janie beside him on the small front porch while he held Molly close in his arms, watching the skies blacken, the lightning livid and wild across it. After the storm, all things were rain-washed and the scent of the air was pleasant and to his liking. His senses were alive with the smell of wet earth and the sounds of birds and wild creatures alike emerging from the shelter of bough and brush and scrub.

His face must have shown his pleasure because his mother's voice broke into his thoughts, asking him what he was thinking. He lifted his good shoulder in an awkward shrug, opening his eyes. He saw her disappointment, though she covered it quickly with idle, bright talk. It was not his intent to hurt her, but some things weren't easily parted with, needing to hold certain memories in a well-guarded box to keep unspoiled and safe, only for his eyes to see. A fear so strong in him that sharing would bring it to ruin, hoarding it like a starving man hunched over scraps.

Again, his mother's voice strode into his thoughts, as she put her hand to his forehead.

"You're a bit cooler now. How are you feeling?"

Nathaniel went to talk, but his voice wasn't there. He cleared his throat a few times, grateful for the cool glass of water she held out to him. It felt good on his throat, feeling the slide of it through him. The water pooled in his stomach, his belly so empty, if he moved around, he'd hear sloshing like the sound of a half-full bull's-eye canteen. He lifted his good hand, indicating to her he'd had his fill, lowering his head down to the pillow, closing his eyes.

He remained aware for only a moment more, uncoiling, adrift.

Slowly, he heard his own heart's sounds, too slow, too hard to breathe. He would have stopped completely and given up, if it was not for the one calling out to him, his only love, his Jane. She was more than desire or dream. And at that precise moment, he refused to believe anything but this – she was alive.

BOOK TWO

Nathaniel

With spring, Nathaniel grew stronger. Each morning the routine was the same and was no different on this very morning. Groggy from sleep, he idly watched his mother rush about his room opening drapes and fussing with bed quilts and blankets. She talked to him the entire time about the ranch, the town, and his family. He nodded to her, but it seemed she was speaking to him from some far-off place.

Taking a spoon from his breakfast tray, she gave the cornmeal mush a stir and then poured him a cup of tea. She lifted the spoon of mush to his lips and he shook his head no. She laughed, and then as she had done every morning since his fever broke, coaxed him to take a mouthful. He complied, eating spoonful after spoonful.

His mother never mentioned his silence, but he could see the worry in her eyes. He looked away, and she gripped his chin, bringing his face in line with hers. She said only one word, a word that brought him back when she did. Over and over, he said it in his head, a need to please her.

This time he surprised himself by saying the word aloud. At the sound of his voice, his mother jumped, spattering the mush over the bedcovers. She didn't seem to care as she hurriedly placed the spoon into the bowl and leaned toward him to touch his cheek. Then she said it back to him.

"Live!" she said. "Live!"

He nodded, but wouldn't say it again, no matter how much she coaxed. When she started to cry, he reached for her hand and gave it a squeeze, but still did not speak.

Mary

On a sunny March morning, Mary strode into her son's bedroom with purpose. In her opinion, it had gone on too long, this sorrow that pressed heavily on her boy's soul. She saw the life slipping from him, recognizing the dark abyss, slow steps, a mere footfall away. Guilt then, reeling from it, when she remembered how she'd been herself, the boy accursed with her own frailties, her malaise. His grief was great, perhaps, insurmountable, but she refused to let it be so. Her intent was not completely selfless, aware if she lost another, she'd surely lose herself.

He'd recently begun dressing himself, wearing the clothes she'd put out for him the night before: brown woolen pants, leather braces to be drawn over flannel-clad shoulders, loving him best in the blue. The others, James and John, were good-looking, quite handsome, but this boy, this blessed child – his beauty always took her breath.

She smiled when he looked up at her. The blue eyes dull, his skin still pale from illness. He coughed, would always cough, the lungs never to be entirely healed.

"Today you're leaving this room," she said to him. Mary studied his face, his eyes, waiting for him to balk, to fight her, but he made no protest. She moved forward and took his arm, helping him to stand. He swayed in her grip, but then steadied himself. He coughed again several times, and then worked to fill his lungs with air.

"Come," she said. "I've made breakfast. There'll be no more cornmeal mush for you. I should think that would put a smile on your face."

He didn't answer, but he did attempt to take a step forward. She smiled, offering encouragement. Wrapping her arm around his waist, he tipped a bit into her, causing her to stumble, but she quickly recovered. She saw him frown, frustrated, no doubt, by his feebleness.

The oak planks creaked under their feet as they continued forward. "Good," she crooned to him with each step taken. "Good."

Nathaniel

That afternoon, Nathaniel sat on the porch in the ladder-back rocker wrapped in a wool blanket. He'd been dozing, dreaming hazy dreams of them, the wind carrying laughter, his heart filling. He floated there not wanting to open his eyes, his mother's humming from inside the house the only thing tethering him.

Memories, moments coming back to him, flashes of dreams, the pictures in his mind riffled there before his eyes as if they were wide-opened. First a boy, then a man, a husband, and a boy again, missing Jane, missing how it had been. He heard someone crying. His chest hurt, moving his hand up under the blanket.

"Mare's my friend...my friend." No one heard him, only his father's angry shouts. When he started to cry, the Indian held his hand. He tasted

80

dirt in his mouth, breathed dust into his nose. His chest hurt. James was there, too, taking his mare away.

His father's voice again, still shouting, "What were you thinking? He's just a boy. Gentling wild ponies, I won't have your Indian ways harming my son!"

"Joseph, please!"

He stared at his mother's boots, small feet, petticoats and skirt, and then his mother's blue eyes, her worried face.

"Oh, my sweet boy, you've taken quite a spill."

Tears blurred his vision, but he caught a glimpse of James, a slingshot shoved in the back-pocket of his pants.

"She was my friend."

Again, he heard crying, and then he saw his mother, her blue eyes worried. "Oh, my sweet boy," she said to him. Her voice was always a comfort. "My sweet boy."

Isabel

Isabel watched Mary and the man for a time before she could muster the nerve to move forward, not wanting to intrude. An intimacy was there between the two, causing a stir of longing in her, something familiar in the color of his hair.

She'd been confined so long at home throughout the winter months the first pleasant day brought her out, riding astride as she had done from girlhood, in want of a woman's companionship, tea and conversation.

81

She immediately thought of Mary, although she'd been told over and over by James of his mother's spells, her melancholia. But Isabel had been certain that first time as she was now that she could bring Mary around, a smile, laughter, always quite pleased on the long ride home, having accomplished something James believed she could not.

Isabel sighed, took a step forward, cleared her throat, and smiled when Mary looked up at her. The older woman had been startled at first and then returned the smile, her face lighting up with pleasure.

"Oh, Isabel! How lovely!"

Isabel waited while Mary pulled the blanket tight around the man and bent and kissed his head of black hair. Saw her dab at his cheeks with a white-laced hanky, gently, and whisper something to him. He nodded to Mary and then shut his eyes. For a moment, Isabel thought he might have been crying. He didn't seem to notice her at all.

Mary finally turned to her and took Isabel by the hand, leading her inside without a word. Isabel looked back over her shoulder at the man, curious. She tried to see a glimpse of his face. *Could he be the one from the cottage?* she wondered. Her heart quickened, her stomach fluttered, an urge to touch him, his face, the hair. Lampblack, black as jet, a black bird. *He is broken*, she thought. *He is broken*.

When Isabel was settled at the dining room table of rosewood with her steaming cup of tea, the finest china brought safely from New York to Connecticut and then surviving the arduous way by wagon to Texas, Isabel could no longer hold her tongue. "Who is he?" she asked, and then felt her cheeks flame, burning red.

Mary smiled and patted Isabel's hand, her eyes closing. Then opened them, vague, distant, and suddenly latching onto Isabel's face. The eyes were bright, the blue of them the color of a cloudless summer sky, boundless, pulling, pulling until Isabel felt the tremble of her hands, the hot spill of tea. She put down the china tea cup, gripping her hands in her lap, her body a tremor.

Mary looked away and spoke in a whisper. "He is my saving grace."

Nathaniel

When Nathaniel jerked awake, James was standing over him. His brother didn't say a word, only shook his head and turned away into the house. Voices drifted out to Nathaniel, but he couldn't make out what was being said. He could hear James, his tone distinct, clipped and self-assured, polished, and then he heard laughter, his mother's and another, a woman. He listened, his ears straining. His heart thrilled, fiercely beating in his chest. He eased himself back, calming, watched the wind in the trees, the feel of the sun on him, the heat of it. He recalled his father telling him that they'd passed on. He knew it to be true, but his heart refused to listen.

He'd sit all his life on this porch, waiting.

Isabel

"James, would you kindly help your brother inside?"

Isabel sat up straighter, immediately attentive. She hadn't been able to keep her mind on their conversation, the whole time wondering about *him*. At first, James had seemed annoyed to see her, although he was cordial. She watched his movements, his gaze stopping on the far window overlooking the porch.

James merely said, "He's sleeping," looked over at her, nodded and walked out of the room.

Mary fussed with the biscuits, the pot of tea, the silver, her eyes cold, tearing up a moment.

After a time, she looked toward Isabel. Whatever was there now gone, a brief storm diminished, calmed, a smile given, conversation resumed.

"Perhaps it's best to let him sleep. He's been so ill. Still so thin, so weak. I worry."

Isabel nodded. "If I may be of help . . ."

"Of help?" Mary looked at her, unable to conceal her surprise.

Isabel felt again the heat of her face, the rise of color in her cheeks. "I spoke without thought. I apologize."

An awkward silence between them stretched on too long, prompting Isabel to stand. Her chair teetered a moment on its back legs from the force of the motion.

"He hasn't spoken since his illness," Mary said at last, seeming to be unaware of Isabel's discomfort. Isabel waited for her to go on, silent.

"His fever was so high. It spawned such terrible dreams, the war, the killings, Jane and the baby."

Mary worried her hands in the fabric of her dress, her eyes bright, fierce with despair and something indefinable, strange.

Isabel grew uneasy, feeling the prickle of the fine hair on her neck. *Had it been a flash of madness?* She wondered then, if James had been right all along about his mother's turn of mind.

"He thinks they are still alive and refuses to believe otherwise."

Isabel gripped the back of the chair, fingers paling, nearly white against the dark wood. "I don't quite understand," she said, growing concerned for the older woman.

Mary stood, moved toward her and reached out her hand. Pushing all qualms aside, Isabel caught the fingers in her grip.

"Of course, how could you? Explaining such things, putting it into words somehow diminishes it, as if it's all ridiculous, absurd. But still I can tell you this, there was something in his eyes, the way he spoke. He believed she was there, Isabel. That Jane was there." Mary was silent a moment and then she said, "And I nearly as well."

Isabel waited, still holding Mary's hand. Mary smiled at her and said, "Come, dear. Come to the parlor and sit with me for a while." The words were spoken with a well-mannered reserve, a practiced and familiar gentility.

They walked together, silent.

Mary sat herself in the Windsor chair before the hearth, Isabel beside her in another.

"I worry for him."

Isabel nodded, feeling far steadier. "It's understandable."

Mary looked at her, the eyes earnest, considering. "And what of James then, if you should help?"

Isabel was taken aback, uncertain of what Mary meant. However, she knew immediately the lie of it. James' jealousy would be expected, aware of his unspoken claim upon her, ashamed to admit something she hadn't discouraged. Isabel forced a smile and without pause said, "He is his brother, after all. Besides, James has never spoken of marriage."

"I see." Mary looked at her, and then said, "So, then you will help."

Isabel

After another cup of tea, Mary began dinner. Isabel was told to retrieve Nathaniel from the porch to the kitchen. She found herself disappointed, he not even sparing her a glance. His eyes were cast down the entire time she helped him stand and then guided him into the house. He was spare, the sharpness of bone evident under her hands. *Oh! The deprivations he must have suffered!* Isabel felt the burn of tears, blinked them away. She had no right to pity him, appraising, as if he were some wretched soul, accursed, and only she with the authority to judge and redeem. She knew nothing of his sufferings, could never know.

Isabel saw his strength, his bravery, abiding still, even when all he'd loved was lost. She closed her eyes and knew in that brief and delicate moment she could love him.

Once in the kitchen, she left him in the care of his mother. Tomorrow, she promised. Tomorrow, she'd be back to help with the household chores, the beating of rugs, the cooking of meals, the washing of windows, and perhaps, if she was fortunate, she might sit with him a moment on the porch, read to him, talk to him.

This was so unlike her. So utterly unlike her. She remembered his face, the hair, how he looked laying there on the bed in the cottage. *He is broken*, she told herself again. *Broken.*

Isabel

"Wait! Isabel! Oh, for God's sake, wait!" James was riding fast to reach her. Isabel reined her horse, stopping. She didn't want to talk, her thoughts still on the other, on Nathaniel. She said his name over and over in her mind. *Nathaniel. Nathaniel.* Mary had told her the name meant a gift from God. The resemblance to her deceased baby brother, Patrick, was stunning, uncanny, she'd said, and to Jacob, the one lost to her. Mary had gone on and on about it. In fact, it was all she could speak of, desperation in her tone. Stiff, rehearsed, defensive, as though it had been explained so many times to so many others. The disparity of the boys explained away before Isabel could even comment. James and

John so blonde, so golden, so broad and strong, and this one, this Nathaniel, so lean, so lost, as if a child left on one's doorstep, a foundling.

What made her think such thoughts? she wondered. She shook her head. The coloring was right, the dark hair so much like Mary's, the bluest of eyes were his mother's as well. The similarities were there without question. So, that wasn't it at all. If she was to put a finger to it, it had been Mary, herself, that gave Isabel pause. Her words saying one thing, her demeanor another. And then at the last of it all, Mary had said, matter-of-fact, defiant, daring Isabel with her words: "I will not speak of this again."

Isabel had said nothing, her mind in a tumble of confusion. She'd only one thought that Mary was holding something close, unspoken and secret.

James rode up, stopping next to her. She smiled with a brightness she didn't feel. "James."

"What the devil are you thinking?"

Isabel looked at him, perturbed.

"You shouldn't be riding alone. It's not safe," he said.

She took a breath, held her tongue. She tried to keep her voice light. "This isn't the first time I've gone riding alone."

"And what would you do if you met up with murderin' savages?"

Isabel sighed. "I don't know what I would do, James. But I do know I cannot live my life in fear."

James shook his head. "Fear keeps you alive, Isabel. Don't be foolish."

She felt the stir of anger but chose not to argue with him. "I'll see if someone might escort me tomorrow, then."

"Good." James eased a bit in the saddle. "I'll ride home with you."

"I would like that very much." Isabel urged her horse forward, James following. "I'm somewhat surprised my father wasn't called on to care for your brother."

James looked at her.

"He was obviously very ill. My father would have been able to help him."

"The Indian took care of him. We all did."

"The Indian?"

"The old Cheyenne," James said. "My father holds great store by him."

They rode on without talking, James' face a scowl. A dark mood had fallen over him, the air heavy with it. She wondered where his mind had gone, what thoughts he had in those black moments. Isabel breathed in and out deeply, forced a smile.

She said, "I think Billy Holmes might be willing."

James gave a sideways glance. "What was that?"

"I said, I think Mr. Holmes might be willing," she paused a moment, "to ride with me tomorrow, I mean. I offered to help your mother."

James was silent. He watched the sky, the lowering sun. "That's quite a burden for you to take on. What of your own chores? And the ride to and from? I think it'll be too much for you," he told her. Then said, "Your father might have something to say about it."

Isabel did not answer right away. It seemed she often censured herself with this man and she was growing weary of it. She simply said, "I believe I'll ask my father to look in on your brother. Though you might think him cured, a doctor may say differently."

"Why do you care so much?" James asked. "Did you take a good look at him, Isabel? He's nearly a savage. I'm certain he's lived among them. And then all those years at war, the killing. After that how could he possibly return to the civilized world?"

Isabel looked over at James, horrified. "He's your brother!"

"Yes, and that's why I can speak so honestly about things," he said. "I saw it with my own eyes, Isabel. Just returned home and he killed two of Caden's men, sweet as you please. He shot to kill those men, nothing less."

Isabel's hands trembled. "I can't believe he'd do such a thing. There must have been a sound reason."

James reined in, stopped, and looked over at her. "If you must, help my mother, but stay away from my brother. He's a different man from last I saw him."

She felt something loosen, a small break within, her heart hurting. Still, she refused to believe it. *You're wrong, James,* she thought. *You're wrong. He's kind. He's gentle.* Appalled at her wrenching need for it to be true.

Nathaniel

By the slant of sun through the windowpanes, he could tell the hour. He'd again slept well past breakfast. No one woke him, wanting him to sleep, to heal. *Live*, his mother had said to him, *live*. Repeated so often his head spun from it. He'd never hurt her, would try to give her all she wanted.

He heard light knocking, the sound of the doorknob turning. It was his mother and the woman from the other day. A man followed behind them, wired glasses set on the bridge of his nose, his eyes deep brown, near black, were bright as crows'. White thistledown hair framed a handsome, angular face, the skin smooth and fair.

Nathaniel watched. His fingers, cold, coiled around the blanket. He'd worn no nightshirt to bed, clad only in his woolen drawers. His heart beat, pitiful, apprehensive. He felt he'd suffocate with so many around him. With a need to breathe air, he flung the blankets off without thought. Both feet on the floor, he stumbled forward to the window. His legs shook from the effort, feeling their stares hot upon him. He didn't have the strength to raise the window, though he struggled with it. His eyes began to burn, and he couldn't breathe. They remained in his room, watching him. He wanted them to leave. He turned to his mother, confused. She held out her hand to him.

They should go, he said to himself. But still they remained. He turned away from them, closing his eyes. He stilled, hearing only his own breathing, and then hearing Jane.

Isabel

Isabel's father, Thomas Langford, had ushered them from the room. Mary had protested.

They waited without speaking over cups of cooling tea. Before, to ease her worry, Mary had talked, unceasing. Again, she'd told Isabel about the fever that had taken Nathaniel's wife, Jane, and the child, Molly. "The Lord giveth and the Lord taketh away," she'd said. "We are left with only that."

Isabel stood and walked to the stove, taking up the kettle. Window light filled the room, warming her, a comfort as she waited. It'd been well over an hour, when she finally heard her father's footsteps on the stairs and then coming down the long hallway to the kitchen. She put the kettle back on the cookstove and walked over to Mary.

Without a word, her father came into the kitchen and began to wash his hands at the soapstone sink. Isabel and Mary watched him, his movements graceful, his concentration keen on each hand, scrubbing palm to finger. Isabel was familiar with the ritual, but Mary was growing impatient, the woman increasingly anxious about her son.

When he turned around and looked at them, Isabel asked, "How is he, father?" Relief shot through her when he smiled.

He directed his reply to Mary. "He is as well as can be expected. Undernourished, which is painfully obvious, exhausted. His lungs are still weak, but with care, he should recover."

Isabel clapped her hands together and raised them to her lips, smiling. "That's wonderful, father." She looked at Mary, the woman's head bowed down, lips moving, silent. She reached for Mary's hand, clasping the woman's fingers in her own. But then Isabel saw something cross her father's face, the sudden shift of expression, catching her by surprise.

"What is it?" Isabel asked. Mary's head lifted, her hand tensed in Isabel's grasp.

Her father sat down in the chair near Mary. Isabel watched him, waiting. Mary was quiet, not moving, sitting tense and straight in the chair.

"Now, now, no need to look so gloomy," he said, smiling. "Your boy is fine, Mary. But, he is to some extent unresponsive. He didn't acknowledge me or speak. Mind you, he is aware." And then, as if to himself, he said, "Perhaps soldier's heart..."

Isabel wasn't sure if Mary heard his last words, the woman merely nodding. Mary then asked, "What can I do for him, Thomas? How can I help him?"

"Do as you're doing," he said to her. He shifted in his chair, in thought. After a while, he said, "He has many scars. From the war, I presume."

"Yes, from the war and gone to it against my wishes and without farewell." Mary stood and seemed not to know why she did or where she should go. She then moved to the window and appeared to be watching the men outside who were working over by the stables. She didn't turn to face them, speaking into the glass pane, her breath clouding it. "Too many years away. Too many years lost."

"Has he spoken of things?" Thomas asked. "Is he troubled by the war?"

Mary laughed, tight with sorrow, anger. "How could he not be troubled?" she asked. She began to cry, and Isabel moved toward her.

At the window, Isabel placed her hands over Mary's shoulders. "Come," she said. "Sit and take some tea to calm your nerves."

"Yes. Yes." Mary patted Isabel's hand. They walked back to the table, Isabel supporting Mary at the waist.

Her father persisted, asking, "Why has he just returned home?"

Mary sat back down at the table, while Isabel hurried over to the cookstove to retrieve the kettle. She refilled Mary's cup and then her own. After taking a small sip of the hot tea, Mary told them of the agonizing months having no word and fearing Nathaniel had been killed. She said he'd been with the 5th Texas Infantry at the start of the war, but then due to wounds he'd suffered wrote to them saying he'd made application for transfer to cavalry. So, began his service with the 8th Calvary. Oddly enough he had made no mention of Jane and Molly which caused them concern, having sent a letter months prior of their deaths. Letter after letter had been sent, but still they had gotten no response from him, never once requesting furlough. As she spoke, she grew breathless, her words all in a rush.

She then told of Nathaniel's nightmares when he was very ill, and the subsequent malaise. Her voice quavered a little when she recalled the night she had watched him while deep in fever speak to his dead

94

wife and child. With only the quarter moon outside the window, she'd squinted her eyes in the dark and gloom to try to see what he saw, had taken no breath to try to hear what he heard. And of another night when it'd appeared he'd been released from this world. And then terrified to see him convulse on the bed, limbs with no control, back arching, to finally breathe in a deep, sucking breath, certain he'd almost died.

Perhaps some things spoken about Jane and Nathaniel's relationship weren't meant for Isabel's ears, but she hadn't been able to bring herself to leave, hadn't been able to keep herself from listening. Throughout the telling, an intimacy toward him grew in her, her heart swelling, as though knowing him for years.

She prayed then that she might one day come to mean something to him, as well.

Isabel

Later that day, Mary began preparing dinner. With floured hands, she worked the dough, seeming to be content in the movement. It was to be a feast, she had said, something she had wanted to do for him the day of his return home. Five weeks gone by since then, perhaps more, she had lost count. Isabel asked to help, but Mary sent her off to tidy up the house and ready the table.

Once in the grand room, Isabel gave great thought to where each would sit. Joseph would have his place with his back to the large hearth at the table's head, her father at the other. Mary, of course, would be beside her husband, James across from Mary at his father's right-hand, the appropriate place for the eldest son, John next to James, and Nathaniel beside his mother. She would sit on her father's side which would leave her near Nathaniel. It was all very proper, above reproach, nothing to cause raised eyebrows or questions or so she hoped. Certainly, there was no indecency in sitting next to *him*.

When all Isabel's tasks were completed, Mary asked her to look in on Nathaniel, wanting everyone to dress for dinner. The men were upstairs washing the grime of a hard day's work off themselves, her father in the parlor reading.

At his door, Isabel gave it a soft rap, saying his name. There was no answer. She tried again, but still nothing. So, gathering herself, she turned the knob and opened it. She looked in, seeing him sitting in a chair, looking out the window. When she stepped into the room, he turned his eyes to her.

Isabel smiled. "Hello."

He nodded, still watching her.

"A bit awkward," she said.

His head tilted slightly at her words, his face perplexed.

She smiled. "This is all a bit awkward, I suppose. Here I am in your room and you not knowing who I am from Adam's off ox. Your mother and I have become quite close, wonderful companions, if that helps at all. She's asked me to lay out your clothes for dinner. I believe she's making all your favorite dishes. She's a flurry of activity in the kitchen. I must say it's wonderful to see her, your mother, so alive. I was worried for her not so long ago. She's overjoyed to have you home."

Isabel stopped to catch a breath, her fingers tightening around the sewing scissors and comb forgotten in her hand. James' words came back to her. *Did you take a good look at him? He's nearly a savage.*

Certainly, his hair was much too long, tied loosely at the nape of his neck, a dark plait, a few days' beard growth. But those eyes lit bright by the sun were so very blue, and the face with its finely raised cheekbones, the angular jaw.

He is beauty blessed, she thought, feeling quite plain and ordinary while he watched her standing there, a stranger in his home, in his room.

Isabel removed her apron, moving toward him.

"Would you very much mind a trim?" she asked, holding up the scissors.

His slender hand rose to his head, long fingers touching a few loose strands of hair. His face was thoughtful as though touching it for the first time, a thing long ago forgotten.

"Perhaps just a bit shorter?" she asked him.

His hand dropped to his lap, nodding his agreement.

Isabel smiled. "Come then. Let me help you."

She, at first, couldn't bring herself to cut it. Only able to do so when she had summoned her courage, taking the sewing scissors and snipping above the leather cording. She held the long, black horse tail of hair in her hand. She at once coveted it like a child would a precious plaything. It had been her first connection to him at the cottage and she was enchanted by it clasped in her hand.

She set the plait on the bedside table and went back to trimming. While she did this, she again told him her name, sharing her stories, a thousand secrets about herself without censor. Her life unspooled and fell around him, as did his hair, black shimmering feathers, ravens' wings, strands of his life entangled in hers. She was unashamed by her forwardness and began to hum, rewarded by his smile.

He lowered his head and Isabel gazed at the exposed white neck. She moved to the side and placed her fingers beneath his chin, lifting and holding his head level. She began to trim the front, layering the sides to frame the face, leaving the back long enough to touch the shirt's collar.

It was all so irrational, this love. It was not supposed to be extraneous, external. It was internal, a thing belonging to the heart and soul, not based on the meaningless, the physical. She expected much more from herself than that. But, she couldn't deny her feelings, standing so near to him, not wanting to step away. Her hand lingered there on his shoulder, her fingers combing through his hair, the unexpected touch of ear, of neck.

His eyes were closed while she combed and fussed over him, working the scissors. He was the earth and sky, tree and rock and water, things grander than she. But he was also sorrow and loss, and she wondered if she would ever be enough for him. And if she was, would he be able to offer her enough for her to sustain? Or would he, as she feared, be forever consumed by ghosts and she forever fighting them?

Immediately, she saw in her mind the woman and child from the daguerreotype. She was easily able to place him with them, could now, imagine them together, happy. She sighed and removed her apron from across his shoulders.

"All finished," she said, bending down to gather the cuttings into a small pile with her hands. She took up a bit of hair and hid it away in the apron pocket.

She stood. "As soon as I'm done cleaning up, if you don't mind, I'll choose something for you to wear."

He looked over at the closet and then at the large armoire, his brow furrowed.

She watched him a moment, suddenly understanding. His clothes should not be in this house, in this room, this childhood place. Certain he must feel as though he'd only dreamed of his years with Jane and the child.

Isabel could not talk about them with him. Not yet. Instead she said, perhaps too gaily, "I'm sure your mother has something here for you."

He looked at her, his hands moving to his head, running his fingers through the shorter hair. She took a breath and held it a moment, waiting for him to do or say something. His eyes met hers, an odd gaze, and then turned away.

Isabel

They sat at the rosewood table waiting for John and Nathaniel to join them. James was impatient, his fingers thrumming on the tabletop. In the kitchen, Mary clattered pots, her nerves showing, anxious to start the dinner. Joseph politely excused himself and went to her.

Before when John had come into Nathaniel's room announcing he was there to help his brother dress, Isabel had grown uneasy. She had not been able to meet his gaze, dropping her eyes. She'd felt him assessing her, keenly exposed. She had been annoyed, irritated at herself and at John. But then had come a flowering of curiosity, wondering if John had thought her intent was to ready Nathaniel alone. Would she have done so if John hadn't appeared? Had she lost all reason because of Nathaniel? Had she become so heedless, so mindless of what others thought? *It would not be the first time*, she rebuked herself. Her father just steps away on the floor below and Mary. *And what of James?* Her virtue with certainty would be sullied.

Slowly, she had composed herself and had shown John the finely tailored dark suit she had found hidden in the far reaches of the closet along with a band-collared shirt, not having found a tie. He had nodded to her and she had left him to it.

Sitting beside her father, her thoughts again slid back to John, remembering his tenderness with his brother. She saw that John had chosen to be Nathaniel's protector. He had whispered something to him, something she had not quite made out, but then had heard him say, *I will*

100

keep you safe. The sentiment had touched her, holding in her heart the very same conviction. But, of course, she could give no logical explanation as to why.

Her father reached over to pat her hand, and Isabel took hold of it. She was greatly comforted to have him there while unfamiliar emotions tumbled and reeled over her, making her reckless and bold, alive with fear. His quiet presence rooted her.

A sudden shift of her father's eyes made her turn to follow the line of his gaze. She turned to see John and Nathaniel entering the room with John leading his brother. Mary, coming from the kitchen, let out a cry. In her arms, she carried a large bowl of mashed potatoes, stark white against the bowl's dark blue lip. When she stopped up short, Joseph, behind her, bumped the platter of beef up against her back, splattering some of the meat drippings on the luxurious imported rug. Mary clucked at Joseph not to fuss, that it was all right, while she went to set the bowl of potatoes on the table. She hurried over to Nathaniel, her eyes shining. She hugged him to her and after a time he raised his arms, wrapping them around her in a loose embrace. Her hand moved up to his hair, stroking the shorter strands.

"This suit," she said, "do you remember this suit?"

Nathaniel stared at her, but remained silent. Mary smiled and wiped at her eyes. She touched his cheek. "You wore it the day you wed."

Hearing this, Isabel gasped, her hand flying to her mouth. *She hadn't known. He hadn't said a word. What a cruelty! How awful for him! She had done this!*

101

Isabel wanted to run, to burst out crying, but instead she kept on with the pretense that all was well. No one to ever know how utterly mad she had become, how little control she now had since she had chosen him. Of course, it was a hopeless endeavor, a fated love, certainly unrequited, no doubt doomed. But it was too late to turn back, much too late. The course had been set for her from the moment she had seen him. Isabel felt as though she was drowning.

"Are you well, my dear?" her father asked. "You're very pale. Do you feel faint?"

Isabel turned to him, smiling her reassurances. "I'm fine, Father, truly. It's just. I hadn't known about the suit, you see. I would not have chosen it, if I had known."

Her father patted her hand. "How would you have known such a thing, Isabel? He hadn't refused to wear it."

Isabel looked at him. "He didn't speak to me, either. But I do know, Father, he had heard me, understood me."

"My dear daughter, you cannot take on all the world's troubles. As a physician, I may be able to cure the physical ailments, but those of the mind are another story. Please, Isabel, let it be. His family will take care of his needs. James is worried—"

"Worried? Whatever about?" Her voice rose, loud enough to draw James' attention. He looked over at her.

"Is there something wrong, Isabel?" James asked, but before she could reply, he looked away to watch Nathaniel. His tone was sharp when he spoke. "Well, are we here to eat or not? Let's get on with it, shall we?"

Mary looked over at James, her eyebrows pinched with annoyance, and then over to Isabel and her father, an unspoken apology in her eyes. Mary looped her arm around Nathaniel's waist and led him slowly to his chair. John and Joseph went to their seats and remained standing. Isabel's father stood then as well, waiting for Mary to be seated. Isabel was dismayed to see James had remained in his seat and was looking at Nathaniel with an unnerving intensity. Nathaniel was completely unaware, remaining fixed and unreachable in some dark place. Watching this, Isabel's stomach clenched, her spine tingling with fear.

Isabel

All through the meal, the conversation was light, the mood easy. James shared endless stories, holding their attention. Isabel feigned interest. She felt trapped, restrained. The others seemed not to notice that James had taken control, directing every thought. Her father became engrossed as the talk turned to horses, Joseph and John adding their opinion.

Mary had gone to the kitchen for bread, and Nathaniel had watched her leave the room. He seemed anxious but remained quiet. He'd barely eaten, though his head had been bent over his plate the entire meal, eyes intent on the mashed potatoes, the pooling of gravy, while he poked his fork at the thick slice of roast beef. Isabel wondered where he was, what he was thinking. Her hand lifted to touch him, but she pulled it back.

She looked around the table, taken aback when she met James' eyes, his gaze unsettling. He had been watching her, and she flushed to know he'd caught her looking at Nathaniel. She'd been exposed, her face most certainly a mirror of her thoughts, her feelings. Isabel smiled over at him and James nodded to her, unreadable. She couldn't think of a thing to say.

The men were still talking, all but James, whose attention was now on Nathaniel. The eyes were unkind, absorbed, and then suddenly turned to look at Isabel. She held James' gaze, triumphant when he turned away first. She eased a bit, but found it was short-lived, when he called out to her father, addressing him not as Thomas as he usually did, but as Colonel. She was surprised when she saw Nathaniel's head jerk up and look over at James.

"Colonel," called James, his voice this time rose above the other men's talking, and the room at once quieted, their animated gesturing halted. A smile pulled at James' lips, and only with a half beat hesitation, repeated, "Colonel."

Isabel watched Nathaniel's face, transfixed. She wondered if her father noticed Nathaniel's response to the military appellation, suddenly coming alive. His interest, of course, excited her, but she was also unnerved by what James was about to say. He seemed strange, high-strung. His voice was tight with excitement, anticipation.

"The war is quite well over, James," her father said, lifting his glass and taking a sip of wine. A smile then to soften the rebuke, he asked,

"What's on your mind, son?"

James settled his elbows on the table, his face serious. "There was recently an article in the Daily State Journal out of Austin. Have you read it?"

"I haven't yet, no. Is it of interest to us?"

"Yes, I'd say very much so. The farmers and ranchers are having a time of it in Llano, Mason and Gillespie counties. They're being overrun by hostiles. They've laid blame on the Comancheros who've been trading repeating rifles to the Comanche in return for Texas beeves and then selling the stolen cattle to ranchers in New Mexico and Arizona. No questions asked. It's a hell of a thing."

"James! Enough!"

Isabel hadn't been aware of Mary's return from the kitchen. The spleen in the woman's tone surprised her.

James turned to his mother, his chin lifted, defiant. "This family needs to join this fight!"

Joseph was quiet, grabbing Mary's hand as she sat down in her chair.

James continued, "Colonel Langford has been quite understanding, a truly patient man--"

"See, here now, James," Isabel's father warned.

James held up his hand, interrupting, "Please, Thomas. You must agree that my father's decision concerning a parcel of land, and then his refusal to help fund Caden and his men, would have been taken badly by any other man."

James glanced at each one seated at the table. "Yet, here you sit, dining so graciously with us, not only after that rebuff, but then another several weeks ago, when two of Caden's men were gunned down, and as I far as I can see it, whose only crime was doing the work they were hired to do. They were provoked into gunplay, which ended up costing a pretty penny to smooth Caden's feathers. And I might add, more so to keep Caden from retaliating against this family."

Joseph stood then, his chair shoved back. "That will be enough! Thomas and I had a long discussion about this very thing some time ago. First and foremost, the land you speak of is your brother Nathaniel's and is not ours to sell. This you know full-well. Secondly, I've made restitution to Caden giving him the substantial bounty paid out on those two men. I shall not lose sleep over their loss nor should you. Furthermore, this is not the time or place for such talk."

He turned to Mary who was dabbing at her reddened eyes with a linen napkin.

Isabel took hold of her father's hand and gave it a squeeze. She looked at Nathaniel. His mouth was set tight, his throat bobbing with emotion, his eyes lowered. Isabel's anger came then, the heat through her, the corners of her eyes feeling the sting of tears. *So, it was this lurking in James, cold, dispassionate, calculating, so certain of himself and the world.*

Beside her Nathaniel suddenly stood, backed up and stumbled. Looking down at the floor, he tried to speak, but the words wouldn't come. He turned and bolted from the room.

Nathaniel

Nathaniel stood outside the fence, a white picket with a fine arbor over the gate. Cut flowers lay at the base of the graves, left by a recent visitor. He'd not known about this, hadn't even thought to ask about such things. From where he stood, he could read the names chiseled in the stones. He didn't want to think of them buried there in pine boxes beneath the earth. Dizziness came over him, and in his ears, he heard the jagged ring from years ago of metal cutting their names into the granite rock. It rent the air, along with his heart.

Jane had come to him, he knew this, remembered this. His mother had said it was the sickness, the fevers. *They've passed on, she had said. You know this.* But, even if it were true, he could still feel her against him, could still taste the salt of her skin, the warmth of her breath on his neck, the soft misting of her kisses over him.

He unlatched the gate and walked under the arbor. He read the names again: *Jane McPherson Keegan; Molly Anna Keegan.* He stared at the inscriptions, but he felt nothing. Lifting his hand to the gravestone, he pointed a finger outward to trace her name. First the letter J, then the A, the N, and lastly the E, and still he felt nothing, only the chill smoothness of stone under his fingertip.

He had left her with just a note. In the letters that had reached him in the first year, he'd read her heartbreak. He had pleaded with her to understand, to love him, to be patient. He had said the war would end and he'd be home, would never again leave her. She had written him that she would abide, promised to wait for him a thousand days, a lifetime. Thinking this, he felt a heat in his belly. Bile rose, and his throat shut tight against it. Shocked by the sudden burn of anger he felt toward her, when it was he who was to blame.

He looked up, closed his eyes, and without thinking called her name. His voice let loose from him like a whirlwind in his anger. The words he spoke made little sense, as if he were possessed. He ranted, cursed, hollered, the entire time beating his fists against the gravestone. His fingers soon dripped blood, staining the stones. His heart was near to bursting, his ears roaring, and he strained for breath. Spent, he dropped to his knees, resting his head in his bruised and bleeding hands.

Even in this place with its evidence, stark and inarguable, he couldn't let it go, let them go.

Nathaniel

Sometime later, from where he huddled against her stone, a hand touched his shoulder and his muscles sprung. Leaping up, he twisted around and swung out, hitting the intruder in the jaw. When he focused, he saw it was James reeling back from the blow dealt, but keeping his feet. James swore and rubbed his cheek.

The anger again rose red-hot from Nathaniel's belly. He cursed inwardly and lunged forward, grabbing a handful of James' shirt and

108

came around again with his fist. Both men fell, and James, the larger of the two, quickly gained the upper hand. James' fists were sledges upon him, the hard blows forcing the air from his lungs.

The pummeling ceased when voices called out, surrounded, their hands grabbing at him. He thrashed and kicked, and let out a sound that was primitive and savage, thick with grief. For a moment, the hands holding him loosened, but then recovered, not allowing him movement. His coat pulled off, the sleeve of his shirt shoved up, feeling a pinch in the muscle of his arm, and then slowly fading, gone away into darkness.

Nathaniel

He was dreaming of horses, running in bands, wild as the earth, without burden, freed, as he was not. He gripped a coarse tangle of mane and pulled himself up onto the long spine. Running flat-out, unencumbered, the horse's feet, as one, lifted a moment above the earth, winged-flight.

He woke thinking his hands were still caught up in the hair at the nape of mane, wrapped around his fingers, his palms. He tried to pull away, release himself, but couldn't break loose. He opened his eyes and lifted his arms to see his hands swathed in bandages. When he shifted, his chest hurt, his ribs tender, his hands and arms aching.

A sense of someone made him turn his head to view the room. She was there again, sitting in a high-back rocker, asleep. He struggled to recall her name. *Isabel. Her name's Isabel.* He studied her face. The lashes were full and dark against smooth, pale skin. Her brown hair was bundled on the top of her head with a tortoiseshell comb. Loose strands framed her face. He thought she was very pretty.

She stirred, a gradual waking, and then opened her eyes. She looked at him and smiled, as if seeing an old friend.

"You're awake," she said and stood, coming toward the bed.

"How long?" he asked. His voice came out a low, dry rasp.

She stopped, her hand rising to her temple, her eyes wide. She looked surprised by something. Her chin lifted then, and she laughed. It was a laugh as soft as moonlight, her face glowing. She seemed to understand what he was asking and responded, "An hour or so."

He nodded, his gaze going to his hands. He wiggled his fingers, and everything came back to him.

"James?"

Again, she understood, and he was grateful. "James is fine," she said, "but, you've a bruise or two."

"Why?" His voice was still very rough.

This time she looked confused. Her brow furrowed. She stepped nearer to the bed.

Again, he asked, "Why?"

She shook her head and frowned at him. "I'm not sure what it is you want to know."

He coughed, his head aching, along with his hands. He closed his eyes, too weary to say more. He heard the sweep of her dress, felt the sudden warmth of her palm on his forehead. He tried to talk to her as sleep pulled at him. Still, he thought she'd heard him ask, *"Why do you care?"* Unaware the words were only spoken in his head.

Isabel

"He woke for a moment," Isabel said as she entered the parlor. Mary was reclining on a settee in front of the fireplace, Joseph sitting next to her.

Before Isabel could tell them anything more, Mary sat upright and said, "I should go to him."

"Now, now, Mary, you should rest a bit longer." Joseph took up her small hand, instantly concealed in his own.

Mary raised his to her lips, a light kiss to his sizable knuckles. "I'm fine, truly. You shouldn't worry so about me."

Isabel smiled, touched by their affection for each other. Her father cleared his throat and looked away, uncomfortable.

She had momentarily forgotten John and James were in the room, until John turned toward James. "Why'd you do it?" he asked.

Isabel walked over to her father, and stood beside him, waiting to hear James' response. Though she knew it was unkind of her, she was pleased to see someone confronting James. It had been John who had finally restrained Nathaniel at the graves, and then had lifted his groggy

111

brother up into his arms, laboring a little under the weight, but refusing any help. He'd carried him into the house and to his room and had stood watch while Isabel's father examined, cleaned, and bandaged Nathaniel's hands. When he saw, Nathaniel would be all right, he had left without a word.

She held her breath when she saw James put down his drink and rise from the plush wingback chair where he'd been sitting. She winced to see his swollen and mottled jaw.

"Why did I do what, John?" he asked. "Why did I speak the truth? Is that what you're asking?"

She saw John step toward James with clenched fists.

"Your truth," John said, "the way you see it."

James shook his head and snorted a harsh laugh. "Are you thinking of having at me, too?"

John stopped, appearing to Isabel to be mastering his emotions. Then he said, "It's not worth it, James. But answer me this, why is it Nathaniel's in your cross hairs?"

James looked away from John's gaze, his eyes locking with Isabel's. "Not true," James said.

"Not the way I see it." John shook his head. "Why'd you hurt him like that? Hasn't he had enough hurt already?"

"It seems to me Nathaniel can take care of himself. Damn near knocked my head off my shoulders," James said, huffing out a laugh, his full attention back on John. "But, I can tell you all one thing for a certainty, the war has gone and addled that boy's brain. On the shoot, he kills two men, easy as you please. And what of him off in his head like he's somewhere else? Jane and the baby are gone and there is no bringing them back. Most days he sits in that rocker and stares down the road hours on end. Who is he looking for?" James lifted a hand to his swollen face and said, "Anyone with eyes can see the boy's not right."

Isabel gasped when she saw John make a lunge toward James, fear growing in her belly. A blow was close to be dealt when Joseph stood up and went between his sons.

She stepped forward. "John!" she shouted. "He spoke, John! He spoke!"

Immediately they all stopped and turned to her.

She smiled and nodded. "Forgive me for not mentioning it right away. But, nevertheless, you heard correctly. He spoke to me. Quite aware, I might add. Of course, the opiate was making him sleepy. He asked for you, James. He was concerned he'd hurt you." Isabel gripped the fabric of her dress. She schooled her voice, working to keep her tone even, desperate to keep her anger hidden from James. "I told him you were fine, and it was he who was the worst for it."

James studied her and nodded. "You saw for yourself, Isabel. He was out of his mind."

"With grief," Isabel countered.

"It's been years," James said. "They've been dead a long time. He knows that and high time he's come to grips with it."

From across the room, Mary said, "You've no idea what you're talking about, James." She struggled to her feet and walked over to face

113

her eldest son who stood a foot taller than her. The woman's ferocity along with the disparity in sizes made Isabel smile, despite the seriousness of the moment.

"It is not so easy a thing *to come to grips with* to use your words. And you upset me so when you speak of fighting so easily, what you believe to be our fight, this family's fight. What part of this fight will be yours, James? What of you? Your brother has gone to war. He has fought for you, fought for this family. All of you, hear me well, there will be no more fighting. There will be no more wars."

The room became silent. Isabel walked over to Mary and took the woman's hand.

Mary looked at her and said, "Take me to my son."

Mary

"I know they're dead."

He spoke as though his tongue was too large for his mouth. From the drug, Mary supposed. She poured him a glass of water from the small pitcher left earlier on the bedside table. She handed him the glass. His hand trembled when he reached for it, the bandages making him clumsy. He drank a little and then gave it back. He looked at her. He seemed to consider something, and then said, "Denying things won't bring them back to me."

Mary smiled, her voice tender. "If only it could."

114

He closed his eyes. "It was like I was walking in two worlds."

"You were very ill," she said to him.

"I can still feel her."

Mary nodded and they both grew quiet. Nathaniel coughed and she gave him back the glass of water. He again only drank a small amount. He looked ill, but before she could ask him how he was feeling, he started to talk.

"I fooled myself into believing God would make things right. That they'd be here. All those years hoping it was a mistake. The longer I kept away, the longer I could keep believing they were alive."

Mary's face softened but had no words of faith to comfort him. She mustered a smile and stood over him, bending down to kiss his cheek. "I promise it *will* get better."

He looked at her and nodded. His gaze held hers for a long time. She was surprised when he smiled at her, and more so when she saw a brief spark of hope there in his face. She vowed then to do everything she could to make it so.

His voice broke into her thoughts and she blinked, her mouth opening slightly. "What is it, beloved?" she asked.

"The woman, Isabel," he paused a moment, suddenly uneasy under her scrutiny.

"What is it?" she coaxed.

His shoulders lifted and then dropped. He shook his head. The words came haltingly, "I just. I don't." He lifted his bandaged hands up to his face and groaned. When he lowered them to his lap, he gave a soft laugh.

"Did she do something to upset you?" Mary couldn't imagine what was bothering him. Isabel had been nothing but a help to her, a Godsend.

"No. No." Nathaniel made a fist, grimacing, and then blurted out: "Why does she care?"

Mary opened her mouth to speak, and then stopped. The answer she was about to give didn't seem to be the entire truth. She was certain, of course, it had been their friendship which had initially prompted Isabel to offer a helping hand. It was her nature to help people, care for people. But now Mary wondered if there might be something more to it. Her belly surged with something indefinable. Excitement, perhaps, or was it fear?

Mary looked at Nathaniel, brushing her fingertips over his brow. "She's very kind."

Mary

Once downstairs Mary fainted, finding herself one moment upright, the next, things graying, her face hot, beads of sweat there above her lip, forehead. She reeled, felt nauseous, and then nothing.

She heard a voice, her name spoken, and she opened her eyes.

"Joseph," she said. She coughed, a glass quickly pressed up to her lips. She drank, the cool water reviving her. She closed her eyes, thinking only of the slide of water through her, the softness of the satin coverlet over her, Joseph always overindulgent.

"Thomas would like to give you something to help you rest."

She didn't respond to him, her thoughts nearly twenty-five years distant, another awakening.

"No one must know," she said.

Joseph looked at her, slowly lowering down next to the bed, kneeling. "Mustn't know what, Mary?"

She looked at him. He seemed different to her, older. It was because of the killing, and the other cruelties. His eyes glittered with loss, sorrow. Because of her of that she was certain.

"About Nathaniel. No one must find out."

"Mary, please," Joseph said, a warning in his tone.

Mary nodded. She began to cry, the pain fresh as the day. "I fear I'm beginning to take delight in my suffering."

"Now, now."

"I'm so afraid, Joseph." Mary ran her fingers over her cheeks, feeling the line of tears, and then how they dried quickly, absorbed into flesh, her fingertips.

"All is well, Mary." Joseph grabbed her hand, taking it tightly into his own. Joseph grunted, shifting his legs, his knees most certainly feeling the strain from where he knelt.

She looked at him and then looked away. "God had His reasons," she said. "You know this as well as I. It had to be. It's all fine. All fine. I can live with it, have lived with it. How could I not really? You know that don't you, my love? In the end God forgave."

117

"Don't talk foolishness, Mary!" Joseph swiped at his eyes, his fingers trembled. "It has been too much for you. That's all, nothing more. What you speak of has nothing to do with any of it. God doesn't waste His time on us Keegans. We make do on our own, get by on our own."

"Blasphemy, you say! Of course, it's all God's doing. No matter that I choose to turn from Him, shun Him, in the end His Will be done. I accept this now. So, must you."

"Oh, Mary darling. Oh, Mary. Don't. I won't listen again."

"You won't listen!" Mary sat up, stiff with anger. "It wasn't you, Joseph. What of it do you know? What suffering have you endured? That wretched savage taking me again and again. A pain so deep, I can't put to words. Ruined. But it was God's Will. My penance. From sorrow and suffering, a babe was begotten. A babe lost to us years ago given back again."

Joseph bowed his head, silent. He looked up at her and said, "Nathaniel is not our Jacob. Jacob was our sweet baby boy died at birth."

Mary pulled her hand from his hold. "You weren't there. I've told you this. He was alive. Days alive."

"Mary, Jacob is dead that is something we cannot change."

She looked at him, his face flushed, eyes wide-opened. *Did he want to tell her something?* They held no secrets from each other, only from others.

"But why would my mother lie?" She spoke it aloud to herself, her eyes narrowing in thought. It was something she had done, something so grievous. She tried to recall what it was, to finally be able to tell him, but again she failed. Mary lowered her head, feeling the anger drain from her limbs, her fingertips. She no longer cared, felt empty. "They mustn't know. No one must know."

"Yes, yes. About Nathaniel. You have my word."

"Make certain the Indian doesn't speak of it. You see for yourself with Nathaniel's return, his love. The truth is on him like a stink, a whisper away. His eyes speak so loudly. I hear it! I hear it! It's plain to me every time I look at him, whenever I see them together. You must kill him first, Joseph, before that ever happens. Before he talks."

"For God's sake, Mary! Don't! Nathaniel is home. Let's find joy in that. Must it all come back to haunt you?" Joseph began to weep. The sobs wracked him as if cut through with each one. Again, it was because of her. She began to stroke his head, her fingers a soft run over his hair. She lifted his face to her face, their eyes meeting.

"No one must know of this. No one must find out the Indian is of his blood. You must promise me this, Joseph!"

Joseph nodded with her hands tight against his cheeks. "I promise you as I've promised you a thousand times before this. No one will ever know."

With his vow, Mary smiled, relaxing back into her pillows. Joseph rose from the floor with the slow ache and roll of age.

The room was still, only their light breathing heard in her ears, a familiar rhythm. The rest was washed away, forgotten, like the ocean's tide come in, full and wide, all things hidden beneath. It was enough for Mary, feeling things might be good again, taking up what she could, not perfect, but a few things left to restore her, restore them. Joseph hugged her, and she felt such love for him.

In his arms, she relaxed, but then tensed when she thought she heard the soft snick of their bedroom door closing.

BOOK THREE

Thomas

Isabel was downstairs in the drawing room. She was playing Mozart on the pianoforte. The music floated up the long staircase and into his room. A soft breeze teased at the curtains and fluttered the papers on his desktop. His eyes strained while he read, the only light coming from the candle lantern he'd the patience to set a lucifer to and illumine. The interruption made him disagreeable and his aging eyes even more so.

Thomas Langford thought about the young man his daughter had taken under her wing, the long hours he suspected she spent with him, as well as, the absurd workload she'd taken upon herself. Nathaniel Keegan, dark-haired, blue-eyed, and as gaunt and played-out as the rest of those Confederate boys had been by war's end, fighting to the nub of them, body and soul. The boy was fortunate to be alive.

Those scars on his foot were no doubt from gangrene that had, at some point, set in and then had been treated with acid. The foot appeared as though it had been broken, to set it straight after its initial healing, a painful undertaking, surprised the surgeons hadn't just taken it. He could only conclude that the boy had put up quite a fight, reminded of the ones he'd no choice, but to give up on, some dangerous as snakes.

There was also a scar running across the boy's abdomen to the hipbone, bringing to Thomas' mind the sufferings of the ones who had been split wide-opened, terrified to see the entrails coiling out of them. It was the thirst, though, that had made them weep like babes, a child in want of his mother, still unable to block out their cries. *Great God! All they had asked for was a mouthful of water and some had died without even that simple petition met.*

As a doctor in the war, he was all too familiar with the suffering, Federal and Secessionist alike. He hadn't turned anyone away. They were all someone's children, so many barely of age. And his greatest failure was he hadn't been able to save them all.

He tore off his spectacles and rubbed at his eyes, his head aching. Isabel would always soothe him when he thought too much about such things. The lopped-off limbs tossed away, the piles raised nearly to the tops of windows. The soldiers fighting him, the fear in their eyes when the bone saw pressed against flesh, as if the loss of a leg or arm would be far worse than the dying. *Fools!* Had they ever been grateful when they woke from surgery alive, breathing still? Had any thanked him for their lives? He was a doctor not a surgeon, but hard-pressed they had called upon him repeatedly, along with a few brigade musicians with time on their hands. He'd become proficient at it, a natural, and he'd done his best, of what he could do for them.

He shook his head and reached for the candle lantern, bringing it closer to his papers. Nathaniel Keegan. It had only taken one look at the man to see it all again, to smell it all again, to hear it all again: The band playing, "The Battle Hymn of the Republic," the drums' cadence like the enormous beating heart of a glorious and brutal creature, this army of men in flawless array waiting their orders: Load rifles! Fix bayonets! Shoulder arms! Forward . . . March! The colors grandly unfurled and displayed, the bayonets glinting in the sunlight of perfect days.

He gagged and retched a little into his throat. He swallowed it down, feeling a burn from stomach to esophagus. He thought of his horses to calm himself. He thought of Isabel. He dreamed of her in that moment dressed in her mother's wedding gown, her slender, gloved fingers slipped through the crook of his arm while walking down the church's petal-strewn aisle toward James. The Keegan men were there, well-groomed and uncommonly handsome. Mary Keegan was a vision, herself, with her black hair worn up and adorned with mother-of-pearl, wearing a wealth of jewelry which bespoke of her privileged upbringing. Her breeding showed in her face, her hands, the back of her neck. Her blue eyes were lit with such joy, all hardships forgotten.

But then he chose to look no further, not wanting the other to disrupt, to wake him from his dream, quickly realizing once a thought exists in one's mind, it becomes nearly impossible to put it aside. So there Nathaniel Keegan stood with his rifle between his spread feet, the bayonet affixed upon it, grimy fingers wrapped, tight-fisted, around the Enfield's barrel. He wore a gray cavalry hat, a gray roundabout jacket and butternut trousers. He wore no shoes. He watched the procession, hollow-eyed. Pale skin, pulled tautly over high cheekbones, appeared nearly translucent. He didn't fight the green flies that swarmed around him nor did he seem to notice the bloated dead at his feet.

Thomas drew his mouth open and was about to scream when his body gave a hard jerk and he awoke. He'd fallen asleep with paper and ledger still in his hands. "Oh, Lord!" The whole of him shook. "Oh,

124

Dear Jesus!"

He was certain he would be ruined for the night. He looked down at the array of books and ledgers, the ink on the pages smudged badly from his sweating palms, illegible, and he cursed. He thought to himself, *I cannot lay eyes upon him again. Never again.* He sighed. *Though, it is through no fault of his own and I am sorry for that.*

He moved to the bed and removed his boots, his trousers, his shirt. Too tired to do anything more, he stood and pulled down the coverlet and sat down again on the edge of the bed. He ran a hand over his face, yawned and lifted his aching legs up onto the mattress. The freshly laundered sheets felt cool against his skin. Isabel's face came to mind and his mouth curved up at the corners. But then his disposition changed altogether when he remembered how hard she'd been working. She would bring herself to exhaustion if she wasn't careful. Of course, it was for Mary. *Dear and lovely Mary.* He felt heat come to his face, blushing. He laughed, chiding himself for being a lovesick fool. *Of all the women!*

He stretched out fully and settled his head into the pillow, bringing the white top sheet up to his neck. He thought of Mary and closed his eyes. He would dream of her and his horses. He heard her voice then, at first too soft to hear what she was saying, but growing louder, *No one must find out the Indian is of his blood...*

He hadn't meant to overhear her conversation with Joseph. He'd merely meant to make sure she was well, to see her again as a friend and as a doctor. He'd no idea of what she spoke, all too aware of her sometimes-fragile state, her nervous affliction. She was such a beautiful and delicate thing. Too tired to ponder her wild imaginings, wanting only to dwell upon good things, he ascended into a different world, an Eden of his own making: his horses, his daughter, married and ripe with child, and the dear and lovely Mary beside him. With eyes closed, it all came alive.

The breeze from the window picked up, the room comfortable, perfect for sleeping. The music still played on downstairs, a soothing lullaby. He yawned and fell into sleep.

Isabel

It only sprung up in her mind when she was too tired to hold it down, to shove it back into those dark places where secrets, so tragic and damning, are kept. Unacknowledged, denied, left to rot, to turn to dust, to ash. But for Isabel, this secret haunted her like an apparition, a restless and vengeful spirit, and no incantation, no spell or prayer, no plea could hold it at bay for too long.

She wondered if it was because of Nathaniel, the caring of him, seeing those scars, those eyes, the war like a pox on him, a stink of the battlefield, so virulent, so vivid, clinging to him a year later. She closed her eyes against it, her fingers kneading her temples where a headache throbbed. She should be sleeping, morning only a few hours away, and her work waiting for her, piling up around her. Isabel's father hadn't complained, hadn't mentioned her time away from the ranch, but she still felt guilty, and slightly foolish. She'd been so certain she could keep up with everything. Mary had needed her more than she had imagined she would, and before too long, Isabel found herself running two households.

She punched her pillow and flipped onto her back, staring at the moonlit ceiling. She thought of Connecticut, the boys she'd spurned, thinking she was above them all and, somehow, still fooling herself and everyone else. That is until *he* would come back to remind her differently.

She had not lived in her father's home for many years, boarding at school, going abroad on more than one occasion, so certain all this would have prepared her for such things. Above all else, she'd been of the age knowledgeable in the ways to counter such advances, to fend off, to have kept it from occurring. But had she truly been the one at fault? Had she truly given him her consent, the right to do such a thing to her?

Always anger when she thought of that time, at herself, at him. She'd met him the summer she'd returned home after the completion of her studies. He'd been a graduate of West Point, a young lieutenant headed off to war, saving the Union single-handedly, as all young soldiers believed they would. He'd been unlike the rest though, somehow different, kind of heart, sensitive, gentle – until that night. Her father had been away, and she'd shamelessly invited the young man to dine with her without chaperon. She'd given little thought to the opinion of others, trusting herself, trusting him. He'd given her no reason to think he'd harm her. He was a man of valor, gallant, courteous, chivalrous.

Later that evening, there had been one kiss, one hand upon her breast. She had resisted, had told him to stop. He had kissed her again, hard, frightening her when his hands had lowered to those areas that should never be touched or revealed before marriage: thighs, buttocks, between her legs. No longer the sweet, gentle boy she had known over those long summer days. She'd fought him then, but perhaps she had not fought hard enough.

She had never been touched like that. Certainly, there had been stolen kisses, fleeting hugs, all sweet, all bearable, so unlike how he'd been with her. *You're not a child, Isabel,* he'd said to her. *What age? Oh, yes, nineteen.* He had laughed then. *You're a woman, Isabel, a woman. And this long overdue,* he had spoken the last as a whisper into her ear.

When he'd finished, he had pulled up his pants, buttoning them, leaving the room. Isabel had remained where he'd left her, a flux of agony coursing through her. Gone for nearly twenty minutes, he had finally returned, lifting her into his arms and carried her to a bath he'd drawn for her. He had watched while she'd bathed, speaking gently, singing songs of such tenderness and caring. *Please know I love you, Isabel. You are my only love, my heart,* he'd said to her, all the while the palm of his hand cupping the back of her head, and then running down her back where her long hair covered her like a cowl.

"You will be my wife." He had stood then, kissing her on the forehead. He'd touched a fingertip to her cheek, taking away a tear. She had watched him, her mind a swirl of feelings she'd no inclination to identify.

She had hurt for days after, bruised, sensitive to her own daily ablutions, angered by her vulnerability. She had not gotten to choose, being subordinate, servile, a thing she had never been a day in her life. Only owning one thing, holding it close, a secret never to be told to another soul, a vow made. Isabel had wished him dead a thousand times over while asking God's forgiveness for such malevolent thoughts. Within a year, she had gotten her wish: The gallant, young lieutenant wounded in battle, only to live a few months longer, his baby born before its time only to live less than a single hour.

Nathaniel

There was a time when Nathaniel would have given most anything to have his father by his side as he was this late spring morning: reaching out to him, his hand hovering, making sure his steps were sound, eyes intent, worried for him, concerned. His father loved him, Nathaniel never doubted that, but sometimes he swore there was something hidden in his father's eyes, some secret. Since his return home, he'd seen a shadow steal across them, a startling lifelessness in green eyes that were normally sharp with intelligence, brilliant with joy. Mostly it would be there when his father watched him, unaware of Nathaniel watching him in return. The child that remained in him wanted to shove down those concerns, felt to him like poking a snake with a stick. He was afraid.

Affection came easy for his father, not unusual for him to give his sons a thumping embrace, a wink, a joke, always with a smile. James had grown weary of it by the age of twelve, keeping his distance, especially at day's end. Nathaniel never minded it though, not even as a grown man. Most evenings, John would occupy their father's time in the after-dinner hours, too young in those days to be working the horses and cattle with them.

After the evening's schooling, Nathaniel and James would sit by the fire and listen to their mother read, mostly from the Bible, but sometimes there would be books filled with astounding tales of adventure. James would quickly fall asleep, but Nathaniel would find himself enthralled, caught up in it, while trying to remember every detail to share with Two Crows. It took great effort on his part to tell the story in the Indian's tongue, struggling to find the right words, a bit unsure if he had succeeded. When Two Crows would nod appreciatively at stories' end, his doubts were eased. Afterward, the Cheyenne would quietly share his own stories of the People in the white man's tongue. Those had been bright days.

"Can you tell me about it?"

Caught up in memory, his father's voice startled him. He stopped and drew breath; it went through him, a quiver. He thought to himself, *No, I can never speak of it.* But he found himself saying something else entirely. "I reckon," he said, but he couldn't stifle a weary groan.

His father stopped walking, Nathaniel, his head down, did as well.

He sensed his father's eyes on him, watching. Nathaniel's thoughts began to wander, walling himself away from his father's scrutiny. He heard Janie calling to him.

"You stay with me now, boy," a distant voice commanded. "Great God! I don't know where you go off to inside that head of yours, but–" the voice broke, a throat cleared. "Well, I might just have an idea."

Janie still called to him. And then the voice was back, "Nathaniel! Listen! You need to be here with us, your family, those that are still alive."

He was grabbed by the back of the neck and shaken. Nathaniel tried to concentrate. *Those that are still alive.* He heard his father talking to him and worked to make sense of what he was saying.

"It's a brave man that can talk about things. Things that aren't easy to talk about, like the killings or all he's lost."

Nathaniel came back completely and looked up at his father. He saw something flicker in the man's eyes and then vanish. Nathaniel turned from it and stared down at the ground. He shook his head and in a soft voice said, "Lord knows if talking helped I'd be doing just that, but it don't." He stopped and gathered his thoughts, saying, "It's done with."

His father stood to face him and grabbed him by the shoulders, holding him in place. Nathaniel panicked and struggled to break free. He shook from the strain. His father didn't relent, pulling him into a tight hug. Nathaniel's ribs at once began to ache from the press of the large arms around him. One of his father's oversized hands was curled around the back of his neck and the other was pressed hotly against his shoulder blade. He felt swallowed up by him, drowning there. He wanted to weep, to find redemption, to be comforted. In his father's arms, he was a boy again, and he at last allowed himself to relax against the larger man. He remained upright only with the support of his father.

A whisper in his ear then, "I don't believe it is, as you say, over and done with, Nate."

Nathaniel could only manage a nod into his father's shoulder. To his dismay without consent, a great run of tears started down his face and into the fabric of his father's shirt. He was too far gone to stop it. Things grew wet, his coughing bringing up mucous from his lungs and his knees buckled when he couldn't catch his breath. His head spun, his nose suddenly bleeding.

"Come, boy, sit down." His father spoke to him kindly while he led him into the shade of a tree. He took firm hold of Nathaniel's arm and lowered him down onto the soft grasses and sat down cross-legged next to him. His father's hand roved a moment in a side pocket, bringing out a handkerchief and handing it to Nathaniel.

"No shame in tears. Not one man alive who hasn't done his share."

His father shook his head, his features drawn with sorrow. He said, "Give it time, Nate. Give it time. I want you to know that I'd give my life if it could change things."

His father gave a rueful laugh and swiped at his eyes. "We're a fine pair." He patted Nathaniel's outstretched leg. "What do you say, we get you back? One look at you, your mama's going to have my head."

Nathaniel dabbed at his eyes with his father's handkerchief but wiped his nose on his sleeve. He stared at the streak of red there for a time. The tears were rising again, and he pressed the heels of his hands into his eyes hard, willing himself not to cry. In a whisper, he said, "Can't seem to find my way."

Large fingers pulled at his hands moving them away from his covered face and then kept them in a tight grip. "Keep a hold of me. You hear me, Natey? Keep a hold. You're home now and that's all that matters."

Nathaniel clutched his father's hand and gave one strong squeeze. He let go and nodded to him. But still despairing, he hung his head and thought to himself: *If only that could be enough.*

John

John had been studying the tracks heavy with unshod pony hoof prints for hours. Cattle had come up missing and a few unbroken colts. With James over to the Langford's, and Nathaniel still off his feet, John was given the task of finding them. Over the past few months, the raids had become more frequent, bloodier. During the war, the Indians had nearly controlled the plains. There had been sixty-two thousand able-bodied young men who had gone off to fight for the Confederacy, leaving only twenty-seven thousand boys and old men in all of Texas. The 2nd Cavalry had been disbanded and the forts in Texas were left abandoned, some burnt to the ground as the Federal troops departed. The Confederate Army took over some of the Forts recruiting the friendlier Indians. The only request was that the Indians not raid, but rather settle the land and farm. It was agreed upon, until the Indians realized the weakness of the white men. While the Civil War raged in the East, bloodshed and terror prevailed in the West.

His family had been fortunate for the most part. Perhaps it was because of the likes of Caden who kept the raiders at bay. He was a man without conscience, cruel, and his men the same, and they frightened John. He shivered and touched fingers to his rifle, resting in its scabbard. At least he was not alone with Two Crows scouting ahead of him. The old Cheyenne was frightening enough to John in his own way. Nathaniel had told him Two Crows had a poke of scalps hidden somewhere, coup from old battles. Some were scalps of white men. Nathaniel had shown John how it was done, but John could see in Nathaniel's eyes that he thought it was wrong, even though, he held a deep respect for Two Crows.

It's not our way, Johnny, he had said, *but in the heat of battle a man might find himself doing things he'd never believe himself capable of doing.*

John had seen Nathaniel fight hand-to-hand and with a gun. He was surprised Nathaniel hadn't been transferred to the Sharpshooters during the war as good a shot as he was. But Nathaniel, John was certain, would take little pleasure or pride in shooting a man down without defense or warning.

Hunting game's different, he'd say, *there's a purpose to it.*

John could see both sides of it. If shooting some important Yankee General dead would have meant shortening the war, so be it. That was purpose enough for him.

A noise to his right stopped him short, and he pulled hard on the reins. He listened, his ears straining, cursing when the sound of his own heart was louder than everything else. Two gray squirrels shot out across the tree branches overhead, chasing each other, chattering. John relaxed, able to bring his breathing back to normal. He urged his horse on, pulling the rifle from the sheath and resting it on the saddlebow. Sweat trickled down from his temples and the nape of his neck, absorbing into his shirt collar. His hands seemed too big and clumsy to manage both reins and rifle. He took several deep breaths, working on staying calm.

A thought came to him then: *Wish that Indian would get back here. He better not of gone and gotten himself killed.*

He shook his head, immediately disgusted with himself. *You're just too scared to be alone is all. You aren't worried about Two Crows no how, only about your own neck.*

John hadn't needed to worry, the Indian coming over the rise in that instant. He rode toward John as though he had something on his mind. With a press of his heels to his mount, John rode out of the brushwood and onto the rolling field brilliantly lit in the morning sun to meet him. He didn't like being in the open, though it was his family's land for miles around in every direction. Somehow it didn't seem to matter who owned the land and what was on it when there was an enemy afoot who didn't

135

give a spit about the civilized world and its laws. His thoughts were interrupted when the Cheyenne reined up alongside him.

"What did you find?" John asked while he slipped the rifle back into the scabbard. He looked at the man next to him.

Two Crows wore his black hair in two long braids hung down on both sides of his chest and grown nearly to his waist. He wore a brown felt hat with a wide brim that hid his piercing, black eyes and the gray along his hairline and temples. For a man of his years, he was lean and well-muscled, seeming to be much younger. Around his neck he wore a cording with a stone arrowhead hanging from it, attached to the arrowhead was a deerskin bundle containing *medicine*. A lock of blonde hair had been woven into a deerskin string hanging from the bundle. A bow case held his bow, a quiver, his arrows, but he fought mostly with an old rifle.

John asked the question again, but the Indian didn't answer him. Two Crows seemed to be deep in thought, eyes only seeing what spooled in his head.

"Hellfire! Ain't you heard a word?" In his impatience, John had lost all fear of the man. "Seein' how you can't see fit to tell me what you came across back there, I reckon I'll have a gander for myself."

John pulled his mount around and was about to start off toward where Two Crows had come when the Indian grabbed hold of his horse's bridle.

"No."

"What?" John looked at the man's hand. "Let go!"

"No."

"What the devil!" John pulled hard on the reins and turned his horse in a circle, trying to break the man's hold. "Let go now!"

"Listen." The Indian's grip remained strong.

"Listen to what old man?" John was angry. "Listen to you impart on what's got you so unhinged?" A rough tug on the reins brought the horse in motion again. By now, the large bay was spooked and ill-tempered. The animal fought against the hand at the halter, meanwhile, nipping at John's leg.

"Enough of this foolery!" John stopped fighting against Two Crows and let his horse settle. He sat there, breathing hard, petulant, but silent.

"We must go." Two Crows looked back toward the ridge. "There will be time to talk later."

Before John could put thought into word, he heard it: the sound of animals in a full run headed toward them.

"You must go!" Two Crows slapped a hand to the rump of John's horse and John set off at a gallop.

"You comin' with?" John had to shout over his shoulder at the old Indian who hadn't moved from where they had tussled. The Cheyenne was standing up in the stirrups, waiting and watching. When the first dark spots appeared on the far ridge, he turned and raced toward John.

"They the ones who stole our beeves?" John asked.

"Yes."

"Well then what are they bringing them back here for?" John scowled, his brow drawing together, puzzled by the situation. Again,

137

shouting to be heard, John said, "Maybe we should lend them a hand."

Two Crows looked at him and then shook his head once with great force. John understood at once what the simple gesture conveyed, more than words. It was not the time to argue. The Indian seemed to be anxious, wary.

Afraid! John thought, *the old man's afraid!* He shook his head in wonder, amazed at the notion that an old warrior like Two Crows would be scared. And then it struck him: *Afraid for you, you fool! Afraid for you!* With that thought, he put heel to rump and rode faster than he ever had in his life.

John

John and Two Crows rode beyond several outbuildings and into the simple courtyard of white picket fencing at a fast trot. Nathaniel sat on the porch in what John currently viewed as the man's favorite rocker. He hadn't acknowledged them, but at closer inspection John saw his brother's keen eyes were focused on the distant horizon.

"Here they come," John said to the Indian who merely grunted his response. "What do we do?"

Two Crows was contemplative. "We wait."

"We wait! That's just dandy! We wait!" John pulled on the horse's reins. His mount was nervous under him. John held him steady while he looked again at his brother.

Nathaniel stood, too slowly, still not recovered. His eyes darted from Two Crows to John. He spoke softly, "Trouble?"

John looked at Two Crows and said, "Not rightly sure."

"Who are they?"

It was Two Crows who spoke up to John's surprise. "Caden."

"Caden?" John's voice rose in timbre, a squeak. He turned to Two Crows. "You never said it was Caden. If'n I'da known that, I wouldn't be racing all over creation tryin' to get away."

Nathaniel stared at John for a long time. The man seemed to be looking through him.

"What?" His voice again came out as a belligerent squeak, and he felt the heat of his face.

Nathaniel shook his head. "Get my gun."

"Now, Nathaniel, I don't reckon that's such a good idea." John's hands shifted on the reins, the horse again dancing beneath him. His nerves were getting the best of him. "Where's Pa?"

The home's screen door opened. His father stood there a moment and looked out toward where the riders were coming in, the dust rising from the fast-moving herd of horse and cattle. He spoke to the Indian with sign, nodding once.

"I need my gun, Pa." Nathaniel held the railing and John could see his legs tremoring. From weakness or from fear, John wasn't clear on the issue. But he dismissed the notion of fear, not believing his brother to be afraid of a thing.

"Let it be, Natey." His father walked over to Nathaniel and grabbed his arm. He walked his brother to the door. "I need you inside. I don't want that fool making any more threats toward you."

"I can take care of myself." Nathaniel pulled his arm from the larger man's grip.

"You think I don't know that?" The older man lowered his head. "Your mama isn't up to any more gunplay. Not here, not now."

Nathaniel sucked in air like he'd been gut-punched. Their father played to win and using their mother against his brother was just the thing to keep him in line.

Not fair a'tall, old man, not fair a'tall, John thought. He pushed back his hat and shook his head, while turning to see how much ground Caden had gained. Coming on fast now with plenty of men, all well-armed. Caden clearly wasn't taking any chances. John looked over at his brother who hadn't yet acquiesced.

"You need me." There was something in Nathaniel's voice which gave John pause. He was pleading, close to desperate.

"Hell, Nathaniel, it's only Caden bringing back our stolen beeves. The way I see it, he's one of the good guys."

"Well, then you're blind." His words were well-aimed, lethal as a heavy charge of buckshot.

John's mouth dropped open and he lowered his eyes, his cheeks once more flaming. He tried not to take to heart his brother's disapproval. "Maybe you're right, Nathaniel, and I'm the fool. But I believe in my gut right now, Caden ain't here lookin' for trouble."

140

Two Crows let out a derisive snort. John watched the old Cheyenne for a long beat. He ran a hand over his face. "All right, I get it. Caden can't be trusted."

He heard Nathaniel laugh. The sound was low, more like a growl. *Rusty as an old fence gate,* John thought to himself. But it was one of the best sounds he'd heard in a long time.

"Ain't as dumb as he looks." Again, the laugh and John grinned despite himself.

"I reckon I take after you then." John laughed at the look on Nathaniel's face. It seemed like how it had been for them as young boys. John looked at his father whose face was split with a wide grin, even while watching the riders coming in hard.

"Time to hole-up, Nathaniel." His father pushed the still recuperating man through the doorway. "I want to hear what they have to say first." He looked at Two Crows. "You best lay low, too. We'll palaver later."

Two Crows nodded and turned his horse away from the oncoming men and headed east toward his lodge. He was quickly out of view. John heard his father let out breath and saw the man's hand shake, as well, when he took up his rifle, taking it to be primal tremors before a fight.

John watched the men come closer and suddenly wanted Nathaniel and Two Crows with them, watching their backs. Nathaniel didn't like Caden, thought the man was lower than a snake. He was a scalp hunter, a killer, and John figured the man didn't rightly care whose hair he snatched off and sold. He shivered and thought how people would say a thing about someone walking across their grave. Never liked the saying,

141

didn't quite understand it, and sure as hell didn't want to think about such things with cold-blooded killers barreling in on him and his father. He almost hoped Nathaniel was drawing a bead on Caden. He grinned, trusting his brother to be doing just that.

Mary

It was early afternoon when Mary Keegan stood in her kitchen watching out the window above her soapstone sink. She turned to see Nathaniel stumble in through the open screen door as if having been given a determined nudge from someone outside. She hurried over to his side, ushering him to her long-departed mother-in-law's Hitchcock chair, one of the few things Joseph brought from Connecticut.

Nathaniel shook beneath her hold and his breathing was too quick. She took note of the bloodstains on his shirt sleeve but remained silent.

"I need my Sharps," he said finally.

"They will no doubt kill you this time." Mary's words were blunt, but her heart flittered at the notion. "I won't have it."

"Ma–"

"What, Nathaniel? What do you wish me to do?" She took a breath and stood full height in front of him. "I had no say when you went off to war, but now I have one. No! You may not have your carbine. No! You may not fight this battle."

Nathaniel's eyes widened. "I'm sorry," he whispered.

Mary touched his cheek. "I know, sweet boy, I know." She smiled. "Jane and I forgave you a long time ago."

He made a strangled sound, not able to look at her.

"We never believed it was your choice," she said. "Perhaps there had been threats made against us. It had been the only thing that we could conclude, the only thing which had made any sense at all. Your father from the North with deep Yankee roots, myself from New York, certainly those things alone would have had garnered suspicion and ire with passions running as high as they were in the beginning of the war. Several distant relatives were graduates of West Point. Of course, all Unionist, which your father and I were as well as your brothers and I believed yourself. I can only imagine the difficulties you must have had to endure, fighting in a war on a side you had no allegiance.

So, my dear, sweet child, Jane and I could only conclude your decision was based solely on your family's well-being. I do so regret you hadn't thought to come to us, to your father, to me, to Jane, as your father had paid a hefty sum to avoid such things. I still mourn for all those years lost, all the horrors you've had to endure. But perhaps your decision was not without merit, not in vain, as I do recall the Martins having been burned out, lock, stock and barrel, everything taken and the father, Walter, never heard from again, along with the boy, Charlie. Soon after, Sarah had taken the girls and had returned to Pennsylvania to her family. And then all those men murdered and tossed into that gruesome Dead Man's Hole. Each one Unionist. Perhaps, your sacrifice was well worth it. But I can't say for certain. Can you?"

His head still lowered, she couldn't see his eyes. She wondered if he had gone off into his head again. She couldn't blame him, and she wrung her hands, worried she'd been too harsh with him. She went to touch his shoulder but pulled back when his head lifted, and he looked up at her for a long beat.

"If it kept you safe, kept them all safe, then it was worth it," he said, standing up somewhat shakily, but determined. "I need my gun." He walked away from her, his mind on other things and she could only watch him move down the long hallway toward the stairs and then listen as he climbed the steps up to his room where his well-looked-after carbine waited for him.

Mary stilled, thought a moment, and then with her decision made, pushed the screen door open and stepped out onto the portico. She eyed the rank and filthy men there in the courtyard, hiding her distaste with a fine turn of her lips, smiling, eyes bright as if with joy, and only those who knew her would see they were lit with the burning anger of her heart.

"Gentlemen," she said. And then to Joseph: "What do we have here?" Before he could say anything, she went on. "Have these kind and brave men come to return all that had been taken from us?"

"Yes, Ma'am, that we have," Caden smiled and removed his hat. He took a grimy hand and combed back his slick hair from his forehead. "It was our pleasure, Ma'am."

"Well, isn't that good of you." Mary took Joseph's hand and

squeezed it. He looked at her and shook his head, but allowed her to continue. "Joseph, these fine men should be compensated for their trouble, wouldn't you agree?" Again, she went on without getting his response. "Perhaps you can talk with the good Colonel and see what Mr. Caden and his men's rate of payment might be for such a service."

"Well, Ma'am," Caden stammered, seeming a bit unsure, a blush suddenly showing beneath the grime and dirt layered on his face. "We was hopin' to get our, well, it was our intention to— oh, hell. I reckon, there ain't no harm in workin' things out with the Colonel."

Mary smiled. "I really do think that is for the best. And as you are aware from recent experience we do make good on our debts." Mary lowered her head, her eyes darkening, her smile fading. She recovered fast, lifting her head, her smile once again in place, eyes only on Caden.

"We heard tell your boy'd taken ill." Caden tried his best to look remorseful. "How's he farin'?"

"Doing well, under the circumstances." Mary tilted her head, her gaze still focused on Caden. "Thank you for asking, Mr. Caden." She turned to Joseph and then looked over at John who had been sitting his horse with his mouth agape during the entire exchange. "John, would you be a dear and remove the cattle from my courtyard. They've nearly trodden over all my hollyhocks and I am now bereft of my roses, in ruins."

John looked at her, not moving.

"John, don't sit there slack-jawed. Do as your mother tells you." Joseph stepped forward. "I'll be in touch, Caden."

Mary watched her husband with a keen eye. The next words, Joseph would speak would be difficult for him, she was certain. He muttered a bit and cleared his throat a few times. Almost inaudible, he gave Caden a gruff and quick thank you.

Mary took her husband's hand and again held it firm in her own, giving it a squeeze. She nodded to Caden as he set his hat on his head. Before turning away, Caden touched two fingers to the worn brim and smiled at Mary.

She stayed and watched the men leave, not taking her eyes from them until they were no longer in sight.

Isabel

Isabel rode up to the Keegan's grand home with James beside her. He had arrived midmorning to escort her, having compromised many weeks before, promising not to ride alone. Billy Holmes, her usual chaperon, had been under the weather for the past few days, leaving James with the privilege of her company. It certainly was not her idea and found the situation to be both ridiculous and demeaning. She hadn't spoken a word to him the entire way, not being spiteful, her mind simply too preoccupied with the household chores left from the previous day and the day's workload still facing her. Exhausted before she began, having already completed the chores at home nearly into the early afternoon. She'd gotten little sleep the night before, remembering things she'd worked so hard to forget.

The boy would have been six years of age this day, if he had lived.

The night the pains came, a Negress midwife had been secreted to the stately white house, all very discreet and handsomely paid. Her father hadn't known of her plight, would never know, away to war, and she alone, frightened, angry, and suffering the pain of Eve. She wished the baby away so often, to just be gone from her that when she heard the midwife's cries of despair, holding the pale, nearly lifeless boy in her large dark hands, it was as a dream come to life, a wish fulfilled. But also, in that moment, Isabel couldn't disavow her hand in its approaching death. Most assuredly, she had killed the child with her unloving thoughts, her despair, her unyielding hatred, her inability to accept the tiny creature sprung from her, even if born of God.

Stop this! She chastised herself again as she'd done all morning. *You must go on, as you have always gone on. You did not kill the child. It was God's will. It is always God's will.*

Isabel focused on her surroundings and saw John working with several men in the Keegan's employ. He was corralling four colts while the others were moving cattle back to the larger herd. She was curious if the stolen livestock James had mentioned had somehow been recovered. She glanced over at him, not surprised to see he was watching the activity, distracted, and she no longer a burning concern. He gave a gruff goodbye and headed off in John's direction. She was relieved, too tired to listen to his diatribes about Nathaniel, certain the

147

subject would have come up at some point.

As far as, Nathaniel was concerned, she hardly existed. Perhaps she was being a bit too harsh, slightly irritable from her poor sleep. She had hoped for so much more, believing him to be, beneath the surface, as refined, educated and well-read as Mary. James and John were knowledgeable to some extent in literature, familiar with many authors and books, and James ability with figures was quite astounding. John was a gifted storyteller, could spin the most intricate and enjoyable tales, leaving her wanting more. She'd given him a handsome leather notebook in which she'd hoped he'd write them down, but as yet, she didn't know if he'd done so. Nathaniel seemed so different from them all.

To be fair, it'd only been a month since he'd begun to speak, to acknowledge those around him. Her father told her to give him time, as she had done for him. She remembered how hard it had been for her father, how much he'd endured, trying to forget the horrors of war, trying to rejoin society, to regain normalcy. It had been a long and difficult journey, and still Isabel wasn't quite so sure he'd completely recovered. Only last night, she'd heard his night terrors. It had been a year without them, his sleep, recuperative and deep. Nathaniel sprung to mind as the catalyst for the nightmares, but she'd hurriedly put the notion aside. She didn't need more obstacles in her path. Her own self-doubts were more than enough to handle.

Isabel hoped she could persuade Nathaniel to take a carriage ride with her and then stop along the way to picnic. She thought if Mary agreed to come along, the two could sway him. A little fresh air and sunshine would do him wonders. She had yet to see him smile or hear him laugh which troubled her.

Oh! Arrogant woman! She silently rebuked herself. *How do you propose to make him whole? What makes you think he could love another, love you?*

Her eyes began to fill and she bit her lip, annoyed at herself. She was acting like a spoiled child, a little girl pouting for what she could never possess, for what very well may be denied her. She thought, *First and foremost, love must bloom between two people, naturally. In time, these feelings will certainly be found out to be truly genuine or just a flight of fancy.*

He was fragile, remembering her words: *broken, he is broken.* It would take time and patience. She had a large commodity of both, or so she hoped. She unhorsed and flipped the reins over the railing and walked determinedly up the steps. Once on the porch, she pushed open the screen door without knocking. She called Mary's name and receiving no response, looked around the kitchen to see what needed to be done. Lovely Spode china dishes were stacked in the soapstone sink. A large skillet sat on the cook stove coated in pork fat, a whitish congelation. Surprisingly, Mary had many fine possessions, by some miracle surviving the rough handling of four men. She smiled at that and began to sing as she found the soap, pumping the water into the sink.

She called out again for Mary, while scrubbing the hardened egg yolk

149

off the dishes.

"She's resting."

Isabel nearly jumped out of her skin, Nathaniel mere steps from her. She hadn't even heard him approach, wondering how loud she'd been singing.

"Oh, my goodness!" She rested her hands on the sink top for support. Her hands sopping, she wiped her forehead with the back of her wrist, pushing aside loose strands of her hair. She took a breath and turned around and smiled at him.

Nathaniel ducked his head. "Sorry for startling you."

She shook her head. "I hadn't realized how loud I was singing. I should be apologizing to you. I'm surprised I hadn't wakened your mother with my caterwauling."

She laughed and turned back to the sink, squeezing out the dishcloth. She draped it over the sink and looked around for a hand towel. She'd forgotten to put on an apron before starting her chores.

"You sing just fine." He moved slowly to the nearby hutch and pulled out a white linen towel. He walked over to her, handing her the cloth.

"Thank you," she said. "For this," she held up the cloth, continuing, "and for the compliment."

"I meant it." He looked at her for a long beat and then as if suddenly aware he'd been staring too long, he cleared his throat and stepped away to look out the window.

She wanted him to talk to her and she struggled to think of something to say. The only thought coming to her was of the stolen cattle.

Genuinely curious, she said, "I saw John cattle wrangling and herding a few ponies into the paddock. James mentioned some livestock had been stolen. Have they been recovered then?"

Nathaniel looked away from the window and over at her. "You could say that."

She was perplexed. "I don't understand."

"Caden." He spoke the name with distaste. "It was Caden that brought them in."

"Had it been Comanche?" She asked.

He looked at her as though she'd two heads, and she felt heat come to her cheeks, certain she was red-faced.

"I know Mr. Caden is clearly reprehensible, but he does seem to do his job quite well–"

"The hell you say!"

"I beg your pardon?" She was not so much stunned by his words as by his anger directed at her.

He looked away from her, standing perfectly still. In a whisper, he said, "Caden's playing both ends." Focused now only on his suspicions. "I'd stake my life on it. Nearly killed us to know a war was brewing back home while we were fighting another. Heard 'bout Elm Creek from a few boys' letters.

"I reckon most believe men like Caden have got the right of it. Chivington, himself, plain out said to kill and scalp 'em all, big and little. Nits make lice." He shook his head and looked her square in the eyes. "Ain't that just fine? Ain't that just dandy?"

Nathaniel's face paled and he swayed a little. Isabel moved forward to steady him, but he held up his hand to her, the gesture telling her to stay back. Her stomach tightened, and she felt unexpected tears.

"I'm sorry," he finally said. "One way or another, things will run their course."

"And where will you stand?" She asked him, not able to hold her tongue.

He looked at her. His eyes were sad. "With my family like always." Nathaniel studied her a moment. "Did you think differently?"

"How could I think any way at all? I hardly know you." She was certain she sounded shrewish. Her heart sunk then, the prospect of a relationship with the man slipping through her fingers. The fact of the matter, it was all her own fault.

"The better for you."

"What does that mean?" Isabel stepped toward him. She touched his arm and then reached up and touched his cheek lightly with her fingers. "What do you mean, Nathaniel?"

He shuddered and closed his eyes. His breath caught in his throat, she saw the vein on his neck pulsing in earnest.

"Are you well? she asked him.

He opened his eyes and she lowered her hand. "I'm fine." Nathaniel took a deep breath and then looked at her. "Why–?"

"Please, proceed, do," she said. "Please, ask me anything."

He hesitated again and then said, "Why do you care?"

She hadn't expected him to ask her such a thing. She had no answer to give him, wouldn't dare tell him the truth of things. It was much too soon, far too inappropriate. She merely said, "I don't know."

"All right then," Nathaniel said. "Fair enough." He turned and left the room, and began to sing to himself, "I leave my home and thee, dear, with sorrow in my heart. It is my country's call, dear, to aid her I depart."

Isabel stared after him, thinking he had a wonderful voice, but more importantly, thinking she truly loved the man. In her mind, there was no doubt, he belonged to her and no other.

Isabel

Mary slept while Nathaniel wandered the house like a wraith. Isabel would catch sight of him from time to time as he moved from room to room. She saw him falter a bit, as though his legs couldn't hold his weight. *Weight, what weight*, she thought, *he is a mere wisp, a feather, a cloud.* She rolled her shoulders, working the tension from her back and then rocked her head from side to side. With the movement, she heard the slight cracking of her neck.

Isabel was exhausted, besides which she was feeling put-upon. She was building up a good burn over Mary sleeping through most of the day while she cleaned and scrubbed and polished and worst of all, pouted. She was angry with herself for being near tears because of Mary's lack of consideration, someone she'd believed to be a dear and thoughtful friend. The entire situation hurt her.

And what of Nathaniel? Not one word was spoken, not one helping hand. There he was roaming around the house like a wild thing, trapped. He seemed as if half-mad, and she was now close to it herself.

"Enough!" shouted Isabel. She tore her apron off and tossed it toward the large oak tabletop. It landed on the floor. She huffed and strode over to it, picking it up. Not being able to stop herself, she folded it and placed it on the table.

Isabel took a breath and swiped at her hair. Strands flew in every direction, but she'd little patience to put them back in place. She lifted her chin and walked down the long hallway.

"Nathaniel!" she called out to him. She continued forward, searching every room. "Nathaniel Keegan!"

Her heart banged fiercely in her chest. *Damn him for making her so— so what? So irrational, so confused, so lost, so frightened, so completely unsure of herself? Just damn him!* Her eyes filled, and she swiped at them, disgusted. Again, she called, "Nathaniel Keegan! Nathaniel!"

"What is it, Isabel? Is something wrong?" Mary asked from the top of the staircase. Isabel regretted causing Mary concern.

"Oh, dear." Isabel rubbed her fingers across her forehead and tilted her head to see Mary better. "I'm so sorry, Mary. Did I wake you?"

Mary started down the staircase, moving at a quick pace. "Is Nathaniel well?"

"He's fine." Isabel paused a moment, and then said, "Well, I believe he's fine. He's been quiet for well over an hour. I'm not sure where he's gone. But I daresay, he's been quite restless most of the day." An idea came to her then. "Perhaps, I might take him for a carriage ride. A good dose of fresh air and sunshine will do him good. Wouldn't you agree?"

Mary looked at her and then smiled. "His pacing can be disconcerting at times. A buggy ride might be just the thing he needs to settle down. He barely has any strength at all, but on and on he walks, hours on end." She lowered her head and said, "I don't know what to do for him." Her head lifted, her eyes locking on Isabel's. "But perhaps you do."

Isabel's eyes widened, and she pressed a hand above her heart. She felt the thumping of it, her breathing as quick. "I–" she began.

Mary smiled at her. "You care for him."

"I– I'm not sure what you're implying." Isabel was flustered. She wanted to tell Mary everything she was feeling, but how could she really? It wasn't appropriate. He was a widower and though his wife had passed almost four years ago, it was still fresh to him, just home and having to face the actual truth of it for the first time. He hadn't moved on. He wasn't ready for any of what she was feeling. Mary interrupted her thoughts.

"I love my son deeply," Mary said. "I believe you can make him happy again."

Isabel raised her hands up to cover her eyes. Tears of exhaustion and sorrow sprung up and rolled down her pale cheeks. She couldn't seem to stop herself. She suddenly was aware of being wrapped in Mary's arms in a hug, a woman's hug, a mother's hug. It was unfamiliar, but wonderful. So very wonderful. She hugged Mary back, a gentle

155

embrace.

Slowly, Isabel released her hold and took a step back from Mary. Brushing away the remainder of her tears, she gave a watery smile. "Thank you." She couldn't bring herself to say anything more for fear she'd begin sobbing again.

"Oh, my sweet girl, it shouldn't be so devastating." Mary smiled, retrieved a lace handkerchief from her dress pocket, and lifted it to Isabel's still damp cheeks. Soft and gentle pats were given, and Isabel allowed the intimate gesture, altogether unaware until this very moment how much she had missed having the love and affection of a mother. She wanted to cry again.

Also, to add to it all, she hadn't forgotten the significance of the day, no matter how much she had tried. *How could she, really?* Pointedly, reminded of it with Mary's embrace. She was once a mother, herself, perhaps for only a mere hour, but still a mother the same, having carried the babe for months, an eternity to her back then. Would she have loved the child, the boy, if he had lived? How could she not?

Liar! she screamed to herself. *You are a liar! You prayed him dead, just like the other. Murderer!* She let out a moan, a sob. She felt her hand being squeezed, her name called.

"Isabel? Are you well?" Mary's eyes were upon her, worried.

"So sorry." Isabel shook her head. "I'm fine." Deceitful again, but not about this: "You are a wonderful mother."

"Thank you, dear." Mary held her hand a bit tighter. "Perhaps things are too complicated at present."

156

Isabel looked at Mary for a long time, trying to glean the meaning of her words from expression or gesture. But she could not and chose not to ask any further.

"Shall we find Nathaniel before the hour grows too late?" Mary asked.

Isabel nodded.

"I think I know where he's gone," Mary said, and smiled at some memory. Isabel hungered for it and was forthwith satisfied.

"When Nathaniel was younger, he'd find a quiet place to hide away. We'd usually find him behind his father's chair. He had an old deerskin robe he'd wrap himself in and would settle down with a book." Mary stopped and looked at Isabel, her eyes filling. "There are moments when I feel such dread, it nearly suffocates. I am so afraid for him." She took in a breath to calm herself. With a feeble smile, she said, "I suppose I'm just a foolish woman, much too dramatic."

Isabel shook her head. "Perhaps you have cause to be afraid, Mary. I don't know. But this I do know, he has abided, he abides still."

"Yes." Mary nodded. "Yes."

They headed toward the parlor and there behind Joseph's soft worn leather chair was Nathaniel, on his side asleep. Isabel's stomach knotted, an ache through her. She felt ill. She thought to herself then: *This love hurts so much. How does one bear it?*

She heard Mary call his name and watched as he swam up from sleep. He woke with terror in his eyes, his hand reaching for something – his knife, his rifle. Coming back to himself, he relaxed, lowering his head back down to the blanket on the floor. He smiled, his blue eyes clear, lit up from the afternoon sun coming in from the side window.

"Time to get some air, my love," Mary said and held out her hand to him. "A buggy ride."

He stared at her a moment and then nodded. He took her hand, a difficult rise from the floor. He grunted as he stood to full height, a hand gripping the back of the leather chair. "Isabel has agreed to be your driver."

He again stared at Mary. Isabel saw the trust he held in her.

He asked, "Are you coming with?"

"Not today." Mary patted his hand. "I think I've gotten away with far too much today. Isabel has not once complained, but I have put too much upon her and I do apologize. It's unforgivable. She must think dreadfully of me."

Isabel went to protest, but before she could speak, Mary said, "Off with you. And, Nathaniel, I do not want to find out that you lifted one finger on this outing. Go now, Isabel, and have Two Crows ready the carriage. Nathaniel will be right along."

Isabel's heart soared. She felt much lighter, and practically skipped out the door and over to the stables, eyes searching for the older Cheyenne.

Once she found him and made her request, though she was uneasy never having spoken to an authentic Indian, it took little time to have the buggy readied for them. Two fancy, grey horses hitched to the gig stood quiet while she climbed as daintily as she could manage up into

158

the seat without assistance. Two Crows was helping Nathaniel, just arriving at the stable, on the other side. They spoke in the Indian's tongue while Isabel watched them, fascinated by the old Indian's care of Nathaniel, his touch, protective and gentle.

When handed her rifle, she placed it at her feet, while Nathaniel's lay across his thighs, fingers gripped around it. She recognized then what James had alluded. Though the carbine rifle remained mute and lifeless upon his lap, she saw it as a slumbering behemoth, once awakened, a dangerous and terrible thing. She imagined the deadly smooth quickness he possessed, finding his sight, pulling the trigger, unremitting and light-fingered as a spider spinning its web. She trembled, frightened by what may have been wrought on those bloody battlefields. When he called her name, she startled.

"Are you all right, Isabel?" he asked.

She smiled at him, her concerns all but forgotten. *It is through no fault of his own,* she thought to herself. *He is kind. He is gentle.*

"I'm well, Nathaniel." She glanced at him. "How are you feeling?"

"Ain't got no complaints."

She was tempted to correct him. She noticed at times when he spoke his words were uncultured, as if he were ill-bred. Again, she wondered: *Had it been all those years at war, fighting with men most whom were boorish and uncouth?* She sighed, willing to overlook it.

"I won't be angry if you doze off," she said. "Please, rest if you need to do so."

He surprised her then by saying, "You are very kind, and I with

159

nothing to repay you."

She laughed. "Your company is payment enough, kind sir."

He nodded once, the old battered gray hat he wore, suddenly drawn down low to cover his eyes, his chin dropping to his chest, at once asleep.

Isabel

The ride was pleasant, the landscape beautiful, Isabel losing herself moments at a time in fancy, forgetting the dangers of this wild place. She dreamed of Connecticut, riding alongside some gentle brooklet, her beau beside her. The leaves of the trees, near peak, were flushed in brilliant hues of reds, oranges, and yellows. Or perhaps, it was early summer on a lazy Sunday morning. There they would journey down a country lane of neatly rowed white houses with black shutters, white picket fences with roses and hydrangeas and rhododendrons in a host of colors. Children would be outside playing with companions, carefree and unburdened from any mortal threat. *Yes,* she thought, *if only it could be as she dreamed it.*

She looked over at Nathaniel who still slept, his hold on the carbine, steadfast. Ridding herself of her daydreams, she was aware with certain regret that he was not meant for the old world of her dreams. They were here together in this place. It had its own certain charm, an untamed beauty, a land so large, so far reaching, making her feel small. A land, no doubt, the life marrow of the one beside her. For him, she would learn to love it, burn a fire evermore in the hearth, name this place as home.

Her musings were interrupted then by the sight of birds, crows and something worse, circling in the sky, a dark swirl of wings, a black funnel beginning to fall to earth. Something lost, dying there, man or beast, and she prayed aloud that it was the latter.

With the hurrying pace of the buggy, Nathaniel woke with a jolt, his gun lifted and ready.

"What's wrong?" he asked, his eyes alert even with the heaviness of sleep upon him.

She lifted her chin to the sky, her hands filled with line and horse. "There."

He looked and nodded. "Can you handle the buggy?"

"Yes." Isabel prodded the horse faster.

"When we get closer, you'll stay hidden in the timber," Nathaniel said in a manner expecting no argument.

She gave none, her heart quick in her chest like a clock. Her throat was dry, her words bottlenecking there.

He glanced at her and grinned, perhaps to reassure her. She found it out of the ordinary, unexpected. For the first time, she noticed he had dimples, though the hollows of his face were much more rugged. Deep lines were carved into his cheeks, amazed she hadn't noticed before a thing so disarming. But then saddened at the sudden realization, this had been the first full smile he had shown to anyone. It seemed as if she

161

merely blinked when his face shuttered closed and he turned away from her. His jaw tightened and pulsed. He looked ahead past the bobbing horses toward the distant hillock. His eyes narrowed looking up at the sky. The crows still came. She felt sick at the sight of the other, not wanting to name it.

He pointed to a stand of trees. "Head there," he said. When she looked, she saw an expanse of thick bramble covering the ground. She was about to mention the impossibility of getting through, when she spotted an opening large enough for the carriage to pass. She had little time to be afraid, simply obeying.

Once stopped, with an easy vault from the seat, Nathaniel was off on a low run, giving only a quick glance back to her. He silently mouthed for her to *stay*. She nodded to him but decided she wouldn't *stay* seated in the buggy. The dark shadows of trees and brush seemed to be a much safer place for her to *stay*. She couldn't keep the smile from her lips, even in this most dangerous and dire situation, aware it was not often she obeyed an order without protest or a need for discussion first. If her father had witnessed it, he'd no doubt be flabbergasted and quite understandably hurt. She shrugged her shoulders with a sigh and knelt low into the black recesses of bramble, the rifle snug against her knees, trying not to snag her stockings, her hair, her dress. All an unlikelihood.

There she waited, hardly breathing, her heart beating hummingbird quick. This was a moment of nightmares, reminding her of those tales of savagery adventurous colleagues of her father had shared with him over after-dinner drinks and cigars. As a young girl, she would listen to them talk long into the night, their voices loud enough to reach her on the stairs, her head pressed against the balusters, struggling to stay awake. The stories were sometimes so ghastly, she would scurry off to her bed, slipping into the refuge of blankets and quilt, while her heart pounded and tears ran down her cheeks, covers drawn over her head. Every noise would startle her: the wind, the creaking of a step, voices raised in sharp bursts of laughter.

She heard a pop of a rifle, jumping at the first one fired, and then another. *Dear Lord, keep him safe.* Isabel gripped her rifle, her fingers white from the tight hold. She couldn't keep the trembling from her legs, her arms, from fear and the need to make sure Nathaniel was safe.

After giving some thought to her next move, she rose into a low squat, pulling back strands of her hair caught in the bramble. The snagged hair pinched at her temple and caused her eyes to water. She was in no mood for the petty annoyance and cursed with vehemence when next her dress caught. With an angry tug, she tore the fabric away from the tumble of brush and then stood up straight.

The next report sent her running, no longer afraid of what she might encounter. It was purely instinct making her legs move forward, her arms like two pistons, the gun wild in her hand, slapping against her thigh. No doubt a bruise would show itself later. She didn't care.

As she ran, her eyes teemed, but this time it was fear that caused the tears to streak down her cheeks. She tasted salt, her nose filling, making it difficult to bring air to her lungs. She saw him as she made the rise. He was in the open on the ground on his stomach, lifeless. But then he

163

moved, the gun lifted, a shot let loose. Her breath caught when she saw several Indians on horseback race toward him.

She couldn't make out what was on the ground next to him. It appeared to her that he was protecting something with his body. Crows and vultures lurked in the low scrub. Others remained on land, cautious and vigilant, waiting. She shuddered and pushed down the bile rising to her throat. She needed to gather her wits, stopping a moment behind the trunk of a large tree. It sheltered her, but she was still able to view what was happening below her.

Isabel counted three on horseback and further back she saw three more with a small herd of horses. Perhaps they would leave with the horses and give up the fight. She realized she was too far out of range to be of help to Nathaniel. With a deep breath, she lowered down to the ground, shoving the rifle behind her into the loose waist of her skirt. The tall grasses concealed her well enough as she trundled along on her hands and knees.

She stopped when she came up to a slight rise close to where Nathaniel fought. While she had crawled toward him, he had managed to hold off the Indians. She knelt and again took a deep breath, checking her rifle. When she heard the report of Nathaniel's weapon, she rose, placed the rifle firm against her shoulder and found her site. She released her breath and pulled the trigger. Grim satisfaction was hers when a copper body, the wild black hair lashing the air, dropped from a pony to the ground.

Isabel saw Nathaniel twist his head around toward the hillock where she hid. He turned back and shot again, though not hitting his mark. Those who remained with the herd watched, black eyes fierce in their brown faces. Their mounts moved back and forth, their arms and hands in constant motion while they spoke to one another.

She lowered her head and closed her eyes. To herself, she prayed, *Please God, let them move on. Spare us. Spare him*

When she opened them, and lifted her head to watch, she whooped to see the Indians turning to leave. But then, she noticed one had stayed behind, her heart rising to her throat when he began to make a run toward where Nathaniel stood in place. Giving little thought to her next move, she lifted her rifle, found her site, and pulled the trigger. Her aim was true and the young, lean body fell from the pony.

She contemplated why Nathaniel hadn't taken a shot and had been missing his mark over and over, a practiced and skillful sharpshooter. When he turned to look up at her, she smiled, but then went cold at the look on his face. She pondered what she had done to displease him.

Even from the distance, she could see his face was gray with fatigue. She ran as best as she was able down the hill toward him. He waved her off and she stopped, her eyes widening in surprise.

"Stay back," he said his voice raspy. "Ain't fit for you to see."

She shook her head and called out to him. "Nathaniel, please! Let me help you."

He shook his head.

"Please! Let me help!" she shouted again to him.

Nathaniel looked hard at her for some time. Isabel stood silent, still feeling fine tremors through her limbs, her hands. Not a patient woman by nature, she seemed to have a wellspring for him.

"All right then, if you're so fired up to help, here's what I need you to do." He stopped a moment and looked away.

She was quiet, waiting for him to continue. She watched him, thinking something was wrong. At that moment, he doubled over coughing, one hand to his mouth, the other keeping a steady hold on his rifle. He knelt or perhaps had fallen, his face turned away from her line of sight. She took a step toward him, hesitated and then advanced closer. She heard the loud beating of her heart in her ears, she couldn't catch her breath. "What have you done to me?" she whispered.

"No!" His shout startled her. "Go back, now!"

At once, it was as if she had sprung to life, again herself, feeling the flush of temper rise in her. "I will not go back!" she shouted to him. "You're not well."

"Please! Don't!" Nathaniel turned his head, his back bowed as he retched.

Still she continued forward, a bit uncertain, and then stopped. "All right, I'll stay back," said Isabel. "But, you *must* tell me what I can do to help you!"

She watched his back shudder, and as he took several breaths, wiping his shirt sleeve across his mouth, his nose. She thought she saw a streak of blood on his cheek, his chin. "Oh, Nathaniel, let me help you!"

He gathered his legs under him and stood up in slow increments. He turned to look at her, his body swaying a little. He lifted a hand to his

166

forehead and rubbed it hard for a time. "Go get the blanket from the buggy."

"What's there, Nathaniel? What don't you want me to see?" she asked, though she was certain of what it must be there by his feet. Imagining seemed to her far worse than knowing. Or perhaps not. Nathaniel seemed horrified at the prospect of her seeing whatever or whomever was there.

And how do you endure such things? How do you go on? She thought a moment and then spoke to herself, "I will keep you safe."

He tilted his head, his eyes dull, confused. "I can't hear a word you're saying."

"It's all right. I'll be right back." Isabel made a move to leave and then stopped. "They won't return, will they?"

He looked out over the grasses to where the Indians had left with the herd of horses. "They'll be back to get their dead."

"No!" she cried.

"We've time, Isabel, besides it wasn't them who'd caused this," he said. "Just go. Double-quick."

She was confused by his words. *It wasn't them? Who then?* she wondered. And then the rise of temper again burned in her belly from the order given, but she tamped it down with a hint of a smile. *You are a stubborn one, Isabel Langford. He means no offense. It is neither the time nor place for gentility.*

In short order, she returned to the buggy, taking the blanket from Nathaniel's side of the seat. It was worn thin, holding the stink of old wool. Isabel was certain it was his from the war. She forced herself to keep hold of it while thoughts of lice reared up, disgusting her. Isabel felt ashamed and balled the blanket up against her chest as if to prove something. It was an empty gesture, no one there to acknowledge it, and she not able to deny her true feelings. It was a fact of war: the death, the sickness, the filth – nits, lice. Her father often spoke of such things, having had endured the infestation during the war. Even the field hospitals had been affected, the wounded soldiers' clothes and hair teeming.

For a moment, she'd forgotten where she was and the need to hurry. "Blazes," Isabel said to the nearby horses and took off in a fast run.

When she made the rise, she froze. Nathaniel was lying on the ground, face up to the sun. She couldn't tell if he was conscious from where she stood. Coming to her senses, she ran down the hill, her feet close to coming out from beneath her in her rush. She'd almost forgotten about what lay near him or his desire for her to stay away.

She kept her eyes averted and dropped down by his side. She cupped his face in her palm. "Nathaniel?" she called to him. "Nathaniel, can you hear me?"

He moaned and coughed, but his eyes stayed closed. She took the blanket and placed it over him. She stood and looked at the sun, marking the time. Her father had taught her long ago how to survive in the wilds, but Indians were something of a different nature. She looked down at Nathaniel, then half-turned to look behind her. When she lowered her gaze, she couldn't stop the rising scream.

There in the tall winter grass was the body of a young boy, stripped of all apparel, the crown of his head dispossessed of hair, hideously scalped, and the sweet, fragile body run through, legs, arms and torso sliced opened, genitalia gone. She felt faint and staggered away, falling to the ground. She was sick to her stomach and began to retch. As she gasped for breath, she heard Nathaniel call her name. Isabel lifted the hem of her dress up to her forehead, wiping the perspiration away and then dabbed at her lips. She was desperate for water.

She made her way over to him, helping him sit. He looked at her and she had to turn away from him. He was the first to speak.

"You shouldn't have seen such a thing." He rubbed a hand over his forehead again, as if it hurt him. He mumbled, "I'm sorry."

The crows began cawing and she was terrified to hear it. She touched his face. "Are you well enough to stand?"

He nodded. "Right as rain. Just need a minute."

Isabel leaned back on her heels, watching him. "We can send someone back for the boy—"

"No!" Nathaniel struggled to his feet. "Ain't leaving him alone. Not letting the crows get to him. Seen too much ..." His voice broke. "Seen too much of that."

Isabel stood up then and took his hand. "All right, Nathaniel. We'll take him home." A gentle smile graced her face. She reached up and pushed damp strands of hair out of his eyes. Her tone soft, she said, "You really mustn't say ain't."

Two Crows

Two Crows took shelter under a small overhang of the stable's roof. He stood watching the darkening sky, his face impassive. He shifted his feet, arms heavy at his sides, his face tilted upward. No sooner had the black clouds billowed and thickened, the skies gave way and the rains surged down in a tremendous whoosh. *A real gully washer*, Two Crows thought to himself, remembering John's words describing such things. He struggled then to see through sheets of water. His hands fisted, his black eyes dimming, the only indication of his worry.

The dirt became deep mud, any hollows in the ground filling and overflowing, a rill. The crows had come earlier to roost in the trees around the graveyard. The loud cawing and restless shunting had made him anxious, his bowels tight with dread. The men had not returned home from the day's work and the woman had not peeked out from window or door. He had expected to see her on the big porch in one of her fine rockers, waiting for the buggy's return. She would be skittish with the rains, high strung as a new-sprung filly in her worry over Nathaniel. He was worried, too. It was a worry edged with fear.

They would be riding in the chill rain, a blanket between them, and the boy not well enough. He strained his eyes, searching the wide dirt road that covered a long stretch of nothing. It was all open grassland, easy enough to spot the horses and buggy. With aching eyes, he cursed and set his stance wider, his head pushing outward and away from his body. He blinked against the great spats of rain, wiping his face with a big palm, drying it in a long swipe down the side of his buckskin leggings.

There'd been trouble, he thought with certainty. *No other reason, Nathaniel would be caught out in this.* He shivered, not happy with the path of his thoughts. He squinted again at the dirt road and this time, where there had been nothing before, bobbed two dark specks. Closer now, Two Crows saw the specks resolve into the shape of horses. The animals were moving at a fast pace, although the road was rutted with standing water and deep mud.

He looked over at the white house and back at the approaching buggy. He made a dash for the porch and pounded his fist twice against the wire mesh of the door. Only hollow thrums could be heard, the weaved metal curving in from the banging. She would not hear it through the glass of the other door. He shook his head and wondered why a man needed such things as these doors. He snorted and banged louder this time on the wood of the door's frame.

A quick glance at the road, he turned back to find Mary Keegan staring at him. Her eyes were glassy, her hair tousled. She looked as if she'd been sleeping. Her mouth was a straight line, her brow pinched in annoyance. With a brusque tug on the inside door, she opened it and stood watching him through the screen.

"What can I do for you, Two Crows?" she asked aloud in words, but her eyes spoke louder, telling him to leave.

He looked at her and felt ashamed. Long ago, she had suffered, but Two Crows believed she had forgiven. Much had been lost to them. But then Nathaniel came, and it had been enough to help them forget for a time.

He turned to watch the road and then turned back. "Nathaniel is coming," he said, his English heavily accented. She looked confused, but then her eyes grew wide.

"Oh, yes, Nathaniel." Flustered, she lifted her hands to her hair and then ran them down the front of her dress, trying to smooth away the wrinkles.

He watched her. "It is raining," he said and waited to see the weight of his words.

She looked at him, her mouth opened and then shut. A small white hand fluttered in the air and then lit against the side of her head. She rubbed her temple. "Oh, my!" she said. "How can that be?"

"They are coming up the road now," Two Crows said. "I will take care of the boy. You must get blankets to warm them. The boy will grow sick again."

"Oh, no, he mustn't!" She looked at him, her eyes angry. "Why do you say such a thing?" she asked.

Two Crows looked at her. He said, "It is rain, not words, that will make him sick. I will go help them now. You must hurry."

To Two Crows' ears, the rain spoke to him with anger. He had gotten soaked through in little time, but he hardly noticed, a man disciplined to ignore hardships. He had endured the Sun Dance many times, along with other deprivations. He had guided Nathaniel in some of these practices, teaching him the ways of the People. The boy had proved himself to be clever, skilled with bow and arrow, knife and gun, much better than Two Crows, himself. But he had never spoken these things to him, only acknowledging Nathaniel's accomplishments with a grunt or nod of his head.

The boy's spirit was strong, very powerful. But the white man's war had taken much of his strength from him, his spirit troubled. Like a river, the sickness of his soul coursed through him, his mind and body ailing.

Two Crows hung his head, his coal black braids dripping with water. He blinked his eyes against the rain. The buggy drew near the porch. Nathaniel was hunched over, his slouch hat nearly touching his knees. The army blanket was not draped over him. Two Crows grunted in despair. The girl's wet brown hair hung to her waist, free of the combs. Her face was red, flushed with cold. Her eyes were wide-open, wild with fear. She stopped the rig alongside the steps, tying off the reins and setting the brake. Her whole body shook when she stood, her hands of no use to her. She looked at Two Crows.

"Please, help him," she said.

Two Crows stepped forward and reached up to help Nathaniel down from the buggy. He stopped when he touched the blanket on Nathaniel's lap, running a hand over what could only be a human leg.

"Nathaniel," Two Crows said, "give to me."

Gradually, the gray cavalry hat lifted, and Two Crows stared into the boy's unfocused eyes. He repeated, "Give to me! *Nehmetsestse!*" He gripped his hands around the blanketed form, but Nathaniel refused to let go of it.

173

"No!" Nathaniel stared at him. He stood up, swaying with fatigue. Two Crows saw the boy was shivering hard enough to rattle teeth.

"No," the boy said to him again, although this time softer, clutching the covered body up against his chest. The look in Nathaniel's eyes frightened Two Crows. He nodded and took a step away, giving him room to climb down from the gig.

Somehow Nathaniel managed, with arms full, to get down without falling. Even though Two Crows feared for the boy, he was proud of his determination, his strength. He followed Nathaniel then as the boy struggled through the sucking mud to the stairs. Two Crows stopped alongside him while Nathaniel rested a moment against the railing, and then followed when Nathaniel took one slow step at a time.

The boy stopped at the door and looked over his shoulder at Two Crows, his brow creased as though struggling to remember something. "My gun," he said.

"Here, Nathaniel. I have it right here," the girl said, rushing up the steps toward them.

Again, Nathaniel's brow creased. "I don't," he paused.

"There, there, Nathaniel," said the girl in a hushed voice. "Let's just get you inside and out of this rain."

"I'm sorry," Nathaniel said. Two Crows saw the boy was near tears. He gripped Nathaniel's elbow and moved him to the door. Mary Keegan opened it and stepped back to allow them entrance. She studied the rain-drenched group.

"You must warm yourselves," she said, handing the younger girl several towels. "Here, Isabel, dry quickly." Mary Keegan looked at Two Crows and then at Nathaniel. "Will you help me with him?" She stepped toward the boy. "What is he holding? What do you have there, Nathaniel?"

Two Crows grabbed her arm, stopping her. "No."

She pulled free, her eyes bright with fury. "Don't!" she said. "Don't!"

He shrugged at her, not dissuaded. "You should not see this." Two Crows looked at Nathaniel, able to make out the contours of a small arm and leg beneath the blanket, the staining seep of blood.

Nathaniel stood watching them, his eyes cold and guarded. The girl was drying herself by the potbellied stove with the towels given to her. Two Crows noticed her hair was drawn up on her head again and her clothing was no longer dripping with rainwater. He was also drying from the heat of the stove, the room growing warmer.

Nathaniel's slouch hat was soaked from the rain. His red flannel shirt clung to his body, the brown leather suspenders discolored, almost black. The boy shook with such force that Two Crows felt his bones might shatter. He moved toward Nathaniel but stopped when he saw the skinning knife appear in the boy's hand.

"Don't take another step!" Nathaniel warned him off, his face revealing his weariness and confusion. "Tell me now! Is this place a hospital?"

Two Crows had no words, but the young girl did. She walked toward Nathaniel, gently. She smiled. "Yes, this is a hospital," she said. "Let us help you."

175

"The boy, he's cruelly hurt." Nathaniel looked at the girl. "Ah, Christ, Lord Almighty."

A sound sprang from him deeper than grief and Two Crows had to turn away, his head lowered, his eyes clouding. He heard Mary Keegan say, "my sweet boy." Two Crows was afraid for her.

The girl moved toward Nathaniel and reached out a hand, stouthearted, taking the knife from him. "Come with me," she said.

The boy went to take a step and then pulled away from her. "No!" He shuffled backward, coming up hard against the wall. "No!"

The boy did not know them. He was not in his family's home, but back in the white man's war. Two Crows spoke to Nathaniel in the Cheyenne tongue. *"You are safe. Listen. Otahe! You are safe."*

Nathaniel stared at him, his face a mask of confusion. "No! You can't be here," he said, dropping to his knees, but not losing his hold on the bundle. "Leave me alone!" He swayed back and forth, releasing a low-throated moan.

"I will not leave you alone," said Two Crows.

Nathaniel looked at him, the eyes seeking, penetrating. "You don't belong here."

The door opened, and Joseph Keegan and his sons stepped into the kitchen with hats and oilcloth slickers dripping. They paused and took in the surroundings.

"Mary?" Joseph went over to his wife, his eyes on Nathaniel. "What's going on?"

Two Crows waited while Mary sorted through things, distracted, his

176

attention divided, an old warrior's mistake. As she talked, Nathaniel sprung up and came at him, giving a hard shove to his chest, knocking him to the floor. Instinctively while falling, he snatched at the boy's pants leg, but only drew air. He hit the floor hard, his head banging soundly. From his spot, he saw Nathaniel dart toward the wide oak table, swiping an arm across it, sending a metal pitcher and ironstone bowls to the floor with a deafening clatter. When Nathaniel placed down the bundle and looked up to search the room, Two Crows saw his tears. The knife still in his grip.

Joseph took a tentative step toward the boy. "Nathaniel," he said. "Natey?"

Two Crows rose from the floor and moved behind the boy. His gaze met Joseph's. He saw alarm and confusion in the man's eyes. Two Crows signed for him to move easy. Joseph nodded and continued toward Nathaniel, saying the boy's name in a soft voice.

Nathaniel looked around the room again. He swiped the back of his hand at his eyes and then tore back the blanket. "Help him!" He swayed and almost went to his knees but righted himself.

Two Crows came closer and when the boy started to go down a second time, he grabbed him. From the corner of his eye, he saw Mary Keegan move across the room toward them. When she looked over at the table, her eyes widened, and her face crumpled. She shrieked, running to Joseph who held her in his arms. Two Crows glanced down at Nathaniel and saw he was no longer aware, and then he quickly took in the rest of the room. John was bent over, breathing heavily, holding back sickness. James' face held an odd look as he made his way over to the table. Two Crows watched him as James studied the mutilation done, and then jumped markedly as the man dropped like a loaded sack to the floor.

He couldn't get to James with Nathaniel clasped in his arms. However, his dread lifted to see the girl and the younger one, John, no longer overcome with sickness, going over to him.

Two Crows sighed and closed his eyes, listening. He heard James' name called out, Nathaniel's reedy breaths, Mary Keegan's lamentations. But above all, he heard the loud rush of rain with its discordant upwelling of ghost voices, withering and censorious.

Nathaniel

In his dream, they rode again into Alexandria, Louisiana on their way to Texas, the war months over. They had no maps, only memory, following trail, road and river. In their travels, they rode alongside a white picket fence. Some of the pickets were missing, but the whitewash was fresh. Beyond the fence was a white house with a simple porch, ordinary in every way, except for the tree in the front yard. Stripped of its leaves, the tree was filled with bottles of every shape and color, branches of various breadths accommodating each one. He asked his pard what it was, and the man, riding alongside him, shook his head

178

and laughed.

"Good Lord, boy, ain't y'all seen a bottle tree afore?"

"Seen plenty of most, but never that," he said. "What's it for?"

"Some say it keeps the ghosts away, evil and family spirits the same,"
his old pard said. "Trapping 'em in those bottles."

He was about to laugh but didn't when he remembered the talismans
he bore himself. He looked closer at the tree, his blood running cold,
thinking of his ma, recognizing a few still bearing elixir labels, draught
opium.

He looked at the soldier who rode beside him, old at thirty-five, and
then he looked back at the bottle tree. He thought of the book of poetry
he'd been given one dimly-remembered birthday, the poetry of Edgar
Allen Poe.

With eyes closed, he began reciting: "On this home by horror
haunted, tell me truly, I implore. Is there– is there balm in Gilead?" He
stopped a quick beat and then pressed on, "Tell me, tell me, I implore!
Quoth the raven, Nevermore."

His pard looked at him, his head atilt and said, "Great God
Almighty! I reckon I should be accustomed to your crazy talk by now.
But truth be told, I ain't."

He wasn't listening as he gazed at the bottle tree. His hand lifted to
touch the small metal crucifix pinned to the tattered lining of his jacket.
He sighed loudly and whispered to himself, "Appears there's not a
person alive without their haunts."

Nathaniel woke then from his dream, looking up into the face of a woman. He said the name, "Janie," aloud, but saw he'd gotten it wrong from the look on her face.

She touched his cheek with her fingertips, and then her palm moved to his forehead. She held it there, her eyes concerned. She leaned over him and kissed his forehead. It felt good to him and he tried to smile. He couldn't tell if he accomplished this or not. He attempted to move, but only managed to lift his right hand. It dropped down to the mattress unnoticed by the woman.

"You're very ill," she said to him. "Hush, now, rest."

"Yes," he whispered. "I'll try." The poem ran through his mind and he moved his head side to side on the pillow. He conjured up his dream again, traveled then through time and place back to the yard in Alexandria with the bottle tree. He remembered what his pard had said about the tree and how it kept away the dead, even the ones dearly loved, and he thought to himself, *going to get me one.*

With eyes open a crack, his lids weighted, he watched the woman for a while. He heard someone breathing. The sound was ragged, harsh to his ears. "Someone is sick," he said. He thought he'd spoken aloud, feeling the movement of his lips. He heard someone coughing from far away, from outside the window, from the great oak's bough, from the distant moon. He wanted to go, to fly, but in his ear a single word was spoken: *Abide.*

To himself he spoke, *I'll try.*

"Was that Poe?" Thomas Langford asked, not able to mask his surprise.

"Yes, I believe it was," Isabel said. "The Raven, if I'm not mistaken."

"Really?" He looked at Isabel, waiting for her to reprimand him for what she might consider a slight toward the young man. She remained quiet, and he wondered if she, too, was surprised to hear the boy quoting poetry in his fevered dreams.

"I suppose I shouldn't be so shocked. James is very intelligent, well-read. Even without schools, Mary must have taught all her boys properly over the years, given every opportunity to learn," Thomas said. He shook his head and looked at her. "But why do I see him so differently than I do the others?" He took off his spectacles and rubbed at his eyes.

Isabel looked at him and back down at Nathaniel. "The obvious difference, of course, is his coloring and he's of slighter build, not as tall." She smiled. "As Mary said, Nathaniel favors her side. I can see it quite clearly."

Thomas lifted his head. His gaze held hers. "Yes, most certainly, it is rather obvious." He turned to sit in the chair by the window. He gazed out at the large oak and beyond to the two gravestones in the family cemetery.

No one must find out ... He creased his brow and gnawed at his lip. *Where had he heard that?* he wondered. And then it came to him. Mary had said those words. *No one must find out ... Great God! Must find out what?* He sighed, silently admonishing himself. *It is none of your concern.*

Thomas stood up and stretched his back. Time had been lost to him the moment John had appeared at his door, frantic. He remembered how badly the boy's hands had shook, hardly able to find his voice. *Yes, of course, he would come,* he'd said, and immediately went in search of the medical bag and essential medicines. In the deepest part of his brain, in the darkest part of his heart, he had screamed his loud refusal. Upon arriving, he'd become detached, working calmly on his patients, as he did for the dying on fields of battle. Distant, remote, to feel, to think beyond his task would be fatal.

All in all, it had been a long night with James' migraine and Mary's spell. Gradually, they had come around and then concentrated solely on Nathaniel. The boy was very sick. He could see Isabel held deep feelings for him. She touched him in ways far more tender and familiar than warranted. He hadn't mentioned her impropriety, simply keeping an eye to things. If she went too far, of course, he would put a halt to it. He was her father, after all, even if she was strong-willed and quick-tempered. He chuckled softly. *As her mother had been. God rest her soul. My dear, dear Abigail, how I miss you.*

"Father!" Isabel bolted to her feet and ran to him, grabbing his hand in hers. "Something is wrong!"

Thomas had never seen his daughter so frightened. His heart sunk. *Great God! Could she possibly love him?*

"Now, now, Isabel." Thomas hurried to the bed and sat on its edge.

The boy's breathing was labored, loud, every breath a struggle. He was growing weaker. The black hair against such pale-white skin was unsettling, the dark smudges of exhaustion under his eyes and on his lids, gave him a cadaverous appearance. Gaunt, sickly, as they all were. *Stop! Don't think of them!*

Thomas shook his head and ran a hand across his face. He looked down at the boy again. *What does she see?* he wondered when he could only see death. The boy's eyes, though, the eyes were Mary's. He'd never seen such blue.

Then, in a flash of memory, the words Mary had spoken to Joseph came back to him. Mary had been upset that day, confused. *You must promise me this,* she had said. It was, of course, something not meant for his ears. But, he could not stop himself from listening outside their bedroom door, needing to learn everything about her. He told himself, *she belongs to another.* But secretly, he continued to hope for a breach between the two.

Thomas took the boy's pulse and listened to the beating of his heart, his lungs. Isabel watched him while she held Nathaniel's hand. He stood up, cleared his throat. "I've done all I can for him," he said. "It's up to Nathaniel now, and God."

He spoke truthfully, using every means to treat pneumonia. Sulfuric ether, aqua ammonia and muriate of ammonia for the liniment to reduce aches and fever, sassafras tea with aconite, flaxseed and cornmeal poultices for congestion, beef broth for sustenance. The depletion of fluids to purge the gastrointestinal tract or bleeding seemed most brutal to him, choosing other measures. He placed two large pillows beneath the boy's shoulders and head, making it easier for him to breathe.

Isabel nodded, her eyes filling. "You can save him." She stood up and walked over to him. "I know you can make him well."

"I will do everything possible, my daughter," Thomas said.

Isabel hugged him. "Will you promise me this?"

Promise me this, promise me this, promise me this. And then he remembered it all, what she feared, what she kept secret. *The Indian is of his blood. Who is this boy named Nathaniel Keegan? Who is this boy his daughter may love?*

He took in a breath, then a slow release. "What of James, Isabel?" he spoke in a whisper too low for her to hear. "What of James?"

Isabel

To her ears, the sound of her crying was like an old woman's. It was not the delicate weeping she'd grown accustomed to, took solace from, at times exploited. The sounds now springing from her were abrasive, ugly, tormented. So much so, it startled her into silence. Unsettled, Isabel wondered when her crying had changed from a young woman's trifling to a grown woman's sorrow. She took a breath and released it, running her fingers beneath her eyes to wipe away the tears.

184

From where she stood on the gallery, she had watched John and Two Crows leave by wagon to bring the young boy home. Once more, against her wishes, she revisited the last few hours, seeing Joseph again as he prepared the boy for his last homeward ride. With a keen eye, he had placed the unfortunate child as the young W. J. Miller who had only recently celebrated his ninth birthday.

When Joseph had left her to gather the things needed for the morbid task before him, he had asked her to remain with the boy. While waiting for him, she had taken a few steps away from the table where the body lay. She had kept her eyes averted, not able to bear the sight, her hands clasped together against her chest, as though the dead child might rise and touch her.

When Joseph had finally returned, he had spread a white linen sheet across the table and had lifted the boy into his arms, placing him down upon it. By then the body had begun to stiffen and what had remained of the hair was matted with blood. John had disappeared for a time, returning with a nightshirt he'd outgrown. When presenting it to his father, he had been unable to hide the tremors of his hands.

Isabel could barely watch and had averted her eyes throughout the task. The daughter of a doctor, she had seen many a sight, but somehow the cruelty, the savagery, the horrid mutilation of such a lovely boy was far more than she could stand. Yet somehow, she did stand it, taking away the dirty, bloodied wrappings, prepared with hot water, soap, sponge and clean cloths before the asking.

Joseph had washed the boy, putting the long night shirt on him. Once he had completed wrapping the bandages around the wretched head, she had seen his hands linger there a moment against the boy's face, seeing his tears.

Isabel had not cried then, nor had she cried when her father escorted her a half-hour prior from Nathaniel's room. He had explained it was for the sake of his patient, needing to bathe Nathaniel in effort to ease his discomfort and lower his temperature. Due to Nathaniel's waking every so often with moments of lucidity, her father was of the opinion if he should wake to find himself stripped bare in front of her, it would cause him great distress. Her father had instead called upon Joseph for help, not allowing her to stay.

Isabel had been near to refusing, but she had seen something in her father's eyes which caused her unease. It was as if he had seen her soul, her heart, her breath quickening, her face flushing. *He knows,* she had thought to herself, *Dear Lord! He knows.*

Outside in the night air, she looked up at the stars and thought about her long-ago deceased mother, as well as, the baby boy. They were of her, of her flesh, of her blood, but she had never known either of them. They were strangers to her. *How then could it be so different with Nathaniel?* she wondered. He should be a stranger to her as well, but he was not. Thereupon seeing him at the cottage and then later as he sat cloaked in a blanket on the long porch, he was of her heart, as though loving him on sight.

Isabel felt the familiar burn of her eyes and tightening of her throat. She pooh-poohed herself as tears threatened, attributing it to her near-exhaustion. Again, it all seemed out of her control as it was when the unborn had been hidden away beneath layers of petticoat and crinoline, silk and satin. Truths buried, but not from God's eyes. In the end, she would not be able to hide away. In the end, she would be accountable.

She was maculate, defiled; a matter certain not to be ignored in the marriage bed. In long ago reveries, she imagined a great love would be hers. He would be without judgment, tolerant. Isabel shivered and let out a long sigh. *Was Nathaniel the one?* she wondered.

She clasped her hands together as though praying. But she would never ask God for such a thing, too afraid of His silence. The disappointment of that would be far too bitter a pill for her. She could not live in bleak despair, without hope. At least in her dreams, it remained. All at once, her stomach leaped, her hands shook. She felt giddy and she laughed, her face lifting to the moon. Her thoughts pushed and prodded, forming words, sentences, a wish becoming prayer, nearly on the tip of her tongue.

"No!" she shouted. "Good God, I mustn't. It will all collapse around me as it always does."

A touch then on her shoulder turned her around fast and she took in a sharp breath. "You nearly frightened me to death!"

"So sorry." James looked forlorn, apologetic. "I needed to see how you were getting on."

Isabel smiled. His hair was unkempt, the blond strands shimmering in the moonlight. He seemed years younger, boyish. The green of his eyes was mesmerizing, but more appealing to Isabel was the vulnerability she saw in them.

"Are you well, James?" Isabel asked. She took his hand and held it. He stared at her for a long beat and then ducked his head.

"I'll live," he said.

She nodded. Her lips turned up a bit when she looked down at his feet and saw he wore only socks. Only one side of his shirt had been tucked into his pants and one middle button was all that had been fastened. On impulse, she hugged him. He smelled faintly of wood smoke and soap. It was comforting to her, resting her head there against his chest, listening to the staccato thrum of his heartbeat.

"Isabel," he said.

She lifted her head up, her eyes fixed on his. "Yes?"

"I need to apologize to you." He looked away from her and off into the distance. "As a matter of fact, I need to apologize to everyone. I'm not sure what got into me. It's just having Nathaniel back after all these years, trying to forgive myself for letting him go in the first place. There are things you don't know, Isabel. You just don't know."

Isabel pushed away from James. Comfort was replaced by panic. "About Nathaniel, then? Is that it?" Anger rose within her. "Are you again warning me away from him? Is that what this is about?"

"Isabel!" James gripped her shoulders. "I asked you this before and I'll ask again. Why do you care?"

Isabel didn't answer. She shrugged away from his hold and looked up at the stars. *Tell him!* she pleaded with herself. *Tell him how you feel!*

"If you're smitten with my brother, it's only fair to tell me straight out." James brushed a hand through his hair. Again, with a simple motion, he captured her heart. *It's only natural she would feel something for James, as well,* she told herself. *Not love. No, not love, but something.*

She shook her head and took his hand. "It's been such a long day. I'm nearly asleep on my feet. Truly, James, we will talk, but not tonight. Please." She studied his face and saw the lines of pain around his eyes. "Let me walk you to your room. You should rest. A bit more medicine and a good night's sleep will do you a world of good. Did my father leave the laudanum with you?"

James allowed her to walk him from the gallery and into the hallway to his room. At the door, he hesitated and then stepped aside to let her pass. His bed was a shambles, blankets and pillows tossed every which way, sheets pulled loose and strewn about the floor as though he'd been in the throes of a bad dream.

"You sit while I remake the bed," she said to him.

She was glad to see him do as he was told with no arguments. She made short shrift of her work and took him by the arm, leading him to the bed. She then took up a spoon from the bedside table and poured out a dollop of the medicine. James settled himself against the pillows and closed his eyes, his lips parting at the touch of the spoon. He swallowed with a grimace at the taste. His eyes stayed closed while she tucked the blankets around him and pressed her lips against his warm brow.

In the faint light from the moon, Isabel watched him for a time. Near tears again, she put her hand over her mouth to hold them back.

Mastering herself, she took a breath and moved to leave the room. At the door, she stopped and turned to watch him again.

"I forgive you, James," she whispered. "But the other question should be, will *you* forgive me?" Without warning, Isabel began to cry, making a blind dash from the room.

Thomas

Thomas watched Joseph cool down his son's hot limbs, chest, and face with a cool damp cloth. The man had not stopped once in over an hour's time. Thomas saw a father's will so strong, a love so powerful, he was convinced medicine was secondary to the boy surviving the night. It was as if he could see Joseph's life force flowing out from his fingertips, his palms, laying hands, as the believers would say, upon his son.

But wait a moment, thought Thomas, *was this truly the case?* From what he'd gathered from the snatches of conversation, the boy's parentage was not as it appeared. *And of no concern of yours,* he admonished himself. *But it is of my concern because of Isabel,* he argued back. *A father must be vigilant for the sake of his child.*

He furrowed his brow, a headache building, his eyes aching. He wanted to sleep, but the role of a doctor too deeply ingrained to put his needs before his patient. He thought himself a good man, but on occasion a trifle judgmental. *But who among us isn't?* he asked himself, satisfied this blemish of character was of little consequence. And more so, he reasoned, *the uncanny ability to judge a man's worth had, oftentimes, saved him both time and trouble.* But then his momentary satisfaction changed to worry.

What of Mary, fretted Thomas, *if the boy's lineage was to be revealed to Isabel? It would most certainly cause Mary much suffering. And what of love? Of mine or Isabel's?* he wondered, choking on such thoughts.

His harsh coughing filled the quiet room. Joseph looked up at him, not breaking rhythm. The boy moaned and lifted his arm. The eyes opened, the blue of them stunning. He looked up at his father, the gaze empty, no recognition in them. The head moved on the pillow, the black hair drenched in sweat, stuck to the skull, to the forehead, and then the eyes turned toward Thomas.

The boy's level stare caused Thomas' breath to jam in his airway, a dull pain filling his throat. He felt as though caught red-handed, the boy reading his mind as easily as a book. The blue eyes were lucid, watching him, waiting for something. Thomas' heart pounded, his temples pulsed.

What do you see? What do you know? Thomas wondered to himself over the whir and buzz of confusion in his brain. *Do not worry for your mother. Surely my feelings for her are quite clear.*

Thomas opened his mouth to speak, stepping toward the bed. The eyes followed him, still aware, still certain, and then at once the eyes emptied, went blank, a candle gone out, only the vibrancy of blue assured Thomas the boy still lived.

191

Thomas touched fingertips to the boy's neck, the heart beating in earnest, the blood still pumping, although erratic. "I am sorry," whispered Thomas.

Joseph sputtered, clenching the damp cloth in his fist, all motion stopped. "Sorry for what?" he asked.

"What was that?" asked Thomas.

"Sorry for what, damn it!"

Thomas looked over at the man. "I'm not sure what you're asking?"

Joseph stared at him for a long beat and then shook his head. "You must be tired, Thomas. Go. Get some rest. John's made up the guest room for you. You know which one as well as I. He will get you whatever you need."

Thomas nodded, for a moment uncertain if he could find his voice. He cleared his throat. "Perhaps thoroughwort for fever…must find some. The Indian would know of it, would he not? The lungs are the concern, but he has youth on his side." Thomas paused and looked levelly at Joseph. "Although of greatest benefit to him is your love."

Joseph nodded and smiled, while rubbing his palm up and down Nathaniel's arm. Thomas judged him to be a man unafraid of expressing such feelings.

"Thank you, Thomas." Joseph stood and held out his right hand to him. Thomas extended his own to Joseph, aware it was shaking. Joseph saw too, saying, "You need to rest."

Thomas looked at the boy one last time and moved across the room. At the doorway, Joseph called to him. "I'll need Isabel's help."

Thomas lowered his head and removed the wire-rimmed spectacles, placing them in his vest's front pocket. "Certainly," he said. "Certainly." His eyes burned, filling.

Great God! Are those tears? Thomas shuddered and shoved his knuckles into the sockets, rubbing hard. *Sleep will cure this folly. The war's horrors were overcome, so too shall this. So too shall this.*

Thomas

Thomas walked down the hallway, wiping at his eyes, caught in a miasma of grief and memories. He would wander forever away from them, if only he could. Her secrets were not as well hidden as she believed. He chose to be kind, not confronting her with what he had discovered all those years ago.

It had been upon his return from war when he noticed things were not right. Her coloring was far too sallow; her eyes dull with sorrow, her lovely hair, limp and unwashed. The draperies covered up windows, the sun seemed an unwanted guest, the house cold and damp, the hearths without fires. He at once turned things around, rallying the servants. In no time, it was again as it had been before he had gone.

Isabel tried to be the girl he loved, her smiles bright, her voice melodious, her intelligence still keen, the stories of town, politics, poetry and literature head and shoulders above any learned scholar. But,

193

the eyes held no spark, as if the light had gone from her. She breathed, walked, and talked, but she no longer lived.

He'd been at his wit's end, unsure of what to do for her, having asked her over and over, what aggrieved her so. But it was to no avail, her answers persisted in denials. On one particularly trying spring night, he wandered the gardens for solace, happening upon a stray cur digging vigorously at the roots of a lilac bush. He hadn't planted it and was of the assumption, Isabel had fancied it, though he recalled they were of the opinion the scent of lilacs was a bit too exuberant.

He had shooed the dog away before any damage was done to it, kneeling to fill the hole dug. The moon had been full that night, the weather lovely, the breeze perfect, the air heartbreakingly fresh. He was of the belief heaven was captured in those moments. He took in a deep breath of night air and began pushing handfuls of dirt back into the hole.

When he heard, the dirt hitting against not earth, but a hard surface, he grew curious. His head tilted, his ears perked trying to identify what it might be striking. He lowered his head down into the hole and strained to see what was buried there. He began to dig, his fingernails quickly blackening, the grooves of his palms and knuckles coated. He finally touched wood and wedged his fingers between the dirt wall and what he identified as a small wood box. His fingers wiggled and wiggled until curving beneath the underside of it. He lifted one end up, his grip around it and then lifted it out, the other hand braced against the ground for balance.

It appeared to be a small wooden casket, a cross carved in the wood.

He laughed at the absurdity of it. *Had Isabel buried one of the house cats in such a florid manner? Though a grown woman, she sometimes acted as a child.* He shook his head and began to return the casket back to the earth when the lid came off into his hands. When he cast his eyes upon what was there, the box dropped from his grip as though scalded. He began to weep without console. *Most certainly that of a servant's,* he inwardly comforted himself. *But then, why hidden away in this place?*

He took up the box again and filled the shallow grave. In his mind, he had no other recourse, but to give the baby a proper burial, not left to rot in a meager wooden box beneath the soil of unconsecrated ground.

So many had been left. So many.

Slowly, Thomas' surroundings changed from a moonlit garden to a dark, narrow hallway. It had taken little time to find out the truth of the tiny wood casket. Servants had loose tongues when silver flowed freely into their palms. Or perhaps it was the threat of losing their employ. Of course, the ones that had talked were terminated forthwith, their loyalty of constant concern. He had sent them off with a generous severance along with a stern warning, intimating their lives would be in peril if they ever spoke of it again.

He had been told Isabel's child, his grandchild, had been buried beneath the earth under a lilac bush by Old Willie, his faithful driver and stable hand. No prayers had been recited, no hymns sung, the babe's soul all those months lost to God.

It had been a cold, miserable spring morning with a persistent drizzle on the day of the second burial. Thomas had been the only mourner. He'd chosen a small, out-of-the way cemetery in Litchfield, several towns over, far enough from prying eyes and wagging tongues of neighbors.

Thomas had wept when the small casket had been lowered into the tiny hole. He had wept for the child, while remembering all the others who had been left buried beneath unconsecrated grounds far from home, many nameless, and lost to the world. He prayed for God's mercy, more than a little dismayed to discover the tears still strong in him. He'd offered no name to be inscribed on the handsome gravestone, a shame burned forever into his soul, instead hoping the words he had chosen would suffice:

"Suffer the Innocent the Weight of Our Sins."

Isabel's secrets were not as well-hidden as she believed all those years ago nor on this day. Nathaniel Keegan would be, with utmost certainty, another misstep for his daughter. He had not been there when she'd chosen to give herself to an immoral man, leaving her unmarried and with child. He would not allow her another poorly made choice. Nathaniel Keegan, with name or naught would never be the son of Joseph Keegan.

Although the son of Mary, he was still illegitimate, still a bastard child.

And, as far as Thomas was concerned, that would not do at all.

Isabel

Finally, Isabel had been left alone with Nathaniel. Exhausted, Joseph had acquiesced to her pleas for him to rest and went off to bed. She stifled a yawn and lifted the pendant watch toward the lamp's light to check the time. Three-thirty in the morning, the night's sky would soon lighten and tinge the hills and flatlands gray. Her finger tapped lightly on the tiny clock face keeping rhythm with its ticking. She watched Nathaniel sleep. No longer restless, his breaths came with much more ease, the heat of fever tolerable. Joseph would never have left him otherwise.

She moved to the bed and studied him. Black hair, thick and long, curled around his ears and neck from the sweat of his fever, the high cheekbones, the well-made nose, his lips, and dark eyelashes, so full and exceptional in length. Her heart began to beat with magnificent thumps, so fast that she needed to take in several, long breaths. Her palms grew moist, her hands shaking.

What a beautiful, beautiful man. She felt her stomach tighten, her heart still banging hugely in her chest. *If only he were well enough. I would love him. Let him love me.*

Isabel knelt beside the bed, her head dropping to the mattress near his shoulder. She started to cry. Until this moment she had denied her loneliness, denied her heartbreak. There had been no one to confide, no friends, dear enough or worthy of her trust, to share all she had endured. She cried in earnest, the sound coming out of her filled the room, bereft,

197

mournful. In her mind, she thought, *please God, please God.* She prayed the language of her sorrow, her tears, would touch the heavens, would reach God's ear so He might know her heart. Perhaps, know more of what she needed than she did herself.

"Of course, He would, foolish woman," she said through her tears, giving a mirthless laugh.

"God is all-knowing."

She lifted her head, her cheeks wet, her nose runny, rummaging in her skirt's side-pocket for her silk hankie. She pulled it free and dabbed at her nose, her swollen eyes. She did not notice he was awake until she heard him call her name.

"Isabel?" His voice was scarcely above a whisper, his throat sounding raw.

She took up his hand, still kneeling beside the bed. "Yes, Nathaniel. What is it?"

He didn't answer. His eyes blinked several times, his throat convulsing. His brow furrowed, as though struggling hard to gather his thoughts. "You're crying."

Isabel smiled. "Yes, only because I was afraid for you." It was not a lie.

"Don't cry," he said, distressed. He rolled his head back and forth on the pillow. "Don't cry."

She stood, releasing his hand and went over to the side table. She poured water into a small glass from a lead crystal pitcher. Her hand shook from the weight of it. When the glass was nearly full, she placed the pitcher back down with a loud thud.

A hand to his shoulder made him look up at her, and he nodded as Isabel showed him the glass. She slipped her hand beneath his head, his hair damp against her palm. She could feel the heat of his breath on the tips of her fingers. When he had his fill, he relaxed his head back into her hand and she lowered him down to the pillow. Then standing, she set the glass on the table.

Unclothed and draped only with a sheet, he began to shiver. Isabel took the blanket from the foot of the bed and covered him. She sat on the edge of the bed, her hip pressed up against his side. She moved her hand without clear thought, rubbing his arm and then rubbing his shoulder.

"Does that help?" she asked.

Nathaniel sighed and murmured, "Yes. Thank you."

Isabel nodded, continuing to knead the muscles. When she touched his face, her fingers moved to his mouth, lingering there. Nathaniel turned his eyes to her. She lowered her head to his and kissed his lips. He didn't respond, but Isabel was persistent. Her kisses grew more urgent, heated. Slowly, he began to kiss her back. Nathaniel stopped himself and looked at her, uncertain.

"It's all right," she said. In her head, she thought, *It's truly not so complicated. Our need is the same.*

"I can't," he began, "I wish…"

She smiled down at him and smoothed his hair back from his forehead like a mother to a dear child. "We all fall prey, don't we?"

He stared at her, eyes still bright with fever. He blinked. "What?"

Isabel smiled and lifted his hand to her cheek, held it there a moment, and then laid open his palm and kissed the center of it. She lowered her head, her mouth pressed to his ear. She said, "Wishing for things we can't have."

His eyes closed, his jaw clenching, visibly holding back his sorrow. "Or those lost to you," he managed to get out in a whisper.

"Yes," she said, "that as well."

Nathaniel sighed and closed his eyes. His breathing softened, as though sleeping.

Isabel rose from his side and moved toward the bedroom door. Once there, she turned the key, hearing the distinct clack as it locked. Her hand stilled on the knob and she took a breath, waiting to hear the recriminating voices, the damning shouts. None came.

With her eyes closed, Isabel turned back to him, waited a beat and then opened them. He was watching her. Tremors began in her legs, her kneecaps jumping. It was the oddest sensation. Her hands clutched at the front of her skirt. She was seductress, wanton and without shame.

No! she screamed inside. *No! Something moves me. Something tells me this is right.*

Her head was swimming. She took a step forward and then another. Nearing the bed, her eyes held his. Isabel smiled at him, her feelings, no doubt, unmistakable on her face.

She reached the bed and picked up his hand, clasping it between hers. Heedless, she sat down and lowered her head to his chest. His heart banged violently within the cage of his ribs. She became worried for him.

"Hush, now" she whispered, hoping her voice a comfort.

Nathaniel shuddered out a deep sigh. His body shook. He spoke to the top of her head, into her hair. "I've been too long lost," he said more to himself than to her. He spoke in a faraway voice, as though talking with ghosts. "This can't be the way."

Isabel sat up and looked at him, unsure of what he meant. She saw his reluctance, but nevertheless said, "Yes, Nathaniel, I promise you, this is the way." She took up his hand and held it tight. He nodded and squeezed her hand once then let it go.

She let down her hair from the combs. Slipping off her unlaced shoes, she tucked her legs up beneath her skirt, fitting on the edge of the bed. Her fingers moved to the ivory buttons of her blouse, undid them, one at a time, as Nathaniel watched.

The blouse slid off her shoulders, down her arms, falling behind her. Lifting her skirt, she pulled back the blanket, and she straddled him. She released a sharp intake of breath when she felt him beneath her, his hardness. Her hands moved under her skirt, working off the remaining clothing.

She grew bold, lustful, tugging at the sheet between them. Pushed aside, his flesh was hot against her. She pressed a palm to his cheek and lowered her forehead to his, kissing his eyelids, his nose.

He began to move beneath her. She gasped, a moan sprang from her, and she shut her mouth tightly against it. He lifted his head, his mouth pressed against hers. She began to suck his lower lip, her tongue searching. She held no coherent thought, only wanting him. It was glorious and terrifying.

Nathaniel slid his hand between them, touching her. She understood what he intended, bringing her hand to help, lifting. Once astride, Isabel started to cry. A violent shiver ran through him.

"I'm fine," she said in a whisper, stroking his face. "It's fine."

Isabel rocked her hips to reassure him, feeling him inside of her. Her palms were placed flat on the mattress above his shoulders, her arms straight, holding her up, able to look in his eyes. She smiled at him as her hair fell around them, a shelter.

"You need not worry for my virtue," she said.

He looked at her.

"You are not the first," she spoke, blunt and without shame, but quick to add, "Though, my consent is debatable."

It took a moment before realization showed in his eyes and his movements stopped, his hands dropped down to the bed.

"He was a Lieutenant in the war. Nine months later, I bore a child who died shortly after."

Nathaniel closed his eyes. "We should stop."

"No." Isabel lowered herself down onto him, her head against his shoulder.

She waited for him to speak; her mouth pressed into his neck. He had not yet withdrawn from her, and then gradually she felt him begin to move beneath her. She was elated when she felt the steady rise and fall of his narrow hips. Isabel smiled, cupped his face with her hand and kissed his mouth.

With their bodies locked, she went on then unfettered. It was a heady rush as she rocked against him, a slow rhythm growing faster. At first, he was gentle, but then his movements became bolder, moving further into her, pushing deeper. She clutched him to her, bitterness and desire, loneliness and loss gathered up, falling into him.

She went on then caught up in a rush, rocking faster and faster. He was tender and violent, driving upward, harder and harder. There was nothing else. *Only him. Only him.* And then she could no longer hold it back, her eyes widened, moaning her pleasure as she filled up and burst apart, a flash, lightning bright, pulsing, pulsing, pulsing, a glorious release, easing to gradual stillness. All the hurt and pain and anger swept away, the sweetest redemption.

"Blessed Nathaniel," Isabel said, smiling down at him. "How happy you have made me!"

Visibly spent, he only nodded and ran his fingers through her hair. His open hand dropped to the bed, his eyes closed, at once asleep.

The low light cast from an oil lamp spread a small, yellow square across the floor. Nathaniel was curled on his side, sleeping. Isabel, beside him, watched him in the lamplight. The sheet covering him hid a scar that ran from his abdomen to his hip. While he slept, she had traced her finger over it.

In the quiet of the deep night, she realized she was stronger than him.

203

This man who had gone to war, killed men, bore wounds, had been afraid. Isabel pushed his long bangs off his forehead. She smiled down at him. She wanted to own his heart, would wish for it every moment. But if cast out, alone, she would not fall to bits. Perhaps, it had been too soon, would be shameful in the light of days. Yet she held no shame, wanting him still.

Tired, herself, she lowered her head to the pillow, spooned herself around him, closed her eyes and slept.

Thomas

Thomas was the first to rise, morning barely breaking. The room was lit gray, the shutters left open overnight as was his habit. Still dressed, he pushed himself up from the mattress, tossed back the covers and rolled his aching hips toward the side of the bed. His legs moved belligerently, his sock-clad feet slowly touching the floor. He reached over, his hands groping for his boots, an effort to lift one leg than the other, pushing his feet down into the well-made boots. He was in a full sweat when the task was complete.

The medical bag, a new one he had bought after the war, sat on top of the mahogany dresser. The old bag had been long ago stowed out of sight. When he had purchased a new kit along with a new bag, Isabel had, without instruction, tossed out the old one. Only by chance had he discovered it in the waste pile and seeing it there had been overcome by sickness, retching in the dirt.

Things were not so easily forgotten, so easily tossed aside. *All those left behind. All those he did not save.* He had kept the old bag. If Isabel was aware of his nonsense, his weakness, she never mentioned it.

Thomas next found his spectacles on the bedside table and set them on the bridge of his nose, looping the wired-arms over his ears. He finger-combed his hair and smoothed the wrinkles from his waistcoat. He took up his bag and headed out the door, his frock coat forgotten on the chair.

Once in the hallway, he hesitated, uncertain of his destination. All was quiet, everyone asleep. He felt odd in that moment, as though he stood in the midst of others' lives, uninvited. But it was short-lived, when he heard shouting.

It was coming from James' room, and Thomas hurried forward. Unhampered by lock, he turned the knob and swung open the door. James was thrashing on the bed, tossing about blanket, pillows and the like, tears running like rain down his face. His words were incoherent, his movements wild with rage.

Thomas stood for a time watching, took stock and then turned to shut the door behind him. He decided laudanum might calm the boy, help settle the nerves and dull the pain of migraine. Foraging through the bag, he pulled out a glass bottle, turned to find an open space on the dresser and set everything down upon it. A spoon remained on the side table along with a glass of tepid water. Thomas measured out a small amount of medicine onto the spoon and poured it into the water, stirring. He moved over to the bed.

"James," Thomas said, his free hand pressed firmly on the man's shoulder. "James, wake up."

James at once seemed frozen in place, eyes wide open.

"James, it's Thomas," he said, his hand still braced against the man's shoulder. "Are you well?"

"No!" James began to shake. "No!"

Setting the glass on the side table, Thomas sat on the edge of the bed and gripped James' shoulders, holding him flat to the mattress. "Wake, now!"

"Mama," it was said in a whisper, "Mama."

"What's there? What do you see?" Thomas took hold of James' hand.

Clear-eyed, James turned to look at him. He said only one word: "Indian."

Thomas heart sped up, leaving him breathless when he spoke. "Did he hurt you? Did he hurt your mother?"

James nodded, eyes closing. Thomas thought he might have fallen back into sleep. He reached for the glass and brought it to James' lips, slightly parting them. "Drink this. It will help with the migraine. And then rest."

After drinking all of it, James turned onto his side, his back to Thomas and his hand lifted to cover his eyes.

He stood and ran his palm down his waistcoat. "A piece of the puzzle."

"What puzzle?"

"Ah!" Thomas said, jumping slightly, not having heard Joseph enter the room.

"So sorry," Joseph said, stepping past him to go to James. He cupped his hand on the sleeping man's head. "How is he?"

"Restless. I've given him some laudanum," Thomas said. "The heavy drapery was well-thought, a brilliant way to keep the room in near darkness." He walked over to one window. "Perhaps we should draw them tighter with morning fast approaching."

Thomas watched Joseph pull the other drapes snug and said, "With all the mayhem last night, we hadn't a chance to confer about James, but I have surmised the headaches, the migraines, are not a recently acquired condition."

"No." Joseph did not elaborate as he sat down on the bed's edge.

"If I am to help him, I must know the history." Thomas moved forward. He stood on the opposite side of the bed and reached toward James' head. He pushed away the long hair covering the man's forehead, exposing the scar along the hairline. "A knife wound?"

Joseph looked up at him, his eyes wet, but he did not fall to weeping. "Yes."

Thomas proceeded, "And what of Mary?"

"What are you hedging at?" Joseph stood up quickly, his eyes dark.

"Dear man, I hedge at nothing. I merely ask as a friend and a doctor. James called out to her in his dream as if she were in danger. I wondered if Mary had been harmed as well during the ordeal."

Joseph walked to the door. In the hall, he stopped and regarded Thomas. "Would you look to Nathaniel?"

Thomas moved to the dresser, reaching for his bag. "Yes, certainly." He took a breath, looked at James, and then joined Joseph in the hallway. "I meant no offense."

Joseph appraised him again and Thomas was unnerved by it. The man's only response was a curt nod.

Isabel

In the large cherry wood bed, on the softest of feather mattresses, cozy beneath a down quilt, she slept, her hand reaching out toward Nathaniel. She was dreaming of him and their time together, feeling her body responding even in her sleep. She moaned, waking herself.

Isabel smiled and stretched her arms out toward the headboard, her toes in the opposite direction. She turned on her side, to find the bed empty. She sat up fast.

"Nathaniel?" she called out, springing off the bed, tripping a few steps over her shoes. Her skirt was off-center and wrinkled. Her loose hair was snarly and fell into her eyes. Her hastily buttoned bodice left a bit of her bosom exposed. She stopped a moment and took a breath.

"He's fine," she said, closing her eyes.

When she opened them, she was surprised to find her father standing in front of her with his mouth hanging and an odd look on his face.

208

Isabel was the first to speak. "Nathaniel's gone," she said. "We must look for him."

"Daughter, cover yourself!" Thomas gathered up a quilt from the bed, sputtering and muttering as he thrust it at her.

"What?" Confused, Isabel looked at him, holding out the quilt to her, and then down at herself. She turned away from him and began fastening the errant hooks, her hands shaking. Buttoned up, she moved toward the bed in search of her blouse, but her father had reached it first, shaking it in her face.

"I cannot bear to ask you why you are in such a state of undress," Thomas said. "To live in ignorance would be for the best, but alas I am not an ignorant man or one who can deny truths."

"Should I feel shame, father?" Isabel asked, not wanting to be unkind. "Do you think less of me?"

Thomas moved to the chair and collapsed down on it. "My daughter, I worry for you, your reputation, your future, but especially for your heart." Thomas looked at her. "He is not the one for you, Isabel. I've seen this in the war with many of the women who had nursed the wounded. They grew attached, developed feelings for them, just the way you feel toward this boy. Trust me, Isabel, it is not love."

Isabel lifted her chin, defiant. "I know my own mind, father. It was what I wanted," she said, while an unspoken *this time* sang like a chorus in her head. "I bedded him!"

Thomas stood with his hands in tight fists. "Stop! Not one more word! Straighten yourself. Joseph will be here at any moment, only gone

209

to check on Mary. Good Lord! Mary! What might she think of this? Well, she mustn't find out. Not a word of this to anyone."

Isabel shook her head, a retort on her lips.

"How many others, Isabel?" Thomas asked, not able to meet her gaze.

Isabel felt her legs soften, swaying. "What?"

"I do understand loneliness, child." He looked at her. This time his eyes reflected kindness, understanding.

Isabel felt heat rise through her, tears pricking her eyes, but she refused to cry. Waving her hand over the mussed sheets and bedding, she said, "You believe I've been with others because of this? All those years you were away to war, you think that I've been..." she couldn't continue.

Thomas stood up, his head lowered. "I know about the child, Isabel."

This time Isabel's legs gave out and she sat down hard on the bed. She closed her eyes, breathless. Her hand went to her throat and she gagged, doubling over. An unintelligible sound escaped from her. She began to cry. "You said not one word to me about this. Why?"

"I was a coward," he said. "I do understand, Isabel. I, too, am lonely at times. My thoughts are not always pure and I am very capable of breaking God's Laws. If given the opportunity, I would--"

At that moment, Joseph entered the room, cutting short her father's words. A confession she had little desire to hear. Her worry, once again on Nathaniel, and she grabbed at Joseph's hand. "He's not here. It had to be very early this morning when I'd fallen asleep." Isabel tightened her hold. "He can't be far."

Joseph lowered his head. "I had hoped James was not right."

"I don't understand…James is not right! Nathaniel only needs time and care," Isabel protested.

Joseph looked at her for a long beat and nodded. "Perhaps," he said, his expression offering her nothing.

She moved to the window with weighted feet. She looked out onto the suddenly well-lit day. Her eyes began to water from the brightness, masking the tears. She cupped her hands against her cheeks, drawing up the wetness into her palms. Joseph and her father talked around her, but she cared not a whit about what they were saying.

She took in a breath and released it, her tears siphoned. Her sore eyes took in the surround of budding trees looping the small cemetery. Blinking several times to gain focus, she began to make out a dark figure pressed up against the larger of the stones. Her heart seemed to stop, guttered a moment, and then sped up at the realization of who it was huddled there. She would have gone down, if not for the sill, grabbing hold, head pressed against the cool windowpane.

She envisioned the slow roll of tears down his cheeks, the words of repentance spilling from kiss-swollen lips, ashamed. In the briefest of moments, she felt a doxy.

Tears for them, for the long-ago dead, four springs gone, if only to be held as dear....

In a whisper, she said, "he only needs time."

211

Isabel

Isabel spoke scarcely above a whisper, her breath fogging the windowpane. "He's by their gravestones ... again."

"What was that?"

Her father came up beside her where she watched Nathaniel from the bedroom window. He looked small and miserable, kneeling on the still muddy ground, hunched forward, his arms wrapped around his waist, as if keeping himself from coming apart.

Isabel, still feeling the sting of her father's judgments, did not want to answer him. Peevish, she took a breath and said, "Nathaniel is at the graves."

"I see," her father stated, but Isabel read far more into the few words spoken.

"What you wish to see, I am sure." Isabel retorted. She turned to speak to Joseph, surprised to find he was no longer in the bedroom.

"Leave him to it, Isabel. It is none of your affair."

At her father's words, she stepped away from the window. His nearness to her was making her livid. She had the urge to lash out at him physically. She wanted to wipe clean the whole mess, angered he had ruined it for her. *What of the absolution she felt?* Nathaniel had freed her, made things right again for her. She would not allow her father to sully something that made her feel clean, reborn.

"You will never understand this thing. You will never know ..."

"I want to know, Isabel," her father implored her.

"You want to know my shame? What I've carried in my heart all these years?" Tears now came to her eyes, ran down her cheeks. She wiped at them, angered by her inability to not feel. "I was ravished, father. Raped! I was forward, perhaps too brazen, I admit, but he went too far. The oddest thing really, how kind he was to me, speaking to me with words so loving, so sweet, I began to wonder if I'd imagined it all, that I somehow had agreed to his seduction, to be carnally known. He was a proper gentleman through it all, but taking me against my will, nonetheless," she said. Isabel turned away from him, walked to the bed, and sat, her hands covering her face. "Now you know."

Her father wept. "I am so sorry, daughter."

"Hush, father," Isabel soothed, "it is not your fault. I was far too bold."

"If only I could take away your sorrow, I would, Isabel," her father said, as he wearily rubbed at his eyes, his glasses jutting from the small pocket of his vest. The near black eyes were red-rimmed, showing specks of hazel. "This boy is not the one for you. He offers you no salvation."

Isabel stood and smiled. "Oh, but he has quite done so, father. You could never know what I have gone through. But by the same token, I know little of what you endured during the war. I only ask you to love me."

Her father walked over to her and clasped her hands in his. He looked rather old to her.

"You are my child, Isabel. You are my life."

Isabel hugged him then, but said, "I am your child, but my life is my own."

Her father pushed her back and looked hard into her face. She did not falter, looking him in the eye.

"As it should be," he whispered, "as it should be." Isabel began to cry in earnest as her father held her in his arms. "I must see to Mary and James. But then, I think we should return home and never speak of this again."

Isabel didn't argue, needing to sort through all that had occurred. *All so absurd, really,* she thought to herself. *The worry, the concern, all for naught; hardly a certainty Nathaniel would ever be willing to start again.*

She jumped when a hand pressed down on her shoulder.

"Come along, dear. I want to be home before midday." Her father took up his bag and walked off down the hallway. She followed him into the hall and watched him as he went up to Mary's door and gave it a single rap. He opened the door and entered the room, shutting it firmly behind him. James' door was closed as well and she felt compelled to sit with him. She needed to talk to someone, but at once realized it could never be him. She scorned the notion of secrets, adding yet another one.

Joseph

It was daybreak and the boy lost to him again. Joseph was ashamed. He had spoken out of turn, his words betraying a momentary weakness. His stomach turned when he saw more hope in Isabel's eyes than he held in his own heart. Joseph understood a deep and abiding love well. Without Mary, he had no life. Nathaniel loved Jane in the same way.

His thoughts wandered to his father. He had been the largest man in town, standing 6 feet and 5 inches tall, but gentle, with a giving heart. He had never once belittled another soul or raised a hand to his children in anger. On a rare occasion, a strapping would be necessary, but only at their mother's prodding. It was never easy for him, ending it with an apologetic kiss to the forehead and a reminder to be good.

Over the years, father, mother, two brothers and a sister had all been lost to him from illness and bad fortune. Alone in the world, he had found and clung to Mary like a man bereft of all dreams and hope, offered a second chance, as though a lottery won. *What luck! What absolute fortune!*

But, it was not to be so simple, so easily given to him. Mary's mother, with all her wealth and refinement, had taken one look at him and closed the door. Not actually, of course, but he had heard the slamming of it in his own mind all the same. Her mother's eyes, as blue as Mary's, were icy cold, voicing her displeasure without an uttered word.

When he had gathered up his nerve and mentioned the silent disapproval to Mary, she had thrown back her lovely head of raven black hair, laughing. "It was to be expected," she had said and then she had kissed him, not appearing surprised or offended, adding, "Although, I must say, I hadn't noticed." Again, she had laughed and had taken up his hand.

His face had grown hot because of her casual attitude. Hurt and indignant, he had nodded and forced a smile. However, he hadn't been able to stop himself from mentioning that her mother's disapproval of him meant she would not agree to their marriage.

"I know," she had said, "I know."

He had turned away from her then, defeated. He remembered his cheeks had been wet with tears when Mary had forced him around to face her. She had been quiet, staring into his eyes. And then she had said, "Elope." One word spoken had breathed into him new life. "Yes!" he had shouted, "yes!" He had known then with certitude she held in her all he would ever need.

Joseph now walked unnoticed from Nathaniel's bedroom and out of the house. Headed to the gravesite, he walked on filled with a sickening certainty he again would fail his son.

Nathaniel

An aching in him like nothing he had felt before and hoped to never feel again. He had gotten sick near their graves. Sinned against her and heaven would know, she would know. Merciful Lord, he missed her, so lonely for the touch of her. It had been too long, and dreams were not enough. Tears burned his eyes, a scream close to the surface. He had told her he was too long lost.

Isabel Langford. Sweet Jesus! What had he done? Oh, Lord! Jane! What had she said to him? What had she called him?

Nathaniel couldn't remember. He only remembered the release, nothing more. He had bit his lip hard so as not to call out Jane's name, aware it would hurt Isabel.

He felt a rise of anger. It heated his belly and sparked his thoughts, hateful words on his tongue. A man, yes, he was that, a man with desires not easily suppressed. But he had remained chaste, had not been led astray, denied himself for years, though the offers and temptations were many. Women had made known their attraction, taken with his appearance, his hair, the color of his eyes. A slow realization that women lusted like men, even more so surprising that they had openly lusted for him.

He had trusted her, believed her. *This is the way,* Isabel had said. And he had followed her, caught up in it. A release from the loss, the pain *…to hell with it, to hell with it!*

217

"Abide! Abide!" Nathaniel yelled. He burrowed his hands into the mud, taking up handfuls and tossing it aside. Then he became frantic, digging and digging in anger and desperation. He started shouting, "You left! You left! Abide, you said. You told me you would abide."

He shivered, fevered still and covered in mud. "I don't know how to go on without you, Jane. Tell me how to go on?"

"You go on one moment at a time. One hour at a time. One day at a time."

Nathaniel looked up at his father. "I don't know how."

"Take hold." His father stuck his sizeable hand out to him. "Take hold and I'll help you. I promise I'll show you."

Nathaniel lowered his head. "It's too late. Jane's lost to me now."

"That's not true, boy."

"I was unfaithful to her, Pa." Nathaniel shook his head. "I couldn't stop. I don't know how it happened. I don't know how it happened. I trusted her."

"What are you telling me, Natey?" His father's voice was gentle.

"Isabel…" Nathaniel couldn't get out the words.

"Did you lay with her?"

Nathaniel began to weep, his tears mingling with mud. "Yes," he said, choking on the word, "God help me, yes."

He felt his father kneel beside him and then he felt the man's large arms wrap around him.

"There's nothing to forgive, son." His father patted his back as if Nathaniel were a young child.

"You did nothing wrong." His father cleared his throat, a nervous tick, but pressed on, asking, "Do you know her intention?"

"No." Nathaniel found himself breaking down again.

"If she wishes to marry…?"

"I'll comply." Something cropped up in Nathaniel then, speaking out of turn when he said to his father, "Weren't the first she'd lain with." And then he had to look away from his father, his shame overriding his sorrow. "Sweet Jesus, Lord forgive me."

"Now, now," his father said. "It's not as dark as it seems."

Nathaniel shook from the cold and regret. At once taken off guard by the line of his thoughts: *But what of James? What of James?*

Joseph

"I won't forgive her for this."

"Mary, please," Joseph sat down in his worn leather chair, closing his eyes for just a moment. It had been a difficult day for everyone. Thomas and Isabel had given their quick goodbyes earlier that morning to Mary and James, leaving instructions for Nathaniel's care, and to Joseph's relief avoided the cemetery. Soon after their departure, he had settled Nathaniel back in his room and into bed after a hot bath and change of clothing.

In the afternoon, James had awoken in good spirits, recovered from his migraine, and Mary seemed to have rebounded, as well. John was running ranch affairs with surprising capability, making a mental note to give the boy more responsibilities. James tended to coddle John, treating him as a child. *How many times had he overlooked John's frustration, not wanting to undermine James' authority?* He had often let things slide, so much easier than upset the cart. Over and over again, the boys had taken second place to Mary's difficulties.

He had given James too much leeway over the years, especially while Nathaniel had been off to war. Many times, James had made decisions without Joseph's input or approval. For the most part, his decisions were sound and Joseph was grateful to him. During those years Nathaniel was away, there had been no one to keep him abreast of things or offer him differing advice or opinion. Nathaniel, though soft-spoken and gentle, had somehow managed to keep James in his place, a tough task at best. Between the two boys, Joseph had felt confident things would remain running well while he cared for Mary.

It was going on five years now that James had been running things alone. Joseph needed to take back the reins. Nathaniel and John had their own mark to make. John would be eager for the opportunity, but Nathaniel had all but shut himself away from life. And now this thing with Isabel … which at once brought him back to his conversation with Mary.

"I'm sorry, my darling, what were you saying?" Joseph asked, rubbing his hand over his face.

"You look weary, my love." Mary walked over to him, pulling the tapestry hassock close to the leather chair, sat and rested her head upon his lap. Joseph began to run his hand over the back of her head. She had let her hair down while he told her of Isabel and Nathaniel. Her face had been without expression while she listened, brushing long strands of black hair.

"It has been quite the time," Joseph said, his hand continuing to rub her head, comforting him.

"She took advantage of him. You know that, don't you?" Mary didn't wait for a reply. "She is no innocent, that one."

"We are not to judge such things."

"I'll damn well judge. Nathaniel is a good boy. Not long ago, he had such vivid dreams of Jane and the child Molly that he thought them still walking this good earth. I'm inclined to believe his thoughts were of Jane." Mary lifted her head and looked at Joseph, waiting for him to agree.

"Nathaniel knew, Mary," said Joseph. "But he was thinking of Jane. He is sick from it and I offered him forgiveness."

Mary's eyes filled at that. "More grief and self-castigation added to his many trials. How do we help him, Joseph? When I sensed Isabel had interest in Nathaniel, I thought, perhaps she might help him move on, all the while, aware of James' unspoken claim on her. I chose one son over the other and because of that both will suffer."

Joseph sighed and said, "The choice was Isabel's and Isabel's alone. I'm afraid she is besotted and Nathaniel barely able to bring himself to

221

go on living, never mind give thought to love again." Joseph took hold of Mary's small hands and spoke quietly to her. "As I told Nathaniel this morning, we must keep this under wraps, not speak of it."

"And what of Isabel?" Mary asked somewhat testily. "Will she keep this under wraps?"

Joseph became angry and his words reflected it. "If she has any shame at all, she will. It took a time to calm him down, inconsolable."

He grew quiet, still running his hand over Mary's hair. "Perhaps, you're right, Mary. For some reason unknown to us, Isabel took advantage of our boy. It is not Nathaniel's way."

"At the earliest opportunity, I want James and Two Crows to ride to the TML and tell Isabel I no longer need her help with Nathaniel or the household chores. Though, I am most grateful. Will it appear too coincidental? I should hardly have an iota of regret here, but I do. Merciful God, I do! Why did she do this? What did she think she would gain? Nathaniel's affection? Well, I think not! And if James gets wind of this …" Mary looked at Joseph. "That will not end well."

Joseph nodded. "No, it certainly will not."

Nathaniel

Nathaniel slept in fitful increments throughout the day. A long span of darkness interrupted by brief flashes of memory and distinct images floating across his mind: Jane, her smile, her eyes, the feel of her lips on his, the warm press of her against him. The likenesses of his mother and father, his brothers, and his sweet child, Molly, were suspended there in the darkness. But then it all suddenly grew menacing as battlefields blotted out everything else.

When fully awake, his mind was a tempest, riddled with pangs of regret and rumination. He was guilt-ridden and felt certain he would be forever ailing. He had seen terrible things in his life and had done his share. It was the way of it in war and was best not to dwell, believing there was not a soul living who could walk through life unspoiled. Scarcely a way on God's green earth a man could keep himself as seamless as a newborn babe and even those said to be born with sin. He told himself that a man must believe what he chooses to believe, sometimes only what he can believe to get by, to find some peace, to feel half-human again.

He had cried plenty after the war. Not always tears seen on the outside, but inside where the hurt was profound and piercing. He had a sickness in the core of him, his mind so bruised he'd forgotten how to laugh. The first time, after a long time, he had heard himself laughing and to his ears he had sounded like someone else, startling himself badly. He understood now, John had the right of it, saying it sounded rusty and rough as an old gate too long beaten by the seasons. The one thing that had gotten him through the war was his loved ones waiting on him back home. It had kept him believing in life, a life sometimes so cruel, so wicked on a man that he would rather die than bear another day. He had every right to be angry and self-indulgent, so grievous was his loss. But when thinking on things got him so mired in the muck, he knew he might as well just give up on living, just curl up in a hole somewhere and die.

During the war, Nathaniel believed the good Lord must not have known the world would soon be coming to an end. Man, brutal, bloody, and violent against each other, making every attempt to kill off humankind. It had been an unspooling of utter and bitter cruelty, a world gone mad. And he a man neither able to accept nor understand, not having the appropriate nature to make peace with such things, and all too aware of his current doggedness to hold close his discontent like a festering wound.

Nathaniel lay there for some time alone in the room of his childhood home, not knowing if it was the fever still burning through him or if he had truly broken, causing his thoughts to run madly through his mind. Instead, he focused for a moment on his body's urges: thirst and a need to use the privy, the latter a more pressing need than the other. He was not in the frame of mind to pinpoint each of the aches and pains of his body, hoping if he ignored them, he could get up and on with things, tricking himself into believing he was fit. But that was soon forgotten, discovering he could barely sit up, his head weightier than a full keg of beer. He decided to concentrate on his legs and began to slide them toward the edge of the bed, kicking off the layer of quilts, his right foot free.

It was day, probably late morning, seeing the sun, edgy and pushy, on the sides of the thick drapes. His eyes swept the room, stopping up short on the rocker pulled up close to the bed. He thought of everyone who had recently sat there, keeping vigil over him. Suddenly, all manner of memory came back in a bright flash. All the oddities he had conjured up in his fevered brain tumbled over him as he struggled to get out of bed. He reached his arm out to grip the bedside table.

With his feet, firmly on the floor, he pushed his body upward and sat somewhat wobbly on the side of the bed. He was worn down to the nub from the effort. His legs shook as he started to rise and he almost fell back onto the bed. He stood and moved about like a man in a slow-moving dream unable to make his body obey him. He found any quick jerking of his head or looking anywhere but level made him dizzy. He was weaker than he ever remembered being, even during the war with all its deprivations. His chest felt heavy and it took great effort to fill up his lungs.

A strong memory of blood came to him, making him lightheaded and weak-kneed. The smell of it to his nose was no longer coppery and fresh, but foul and decayed. He gagged at the vivid remembrance of it, seeing in his mind's eye the blood stains on the wood floor below the window of his parent's bedroom. He forced himself not to drift, not be drawn back to the battlefield. He thought of the story of Jesus at the wedding in Cana of Galilee. Nathaniel believed it to be a story of a son honoring his mother. Close to faint, he continued forward, mumbling to himself, "*water to wine, wine to blood.*" He stood there a moment and then without warning, dropped to his knees, everything going dark.

Joseph

"Joseph, it wasn't your fault."

"I should have been with him."

"You stayed with him the entire night and most of the morning. How were you to know he'd awaken and decide to wander?"

Joseph smiled at Mary. "Well, I should have known. It seems to be his inclination. The boy hasn't been thinking straight from the fevers."

"We still see him as a child, though he's a full-grown man." Mary placed her hand against Nathaniel's cheek, studying his well-favored face. "He is a man who has survived a war and the death of his wife and child, a man who is accustomed to doing for himself."

Mary smiled and turned to Joseph, looking in his eyes as she spoke. "I see how much you love him." Her eyes filled up. "For that I am so very grateful. Don't let things get in the way of that ever."

"Mary …" Joseph looked at her and shook his head. "I won't," was all he said. Mary smiled. It was a tentative smile like spring before the full bloom of summer. She reached over and gave a light squeeze to Joseph's hand.

"I'll get broth for him. If he roused once, he will rouse again. He needs nourishment to recover." Mary nodded to Joseph and then left the room.

Isabel

It had started in her the first morning home after being with Nathaniel, startling and unexpected as a pinch. Isabel had been euphoric, her dreams in clear reach, her mind as quick and light as a hummingbird. Ever hopeful her father would have a change of heart over time, but more so, Nathaniel.

Isabel trusted her father, believing he loved her enough to sacrifice his own needs, his own dreams. However, scarcely a day later, she realized it was all a lie, a successful bluff. Her father did not intend to accept Nathaniel, though she could not understand what drove his disapproval. *Was his hatred so strong for those who took up arms against the Union, a secesh?* she wondered. As a doctor, he relentlessly fought for all the wounded, no matter their allegiance. It made no sense to Isabel.

Her father, without question, favored James, and she had to admit after their brief chat on the portico that horrific evening, she had seen a very vulnerable, sweet, and gentle side to the man. If Nathaniel had not come home, it would have taken little sacrifice on her part to accept James as her husband. But Isabel had been drawn to Nathaniel, beyond all reason, as though enchanted. She could offer no logical explanation for it. She was not a woman who put great stock in the sentiment of the heart. She possessed an uncanny ability to rise above emotions, sensible-headed, which often led others to believe her to be cold and aloof. Nathaniel had changed all that the moment she set eyes upon him.

Her father's resolve was far stronger than she had imagined it to be, as he allowed her everything she desired. Unfamiliar feelings warred in her, making for restless nights, and she wandered through her days, bleary-eyed and withdrawn.

Soon, after too many sleepless nights, she fell into a deep depression, her grief becoming unbearable. She was so close to having all she ever dreamed about, ever wanted, only to have her father deny her this, placing another hurdle in front of her. As if, Nathaniel alone wasn't challenge enough.

Although she refused to give in to her melancholy, struggling against it, she could not keep it at bay. Her decline came at once, though it was not evident on the surface, only to her, as she raptly watched the skin of her limbs begin to shrivel, curling back from her bones like aged-tree bark, overly sensitive to touch, buzzing and shivering beneath her fingers. She could no longer sleep, the pounding of her buirdly heart too loud in her ears, pulsated its strong, frenetic beat.

To her eyes, she was translucent, seeing the outline of each organ, the curving bones of her ribs exposed as if only swathed in gossamer, which was both frightening and thrilling to her. Into her womb, she could see—giddy with promise, desperately wanting life to be there, fragile and embryonic, a nebulous dream child, tamping, burrowing, and latching onto her secret fertile walls, *Nathaniel's child.* However, she suspected it would remain empty, barren, its vacuity as malevolent as a cancer, a befitting punishment for the other.

On the seventh day after being with Nathaniel, she had cut away her waist length hair to her shoulders, to her father's displeasure, too afraid the strands would come to life, snaking around her neck, choking her as she lay in her bed. She imagined a web spinning around and around, becoming shrouded in a thousand silken filaments, unable to break free, unable to move. She would lay there for hours paralyzed beneath the bed's well-tucked covers.

Isabel no longer prayed to God or the sainted, knowing all she had done had been seen. The sin of fornicator was hers to bear. *To whom could she profess? Would she one day be exposed with the public unfurling of conjugal bed linens? Of course, Nathaniel would never stand for such things!* In that she felt hopeful.

When she was young she had only her father and she had clung to him with a childish desperation, fearful he would leave her, too, as her mother had left her in death. But in the end, it was she who had left, sent off to boarding school. All those comely, vacuous girls, with very little knowledge of the world, choosing to be submissive and worse, sycophantic to all men, had promptly distanced themselves from her. Isabel had thrown herself into her studies, finding solace in her books and her poetry. Sad, lonely, her open-eyed daydreams became more and more authentic. With the hours spent alone in her room, she began to withdraw inside her mind for camaraderie and love, reaching out to her long-ago departed mother. That had been the start of her first decline; the second had been after the baby. But each time she had made it back.

Now on the eighth day, tucked away in her room, dreaming of Nathaniel, the world outside her window had dissolved–featureless, hazy, and insignificant. She was safe within her walls, a womb, suspended by an umbilical thread within the amnion. Her father battered at her door as he had done before, intruding, and slicing open her safe world, a Cesarean.

Each night Isabel cried without pause in her sleep, feeling the tears dribbling down her cheeks, into her ears, swelling from her, bitter and enduring. *Was it real? Or only crocodile tears, crocodile love, crocodile life?* She told herself it was far easier not to feel. She viewed herself as a motherless child, alone. Nathaniel to her was a waif, lost and broken. They were a pair the two of them. *Was that the draw?*

James

It hadn't been lost on James, aware Isabel had feelings for Nathaniel. Thinking it, going over it in his mind, didn't hurt as much as he thought it would hurt him. More so surprised, there was no anger. Something seemed to break in him after seeing the brutalized boy, giving way to an odd sort of peace. *Had it been the laudanum?* Muzzy-minded for a day or two, but this had been different. He felt like he was swaddled in cotton, the soft wind as delicate against his face as a kiss, the sun seeping into the marrow of him, warm and reviving. He had a sense of second chances.

A memory was there, unclear, but on the edge of something big, something important to him. The sight of the scalped boy had felled him. The pain in his head had been without warning, swift and debilitating. He held little stock in dreams or signs, but his inner voice told him to take heed, there was something of import he needed to puzzle out, a spun tale he needed to hear, though without doubt gruesome, held the answers. The boy had died. He had not.

And thinking this without prompt and with deep surety, led him to believe that he too had suffered a similar assault. He floated above the notion from a safe remove, unbelieving, but still not with complete dismissal, lifting a hand to his forehead.

One day followed another. A week had gone since his migraine. Isabel had not returned. His mother, in seemingly good spirits, sent him off, laden with breads and baked goods, canning jars full of green beans and tomatoes, sacks of potatoes and beef as thanks. James, also, carried a gift, a bit more personal. He hadn't formally presented himself to Isabel's father as an interested suitor, but he was well aware of Thomas' unspoken approval. Clearly, Isabel held some misguided romantic notions about Nathaniel as widower and war hero. James wasn't certain how deep those romantic notions went regarding his brother.

James shook his head, grimacing. Such thoughts were lowering his mood, his outlook darkening further when Jane came to his mind. Her image broke over him like a crashing wave, seeing her with startling clarity, hearing her words, harsh and angry.

Even in her last hours, the fire still raged in her toward him. It had only been a week since James' last visit, sent off by his mother teeming with food and books and winter clothing, blankets and, of all things, hair ribbons and silk dresses, fine china dishes, booties and a porcelain doll for the child. His mother had been distraught, forbidding James to return home without them, needing Jane and Molly under the Keegan roof. It had been a request of James from the onset of Nathaniel's departure, but Jane had slapped his face, her boot heels dug into the earth, defiant and accusing. And still the anger, the defiance, continued, a year later, into the bleak and desperate hours of her dying, no utterance of forgiveness for him, no absolution forthcoming. At the last of her breath taken did his heart turn to stone, as she had believed of him long ago. Her words, years after her death, were still a thing hard for him to forget.

"How many deaths will be on your head, James?" Jane had asked

him. *"Are we nothing to you then? Is God no longer a reckoning?"*

She quieted, sucking in air through her ruined lungs. "I fear my Nathaniel has succumbed to a horrible death, a malady wrought, and him alone in his time of passing. You have wreaked destruction upon my family and I am hard pressed to understand the why of it. Is your envy so potent, poisoning your heart so against us, this helpless child near death, your niece, your blood, Nathaniel, and I, a woman you had once admired? It is that then, isn't it, angry I gave you the mitten?"

Jane shook her head and then continued, "Coveting, always coveting. Why do you envy him so, this brother who would die for you, perhaps has died for you? I should be the envious one, Nathaniel off to do your bidding, while I am alone in my grief, my time of dying. . . Go, now, James. There is no more hope for me. But, first take this and if you have a soul yet in you, heart not yet of stone, give this letter to your brother if he should survive the storm of war. It is only for his eyes. As I have no one else, I place my trust in you this one last time, do not fail me again."

James thrust his hand into the side pocket of his vest and fingered the worn letter, his body giving a hard shudder. After Jane's death, he could not bring himself to go against her wishes, but he feared exposing the truths he believed were written there. James scoffed at the ridiculousness of it all. There was nothing and no one to fear. He had done nothing to warrant her hatred, her accusations, and to think he had once thought to have cared for her. Blinded, no doubt by her comeliness, no one in the county had compared, until now, until Isabel.

233

But Jane had only eyes for Nathaniel after their first encounter, James pushed aside, given the mitten as Jane had so callously called it. His stomach jumped and his breathing caught. *Was history repeating itself?*

James pushed the damning memory aside, instead recalling the conversation with Isabel on the portico. It was as though she had seen him for the first time, and had understood the man he was, allowing her this as he allowed no one ... but Nathaniel.

The thought sprung from the back reaches of his brain, unfettered. He did not try to contain it or deny it. There had been a time when he had loved Nathaniel like no other, as a brother loved a brother. Nathaniel loved him as well. No doubt, still did, even after everything.

What had sparked the change in him? With that question, an image flashed in his mind of Two Crows, lifting Nathaniel into the air and settling him on a broad, copper shoulder. Nathaniel was smiling down at James, blue eyes large with excitement, slender fingers grabbing hold of the long, black braids.

"Where's Nathaniel going, Pa?" he had remembered asking. His father had taken hold of his hand, appearing surprised to find it to be nearly as large as his own, a boy of nine years, long-legged and thin as a marsh reed. "Your mama's not feeling well," had been all his father had said. James had watched Nathaniel go, eyes fixed on the small, pale face framed with the blackest hair, until Nathaniel had vanished from view. His father had watched with him and then had squeezed his hand, saying, "It's not forever."

Maybe not forever, but it had been a defining moment to James, the moment the breach had begun, a clear betrayal. It had been on that day, James supposed, he had commenced to hate Indians. He had always carried a strong distrust, an almost paralyzing fear of them, yet he had no specific reason as to why, only going on instinct, a gut-feeling. He had heard all the grisly tales as a boy, the killings and abductions, but this was different, this was keenly personal. He had come close to grabbing up his Pa's rifle that day while he had stood watching his much-loved brother being carried away, taken from him.

After a month's time, Nathaniel had returned to them, brown as a papoose, but unharmed. He had not let the boy out of his sight afterward, daring to demand Nathaniel be left with him, his responsibility only, during their mama's spells. But worst of all to James was Nathaniel choosing to be with Two Crows of his own accord when he was older. It was to James the most brutal of betrayals.

Riding side by side with Two Crows on this late spring morning, headed toward the TML Ranch, James started at the realization, it had been that day his hatred had gained a face. Glancing over at the man, James could not dismiss a growing feeling, powerful and overwhelming. The Indian had secrets.

"It's grand, isn't it?" she said.

"What?" James turned to look at her, wondering about her shorn hair. Though Isabel remained beautiful, the length was an oddity.

"All this before us …this land, this sky…so, so big, so, so grand," she said. Her smile covered her face. Her eyes were opened far too wide and her hands' movements were far too agitated, paroxysmal.

"Are you well, Isabel?" James asked.

Isabel paused her gesturing, her mouth forming a perfect "O" of surprise. "Do I not seem well to you, James?"

He dug his hands into his pockets, his shoulders raised in tension.

She smiled, turning to look again over the sweep of land.

They stood together, close, but not intimate. The portico, once again, a place they had ventured without thought. This time it was her home. A white bench swing hung from a wooden rafter and scrolled cast iron furniture had been placed in a far corner. It was a beautiful spot to watch the world.

"It looks so peaceful to the eye, but it's all a ruse, really." Isabel stopped and looked up at him, her body stayed facing forward, her neck swiveled, her head tilted back.

"You'll get a crick." It was all he could think to say.

"What a charming word. Crick, crick, crick," she repeated, and then laughed.

The sound of it gave James goose bumps. He calmed himself.

236

"What's going on, Isabel?" James asked with a serious tone. "You seem to be chawing on something. Best spit it out then."

"I speak of secrets, Mr. Keegan, horrible, horrible secrets." She giggled and then said, "Chaw on that."

James insides churned, his breath caught. "I reckon we all have a secret or two."

Isabel watched him. Her eyes fixed on his; the intensity was disconcerting. "And you live with them?"

"You can control what you choose to reveal or not reveal, Isabel. Besides, I'm sure your secrets are quite benign."

"My, my, Mr. Keegan, you surprise me so often. Benign. Benign."

"A girl like you couldn't possibly have done anything so objectionable to fall into disrepute."

"If I were a man …"

"What if you were a man?"

"If I were a man, there would be no secrets." She laughed.

"What's funny, Isabel?"

"Do you care for me, James?" Isabel turned to face him, her eyes burning him.

James felt his face heat, knowing his cheeks had colored. Her forwardness had caught him off-guard, a feeling he hated. The word no was on the tip of his tongue, wanting to hurt her. *Did he care for anyone?* He had shut himself away from such things long ago. It only caused pain. Jane had the right of things, calling him heartless, inhuman, hateful. Her screams haunted his sleep for years. He knew how it felt to hate and be hated. *Did he know love?* Nathaniel loved without condition. Even as he walked down the dirt track away from his wife and baby, his mama, and pa, and his brothers, his love for James shone bright as the moon. James could still feel the light breeze of the night, how it tried his silent tears, watching his brother become smaller and smaller, until he was completely out of his sight. He lived with the lies, the secrets.

"Yes, Isabel, I care for you." James took her hand and kissed it. He pulled her toward him, holding her in a strong hug. He felt her head nodding against his chest.

"Good," she said to him. "Good."

Joseph

Joseph stood beside Nathaniel on the porch in the late evening light while they watched James and Two Crows ride under the arch toward the main corral of the barn. Joseph was in high spirits to see the boy in better health, even though a low-grade fever seemed unremitting, hectic. He felt the press of Nathaniel's shoulder against his own and couldn't keep from grinning when James gave them a quick wave. Joseph felt content.

His sons were home.

Breaking the silence, he asked, "How is it with you and James?"

"Fair to middling, I reckon," Nathaniel said.

"It's that good?" Joseph smiled and bumped his hip against Nathaniel.

"I don't rightly feel one way or the other about it." Nathaniel sighed and looked up at the darkening sky.

"He loves you," Joseph said, never surer of a thing.

"Funny way of showing it," Nathaniel said. Joseph saw a slight upturn of the boy's mouth, not quite a full-on smile, but close enough.

"Let's sit," Joseph said while guiding Nathaniel to the high-back rockers.

Lowering himself down into the chair, Joseph let out a groan. The ache of his bones always surprised him. His knees, especially, were a bitter reminder of age. Nathaniel showed no notice to Joseph's grunting or the cracking of his joints as he settled in the cushioned rocking chair. Resting his head against the high-back, he took in a deep breath, releasing it, and closed his eyes.

"What I'm about to ask might be a bolt out of the blue, but I need to ask all the same." Joseph opened his eyes and studied Nathaniel, the track of his gaze, the convulsing throat, and the tight-fisted grip on the rocker arms. After everything, he deserved the truth, or as much of it as he could tell.

"Have you ever pondered James' scar and how it was done to him?"

Nathaniel glanced at his father. "Plenty of times," he said.

Joseph was silent for a time and then cleared his throat, blundering forward. "Have you spoken with James about it?"

"We've spoken some on the matter."

"You have?" Joseph's heartbeat ramped up. "Does he remember how it happened?"

"No, he couldn't recollect," Nathaniel said. "But his nightmares were powerful bad. I reckoned it had something to do with it."

"And he remembered nothing?"

He felt Nathaniel's eyes on him then. His heart felt near to bursting from his chest as he waited for Nathaniel to speak.

"You mean about the *scalping*?"

Joseph sucked in a breath and then released it, gaining his composure. Before he could answer, Nathaniel began talking, looking off into the darkness.

"Two Crows familiarized me with the ways of such things as a boy and it got me to contemplating. I didn't inquire about it though, and never told James what I thought. James warned me against it anyway. Mostly, I didn't want to cause him any more hurt." After a pause, he said, "Appears you were of the same mind."

Joseph dropped his head and sighed. "Your brother asked only once, but it gave your mother such a virulent spell, the worst I'd seen. Two Crows took care of you for well over a month then, longer. I'd lost count. You were a little dote and needed more care then I could give you." He rubbed at his eyes. "James never asked again, and I gave your mother my word never to speak of it."

Nathaniel looked off into the distance. "Reckon there's no more need to speculate. He doesn't remember it though. He'd yell out in his sleep,

240

calling for ma, and I'd snug up to him and tell him he was safe. I hardly slept after those terrors of his. The headaches would come on him sometimes. I could never make it right for him."

"You were just a boy. It wasn't your place. It was mine. I'm sorry," Joseph said to Nathaniel.

Nathaniel nodded and said, "I understand why he hates, why he's so full of anger. It must devil him some, the not knowing. Must make him loco."

"When you were born, you brought us joy. James wouldn't let you out of his sight."

"No matter that, something happened." Nathaniel looked at Joseph. "What was it pa? What changed?"

"You're right," Joseph said in a whisper. He sighed and rubbed a hand over his face. "I noticed a change when Two Crows brought you home. James was so angry at me, at Two Crows, even at your mama for taking you away from him. I saw something in James' eyes when he looked at Two Crows." A shiver coursed through him, remembering. "I knew it wasn't Two Crows he hated, but the one that hurt him."

"And mama?" Nathaniel spoke so low, Joseph had to lean toward the boy. It took a while to grasp what he was asking him.

Joseph heard himself speaking, knowing his answer for the half-truth it was. "Your mama was brave. She fought back, stopped him. I wasn't too far off. When I heard screaming, I turned back double-quick, and I shot him dead through the heart. Then what he tried to do to my boy, I did to him. Wasn't near enough to what he deserved. God's forgiveness,

241

be damned." Joseph let out a small laugh. "More likely Joseph Keegan, be damned."

"No!" Nathaniel shook his head. "No!"

Joseph reached his hand out and squeezed the back of Nathaniel's neck. It felt too warm against his palm. "Now hold on there, Nathaniel. Calm yourself. I do believe God may not judge my actions too harshly."

"You did right, pa," Nathaniel said.

"I thank you for that, boy."

"You protected your family, kept them alive."

"I know what you're prodding at and I want you to stop."

"I should have been with them."

"Nathaniel…"

Nathaniel stood up fast, his eyes bright with the beginning of tears, his watery gaze intent on his brother, walking toward the house. "Not just myself I blame…no, sir!" he yelled it out into a gust of wind just then sprung up.

Joseph turned his head a fraction, seeing sorrow cross James' moonlit face as he approached them. Bereft, Joseph looked up at the night sky, giving a silent prayer. *"Dear Lord, please do not visit my iniquities upon my sons."*

Isabel

Isabel entered the study where her father sat at his desk bent over his ledgers. It had been several hours since James had left from his visit and her father had not once asked about the time they had spent together. A ploy really, she believed, but his feigned disinterest pressed on her to such an extent she now stood watching him, wishing she could know a person's mind without having to converse. Her pride made her hold her tongue, turning her back on him and leaving the room.

"Isabel?"

She heard him call to her as she paused to look out the parlor window. Her attention was drawn to a line of horsemen riding the wide dirt track toward the house. She sighed. Caden and his men were returning from their debaucheries and murderous deeds for which her father paid handsomely. She was of two minds about the Indian killings, more so after the Miller boy's death and mutilation. It made her angry and frightened, finding it hard not to want them all to go far, far away and leave the ranchers in peace. Nathaniel cared deeply about it, though, able to see both sides of the issue. Yet, she supposed, he had made it clear, his family would come above all else.

She hadn't given it much thought. But now watching the wretched lot enter the corral and lower themselves to the dusty ground from their horses, soiled in blood and dirt, everything came back to her. No matter the many scalps, the spoils of their kill, strung out like black woolly flags on strips of rawhide, Isabel was no better, as she recalled the quick, seamless shot that had felled two men only several weeks past.

Even after Nathaniel had later explained the young Indian was simply looking for coup, Isabel hadn't swooned or felt aggrieved by the killing. Her only thought was to keep Nathaniel safe. The Indian had been a threat that had to be dealt with swiftly and without sentiment. It was as simple as felling a winter geese, deer or turkey. Perhaps, if the threat had been from a white man, she would have been overcome. Perhaps, but she couldn't be certain.

Caden was making his way to their front door and Isabel went to her father's study to alert him.

"They're back," Isabel said. "I implore you, father, not to invite that horrible, little man into this house. It was nearly a week before the odor cleared."

Her father rose from his chair at the sound of heavy-fisted thumping on the front door. "Isabel, please ask Cook to see to dinner. I'm famished. My business with Mr. Caden won't take long."

Isabel did as she was told, scurrying away before her father could open the door and allow the wretched man entrance.

While the stench of Caden still lingered throughout the house, Isabel made her way out to the balcony off her room, enjoying the fresh air. She searched the night sky and land, wished on the stars. If Isabel had been told she was of a similar disposition as Mary Keegan, she would have been shocked. But after her recent bout, again at a loss as to what to name it or worse yet claim it as a part of herself, she very likely would have agreed. But she was strong and therein being the distinct difference. Her mind was quick, clever and yes, rational. *Dare she put name to it, dare she voice it?* Yes, she dared. "I, Isabel Langford, am inarguable of sound mind."

And with that spoken affirmation, she refused to acknowledge otherwise. She was strong, independent, and needed not be ashamed of the choices made as any man would have made without ridicule or judgment. It was her decision, her right to be with whomever she chose. A vow made years ago to never allow any man to lord over her, control her, demean her. She would hold all power, of course, best achieved when the man remained unaware. Again, she was clever, of similar intelligence, dare say of greater intelligence than most men. Yes, she would say it and would lay claim to it with confidence, although with utmost humility.

But her confidence faltered when thinking of Nathaniel. Certainly, Mary was aware of her transgression. James' visit surely was meant to be the polite thank you, but no thank you. There was something unspoken. She had seen it in his eyes: fear, admiration, need, caring, perhaps, love—for her. It had been far more than she had seen in Nathaniel's eyes. Oh, yes, there had been fear and uncertainty, yet there had been longing, as well. She lifted a hand to her heart and pressed her palm against her chest for a time, tears welling. Sorrow and loss had been the string pulling them along, a need in them far greater than the physicality of the act. Nathaniel had been conjuring ghosts and she had been laying hers to rest. *That was it then, wasn't it, clever girl?* It had been mutual really. Power was one thing, but never let it be said, Isabel Langford was ruthless. No never. Given time, Nathaniel would see the choice was not only hers, but his as well.

Where did that leave her then? Had she tricked herself into believing Nathaniel was her true love, her saving grace? The clarity and certainty of the moment, freeing her from the grip of the other's hold was redemption enough for her. *Had he served his purpose? Had they been meant to come together in that moment only to purge and begin again?* That certainly must be it and she would explain it all to Nathaniel as such, sort through it all. Mary would come to understand how it had to take place. It was a new day of possibilities, whether it would be with James or Nathaniel. Isabel believed with great certainty she could make them both love her and the choice between the two only hers.

BOOK FOUR

Mary

Mary had hoped the Spring Social in town might set things right with her family and allow her to bask in the admiration and envy of her neighbors when she appeared in the hall, adorned in her jewels and finest gown, escorted by the most handsome of men. Every woman, young and old, would gape at them, not being able to help themselves. Mary understood as she, too, admired her boys openly, prompting James and John to preen and strut and tug at their coat lapels, while embarrassing Nathaniel to no end, and she unable to keep from laughing at his discomfort. It seemed it had been years since she had laughed with such abandon.

But now, weeks later, it looked grim at best to hope for such simple joys as she stared straight ahead into the eyes of Isabel Langford who rode in the barouche with her. The young woman, seated across from Mary, sat far too at ease beside James, her escort–the invitation accepted months ago. Joseph, sharing the carriage seat with Mary, held her hand giving it an occasional squeeze. It both annoyed and reassured her. She looked up at the driver seat and sighed. There Two Crows sat with reins in hand dressed in Joseph's old frock coat and top hat, looking both regal and ridiculous.

Alongside the carriage to Mary's left, rode John, her youngest and to her right, was Nathaniel riding with such effortless grace on his black gelding with all its Indian trappings. Again, she released a long sigh, feeling on cue a gentle press to her hand. She pressed back, not having the heart to worry Joseph. It had taken everything she had, every ounce of bravado she could muster to face Isabel Langford. Nathaniel had not spoken a word to the girl, his eyes kept averted from the barouche and even when Mary called to him, he seemed to only hold his gaze on her for the briefest of time. She decided it was best to leave him to his thoughts, grateful he had agreed to come along with them at all.

Mary was certain each of her sons would be on all the available young ladies' dance cards. With that thought, she immediately remembered another such dance from another lifetime it seemed, and how Jane's card had only Nathaniel's name written upon it and she able to have any man's favor. James had envied Nathaniel then, perhaps had always envied him. Mary had seen the jealousy so often in her eldest, but not understanding the cause.

Her mood had turned decidedly dark, wishing for a taste of laudanum to soften the edges, to lighten her gloominess and lift the shroud like a heavy fog from her mind. She came out of her reverie to the sound of Nathaniel's laughter. It made her catch her breath. He was riding next to Two Crows and was speaking to the Indian in that awful dialect which annoyed her, but his laughter atoned for it. She could see Isabel's head angle ever so slightly, the young woman trying to be discreet, eager to catch a glimpse of Nathaniel. Mary saw James tense, shifting his leg closer to Isabel's, engaging her in conversation.

In that moment, anger rose in Mary toward both Isabel and James. But then she took in a breath and released it, aware the blame lay at her feet alone. She had wanted this young woman to care for Nathaniel, to do whatever it would take to make him whole again. She was not naïve, knew the ugliness of war, the deprivations and depravity. Years without the needs a wife would offer a husband, not only the carnal, but the emotional needs, to feel human again, to feel a part of humankind. *Had she secretly wished for such a connection between Nathaniel and Isabel?* The coward in her perhaps wanted such things; the selfish part had with surety, not wanting to endure his sufferings, not wanting to work through the detritus of war. She had placed it upon Isabel to tidy things up for her, to remove the tares and bring forth only wheat. Joseph had been so dependable with such things. A prayer of sorts sprung up in her, though God had been deaf to her for years. She could not hold it back, thinking only of all wickedness being blown away as chaff in the wind.

Nathaniel

For the first time in months, in truth, years, Nathaniel was content and the sweetness of it frightened him. Through the open windows, he could see the colorful paper lanterns lighting up the night, the laughter and chatter in the room a warm hum through him. The music was lively, his mother and father taking a turn on the dance floor. They looked in high spirits. James was dallying with Isabel Langford, a rare smile gracing his brother's face.

Naturally vigilant, his sharp-eyed gaze ran a quick circuit around the hall. He saw Caden looking in his direction, his steel gray eyes unflinching. It unnerved him for a moment, knowing there'd be a fight to be had soon. Though not wanting to upset his mama, a part of him was looking forward to it. He just needed to work out the odds to be this side of fair. He chuffed at that aloud, his thoughts sliding to another dance; surprised by the fact he could think of Jane a little easier, the pain not as sharp. Though he fretted something terrible over his infidelity, he realized it had been a turning point, a choice clearly presented—die or abide.

It had come to him in a dream a few days after he had lain with Isabel. Jane was there burning in his brain, bright as the moon, eyes deep blue, nearly black. Some called the color midnight blue and he had liked the sound of it. It was a dream that had visited him many times before, but this time Jane's message seemed clearer to him.

He had dreamt of the time when they had conceived Molly in the early hours of a new year, six months into their married life. After their love making, Jane had held him close to her and had said with certainty, "it will be a girl." The half-lit room, the play of shadows on the wall, across Jane's face and exposed breasts had made him ache for her again and she had smiled at him, Madonna and temptress all at once. "Always," she had said to him then and again this time in his recent dreaming. To him it had trumpeted absolution.

He smiled at the memory, his sorrow and discontent appeased, at least, for the evening. Isabel had called him blessed and it had seemed as if in that moment she had been washed clean, a baptism. As to why it had been him, Nathaniel had no clear answer, but aware if James got wind of things, there'd be the devil to pay and he was done paying, brother or not.

He had little time to ponder more on all that weighed on him, for in that instant he found himself surrounded three-deep by women of various sizes and complexions, their dance cards swinging from fine-boned wrists. He cleared a path through them and one-by-one began to dance with each to the best of his ability, though his bad foot caused him to falter now and again. Indiscernible to his dance partner but had sent a terrible shock through him.

Much later, damp with sweat and a strong thirst, Nathaniel politely begged off the next in line, promising he'd soon return. When he turned away to leave, he saw his mother and waved over at her. She was as regal as a queen and looked quite beautiful. As she moved across the dance floor toward him, all eyes were upon her. He grinned, burning with deep pride.

Behind him, he heard the murmuring of the young, impressionable women, moving like small birds on a branch, wings flaring, twittering with bright song. Quickly they skittered around her, offering her greeting. Nonplused, his mother's eyes shone addressing each girl by name and asking after the families who had not yet arrived at the dance.

She excused herself and Nathaniel, taking his arm and propelling him over to a table filled with cakes, pies, and several bowls of punch. John and his father were there, John handing him a small cup of punch.

Nathaniel drank it dry, looking for more, his tongue thick from thirst. His father took the cup from him and refilled it, handing it back.

"Hard work, ain't it boy?" his father said, with a wink.

"All folly," Nathaniel heard himself say without putting much thought to his words.

"Never felt that way before," John said, grinning at him. "Must be old age settling in."

Nathaniel smiled, dipping his head, not wanting to recall the unspeakable reason why things changed, he changed. He watched John's eyes shutter, deeply thinking, a play of emotions dappling his face. Before John spoke aloud, Nathaniel put an abrupt end to it by excusing himself in want of some air. John followed him without invitation.

Outside, Nathaniel made his way over to a group of men he recognized as friends and neighbors. On sight of him, a hand or a hat was lifted in greeting, smiles large on wind-hewn faces.

"Well, I'll be damned, Nathaniel Keegan, large as life and twice as ugly," one shouted while the others with good nature, hooted and catcalled. But it was Ferguson McPherson who pushed through the men and without fanfare uncoiled and landed a head-jolting punch. Nathaniel's jaw was nearly unhinged, his cheek splitting from the raised crest of the man's ring. Nathaniel remained upright, but his ears buzzed, and the lantern light appeared like the tails of comets, scattered traces across the night sky. He could see John from the corner of his working eye, a look of horror on his brother's face. McPherson had been drinking.

"Your fault she died. All your fault...my girl's dead. You son of a bitch!"

Nathaniel could barely speak, only able to bring up bile and two words. "I'm sorry," he said, as if Jane's father's accusation was the verdict needed. A relief to him really, after so long putting his anger and judgment on James when all along it was he who had left her, had done his brother's bidding, knowing well Jane would have demanded differently of him. Blaming her, the worst of it for dying, not abiding as she had promised him.

One man pulled McPherson away, coaxing him with a bottle of whiskey. Jane's father grabbed for it, staggering into the darkness without a glance back.

A rancher by the name of Johnston clamped a hand to Nathaniel's shoulder. "Nothing you didn't know about him already, son. He was a drunkard when he'd first come to town and remains as such. You gave Jane everything he never did."

Another man stepped forward. Nathaniel recognized him as a former soldier of the 15th Texas Cavalry, discharged at the onslaught due to illness before a battle fought or so Nathaniel's mother had written him. The man stood in front of him for a beat and then took up Nathaniel's right hand in his, giving a firm handshake. "Thank you," he said and moved aside to allow one man after the other do the same.

Each stood with hat in hand, some near tears. A bottle seemed to appear from thin air and the men began passing it amongst themselves.

One man spoke, raising the bottle high above him. "To Texas," he shouted, and all intoned the same toast. Once more the bottle was raised high. "To Nathaniel Keegan," a second man shouted. "Nathaniel!" The men agreed in unison.

Nathaniel stood impassive but took the bottle when offered to him. He lifted it to his lips and gulped down several mouthfuls of burning liquid. He wiped his mouth and handed it back, nodded to the men, then turned and walked away into the shadowed night alone, John having the good sense not to follow.

"Ain't that something," a voice spoke to him from out of the darkness.

Nathaniel searched, eyes adjusting to the gloom. Caden sat on a makeshift bench in front of the mercantile. He lit a Lucifer match, the light flaring, and set it to the tip of a cheroot. The smoke plumed from his mouth, thick and pungent.

Nathaniel stilled, a wild thing cornered. He waited.

"All those men thanking a half-breed don't make any sense at all. But here's the thing of it, they ain't as knowledgeable about the truth as I am. My instincts never been wrong. I knowed you was a breed the minute I set my sights on you. The Colonel said as much last I saw him."

Nathaniel took in a breath and released it before he spoke, holding back temper. "Well, Caden, I wouldn't feel no shame in it if it were true. But you got your facts jumbled, the Colonel as well," said Nathaniel, waiting to see the course of things and how it would all unspool. Though there was one thing of note: his words did nothing to change the little

255

man's mind set, no doubt, on killing. But not to be done alone, Nathaniel decided, his men nowhere in sight. Hadn't thought Caden the gall to take him on as such, but clearly, he'd been mistaken, though never to be again.

"You been warned. You and that old Indian, both. Folks don't cotton to him strutting around in his frippery like a peacock, roaming free." "Ain't no never mind to me, Caden, what you or folks think about that Indian. He ain't going nowhere, no how. You touch one hair on his head, I'll kill you." It had come to that now, seeming to be a natural thing to Nathaniel, to voice killing with no qualm. There was a hard and honest truth to his words, plain to Caden by the flash of fear in his eyes, the intake of breath.

But the little man kept up the bluster, saying, "We'll see about that. We'll just see about that."

Nathaniel nodded, turning his back on the man, his short hairs raised; not doubting for a second the man would put a bullet in his back. He made his way over to the town hall, and stopped near an alleyway, leaning with ease against the planked building and spoke into the night. "That man's on the prod. You best watch yourself."

Two Crows broke from the shadows then, top hat still set on his shiny black head, amusing Nathaniel. But tension crept up on him again, more so when he heard Two Crows' words.

"I take scalp," he said, matter-of-factly, without sentiment in his heavily accented English.

"No," Nathaniel censored, but wishing to appease the Cheyenne, said: "It's my kill." Two Crows nodded once and then spirited away, a ghost. Nathaniel's eyes brimmed, weary, but his heart held no fear.

Nathaniel

The moon was out in full view, clouds skirting its edges. It lit the town up palely. The scent of cinnamon and vanilla and women's perfume intermingled with the outdoor scents of manure and dirt, lamp oil and smoke. It had been years since he had been to town and he studied it now with a discerning eye. Texas Hill Country, no better place, and he had sorely missed it.

Nathaniel smiled and breathed the air in and out of his damaged lungs. No better place on God's good earth with its rolling hills covered in wild flowers, blue bonnet, and black-eyed Susan, oak and cedar and cypress trees, as well as, an abundance of clear, running rivers and cold spring-fed streams. Though he'd seen some fine country in his travels, this land stirred his blood, spoke to him of home. He held a joy beyond all things to be back in these lifeblood lands, a land touched by God. On impulse, he held out his hand to the stirring winds, the star-lit skies, and he felt heartened. He then thought of Jane and the child borne of her mother and his heart began to ache, would always ache.

Long ago, he had vowed they would spend the remainder of their days in this place. And even though everything good had been taken from him, nearly felled by the loss, Nathaniel would abide, secure in knowing she had forgiven him, and even now waited for him to be together a thousand lifetimes, infinitival years—*always*.

He canted his head then, hearing his name called and he braced himself up and pushed away from the building. He lifted his hand to his hair straightening it as best as he could and then tugged at his coat, adjusting it. He lifted his foot, one then the other, wiping the dust off his boots on the back of his pant legs.

He heard his mother talking, her words carrying outside to him, saying something about being true to his word, keeping his promises. It made him smile to hear his mother say such things, even if it rang false to his ears.

Nathaniel was halfway back to the double doors of the town hall when a woman called out to him. The voice was the voice of a ghost and he became panicked. It was the clearest he had heard *her* speak to him, even in the fevers. He remained stock-still, breathing heavily. There had been for him far too much tempest in one evening.

He mouthed her name, fear holding back his voice. He hadn't moved, not one twitch of a finger or eye, only the sound of his harsh, guttering breaths. She came up beside him, a hand to his shoulder, traveling down to his forearm. Small white hands with ragged nails, though well-cleaned, clutched at his wrist. She wore no jewelry.

"Nathaniel," she said. "Are you well?" The voice was softer, a higher octave than he recalled, the fingers, thinner, smaller.

"It's me, Nathaniel," she said. And he began to shake outright at that, not daring to look at her face.

"Please, Nathaniel, you're frightening me," she said, her hand grabbing his.

"Jane?" It was all he could muster.

A gasp emitted from her and her hand lifted from his as if touching fire, burnt. "Oh, no!" she said.

In that instant, he moved to view her and saw the woman standing there, small hands the color of milk lifted to her pale white face. A replica of his Jane, but off somehow, not quite the same. It was the eyes, he reasoned, the blue of them not as dark, not midnight, but the color of cornflowers. He thought in that moment of the folklore about such fading flowers speaking of unrequited love.

She gathered herself first and spoke to him. "It's Adair, Nathaniel." She took a step closer. "Don't you remember me?"

He sighed and closed his eyes, limbs still shaking and clattering like skeleton bones strung from a tree, though upon gaining his senses, realized it was only the sound of his chattering teeth. "You gave me a fright, Adair," said Nathaniel. "You've grown some and pretty near to Jane's likeness."

"I've been told," Adair said, nodding. "I am sorry."

"It's no fault of yours, Adair. It's just five years ago, you were no taller than my elbow, dressed in coveralls and hair in pigtails, all the while poking Charlie Monroe with a stick and making him cry." Nathaniel grinned. "Still making the boys cry?"

Adair laughed. "Not hardly."

259

Nathaniel tilted his head, eyes considering her. "Breaking hearts no doubt. You've grown up fine."

Adair lowered her head. Her pale cheeks surged pink with color. "Thank you," she said. "Other than you're being skinnier than a rail and the bloody gash on your face, you look fine yourself."

She foraged through a small beaded bag, taking something in her hand and quickly pulling the drawstrings closed. He watched her as she lifted a white hankie edged with blue stitching and fine pink flowers embroidered in the center to his face. She began dabbing at the cut before he could protest.

"It's almost stopped," said Adair, her head angled to the right, her light eyebrows crimped in concentration. "Whose fist did you run into?"

Just then the music swelled up in the room and rolled out through the windows and doors over them. It was a spirited Texas variation of a Highland Schottische.

"Would you care to dance with me, Adair?" he asked. "Or is your dance card full?"

"Why let me see...oh, yes, your name's right here, Mr. Nathaniel Keegan, as plain as the nose on your face. It would be an honor and a pleasure to dance with you."

Nathaniel smiled and took her hand, escorting her into the hall. He was unmindful of the stir they caused when they came into the room or when they proceeded to move across the dance floor to the music with perfect cadence and ease.

For the first time in months, nay, years, Nathaniel was content.

Isabel

Isabel was in high spirits after the Spring Social. Mary had invited her for tea and light fare in the hotel dining room before retiring for the evening. James and John, as well as, Joseph had sauntered off to the small bar for a nightcap, which catered only to the guests of the hotel. Nathaniel had left to escort the young woman home whom Isabel had soon discovered was Adair McPherson, Jane's younger sister. The resemblance was uncanny, calling to mind the daguerreotype of Jane.

Of course, Isabel intuitively knew who the woman was as she watched them dance. It was as though they had danced in each other's arms many times before, so in tune were they with every step and turn and sway. They had made a stunning sight, every eye upon them, even those promenading around them on the dance floor. But oddly enough, Isabel felt no envy. In fact, her heart ached for the love Nathaniel had lost, very much aware Jane was the true and natural fit and this woman though seemingly a perfect match was only an imitation. So deeply it must cut to see a near replica of the one most loved, but never to have again on this earthly plane.

She thought herself better than to ever be second fiddle to the dead. If this woman wished to be as such, so be it. Isabel preferred to be the one set upon the pedestal and not the other way around. Of course, she was not of a spoiled disposition, only thinking this way because she had pined for so long for a true and enduring love. Seeing Adair and

261

Nathaniel on the dance floor was of greatest revelation to her, far more convincing than the dire warnings and forbidding of her father. She recalled her own words, the logic of what had transpired between herself and Nathaniel, knowing it was a thing both necessary and beneficial. At that instant, a pang of emotion rapped upon her heart, sorrow uncoiling within, her throat aching at the first hint of tears. The act between them was logical and purposeful, but impractical in the long run, and yet she still wanted him. She huffed and shook her head, a smile on her lips.

"All the women wanted him," she whispered ruefully, remembering the throng three deep around him.

"Wanted whom?" Mary asked as she came up behind Isabel.

"Oh, my," Isabel said, her face heating, aware her cheeks would be flush with color.

"Why, Nathaniel, of course," Isabel said without thought, disconcerted.

Mary sat, motioning to the wait staff and looked at Isabel for a long moment, causing Isabel considerable discomfort and regret at her flippant response. She took a sharp intake of breath, deciding to get to it, the hurdle to be vaulted, if anything was to be salvaged between them.

"I am fully aware things are not easy between us now which I dearly regret and take full responsibility. I fault myself and not Nathaniel. But I do wish you would hear me out, and try to understand my heart, my motivation. I beseech you to do this one thing for me, for our friendship which is everything to me. Will you listen, dearest Mary? Will you do this for me, for my sake?"

Mary lifted her hand and placed it on Isabel's, a soft pulse of fingers given as answer.

"Thank you," said Isabel, her eyes lowered and then lifted, meeting Mary's gaze. "Thank you."

Mary

Mary brought the teacup up to her perfect mouth and took a deep, yet decorous sip of the brew. Tea soothed her, made her think of pleasant spring mornings in her garden beneath the white pergola on the grounds of her Connecticut home. Joseph had constructed a perfect replica of the one from her childhood home in New York. He understood her well: a small consolation for releasing extravagance and embracing economy and frugality. She had done so easily, having a faith strong in him and in his nature to please her, to work hard for her. He would often refer to her as his good luck, his fortune won, and though it had only been words and a wish in the beginning of their lives conjoined, it bloomed and flowered into modest riches, sprung from the fertile earth of river valley soil, after having toiled without much success in the rockier terrain of northern Connecticut. At her suggestion and with the sale of Joseph's family farm and a few baubles of value of her own, a tobacco farm had been purchased.

Several years later, wealthy in their own right, and eight months pregnant with their first child, Mary traveled alone on a hot summer morning along the toll roads heading south unbeknownst to Joseph. She shambled on foot until she reached Danbury, encountering an old man with a long gray beard and a shrunken and withered woman who persuaded her to ride along with them in their wagon of chickens. They were headed to Norwalk and in that instant, she seemed to have shocked herself awake, a jolt so strong with the realization she had gone miles from her home and her husband. Distraught and exhausted, she chose to journey onward with them, catching a steamboat to New York City. She arrived at her mother's door, filthy, sweat-stained, and reeking of chicken excreta, not having a change of clothing or a desire to wash. At this her mother, when the butler presented Mary to her, thusly turned her icy blue eyes upon her, nodded and led her forthwith to make herself presentable by, though said with a thin-lipped smile, a good hosing.

Of course, that would not be the case as the O'Brien household had the good fortune of indoor plumbing and a hot bath awaited her in an exquisite porcelain tub. Memories of her husband skirted to the back of her mind at her momentary pleasure, until the next day, after a deep dreamless sleep, when a tremendous pounding nearly battered down the front door.

Mary categorized and recognized later the time as a period of dark and deep confusion. *Why had she remained with her mother? Why had she turned Joseph away?* Her mind did not seem to be her own then, controlled by some hurtful, selfish creature with no sense at all. Joseph could not make her care about their life together, could not make her feel their love, any love at all. She wandered the edge of an abyss. In her mind, it was as though looking down the black expanse of nothingness, a coal black well where she scaled the side and sat on its rimmed edge with feet dangling inside, whispering one line over and over from a childhood rhyme: *We all fall down, we all fall down.*

Her mother reveled in it, kept her confined to her room.

And then next Mary remembered the laboring and the babe coming forth, squalling and whole. She had watched her son being lifted into a shaft of light, limbs flailing, able-bodied, and fierce. "No," her mother had said to her later, "the babe was lost."

Lies! She had seen him, had heard his cries, the wailing and then nothing. His name is Jacob Joseph, she recalled saying, seeing the babe's full head of black hair. The priest had been called. *Last rites for her or had it been a baptism?* Consecrated droplets spattered about, on her lips, eyelids, running from her nose, salty as tears. *Her tears? Had she cried?* No, it had been sweat and blood flowing like wine, piercing, bleeding out, a roil of placenta, so much blood, her legs dangled over the edge, kicking out and back, her patent leather shoes banging together, *thump, thump, thump.* She saw she was smiling, singing that old song again, pushing off and letting go, and we all fall down.

"So, you certainly understand my reasoning for this. Please tell me you do, Mary." Isabel's voice though soft, felt like a prod to the senses. Her eyes, while opened, were looking inward at memories, now widened and latched upon the girl's face sitting across from her.

"Well, of course, child," Mary replied, lowering her tea cup to the saucer, the tea cooled, near cold. *Had Isabel noticed her detachment?* Perhaps not, so caught up in her own tales, spinning them out before her unaware her audience of one was off elsewhere.

Isabel appeared relieved. Her hands reached out to Mary, but recoiled like strung wire cut when Mary said, "I want you to tell me your reasoning once more, but to the point this time, if you don't mind."

And so, Isabel began again, and Mary listened as the girl explained how she had been taken advantage, a seduction, by a young officer headed to war. Though it was not her wish, she perhaps had given him reason to believe she had agreed to such a thing. But in the deepest part of her heart, she had not. Shortly after, she had grown big with child, losing him soon after birth. Then it was some such about renewal and rebirth for her and Nathaniel, and something about conjuring ghosts and putting them to rest. But mostly it was about redemption.

"I see," Mary said after listening and understanding more than she would ever convey. Mary rose from her chair and stepped over to Isabel. The younger woman, rising from her seat, stood before Mary, expectant.

"And what of James?" Mary asked.

"I will never speak of this," Isabel said, a veil of worry on her face, biting the inside of her lower lip.

It was endearing to Mary, moving her to take Isabel into her arms, embracing her. "Good," she said. "It is for the best."

Nathaniel

Later that night, Nathaniel commenced dreaming about her as he fell into sleep, an intercrossing of Jane and Adair, an eerily striking beauty. He became enervated in his dream, steeped in the mire of shame, loneliness, loss. The part of her who spoke in Jane's voice told him to hush, all would be well and the part who spoke with Adair's voice told him to believe, to trust. He watched the hand moving Adair's hand forward towards him and recognized it to be Jane's hand. They smiled at him from the same face. Even though the dream was joyful and moon-bright, he shielded his eyes, unnerved.

Hearing a voice beckon again and again, he lowered his hands, his fear lessening. It was Jane alone now, to Nathaniel shining as bright as God's face when shown to Moses on the mount.

"Bring her home," said ghostly Jane. A ribbon of light like smoke, a mist, rose and then dissipated into the night-black room. Nathaniel woke then, an ache so dreadful through him, he moaned. Aloud he said into the darkness, "I cannot…" But in his mind, he simply said, "yes."

Adair

Nearing four o'clock the following morning after the dance, Adair McPherson, still a young woman of twenty, though considered by many a spinster, stood on the rotted wood stoop of a small poorly built shack. There was a pervasive stench around her, the smell of stale beer, whiskey and vomit. Inside, her father lay flopped on a pallet of straw in a stupor, unkempt and snoring. A pot of strong black coffee awaited him, warming on the cook stove. Adair started, wondering a moment where she had left her mother's tea towel, but chose not to return into the house. A niggling of something gnawed at her then, a spark of remorse, flaring into panic. Even so, she dismissed it and jumped from the stoop. A puff of dust lifted from the dry earth and settled on her shoes. A hard wind blew into her face, taking her breath. She turned her back to it and the small shack, walking away without direction.

Adair had remained with her father in this place, even after Jane had implored her to do otherwise, offering her shelter, a haven with her, with Nathaniel. Oh, how she had wanted to leave, to escape the vileness, the pitilessness of her father's existence, which had been slowly smothering her, encroaching upon her life, seeing the proof of it fully in the town folks' eyes.

Her sister Jane had never felt ashamed, never belittled by her circumstance, her pride, her confidence outshone everything, as she, herself, a stunning beauty, out shone everyone. And because she had believed in her worth, the town believed as well, saw it as truth. Their father had little control over Jane, since she had refused to acknowledge him even as a child. He had never set eyes upon his granddaughter. At the thought of her niece, Adair heaved out a dry sob. Her father had gone on a binge when he was told of their deaths, but had grown mean-spirited and surly, yelling in the street, *Good riddance to bad rubbish!*

Adair had been emboldened in her sorrow that evening, locking him out of the shack. He'd found quarters in a jail cell, Adair wishing they had lost the key.

She now recalled the steel in Jane's dark blue eyes, her resolve when she had talked to her. "Leave him," Jane had said. "Let him rot here. It is his yoke, not ours. Mater died shouldering it, but I shall not, nor shall you. Leave him to it, Adair. Let him kill himself. I am through with him and well you should be."

Take me with you, Adair had screamed inside her head, take me away from this. But she had remained silent since she couldn't bear it any other way, couldn't bear watching him loving her, loving Jane. Just a girl then, a child really, but no matter, she had loved him first and, in her imaginings, had loved him best.

From the onset, Jane had been preoccupied with her other suitors. She'd had so many, James Keegan, her first choice, until that day Nathaniel had appeared at their door with a variety of supplies and medicine for their mater who had been suffering through a long and arduous labor, eventually losing the boy-child and days later her life when a bleeding so vast and hard had sprung from her, the mattress ticking weighing heavy with it, the floor boards stained.

This, she had thought to herself afterward, begotten from loving a man. But then she had amended, thinking of Nathaniel, no, this came from loving the *wrong* man. She avowed right then on her mater's deathbed, to remain all her days alone before making the same mistake. And alone she had been while admirers came and went, not one could compare.

So then, what now? Adair wondered, as she walked beyond the sleeping town and into the wild. Her sister's husband, a widower—it was not uncommon for the wife's sister to come into the household, care for it, for the widowed man. *Would Nathaniel become her kinsman redeemer as Boaz had for Ruth?* It didn't bother her in the least to be second to Jane, something she had always been, assured by the fact, in her heart, she had loved him first. A soft breeze riffled her hair, her dress. Adair smiled. Perhaps, she thought, it was finally her time.

Nathaniel

The shouting was frantic and loud from the street below and boomed upward into the open hotel window where Nathaniel slept. He roused taking in a deep breath and then began to cough from the smoke that hung in the air like a fog. A fist pounded on the hotel door, and his name was called. He recognized the voice to be John's.

"Hold on," Nathaniel croaked out as he threw back the blankets and grabbed up his trousers tossed across the chair. He hopped one footed, left leg than right, into the legs of his pants and then worked the buttons. He took off the latch and swung open the door to find John, James and his father in the hallway, looking disheveled, but clothed.

"Fire," his father said. "Looks to be the McPherson shack."

Nathaniel's stomach flipped, close to gagging. He looked away from the concerned eyes of his family and headed back into the room, gathering up his shirt and boots.

"Let's go," he said, now fully awake and dressed.

Nathaniel recalled his dream as he ran down the flight of stairs. Bring her home, Jane had said. Bring her home. Perhaps he would never get the chance to do Jane's bidding, this to be one more failing upon so many. He had balked at the idea of Adair coming into their home without Jane. It didn't seem proper, still seeing Adair as a child. Jane had desperately wanted Adair away from their father, a disgrace and a drunk. She had held little compassion or sympathy for the man, no love or respect. It had not been a stretch to believe Jane would have put a bullet in his heart, with neither guilt nor conscience. Though it frightened him to think of Jane like that, it also captivated him, her strength, her fire, her capabilities. It was easier to leave her for the war, remembering her this way. He had left his well-favored rifle along with other weaponry and ammunition. She had been a fine accurate shot. He had made certain of that straight away, due to the roaming war and hunting parties that more than not would take a liking to beautiful light-skinned and light-haired creatures such as Jane. Nathaniel respected the Indian, but he would kill those that harmed the innocent. He had seen the aftermath,

271

the horrors by both white and Indian, grateful and at ease with Jane's fierce and abiding inclination to survive.

He immediately shoved away the voice that mocked him, spoke aloud what he chose to ignore, asking why then had she died? It had been a foe unseen, no preparation, no gun, no blade, could thwart it. He had thought things out, planned it through, but it didn't matter how thorough he had been to ensure their safety, their well-being. He could only view it as God's will, a penance so virulent, so odious, to be unbearable. But he must bear it, must wait out his natural days so salvation might be his, reunited with his wife and child, if the Lord saw fit. It was all he had and he clung to it like a man in a desert, long-suffering, tongue thick from thirst, step by step, moving toward the promise of water. He chose not to believe it to be a mirage, a shimmering illusion. He mustered up his faith, at times the size of a mustard seed, but confident in his nature to be just as strong willed as the Almighty, no matter if it was sacrilegious to have such notions.

When they reached the shack, it was burnt to the ground, only the cook stove stood center among the charred and smoking ruins, the remains of a man were seared into place along the west facing wall. The crowd split and let them pass forward. There in front of them kneeling was Adair, face black from tears and ash. She looked up at Nathaniel and said, "Please bring me home." And at that a chill ran down his spine and his hair raised nearly straight on his arms. But more unsettling was the quick chevron of a smile and the firefly brightness in her eyes, though brief, was recognizable to him.

Joseph

Joseph worried about how the fire might affect Mary as he tugged Adair along by the arm down the town's smoky main street. Nathaniel, shaken, walked a few steps behind, his face turned down, and his thoughts more than not a scramble. Ferguson McPherson was a miserable human being, but to die in such a way for any man was difficult to stomach. The county law was mainly upheld by Federal soldiers. They came soon after the fire from the east side of Oatmeal, a Negro settlement nearby.

Upon their arrival, Caden and his men quickly dispersed, but not before working the folk into a frenzied mob, shouting his vile about the Indian parading around free as you please in his frippery and frock coat and how he had spied Two Crows skulking in the bushes behind the McPherson place just that morning.

It was quite the time holding Nathaniel at bay, but Joseph, a well-respected and generous man to his neighbors, was soon able to talk sense into them, persuading them to wait for the law, a military law no one respected, mainly resented and despised. Though aware, at the beginning of the war, the ordinance to secede did not pass in the county as the issue of slavery held little sway as very few kept slaves, but then again most still contributed to the Confederacy, many in the Confederate Army remaining on the frontier fighting Indians. To Joseph, life's circumstances often seemed to be being caught between a rock and a hard place.

John appeared and walked on the other side of Adair, a year off from her age, aware of each other from John's rare occasions in town. Mary, though revolted by Ferguson, would send John with money and provisions and strict instructions to give everything directly to Adair and if the drunken scalawag was about, to wait until he had blacked out or had gone off to his usual imbibing past time. It was all spoken with a rigid delivery, her voice low and blunt.

Mary had been fast friends with Jane and Adair's mother and it had taken all Joseph's power to keep Mary from loading his Yellowboy and heading off to town to put that dog down, in her own words, after learning of the woman's untimely death in her begetting. It also set off several weeks of Mary's darkness, asking again about the babe, Jacob. The house reverberated with her cries, keening her loss. John had been touched the strongest by it, Nathaniel busy at the McPherson home, helping them out, and James, whom Joseph had thought fancied Jane, went once, never to return. His mood had been as dark as Mary's, and Joseph, believing himself an even-tempered, jovial man found he was at wit's end.

Mary's black days fortunately lifted at the announcement of Jane and Nathaniel's courtship, having dreams of a wedding and grandchildren. It pleased Joseph very much as well, but not James. No matter what Nathaniel did for James there remained a breach between his two boys. Joseph understood full well what the trouble was, though, it was a secret he held close to himself and had promised to keep to his death. The other secret about another son, well that secret he had kept for years from his

274

beloved, his Mary.

He could not tell her of that time while in a dark, malevolent place she had taken a stickpin, a gift from her mother, a diamond encrusted heirloom, and had slowly pressed the long length into the beautiful, tender spot, the fontanel, on their precious boy's head of dark curls. Joseph again could see the large blue eyes closing for the last time as he had envisioned it in his nightmares that night and every night since he learned of the death, as well as, the cessation of those sweet small breaths. He had imagined this scene over and over in his mind after Mary's mother, in minutiae, told him the particulars, her icy blue eyes casting blame upon him for his multitude of sins against her and Mary. He had held his son only once, a brief time before he was set in the smallest of caskets, an ivory blanket wrapped around him, perfectly formed from brow to fingertip to toe.

He was an angel lost to them. *What had overtaken her? Had she been out of her head from laudanum?* Joseph refused to leave Mary even at her mother's insistence. Days later when Mary could travel, he stole her away in the night, his heart thunderous in his ears, his fear the strongest he had ever known in his lifetime. The absurdity of it made him weep with laughter after they had trekked miles without pursuit.

Joseph had thought of it often, of Jacob's death, and wondered if it had been Mary, addled by laudanum and a dark heart, or if it had been Mrs. O'Brien, herself, who had done the horrific deed, when he had spotted the long heirloom pin, stationed ghoulishly in her veil, during the funeral service, attended only by a few household servants. He became even more so suspicious when she had seen him watching her, a macabre smile tugging at the corners of her tightlipped grayish mouth. He had known no one like this woman and he was gladdened when Mary, a few years later after the birth of their son James, decided Texas would be their home, as though eighteen hundred miles of landscape could keep the devil at bay.

Now as they trundled along Main Street, Adair between them, Nathaniel trailing behind, Joseph was shocked and perplexed by his mind's meanderings. Perhaps horrifying scenes conjure other horrors, other ghosts, and if he a man of a strong constitution can lose his footfall what then of the others?

He looked up at Mary's hotel window, seeing her watching through the wavy glass pane. He gestured to her and she waved to him. He heard Nathaniel stumble behind him and he turned to see if the boy was steady. Nathaniel nodded, but as though from some remote place. Horror begets horror and it was Joseph's place to drive it all away as he had done before and would do again.

"Come along, child," he said to Adair. "It will be all right. We will bring you home if that is your will."

"Yes, thank you," Adair said, looking back over her spare thin shoulder at Nathaniel, her face streaked with ash like war paint. "Yes, that is my will."

Two Crows

Two Crows left town in a hurry on John's horse in the middle of Caden's rumblings. When the mob of white men began to chant, kill the Indian, he watched as Nathaniel struggled against his father's grip, a fire in his eyes to kill, a fire, Two Crows had not seen in the boy before the war. He, at first, thought to blame the bad medicine of the war, but it had not been this that had turned a gentle heart, fierce – it had been loss. Two Crows understood such a thing, had felt it for many seasons since the murder of his son and the death of his wife. At the thought of his woman, he touched the plait of blonde hair twined in his own. For over twenty-five winters, he had kept his fire banked, waiting.

He stopped and lifted his nose to the air. The one he had saved, the boy James, hunted him now and Two Crows would soon let himself be found. The anger in that one ran hot, seeing evil shadows in his eyes, memories like ghosts, haunting him, though the truth never spoken, the questions never answered. The time had come. Two Crows did not know how he knew this. Perhaps it was the return of Nathaniel – perhaps not.

Two Crows, like Nathaniel, had a gentle way about him as a boy. His father called him weak, having the heart of a woman. Years later he had taken a wife, a white captive used by many before she came to him. She had been beautiful, but wild. He had grown to love her as she loved him. The men of the tribe began to envy him. They each had their chance for such a magnificent creature, but only saw with their eyes and not their heart. Two Crows worked with her, helped her with her chores while the

277

men and women of the tribe jeered at him, belittled him, but it did not trouble him.

He was patient with her, as he was with his horses of which he had many and again that confused and caused envy among the tribe. But soon the people began to recognize his strong medicine and would tell stories of Two Crows' way with the horse at the night fires as he was too humble to speak for himself. They said he talked the language of horse and this pleased him. He became a great man in the tribe and much loved, giving each boy a gift of a horse on his birth. It had been many seasons of happiness. His father, upon his death, spoke to him of pride and love. The same winter of his father's journey, a son was born to Two Crows.

The boy-child had a wild mane of flowing black hair and blue eyes the color of a winter sky. The people, upon seeing the child, smiled and said his woman had given birth to half boy and half pony. Two Crows liked that very much. He loved this half child half horse with his full, thick mane of black hair and the wild blue eyes of a stallion.

Through the passing seasons, the only thing that saddened him was the hostile heart beating in his son. As the boy grew, he became more and more angry. The one spirit Two Crows could not gentle, could not tame. The boy's hurtful pranks became more vicious, molesting young girls, fighting with the other boys, hurting the younger children with rocks and sticks, having one time plucked out the blind eye of a child not more than three seasons, and so much more, that Two Crows had to turn his eyes away from the memories as he rode.

Two Crows' father had prayed each night for Two Crows to become a brave warrior, a fierce hunter, and though Two Crows had not become such a thing, he believed his father's prayers conjured in him, in his blood, in his loins, in his seed, this ferocity and it formed in his wife and sprung from her onto the earth as a wild horse beast. His horse child could not be tamed and soon he was banished. Two Crows' wife was without console until he took her and his horses in search of the boy.

Again, he stopped and lifted his nose to the air, listening. He thought of James, the one he had saved, and then acknowledged with a sharp nod that the story was not yet finished. Two Crows looked up at the sky through the trees. He thought of his wife, long ago walking the hanging road, his son as well. His horses were gone and his people no longer remembered his name or spoke of him around the fires. He did not know if he would die far from his tribal lands. He did not seem to care when he pressed his heart for answers, his mind for clarity. He knew only this: the end would be vengeful and bloody.

James

James had set off on his own to hunt for the Indian without giving word to his family of his plans. He was not in the mind to hear their reasoning about any of it. Caden, straight off, was a murderer, his men the same. James had been aware of this from the onset. Some of Caden's men carried brands of their offenses on their foreheads and faces. Most had spent long periods of their lives incarcerated, all would lie, cheat, steal and rape, all would and have killed. And yet he chose to believe the worst of the Indian, of Two Crows, over them.

He'd gotten wind of the altercation outside the town hall. Ferguson McPherson, drunk, had sucker punched Nathaniel and, of course, he was told it had been his brother apologizing. It was typical behavior from his brother, which set James' teeth on edge.

All those years, all those times, he wanted to put his hands around the boy's throat, throttle him, to get him to fight back, fight him. It infuriated James to no end, confused him, and made him uncertain of his own mind, his own feelings about life and death, about right and wrong.

"Fight for yourself, damn it, stand up for yourself," he had shouted often enough, giving Nathaniel a good shove for emphasis. It was all a man had. It was all James had. *What was it about his brother's gentle ways that turned his stomach?*

He had seen Nathaniel shoot and ride, and fight—when he had no other recourse—and he was good at it all, better than James. So, it wasn't as if he was incapable. He had even saved James' neck a time or two. But that weakness, that unwillingness to fight tore at James, drove him to madness and on occasion in his youth to tears while barricaded in the privacy of his room. The anger, repulsion, disappointment seemed to turn like the bore of a gun on himself, as if he was the weakling, the one who had failed.

Nathaniel had a way of turning James' world on its head, spinning haphazardly, along with that damn Indian. It was time to get answers, once and for all. The Indian had secrets; he could feel it, taste it. It'd been time enough letting things ride. Ferguson McPherson was better off dead, should have died a long time before this. The loss of the man, murdered or accidental, wasn't the issue. There was much more that the Indian had to answer for, something deep and familiar, something which might very well shatter everything.

Stand up for yourself, the voice in his head jeered at him, his entire body shaking, *this time.*

Thomas

Three days after the Spring Social, Thomas walked out from his bedroom onto his portico, pleased with the world and the order of things, all coming together as he had envisioned. Isabel had arrived home from the dance replete with stories and a love-struck heart, not for Nathaniel, but for James as it should have been from the start. Of course, Isabel was a spirited woman, set on making up her own mind. His influence, no doubt, had set her on the wrong course, doing the opposite, her need to do the choosing. He had never quite mastered the ways of negotiating with her. This day he remained silent, but joyful, trying not to appear too self-satisfied.

He inhaled deeply and stretched out his stiff arms above his head. He coughed and then coughed again, bringing up a wad of phlegm. He spat it out into a nearby urn. His body was growing older, the time at war doing him no favors. It seemed only fair and reasonable to take chances at this point of his life, to achieve his heart's desire before he died. *Though dare he, do it?*

The Keegan men would be miles from the ranch, the Indian off somewhere in hiding from Caden and his cohorts after the McPherson fire, remembering Isabel's dramatic retelling of the tragedy. There had been quick mention of Adair McPherson remaining at Nathaniel and Jane's homestead, a wish of Jane's from years ago now fulfilled, though this day ringing hollow. This prompted thoughts of his own life as being a succession of events strung together, streaming forward and aft like a ribbon in the wind, fluttering, soaring, then suddenly plunging, heavy and inert, only to rise again. He had hung on, never letting go through it all, following its fluid trail to Mary's door. Although he had to admit his one recent error of judgment due to his frustration and worry for Isabel over Nathaniel now dogged him considerably. Without thought to the corollary, he had blurted Mary's secret to Caden, of all souls, immediately horrified and remorseful of his betrayal. He bribed the man with several fine horses and a rather large sum of money. "Do nothing," he had commanded after Caden had scowled saying, "knowed he was a breed," and then had made a lewd comment about his Mary being ruined, no longer too good for the taking. Thomas' hair had risen on his neck with those words and his stomach had clenched. I will kill you was on his tongue, but his mouth had become too dry to form and release his sentiments.

It had been almost four weeks later, when Thomas had overheard Caden speaking of the Indian attacks, boasting about the killings of the young Miller boy and Ben Thomas' wife after raping her. All of it had been *their* killings, *their* cattle-thieving, disguising themselves as Indians.

The men had been drinking that evening, loud and raucous and smug, calling Thomas names, toasting to the fool, Colonel Langford. It had taken all his self-control not to confront them, then and there, but he saw it as foolhardy, thinking only of Isabel and what might become of her if they should murder him. It was a certainty; her wellbeing and their home would be in peril. Without doubt they would murder them all, take off with the stock and place it at the foot of the Indians.

On the morning of Caden's dismissal, Thomas had gone to his desk and had written a check, a goodly amount and had handed it to Caden. It was to be the last payment made, no longer needing their services. Thomas had been afraid when Caden had looked upon him from his horse before leaving, gray eyes like steel bayonets, piercing and lethal. Thomas' ranch hands had gathered around him, all good men, all veterans of the war, and all of high principles unlike Caden and his band of vipers. Isabel had been opposed of hiring them from the onset, had believed terrible things were afoot, no good to come of it, she had warned him. She, of course, having the second sight of a woman, had been right.

Not that long ago, he had chosen again to ignore Isabel's warnings, disregarding a recent conversation with her when she had told him Nathaniel Keegan believed Caden had been, in his words, "playing both ends." All the lives lost, and he had paid them for the deed, for the killings, the murder. He had been a fool, and he felt his blood heat and curdle in him, his heart thumping against his ribs so hard his shirt moving with each beat. His bones grew heavy, rooting him to the ground like an ancient tree of petrified wood, leaves shivering in a bad wind.

That night four weeks ago, as the men drank and disparaged him, he felt as he did now, not able to budge from his spot and only able to move when they fell into a harmless drunken stupor. Far too much time had gone by before he had worked up the nerve to dismiss them and finally send notice to Austin and the local authorities, causing him again to feel the sting of shame. It had been on the day of the Spring Social, waiting far too long, but at last, it was done, finished.

Thomas inhaled a deep breath, twisted his torso to the left and then right, raised his arms again over his head, bent down and touched his toes, and then stood upright. As he straightened, he heard Isabel calling for him. Breakfast was waiting, and he smiled at the simple pleasure of it and his good fortune. He had hopes of James soon joining them in their morning ritual, once married to Isabel, gladly signing over all his worldly possessions to him, though reverting to Isabel upon James' death or the unlikelihood of divorce. He was certain after he talked with Mary that all would be in its perfect and proper order.

Mary

Mary sat holding the large, brown envelope Joseph had obtained from the Overland Mail Stage while in town for the Social. He had quickly tucked it away from sight before she could question him, distracting her with trivialities about their neighbors and the chance of running late if she didn't hurry. Of course, she had made her entrance at precisely the right time, her moment upon entering the town hall now recounted in her mind. It had been thrilling when all eyes had turned to her and her boys, bringing on envious gasps, a wonderful stir, and then quick composure and congeniality, the women never forgetting the social graces, even in the wilds of Texas Hill Country.

It had all been quite wonderful, one of many grand moments she recalled over and over while sitting on her wide front porch in her favorite seat lulled by the breezes and the sweet sway and rhythm of the rocking chair. But now after having read the words penned by her mother's hand, she sat shaking, near apoplectic. The short note had been written long ago, her mother deceased more than ten years, leaving Mary the New York City home and nothing more, all else going to the Church. It was dated the day her mother had died, the postscript bearing witness to the fact. Overcome, she felt as if her mother's ghost sat beside her, the wind shifting the nearby rocker to and fro.

Her mother had never loved her the way a mother should, had never loved her baby brother, and had never loved her kind, gentle father who had died too young under curious circumstances. All his wealth, which

285

had been vast, went to his widow, a beautiful woman who bore the cold, dead eyes of a killer. Or so, Mary had believed her to be in her wild imaginings regarding the tragic night of her baby brother's death and then soon after, her beloved father's. *If true, why had she been spared?* she had often wondered.

Curiously enough, she had never thought to blame her mother for the death of her own child, Jacob. Until now, until she read the sinister and cryptic message along with the lost diamond hat pin which had dropped into her lap from the brown envelope. *Where had this parcel been all these years?*

The family lawyer, Jonathan Blackburn, esquire, who had seemed a bit too concerned, too solicitous, lacking a certain decorum and distance from her mother before and after her father's death, had been known to spend many late evenings at the house and was often seen by Mary emerging in the gray light of early morning from the side garden gate. Her mother had never remarried, although her relationship had remained strong with Mr. Blackburn right up to her death.

Mary looked down at the envelope in the bowl of her lap and noted the return address was that of Blackburn & Associates Law Firm in New York City. She had read the man's obituary in The New-York Times, a newspaper she faithfully subscribed to, especially of value to her, the Sunday edition with its coverage of the War, though the news was delayed, it kept her far more abreast of things than the bias drivel available to her in Burnet County.

She lifted the note to read again, feeling no guilt or shame by the fact it was addressed to her husband, Joseph. It was the most peculiar thing really, not a letter at all, but a poem and she began again reading it aloud this time:

A kiss, a hug
A baby's cry
A diamond plunged
Into an eye
A baby, a husband, a baby again
One stick of a pin
Has wrought their end.

Was it a confession? She held the hat pin up to her eyes, the diamonds shining in the sunlight. It was over ten inches long, tarnished with brown stains along its length. The significance of the correspondence, the odd poem and the pin, seemed to strike her all at once and she howled in anguish, screaming until her throat became raw.

Suddenly, she sprang up from the chair, pulled back the screen door and ran into the house to the soapstone sink. There she vomited until she had nothing left in her. She wiped at the string of spittle, the smear of sickness on her hands, with the material of her dress. She inhaled and exhaled with deliberation and then began to laugh, at once clasping her mouth shut with her hands, as she thought of one line from the poem: *A baby, a husband, a baby again.*

All those years she had worn a hair shirt, needing absolution, pardon, conjuring up the notion her redemption had finally come upon Nathaniel's birth, believing her molestation and resulting pregnancy had been her punishment, her penance doled out for her sin, a sin unknown and elusive, years beggaring description. Mary had remembered very

287

little from long ago, but a single voice in the darkness of her vapory laudanum dreams, chastising her, calling her sinner and her mother telling her the baby had died at birth, even though she had seen his beautiful chubby limbs flailing about, the dark full head of hair, so rare on a newly born babe. Jacob had been precious, and her mother had snatched him away from her.

And Mary with no way to retaliate, no way to avenge, but perhaps she had done so long before, marrying Joseph and leaving her mother against all her threats and protests, leaving her to die alone with the weight of her sins upon her soul, never to find absolution and worst of all never to see the face of God. Yes, perhaps, God was good after all. Mary had lost a child, but He had given her another in the likeness of the one lost to her, though she had to prove herself worthy, had to endure great suffering.

Mary stood and cranked the water pump handle as a rush of liquid poured from the spout. She cupped her hands and splashed water on her face, drank it thirstily. She thought of her mother not able to make sense of the inner workings of such a mind. Mary shook her head and raised her fist into the air, though it felt false to her, a charade, nothing more than empty gesture. She dropped to the floor and wept.

Mary

After Mary had finally collected herself and had carefully returned the peculiar verse into the large brown envelope while placing the hat pin in her dress' pocket, she had for a time positioned the envelope over the hearth's fire until the heat of the flames brought her around to make a choice. It would be easiest to be rid of it, to burn it all away, to forget. *But could her mother's sins ever be forgotten, be forgiven?*

In all the detritus of loss, she had surprisingly gained something, something she had not had for well over twenty years. She had been vindicated, freed from sin, from the weight of guilt. Remorse so deep and encroaching, debilitating, destructive, had all been lifted. But the price they had all paid, the path she had chosen to run from her imagined sin, the pain her sons had endured as well as her dear, loving husband, had been costly. And yet she could now breathe unencumbered, no longer a yoke upon her shoulders, placing it squarely on her dead mother for all eternity.

Again, she tried to parse things out, tried to find those moments of the irrational, the cruelty, the madness that had lurked in her mother, the one who had held her as a baby giving her life's milk, caring for her, sheltering her, loving her as she believed all mothers loved their children. By the age of five, she had spent most of her time with the nannies after she had started her schooling at her father's directive, contested daily by her mother. Mary had been a voracious reader, quite bright for a female she had been told, spending hours in the family's

289

library. Her father had become her confidant, her friend, discussing all and sundry subject matter.

Her mother had hidden her jealousy, her resentment well. The night her brother had died, an infant not quite two months of age, there had been a heated row between her parents in the early hours of that morning with her father stomping his way down the hall and out the door, saying, "…the last straw…" and "…divorce…"

And then her brother had unexpectedly died, and her father returned straightaway when he had gotten word. Everything seemed forgiven in their mutual grief and loss, until the next hue and cry by her mother. This one had ended him, had ended the life of her beloved father. So clearly, she could see it all now in the morning light—her mother loving another man, though loving another's fortune far more. Her mother had stolen away Mary's own son out of spite, out of anger, for Mary's disobedience, rebellion against her. Worst still, her mother had led Mary to believe she had gone mad, letting her think it had been her delusions which caused her to believe her son had been healthy, vital, whole, alive at birth and she very well may have played a part in the baby's death.

Mary sighed and lifted her hands to her face, but her eyes remained dry. She lowered them, surprised at their steadiness, her steadiness. She tried to rebel against a sudden thought, a voice in her head saying, *well, to be fair to the woman… But why should she be fair? Why should she be reasonable?* she silently asked. Yet Mary could not deny that it had been her own guilt, her own dark thoughts imposing the sentence of murderer upon her soul at each startling, corporeal memory conjured in her mind's eye and ear. *How many days, months, years, had she wandered her home in search of a crying infant, her baby?* It was an incomprehensible question, sparking her anger.

"Damn you, Mother!" Mary shouted. "Damn you to a burning hell!"

Mary still had much in her life to be grateful. Three fine sons and a loyal, enduring love from a man who believed in her, tolerated her madness because—and then a most traitorous thought came to her, a thought she was hard-pressed to ignore—because he had believed it had been her who had unwittingly in a laudanum haze, a stupor, had killed their son, their first-born child. Mary became angry, agitated by this, but then immediately relieved and amazed at his love for her. Joseph had lost a child, presuming by the murderous hand of his wife, but had forgiven her heinous crime, her sin. She was blessed, and she refused to lose sight of such a thing in the malevolence of this truth, this revelation, this unveiling of her mother's depravity.

To be weighted and then uplifted, reeling from a disparity of emotions, she began to feel the familiar pull of her need for laudanum, its distinct taste on her lips, the familiar muted vapor, the nothingness, of floating without fear or anger or pain. *Oh, how oblivion would help her heal, help her remain on this earthly plane intact, whole, though separate, a safe distance from all the unpleasantness.* The drug had kept its hold on her for years, struggling to overcome its dominance on so many occasions. It had been a constant back and forth, winning and losing.

After Nathaniel's birth, she had lived wholly and life for the most part had been golden, until the war and Nathaniel's leaving. The loss of Jane and Molly and her beloved son sent her spiraling out of control, reliving Jacob's birth, dovetailing into the memory of her rape and James' ordeal. Her dear boy, James, an angel in demeanor and appearance, blooded, marked, never to be the same. The image of a fallen angel would often come to her thoughts, though she tried not to reveal her feelings, her judgment upon him. The scar he wore seemed to fester, not physically, but deep in the core of him, his heart. She had saved James which had given her some solace, though she had paid for it dearly. When she had learned, she had been with child, nearly four months on, attributed to her laudanum trance, she had chosen to see it as a gift from God. She had been punished severely, but in His Benevolence, had given her the child lost to her. She had been forgiven. She had been blessed.

Nathaniel was her light, her saving grace, even though he was of the Indian's blood, Two Crows' grandson. All the years a secret kept from them, a bond between Joseph, herself, and Two Crows whom she owed dearly and despised vehemently. Nathaniel loved the Indian and Joseph, in fairness and gratitude to the man for saving James, allowed him a familial relationship with her boys, especially Nathaniel. Of course, in her eyes, it was borne of guilt as well for having killed Two Crows' son, a murderer and rapist who did not deserve a whit of compassion. Mary had not been able to alter Joseph on this course and Two Crows took hold of each opportunity as she watched a wedge grow between her sons.

But it was much better these days, light in the darkness, and where there was once despair, joy and promise. They had all endured, overcome because Mary would have it no other way.

With that reaffirming thought, came a knock on the kitchen door and she turned to see the man called Caden peering through the wavy glass panes directly at her. A reflexive urge to run impinged upon her ability to think. She remained still, rapt, like a deer in crosshairs.

"Hello there in the house," the man called out to her and then the unthinkable occurred when he turned the doorknob and walked into her home.

"Ma'am," Caden said in greeting, removing his hat. "Sorry for intruding, but I'm here on business in relation to the Indian that squats hereabouts on your land. My boys have been tracking that snake a couple days now and I got this notion to check closer t' home."

Mary composed herself, moving her hand along her side, recognizing the shape of the hatpin in her pocket. There was something different about him. Namely, rather than the rancid odor of the unwashed there was only the light scent of sweat, horse and tobacco.

With his hat removed, a new one at that, she noticed his hair had been washed, his clothing, too, all newly purchased. Caden was not a large man, measuring only a few inches above her own diminutive height. He could easily be mistaken for a young boy from the back, though his face told a different tale. His eyes were cold, gray in color, frightening. In those eyes, she saw a vision of her death and it paralyzed her, summoning a time when she had been facing the same danger. She had fought then, and she would fight again, refusing to be cowed. Her back straightened like a ramrod, running her fingers along the pocket edge of her dress. Mary looked at Caden and watched him while he settled himself firmly into the room, moving closer to her.

"You might not see me as anythin' special," he said, turning his hat around and around by the brim like a nervous schoolboy. Another step closer and Mary tensed, eyes alert for an escape, a weapon. She speculated on the chances of Adair or Isabel or even a ranch hand to appear at her door at that moment, wondering if God would be so cruel as to allow such violence rendered upon her again. She called out to the angels, to Jesus, Himself, to smite Caden down where he stood, a lightning strike, an apoplexy, his heart to cease its beating, anything to keep him from taking her as no woman should be taken.

His hand reached out and touched her hair, falling loose to her shoulders. He seemed entranced by it which gave her a spark of hope to save herself by her wiles. It seemed he was enamored by her and perhaps would prefer her consent to the act rather than force. If somehow, she could keep her wits about her, use this small unearthing to her benefit. Her only thought was she would kill him if necessary.

Her gaze went to the door, still hopeful, and her heart lifted high in her chest, shocked to see Thomas Langford standing there in the door's threshold.

"Here, here Caden, what is the meaning of this?" Thomas asked as he took several quick long strides into the room. "Are you well, Mary?"

Before she could answer or call out, Caden, a gun appearing in his hand, turned and fired once upon Thomas, felling the man like an ancient, noble tree which made a great thud as he landed hard upon the fine hewn oak floors. An unearthly sound roiled up and out of her and she turned to run. He leapt at her, grabbing her with the gun still in his hand, knocking her to the floor. Her head was spinning as she turned to look over at Thomas, his eyes wide open, his body now a riverhead to a slow and bloody riffle, sluicing over the wide oak planks.

"You ain't no better than a squaw what was done to you. The Colonel told me your little secret. I knowed I was right about that boy being a breed. I reckoned a better man can enjoy the same pleasure of a buck. Now don't get me wrong, you're one hell of a woman, fine and mannerly, beautiful to boot. It's a crying shame what been done to you. But fact is fact, you're ruined, sullied and ain't nothing goin' to change that."

His words astonished Mary, amazed her in some cerebral, detached way at how Caden truly believed in his right to take her, to rape her. If things were not so dire she would have sneered at him, flailed him with her words. But she was powerless, brawn far superior to anything she possessed. Mary refused to be defeated, beginning to fight him, the hem of her dress clutched in his grip, shirred up her stocking legs. The tip of the hat pin stuck her in her hip, the cap coming free with her struggling. It was long and sharp, the tip pointed.

Caden was small and lean, but too heavy for her to lift, too strong for her to fight. While he nuzzled at her neck, tore at her bodice, she punched him with her right hand while searching for the hat pin with the other. It caught on the inside cloth of her pocket and she nearly wept, giving up on it, until she felt his hands reach between her legs, pushing them apart, touching her, a rough exploration. She gagged, retching, and he pulled his hand away and looked at her for a time.

"Don't be gettin' sick on me, now," Caden said, continuing to pull at her garments.

The hat pin finally came free with one strong tug and she fisted it tightly, the diamonds cutting into her palm. Without further thought she raised her hand in a long arc, sweeping the pin at Caden's face, his steel gray eye, missing and grazing his cheek. He slapped her soundly, fighting her for the hat pin, but Mary held fast to it, the sharp tip pointing upward at Caden. She bucked hard off the floor, taking him unaware, toppling him forward, the weight of him crushing her, and growing steadily heavier. She waited for him to fight her, but he was silent, not moving. She took advantage of the moment and pushed up at him, realizing she no longer held the hat pin and more so surprised to see it had pierced his body, plunging into his heart.

Weak with relief, she crawled out from under Caden, stood, neatened her clothing a moment, her hair, and then walked down the long hallway, up the stairs and into her bedroom, locking the door behind her.

James

James found Two Crows by a clear blue creek with a neat fire laid out before him. The camp was surrounded on three sides by a copse of trees. The Indian sat there, still, quiet-like, unperturbed, with his back burrowed up against a madrone tree, tall and near to a hundred years old. It was a rare one, a real beauty with its smooth light bark and mottling of tan and terracotta.

He scoffed aloud certain the old Cheyenne believed the tree to be a sign. James didn't speak, dismounting and drawing his carbine from its scabbard. He walked toward Two Crows waiting for the old man to acknowledge him. The silence was soon broken with the rumbling of James' stomach when the wind shifted, blowing the scent of roasting deer on the campfire spit over to him. His hunger urged him forward. The old man looked up, grinning.

"Eat," Two Crows said. "Eat first then we parley."

James wanted to argue, but he had been riding hard for over three days and he was tired, filthy and hungry. Deprivations he wasn't familiar with, having had a near privileged childhood, spoiled, one might say and recalling the words of some, they often had. He made short shrift of the roasted meat, wiping his hands on his pants and gulping down teeth-aching cold creek water. It was a feast after days of jerky and pemmican he'd stolen from Nathaniel before lighting out after Two Crows. His thoughts turned near-pleasant, though it was a short-lived respite.

"It is time for your questions to be answered, but know truth comes at a cost," Two Crows said. He looked at James with lampblack eyes, his gaze unflinching, direct, his stillness unsettling.

James nodded from where he sat by the fire Indian-style and chose to begin as memory prodded his mouth in motion, a tidal rush.

"I remember…" and so he began recalling a time as a five-year-old boy, well-nigh six, watching two men fighting, the Indian and his father. He recalled the smell of his father's breath, the way he moved, lurching back and forth, his words tangled, garbled. He remembered the long dark bottle his father had been drinking from tossed into the dirt, empty, and how he had lifted the bottle to his own lips, tasting the stinging liquid, making him gag and bringing tears to his eyes. The fight had gone on between the two and every blow his father had dealt, a joy had erupted in James, a perfect satisfaction, deliverance, justice served, in the late hours of a dark, bleak night. He recalled the words, making no sense to a young boy.

"The child is a Keegan! My son! Heed me well on this, choosing not, no stronger enemy will you find."

The Indian did not answer, shrugging his shoulders with a grunt, as he lifted himself out of the mud.

"Say it! The child born is Keegan! I want to hear you say it," his father shouted, howling with rage and James went to him, tugging on his shirtsleeve, helping him stand.

"It's all right, papa," he remembered telling his father. "It's all right."

His words made his father weep as the man stood and leaned heavily on James, making their way back to the house.

James sucked in a breath at the vivid memory, held it for a moment and then blew it out, his head swimming. *Why was everything coming back to him after all these years?* James looked at the Indian, an old man now, and he was no longer afraid.

"It was about Nathaniel, wasn't it?" James watched the old man's face, searching for answers, for lies.

Two Crows nodded. "Yes."

James said, "I don't savvy!" Struggling to remember things, he knocked off his hat and ran a hand through his hair, exposing the scar there. He put his fingers to it, worried all of this would set off his headaches. "I'm sick of the questions, the not knowing. Now you give me the answers."

The Indian nodded. "As I told you, it is time. My people are great storytellers. I will begin by telling you a story of a wild horse boy, my son. He was born to us half-horse and half-Cheyenne bearing a ferocious heart. He scorned being a man, being captive to the people. I could not tame his heart, gentle his spirit.

He was sent away, and his mother mourned for him. I took her and my horses in search of the wild horse boy. His mother, my wife, grew ill. One black night with no moon, she walked the hanging road. I lit the way for her with many fires to guide her path. I had been afraid she would be lost. I still searched for the horse boy alone, his mother's wish. It was during the Moon of Budding Trees when I found him, murdered by your father's hand while taking scalp of a boy with moonlit hair. His

299

death came before he could do this thing, but he had left his mark on the boy and the mother."

"What do you mean by that? How did he leave his mark on the mother?" James asked, confused and fearful of the answer.

Two Crows held up a hand. "Listen," he said, "your answers will come." He continued the story as James scowled, rubbing the scar on his head, knowing it all to be truth.

"The horse boy's spirit in death had passed into the bleeding gash, and once there was trapped. Because of this, the moon-haired boy's head often ached, his eyes blinded, when the spirit kicked and ranted, wanting freedom.

The moon and sun wheeled the earth and during the Midwinter Moon the mother labored, giving birth to a boy-child. The father worried the infant was not from his seed, but from the wild horse boy's when he had taken her.

I am a medicine man and could not refuse when the father had begged me to heal the boy and the mother so long ago. I saw the mother had been with child, before my son came upon her. The father and mother had not known this, the mother often ill and not of clear mind. After his birth, I took the baby, a boy, to my teepee many times…a son for a son."

Two Crows closed his eyes and dropped his chin to his chest as if sleeping. James sat quiet for a time, making sense of the story and then sprung to his feet, hurling himself forward.

"You dirty bastard," he said, hitting Two Crows in the face hard with twenty years of gathered rage. He didn't hear the hard crack of skull against the madrone tree like a lightning strike and did not see the rill of blood running from the man's head nor the streaks of scarlet deepening the terracotta of the tree truck, turning it into the color of fire. He pummeled the old Indian until he was exhausted, resting his head on the man as if a bolster. He began to cry, deep wracking sobs.

Twenty minutes later, still breathing hard, his ears roaring, James dragged himself up and walked to the creek. He plunged his hands into the clear water and washed the blood from them, the sweat and tears from his face. He stopped a moment, shifted, and tilted his head, briefly hearing Two Crow's voice in the riffling of the madrone tree's leaves.

Adair

Adair was surprised to see Isabel at the door of Jane and Nathaniel's house, a sweet home, tidy and neat with floral curtains and family portraits in silver frames and Jane's china placed orderly in the walnut hutch, a wedding gift from Joseph and Mary ordered from New York City. Their wealth was beyond Adair's ability to weigh, put in terms, measure. She had nothing the whole of her life, merely handouts from Mary and Jane. Anything of value had been sold for liquor, everything gone, her father even snatching the gold wedding band from her mater's stiff finger before she was put into the dirt.

Adair had carried that image in her thoughts the day through and when the mourners had left, Jane pleading with her to leave him, persistent, but wearied by her refusal, leaving as well, was Adair finally able to run from the shack into the swell and hum of a humid Texas night, heaving and choking out her hopelessness, her heart heavy as stone, weighted, realizing her mistake, the choice made and she, well and truly, alone.

Again, the knock sounded, and Adair's heart leapt, her hand shaking as she bracketed her finger around the knob, pulling back the latch. The door swung open.

"Good morning," said Isabel, impeccably coiffed, despite the fact she was wearing trousers and a worn wool coat. Though it was overcast, the coat would be too heavy for the warmth of the day.

"Do come in," Adair mustered, moving aside to allow Isabel a path into the home.

"It seems it was only yesterday that I had happened on the house. It was sorrowed, this place, but still it drew me to it," said Isabel.

"Well it is lovely now," Adair said, pointing to the curtains and tablecloth, cushions and pillows. "All sweet and pretty, wouldn't you agree?"

Isabel turned to look at Adair and then glanced around the room. "Yes, I agree, although I should be more modest about my handiwork."

"Ah, so this is by your hand then, all this?" Adair was taken aback, feeling a pull of something, as if trespassed upon, encroaching on the sanctity of all she held close, namely Nathaniel. Adair waited a beat to feel the bright flare of guilt she felt when she thought in that way about him, yet none came, and the sides of her mouth curled slightly into a very small smile.

"Does it please you?" Isabel asked, studying Adair before removing her coat and dropping it on a ladder-back chair by the kitchen table. "I often felt an intruder here, but I was still compelled to restore the place."

"And so, you did," said Adair. "It is as I remember it. Of course, the fabric is different and the placement of furniture. Even so, it is as charming as I recall it to be. Initially, it had given me such an aching, a pining for my dear sweet sister, Jane, I can only imagine how Nathaniel had felt to see it."

Isabel turned to her, eyes dark with a sentiment Adair could not name. "He will love no other ever again, trust me," Isabel said, showing all her white straight teeth in a full smile.

Adair shivered at the menace it augured. "Perhaps," Adair said, gripping the apron strings at her back and with a sturdy tug released it from her, its front dipping to the floor. She placed her focus on the folding of the cloth and was tempted to snug her face into it, a comfort, evoking the memory of her mater. She gathered herself and said, "Please sit, Isabel. We'll have tea."

"Lovely," said Isabel. "So very nice to have you here, a woman of my age or near to it. Mary is as a mother to me and a fine companion, but a bit uncomfortable and, I dare say, inappropriate to speak of the physicality of love." Isabel tittered into her cupped hands, delighted

303

with some thought unshared. "Those Keegan boys are quite something."

Adair smiled. "Yes, they certainly are, indeed."

"Would it be John then who has captured your heart? He is handsome, very tall and becoming quite the man." Isabel watched her, brown eyes, latching fast. Gooseflesh rose on Adair's arms, the fine hair bristling and shining a moment in the weak sunlight. *Who is this woman?* Adair wondered.

A shutter banged, and Adair visibly jumped, her heart rabbiting in her chest. Isabel laughed, rising from her seat at the table. "Please sit, Adair, you have had a time of it lately. Such horrible loss. Let me care for you."

After taking the kettle from the flame, Isabel moved to the hutch and brought two small cups and two saucers to the table, setting them upon it, going next to the mounted wall cabinet, finding the tea, as well as, spoons and sugar, as if, Adair thought to herself, it was a place of her own, her home and Adair the stranger.

Isabel sat, smiling across the table at her. "We all fall prey to it," Isabel said.

"Fall prey," Adair questioned, "to what?"

Isabel sighed, gave several light taps to the top of Adair's hand and then pulled it back as if nipped. She composed herself and looked in Adair's eyes.

"Wishing, of course," Isabel said, "wishing."

Nathaniel

Men like Caden were a dime a dozen in Texas. A bully when his men were gathered close to heel, but a coward alone. Nathaniel thought this as he stood over Two Crows, numb to all feelings, even anger, which was tamped down, did not stir. The old man was a second father to him, teaching him the means to survive in the wild which kept him alive during those dark days of battle, surviving on little, and knowing the ways to make due. He dropped down on his haunches and touched his fingers to the man's throat. Two Crows' life blood seemed to have painted the earth, the tree of white, a gruesome, but beautiful spectrum of color, aware the tree signified balance between light and dark. *Or truth and lies,* he thought.

He, at once, blamed Caden, seeing a cluster of horse hooves and boot prints as well as the scalp taken which should have horrified him most of all, but still it remained caged inside him, locked away with the other horrors witnessed. Perhaps it was God's way, setting him at a distant remove, in order, to make decisions, choices that would be right and just.

He scoffed at the notion as his soul carried a pox of sins so dark and copious, no penance, no rebirth, and no redemption would be able to turn things proper. At the thought, he gagged, hawking up bile, phlegm, and blood. He spat it out away from the body. A notion like that had to be put down, laid to rest. Redemption was all he had. He needed to stop thinking in such a morose manner. Certainly, war, wife and child gone, and now Two Crows murdered, along with a brother's hatred wasn't the perfect fodder for pleasantry, but he'd have to make himself move past it. He was abiding, living, and God's grace might still shine down upon him. He had faith enough, though he needed to remind himself of it every so often. He was surely sorry enough for all he had done. *Still was it so wrong to try to remain alive, to survive?*

"Thou shall not kill," he whispered out into the night. But promptly reminded himself of the mistranslation of the original Hebrew, lo tirtsah, which meant *you shall not murder.* An interpretation to him as different as night to day.

Nathaniel shook himself out of his ruminations. He had been tracking James, who had been tracking Two Crows. The moment James had come up missing and days later still not home, Nathaniel reckoned his brother believed he had the law and the right of it behind him, now justifying what he had hoped to do since boyhood.

He took a step back, then several more, looking around, but there were too many tracks and boot prints to make sense of it all. Yet one fact was certain, Caden's men had done the scalping, and while James most surely dealt a few blows, the fatal ones had not come from his brother, eyeing several knife wounds to the heart and chest. James' hand in it would be his tale to tell. Rather than anger—again he couldn't quite place why—there was a certain peace, calm in him when he should be feeling much more.

Where was the sorrow? Where was the rage? Had he lost all capacity to feel?

306

Suddenly his stomach lurched, a worry, strong and invasive, ran through him, as intense as a bolt of lightning striking a tree. His hair raised all over his body, tingling, and he looked up at the sky thinking it was certain to be tinged green, a warning of a tempest brewing. He was surprised to see the crystal blue of it through the lattice of leaves and branches, and to hear the continued thrum of cicadas and birdsong. Nevertheless, something was wrong, though it wasn't by the hand of God or nature.

Nathaniel walked to his horse, untied the rawhide strings and removed the wool army blanket coiled in his blanket roll. It was all he had for the body as Two Crows had nothing in his possession. John's horse was nowhere to be found and the frock coat and beaver top hat had gone missing as well. Nathaniel quickly got to it, hearing Two Crows voice as he worked, saying this duty belonged to the women of the tribe, one of many views Two Crows and Nathaniel differed.

He tipped his head back, searched the madrone tree and soon spotted a fine resting place for the old man in the fork of two broad boughs. He began to wrap the man snuggly in the army blanket, washed clean by Isabel the night of finding the mutilated boy. He stopped his work and slapped his leg to chase the face of the boy away. He shook his head and focused on the chore at hand. He had tied rawhide strings to Two Crow's ankles and wrists to keep his arms and legs in place before he had encased the body and now began tying the rawhide at the top and bottom ends of the blanket.

As Nathaniel stood, he surveyed the tree and then looked down at the blanketed body. He returned to his horse and retrieved the lariat lashed to the pommel, working the lasso open. On his knees, he slid the lasso midway around the body, pulling the rope tight. Next, he stood and tossed the end of the lariat over the limb and went to get his horse. Once there, he tied the end of the rope to the saddle horn and commenced to pull the dead man up the smooth bole of the tree. It was fast work as the body fit well in the crotch of the branches like a ready-made cradle, facing toward the east. He then took out his skinning knife from its scabbard and sawed through the rope while balancing on the horse's rump, which blessedly remained still and steady. Even the blood had no influence on the fine cavalry horse.

When he had gotten down off the horse, he lifted the knife to his hair and cut a length of it, letting the wind snatch it from his fingers and scatter it in its wake. He then rolled up his shirt sleeve and sliced a deep cut into his left arm to join the other two healing scars, his blood running into the earth with Two Crows'.

He again searched the ground for sign, studying the blood on the tree, the boot prints and hoof prints, deciphering it to be as many as five men, perhaps more, he couldn't be certain. Though something inside of him spoke loudly and most assuredly, James had been taken by them from this place.

The horse remained by the tree and he went over to it, taking up his bull's eye canteen he had scavenged a lifetime ago from some long dead soldier. With his back against the tree, he slid to the ground, drinking the tepid water while thinking of the clear running creek not more than a stones' throw away.

He was hot, tired and feeling the weight of his emotions, an anvil on his chest, but he had no time to rest, to dally. His brother needed him. As he stood up and looked one last time at where Two Crows was laid to rest, and then back to the bloodstains on the trunk, he spotted lettering scrawled into the farthest right side, nearly to the back of the tree.

The words carved there were not at eye-level, but low as if someone had been on their knees. *How had he missed it?* he wondered. The words were in Latin and it read: *Lex taliones.* Nathaniel held little doubt it had been written by James'. *But why?* He searched his memory for the meaning and his breath caught, his heart seized. *Lex taliones—the law of retaliation.*

Adair

Adair had been the good one, selfless, sainted in her mater's image whom she had loved and loathed with same volition, although she remained staunch, believing her mater to be lofted above all others, nearest the Lord. She was thinking this as she walked into Mary's home with Isabel one step behind, practically on her heel backs. Adair felt a stir of ire toward the woman, an intruder, clearly taken into the Keegan fold. Isabel had a secret in her eyes, in her smile, more so noticeable when she spoke of Nathaniel. A nuance in her tone when she said his name, an intimacy as if lovers when she held a shirt of his in need of mending. Her fingers were as sensual a thing Adair had ever seen, arousing her with just the barest of touches across the hem or a small moment taken to caress a button.

Adair needn't ask if they had been together. She had sensitivity in her, insight, perhaps a seer. This ability had saved her on more than one occasion, reading things, people. Life was hazardous, treacherous. Though by rights she was tied to the Keegan clan, her father, a blight on her, on the world, was her blood, her family. It was her yoke to bear, even though Jane had given her choices long ago more than once. But she had been angry at Jane, angrier than she allowed herself to admit. Guilt, always guilt, rose at the admission.

A good man, a kind man as Nathaniel Keegan should not spawn such vile emotions. Her thoughts, her feelings tainted her love for him. He did not deserve a sinful, pitiless woman like her. No, she was no saint, no holy vessel. Dearest Nathaniel clearly carried a light within, an ability to make clean even the lowest of God's creatures, perhaps even her, a sinner so abhorrent, though her misdeed went unspoken, unacknowledged in her heart and in her mind. Yet in her sleep, in her dreams, she had smiled knowingly, skipping down the narrow dusty trace with the slow burning heat of the home fires behind her.

In that moment, the jolt of acknowledgement horrified Adair far more than the scene before them, blood and death splayed out across the polished oak floor boards and then the screams from the woman at her side. As well they should, the screams did not stir her, and for the first time Adair, indeed, understood the extent of her deadened heart.

Nathaniel

Nathaniel had traveled accordingly by the stars, a waning moon giving ground, intensifying their glories. He had no plan, only intent. He loved his brother even through the miseries, the love strong in his heart. It was a feeling more than memory, although dappled. Nathaniel rode on as he had in his days at war, holding neither fear nor judgment.

He remained on point. They did not hide their trail, easily read even in the dim light. There before him lay a wide swath of snapped branches, torn leaves, rocks flipped and scattered, hoof tracks imprinted into the soft dirt, excrement of both man and horse. This was the action of men who held no fear; arrogance in them conjured when running in packs, a violence deep and primal. No matter to Nathaniel, he had dealt with the likes before and he, a wolf alone, would kill them all.

Adair

Adair stopped at the threshold and watched Isabel run forward into the room, slipping on the blood, arms pin-wheeling briefly, regaining her footing. Throughout it all, the woman sustained a high pitch screaming, wordless and peculiar. It would have been comedic to Adair if it weren't for such a brutal scene splayed out across the brilliantly polished wood floors.

"Isabel!" Adair shouted, as she moved toward the hysterical woman, avoiding the rivulet of blood, and over to the dead man she ascertained to be Isabel's father. "Isabel! Stop this!"

Isabel's arm flailed and struck Adair hard in the face. Her ears rang and her eyes started tearing. "Blast, woman!" yelled Adair. "You've broken my nose for certain!"

When she gained her senses, she saw Isabel had dropped to the floor on her knees sobbing, and Adair's dead heart returned to lively beating, filling her with such immediate and powerful compassion and sorrow. It was a deep-down, soul-stirring sorrow for her own losses she had never put name to for fear of never coming back again to know life and its possible joys and small graces.

So there Adair found herself, on the floor, arms encased around this woman who by all rights and circumstances might very well take everything from her as Jane had done before her. And as Adair cried, hard sobs wracking her small frame, loosing every hurt and suffering out into the world, she found herself embraced and held close, a thin arm encircling her waist and Adair's head finding its way into the narrow hollow beneath Isabel's chin.

There they remained embracing each other and sobbing and not releasing hold of each other even when Joseph and John entered the home. Adair did not look up at the men, did not care to take on questions, to sort through their worries, their concerns. She simply wanted to remain in the comforting hold of another, gone without for so many years. *Sweet mater! Dear sweet mater! All the blood! All the blood! And all the fault of mankind!*

"Listen to me now!" Joseph shouted, "Girls, where is Mrs. Keegan?"

Adair lifted her head and looked at the man but couldn't speak. She lifted her shoulders in a shrug. Adair felt Isabel begin to tremble and she held her tighter and began to stroke her hair. It was now Adair's time to offer comfort. A brief wish passed through her thoughts to be well shot of the blood, but she remained steadfast.

Adair watched from the edge of her eye, John grabbing hold of the man Caden by the arms and dragging him across the floor. An odd thing caught her attention, a glint of something in the left breast of the man's shirtfront. Diamonds, she thought to herself, a thousand diamonds like small stars. *Had she lost all reasoning? Had it all finally drove her to madness?*

John was watching her. She felt his kind, green eyes assessing her. "A stick pin," he said with a wide grin that changed forthwith into a grimace, his cheeks reddening beneath tanned skin. "Forgive me, ladies," he said with such formality, she felt Isabel's shoulders bobbing and then heard a slow soft chortling. Adair couldn't keep herself from laughing as well, recognizing the absurdity of such civility from the boy while dragging a dead man across the floor, the boot heels marking a path through the blood.

Once John was outside and their laughter nearly subsided, she dared to look over at Isabel.

"A bit better now?" asked Adair.

313

Isabel hiccupped, inhaled, and hiccupped again, rubbing her face. She nodded and put a hand to her father's chest. "I rued the day he had hired that man. I gave warning. Told him of Nathaniel's suspicions, but he wanted no talk of *that boy* is how he had put it. He would shush me at every mention of Nathaniel's name. I thought it was because of the war, Nathaniel being a *Sesech,* a Confederate. It wasn't that, though. My father knew something. I could see it in his eyes. But there could be nothing so bad to keep—" Isabel stopped abruptly.

"To keep you from loving him," said Adair.

"Yes," Isabel said, looking out the window which offered a view of the graveyard, although a fair distance away from the home.

"Jane is gone," Adair heard herself saying, "been gone for years now."

"Not to him, not to Nathaniel," Isabel said, choking back a sob.

"Have you been with him, Isabel? Have you lain with him?" Adair asked, suddenly having the oddest sense of her sister within her, the one asking those questions and Adair speaking, but watching it all from a distance.

As she was thinking this while her mouth was speaking words she hadn't formalized in her mind, Isabel began crying. "Will you treat him well? Will you love him always?"

"I will," Isabel said, between sobs. "I loved no other as I do this man."

As she listened to Isabel speak of love, inside her head, Adair was screaming. *No, he is mine now, Jane. Not hers. I will not lose him again.*

But from her tongue, the foreign words came again. "Are you with child?" she asked.

Isabel gasped. "How..." She looked curiously at Adair, deep into her eyes. Adair turned away from the penetrating gaze of the other woman. *It's happening again*, thought Adair. *Will I never find happiness?* At that, she felt a touch on her cheek as soft as a kiss and her sister's voice as if she knelt beside her, speaking into her ear. *I promise you will,* were the words spoken.

Aloud, Adair asked, "He is not returning today, is he?"

"Who are you talking to, Adair?" Isabel was staring hard at her. "What does that mean? What are you saying?"

Adair shook her head and said, "No one and it means nothing. It was just a feeling that came to me." This gift, her mother had called it, had never once brought joy. "I have lost. You have won."

"Adair," said Isabel, wrapping her arms around her waist. "You're not making any sense."

Adair shook her head and smiled. "It's all right, Isabel. I understand everything now. I do know how it feels to wish for a thing for so long and not having it come true."

Isabel started to laugh as if mad, her eyes wild, staring at her hands. "Here you speak of love and wishes while I swim in the blood of my murdered father. I am alone and yes, Great God, yes, with child again. Again, again..." Isabel began to rock back and forth, her legs folded beneath her.

"Isabel," said Adair. She lifted her hand and slapped the woman's

315

cheek hard enough to bring her back. "You are not alone, I promise." Relieved it was her own words coming from her this time and more so of the sincerity in them. "You and I, we are not alone."

Isabel started to sob. "I have behaved so badly towards you. I was envious of you, your beauty, and the way he would look at you."

Isabel covered her face with her hands and Adair wanted to protest, to pull them away, wanting to shout, *the blood, the blood*, but she remained silent.

Adair looked away, watching John through the window, his head bobbing in and out of sight as he labored over the corpse and then as he walked the length of the porch and finally stood in the doorway, looking directly into her eyes.

"I'm headed into town to get the law out here," John said, sounding quite like a man in that moment.

"Yes," Adair said. "Of course, someone should." She nodded. "I will tell your father."

John smiled faintly and lowered his head. "He knows I'll be headed out."

"And what of..." Adair lowered her eyes to Isabel's father.

"If you could, eventually...just cover the Colonel when Isabel is ready...the law will need to see such things, I reckon," said John. "It's not my place to ask, but if you are up to it..."

Adair understood. Clean up the mess, the blood. Hours spent as a child wiping away her mother's blood, doing the task with her father on a bender. Jane had been with a gentleman caller, refusing to cry, so angry at the world, until Nathaniel. He had changed her, bringing the kindness, the softness, back in her. Adair sobbed, and John's brow furrowed, concerned.

"Don't trouble yourself, Adair," said John. "I'll handle it when I get back. It's been a shock for the both of you. Helping Isabel is enough for you to handle. I am awful sorry for putting that on you. Pa wants you both to wash up. If you need anything, find him. He will help you."

Adair's lips formed a smile, hopefully reassuring to John. "I'm fine. Go on now. I will tend to things here."

As John went to leave, Adair heard him speak more to himself than her. "I wish my brothers were here…"

As do I, Adair thought, *as do I.*

Nathaniel

Nathaniel came upon the camp hearing the men in boisterous folly, jeering at something, someone. Immediately, he discerned it to be his brother in bad stead close to being tortured, hanged by thumbs or toes. There were many in the group who would know every means to keep a man alive for days of merciless cruelty.

In his mind's eye, he saw himself with blade in hand, slicing each throat to the spine. His blood simmered, his heart an inferno burning, white hot with rage. He would have no guilt, no regret, an avenging

317

angel, the sword of Michael.

Nathaniel took a breath, several more, and gained composure. He would wait for nightfall; wait for the vermin to crawl into the folds of their rank and moldering bedrolls, bottles to their decaying mouths. He would hew the vile creatures for the sake of many, for the sake of his brother, as he had always done.

James

He was a fool and a killer and judgment would be harsh. James knew that and thought maybe it was upon him now. The stinking men milled around him in the makeshift camp, spitting at him and kicking him in the most susceptible parts. Well-deserved, James supposed, after what he had done and justifying it as retaliation, eye for an eye.

Son for a son...

Why had it meant so much to him? Why did he hold so tightly to the anger? Anger from an injustice, an abuse, he had not remembered. Or had he remembered, yet refused to acknowledge? James' hatred was formidable, blind, without conscience. He had the death of innocents on his hands, his soul.

Dying now, a definitive sign from God of his darkness, his malignance, would seem appropriate, well deserved, yet his head raged against it. James began then to bargain, asking for forgiveness, working out a thousand ways to make restitution. *Would anyone come for him?*

He had left without word, only snagging provisions from Nathaniel's possibles bag. Maybe his only hope would be from the one soul whom he had wronged the most, the one soul who loved him unfailingly.

James moaned, sick of heart. He could never make things right nor ask for forgiveness from that quarter and with Two Crows dead... James felt devoid of hope, heavy-hearted, lost, and bleaker than a Texas night without star or moon. *Was this hell or that odd nether world of Purgatory?* War was said to be hell on earth and he had sent Nathaniel to it because he felt a grievance needed to be settled, a score to be paid, and all derived from some dark-seeded sentiment, some raging, though elusive insight of being wronged.

His father tried, a good man taking him to task for his pettiness, his mean-spiritedness. But it had done little good, so determined, so focused to pay them back. At once his scar tingled and itched, James fearful the blindness of a headache would render him helpless. He smirked, finding he still had fight in him, not yet considering himself done for, finished. He was not quite repentant, not quite ready to submit himself to his just punishment, not able to surrender as placidly as a sheep to slaughter.

Oh, he knew he'd need some serious penance, some balm of Gilead, some cleansing of his sins and he hoped he'd get it. But today was not the day of his reckoning. The likes of these beasts, these sinners were not to render his sentence, his judgment for all eternity. God would never use these men as His instruments.

And then his heart jumped against the cage of his ribs at the sound of gunshots, laying everything to waste.

Nathaniel

Nathaniel had come then in the dark, slowly taking his Officer's LeMat Revolver from its scabbard, a glint of moonshine off its barrel, the moon no longer hidden by cloud. Although it was brighter, nearly daylight to Nathaniel, accustomed to warfare as well in darkness as black as pitch, he was at the ready with his revolver and skinning knife. He had moved up the military ranks as the head count of officers became less and those capable of reading and scribing an advantage. But Nathaniel, though genial, was more of a loner. His greatest virtue was the need to keep his men safe, keep them alive and breathing. Well, now for him the stakes were higher—his brother's life.

Quietly, Nathaniel moved, every skill taught by Two Crows along with several of his own came to him. He recalled the tracks, the number of horses. Six men at the most, he reckoned, seven including his brother who would be tied close by them.

Nathaniel knelt behind a knot of brush and shrubs. He had left his boots and horse a fair piece back, changing into moccasins before he set out, following their trail with ease. There was no subtlety in war when thousands of men marched along muddied roads and dusty pikes, no hiding, but the men he tracked now were dim-witted and arrogant. His pistol was old and he longed for his Sharps, but the fighting done would be immediate and tightly quartered. Knife and pistol would serve him well. Old thoughts emerged, a ghost of who he had been those years in war took possession of him. For the good of all, he thought to himself, if such a thing existed in killing.

A guttural sound took hold of his attention and then a man's cursing, a valiant attempt not to cry out in pain or terror. Nathaniel's heart pounded in the cage of his ribs, his hands shaking, and he took in a hard breath and released it. Over and over he repeated this, until he felt the slowing of his pulse. He tugged at his collar and loosened a button, drawing out the rosary beads he had placed around his neck. He felt for the crucifix and brought it to his lips with a quiet prayer. "By the grace of God," he whispered and then quickly shoved it down into his shirt, feeling the metal pressed against the taut skin over his heart. He had fought well for his men, his comrades, in a war against men he had no quarrel, against a cause he espoused, leaving him with no true compass other than to keep his pards alive so that all could return home to their mothers and fathers, their wives and children. He had saved many but had lost many more.

Another guttural roar spurred Nathaniel forward through a brace of trees, the dark leaves dappled by moonlight. As he got nearer the camp, Nathaniel forced himself to wait, to hold steady, until the men drank themselves into a stupor, soon to be an eternal sleep. But perhaps there would be no need for killing, these men to be the Cavalry's concern, perhaps... those thoughts were soon put to rest when Nathaniel saw in horror a man slowly rise and stumble toward his brother, pressing a knife blade crosswise against his brother's throat. As though removed from his corporeal self, he lifted his pistol like air, weightless, and fired a perfect straight line into the man's beating heart. And then hell opened up around him.

321

James

After it was completed, they stood together, sweat, blood, various matter covering his brother, chosen not to be examined too closely by James. He remained tied, hands numb, pants long ago soiled from fear and a pressing bladder gone unheeded, remembering another time, another humiliation as a boy with an Indian hunting party looking for amusement, men of the same bent: mean-spirited, cruel, menacing, every single one a killer. Nathaniel had saved him then with Two Crows help and James hatred had ratcheted higher, but that was all before knowing the truth.

The stench brought him back around and the whispered, "Are you well?" from Nathaniel. He nodded his head and then spoke, throat raw from the previous night's angry outbursts, cursing them all. The welts, the burned and oozing skin, and the knife cuts caused him discomfort, pinching and stinging against the fabric of his shirt. But no pain was greater than the pain of his heart. He wept, tears rolling down his face and he saw Nathaniel's misunderstanding, believing him to be far worse off than he had admitted. James cut his brother off, and took a step forward, lifting his bound hands, still unable to control his tears.

It felt to James as though all his life's pain, all his agony, hatred, frustration, helplessness, his suffering came loose in this place of carnage, unfurling, a ball of string untwining and James unable to stop its rolling, each hiccup, each breath, was like a tug on string reeling away from him. With a sharp yank at his wrists, his hands were released, the separation and freedom causing him to hitch in a breath, deep and rich and curative, though it only lasted a moment.

When he looked at his brother's face, James saw the man's eyes which remained as guileless and loving as in their boyhood days, far kindlier than James deserved. When he settled, and found his voice, he moved toward Nathaniel and pulled him into an embrace, a piercing pain in his abused arms and body. "I am sorry," he said. "Forgive me." James' voice was ragged, harsh, penitent. "Please...forgive me."

He felt Nathaniel's forehead press against his shoulder, shorter, leaner than James.

"There is nothing to forgive," said Nathaniel.

And precisely in that moment, the world went dark.

Mary

"I have always placed too much upon Nathaniel," she said when Joseph entered the room and sat beside her on the edge of the bed. "As a boy, he was so intuitive, shouldering it all, and I allowed this. Will he ever forgive me, Joseph?"

"He loves you very much, all of us," Joseph said. "There is nothing to be forgiven. I have always tried to protect him."

Mary watched Joseph closely, his eyes red-rimmed, wet with unshed tears. She tapped his hand resting on her thigh and then brought her hand to his clean-shaven face. "Yes, you did and for that I am grateful. But still we failed, although you kept your secret well for my mother, didn't you, my husband?"

She closed her eyes a moment, and then looked at him as she spoke. "As you must have surmised, I discovered the letter, the hatpin."

A groan emerged from his closed mouth, muffled and sorrowed. He took her hand and kissed it. "I am a fool." And then she watched as he cried.

"Come, rest your head, my love, my dearest," Mary said. "We have done well with our lives, haven't we? Three beautiful sons, a lovely home, more wealth than is needed in a lifetime…You have cared well for me, Joseph. I bear you no ill will. It is I who must be forgiven. I have taken a man's life tonight."

Joseph lifted his head from her shoulder. She listened to his breathing and then the quiet snuffling, composing himself.

"Did he hurt you, Mary?" he asked in a whisper.

"I would not be taken again." Grim-faced, she said, "So perhaps, I shall never be forgiven."

"You did nothing wrong," said Joseph. "God is merciful."

"And what of Nathaniel?" Mary looked at Joseph and saw his confusion. "Though we did not ask it of him, he bore our crosses since birth."

Joseph lowered his head, not able to look at her or speak.

"We all are guilty of it and though it is painful to admit, even yourself, Joseph." Mary placed her fingertips under his chin and raised his head, so his brilliant green eyes looked directly into her own. "We must be strong for him and we must ask to be forgiven."

Joseph turned to her and hugged her with his broad arms. She would have loved to remain embraced like this for the rest of her days.

"Mayhap he has carried a cross for us, sacrificed for us, but if so, it was of his choosing. Never once have we asked this of him. I love the boy to the marrow, would die for him, bargaining my soul to change the course of things, but God was indifferent to my pleas. But do not fret, Mary. It will be well. We have survived wicked sedition and great loss. But we are strong. You, my most courageous wife, are the most steadfast of all. Your strength is greater than my own and you have triumphed. You live, my love, my wife. You live, and I am forever grateful you found the strength to make it so. I say this with the utmost truth: I will not live in a world without you."

"And I without you, my darling, Joseph, and I without you."

Joseph smiled at her and moved his head close to hers, pressing his lips against her lips for a very long time. When he released her, they began to laugh together as they did when they were young.

James

It had been going on seven days, nearly a week since he had gone off with intent to kill. *No*, he screamed inside his head, the word, *kill*, reverberating through the pan of his brain. "NO!" he said aloud, putting things to rest. "Justice, it was justice."

325

When he had confessed to the killing, Nathaniel had sworn to him that Two Crows had not been murdered by his hand, but by the men who had followed him, Caden's men. Men, not a word close to what they were: Animals, vipers, worse. *What was worse? he wondered.* James couldn't think, dead tired from being on the trail and then taken.

And then saved … he slowed his horse, reining to a stop and dismounting hurriedly, overcome with an urgent retching sickness. No food for days, barely any water. Nathaniel tried to feed him, make him eat. He couldn't seem to hold it down, all manner of memories rushing into him, oozing out his pores, destroying any peace he had ever found in his dreams. Sleeping was no longer a thing he could count on, his dreams far too real, feeling the sharpness of a knife pierce his scalp, though at first just the coolness of blade without pain and then searing, searing. His mama was there beside him, fighting, screaming, crying, and James no longer wanting to know or see it all ever again. It had been better not knowing, not remembering.

But, of course, all this had to be recalled, and James was glad of it, really. He understood now, saw the true enemy, and he had gotten his brother back, the love between them so important to him in those boyhood days. The small sufferings endured now in his mind, in his thoughts, were not as a physical blow, no marks appeared, no blood drawn. It was a compassionate, gentle punishment for his sins. He had gotten off lightly. James mounted his horse and rode on seeing again the dreadful look on Nathaniel's face in his mind's eye while he had told of Two Crow's deception. Their father had paid dearly for it, for saving him, saving their mother. *And perhaps Nathaniel*, he thought to himself, *yes, most assuredly Nathaniel.*

As he continued making his way back home, Two Crows' words tumbled across his brain. Over and over, he heard his own voice in his ears saying it to his brother. *A son for a son…* Nathaniel had stood and walked toward a thick stand of trees, vanishing into the dark night. Much later, he had heard Nathaniel howl with such tormented sorrow that James had fallen back into weeping. He no longer recognized the man he was becoming, the tears, this love locked away so deeply, he'd not known how to retrieve it.

Without announcement, Nathaniel had emerged from the darkness like a wraith, giving him a start and a bracing hug, and then placing a fine hand on James' shoulder had said, "I *am* your brother. I *am* a Keegan."

James had nodded, smiling, gripping the hand there. "Yes, Nathaniel, yes."

He looked ahead at the grand white clapboard house, his home, coming into view. Nathaniel had asked James to do one thing for him, a thing Nathaniel could not do, although he had told James that Jane had asked this of him when she had come to him in a dream. James had only smiled and agreed. Perhaps, Two Crows had been right in the telling, believing the spirit of his son had entered him and only God's truth and the remembered horror could expulse the specter from him. James shook his head and grinned, amused by the idea he was thinking akin to Nathaniel. He immediately grew somber, his lips tightening in a thin, firm line. His brother had made a promise to him. *So at least that was something.* At least James had that to give them upon his return.

James

It was Adair who greeted him on his arrival. She told him of all that transpired in his absence and he spoke of his own. For a moment, he reeled inside at how easily they spoke of death and killings, but how they must be this way to move forward. Nathaniel as well as his mother had done so out of necessity and he would walk the road of perdition, offering his soul for them.

On the long porch, James sat in his mother's rocker, filling up with memory, but this time of her love. So much sweeter life seemed to be to him. Even after all the killing...

Adair interrupted his thoughts. "Will he come back to us?"

"Yes, he promised he would. But when, I don't have that answer for you." James leaned his head back against the wooden rocker, closing his eyes. He was so very tired. "I have sinned against him and he has forgiven me."

Even after all he had done, even after he had at long last given Jane's letter to Nathaniel, his brother reading it over and over by the glimmer of firelight, his eyes lit, flickering with ever changing emotion like the shift and spin of night skies.

"What have you done, James?" Adair asked. He heard the fear in her voice, a quaver. Not so long ago that concern for Nathaniel would have made him enraged. He had resented how intensely they loved him.

"I've wronged him all of his life and it was me who sent him off to war. I convinced him the family would be in harm's way, maybe slaughtered in the night in our sleep while the house burned around us to the ground," James said, but couldn't help himself from adding, "it wasn't all falsehood. There'd been many innocent people killed in the county."

"Yes, it is true, that," Adair agreed. "Well, I have committed a far greater sin and I must speak of it or I'll go mad."

James opened his eyes and looked over at Adair. She was as beautiful as Jane, even more so because of her childlike demeanor, her guilelessness. He was near to ten years her senior but not so old to be a good husband.

"Tell me, Adair, I won't judge you," James said, taking her hand in his own. She began to cry then, and in between the sobs, he began to parse her story. He hugged her at the end of it, understanding it all, offering her solace.

Nathaniel

It had been nearly five months to the day when Nathaniel had left after the butchery, two seasons passing, having a need to take stock, sort things through, learn to forgive the others as well as himself. His heart had been broken, but he had discerned the spirit and the organ were each able to mend by slow degrees. Over the months, his hair had grown out past his shoulders and on the morning of his return home, he had plaited it neatly after he'd bathed in the cool waters of a stream, a baptism. Oh, how he had wanted to die back then, and so easily to do so. But still he remained, still he breathed life in and out, felt hope smoldering and finally heard Jane speak to him.

She had told him her story every night in those months of his wandering. Her thoughts, his thoughts woven together as fine threads in a tapestry and realizing she was in him, with him forever. Perhaps it had been the many nights of draught opium dreams, but fiercely believing in visions and of God's angels coming to earth whispering truth in the ear of man. He had seen her days lived out, come to life, during the time he had been off to war, all he had missed, and he had heard her speak her heart as clear as a bell in winter's silence.

As he rode toward home, her story came back to him. He understood now the pain he had caused her, and he had nearly thrown himself from a canyon rim to circle briefly as a blown leaf and then descend into the waters, carried downward. Though he had never been strong enough.

Several times death had nearly caught him, and instinct became his enemy, fighting to remain with heart beating, blood coursing. After many bad nights when each breath taken was laborious and heavy with despair, Jane had talked to him once more. She had whispered their pledge, their promise to each other. *Abide*, she had told him, *abide* and then she was gone, the specter resolving slowly into that of his mother, seeing her again all those months before, requesting one thing from him. *Live*, she had pleaded, *live*.

So now five months had gone, and he had pared himself down to mere bone and sinew. A month, forty days going without food, but on those days of weakness he had allowed himself some berries or pemmican, a mouthful of water. He had waited for a vision, his path, remembering months before telling his father, he had lost his way.

He recalled on one particular night of deepest despair, a roiling of sorrow so vicious, Jane had come and had kissed his mouth, telling him to go out from this land and travel home. "I do not want to go," he had said aloud and then had asked with tenderness, "Do you want me to go?" She had lain upon him, holding him close. "Yes," she had said to him, "it is time."

Nathaniel

On his return home, the welcome had been sweet, the tales had been spun, the love there for him as strong as boyhood, perhaps more so with such immutable losses endured, most recently Isabel's, which he hoped to remediate in some small way.

His father had mentioned her circumstance and Nathaniel had felt burning shame. Between himself and his father there had been a moment of unspoken reassurance, a silent exchange of understanding. There would be time to talk later as the nurturing years had been the true barometer of love, not seed, not the begetter or the begotten. He no longer saw the fleeting shadows cross his father's eyes. He now understood.... *a son for a son.*

Nathaniel chose not to pass judgment on Two Crows. He had been a kind and decent man, saving his brother, James, and his initial intent, whether it be vengeance or loneliness, had brought him to this summit, this precipice, only to lose his ground. Nathaniel had been loved well by fine men and was, without doubt, dear to them. In the grander details of this world, under the glorious shine of God's moon and stars, man's final tally would be only that of love and how the scale balances. Nathaniel was comforted knowing he had mourned and guided the man to *Seana*, assured he was at peace.

Some time had passed before he felt able to see Isabel Langford. But when things became too quiet in an unsettling sort of way, a quiet he had seen before, the calm before storms, before worlds fell apart, his decision was made. Not in the mind to recall any of those times, Nathaniel focused solely on Isabel and the child as he rode.

When he made the bend, he saw Isabel in her rose garden. Her brown hair worn long and loose was parted down the center, the front strands tucked behind her ears away from her pale face, translucent as moonlight. His heart rose and pressed against his breastbone, watching her, his breathing quick.

Isabel saw him coming, raising a hand to shield her eyes from the sunlight. Her white dressing gown floated and billowed in the breeze. The sight was more than he could bear, looking as though she belonged in holier worlds. He had to look away. It was late afternoon, nearing evening, and though the days were shorter, Nathaniel found it odd that she was dressed in nighttime attire. He worried he might be intruding on a private moment.

Still, he unhorsed and tied the gelding at the fence. When he pushed open the gate he felt Isabel's gaze on him and when he started up the stone walk toward her. She hadn't moved, standing there like a picture in the long shaft of light, illuminating her face. It was unbearably sentimental, causing him to feel discomfited and out of place. He had never dwelled on his appearance but was aware he possessed a measure of good looks, emboldening him as he approached her.

Isabel still hadn't moved, her hands filled with freshly cut roses. She lowered her head to breathe in their scent before she looked back up at him. They stood silent for a moment and then she walked toward the house and climbed the porch steps. Nathaniel followed her.

When they entered the house, he stared at her and saw how pale she was, but then she colored a bit from his regard. She dropped her eyes down to the roses she still held in her hands and walked to the settee, sitting down with effort under the weight of her swollen belly.

Nathaniel smiled. He was content to just look at her, aware there were times in a man's life which had to be watched closely so those moments could be remembered over and over in the mind's eye. He knew then he would remember, years later, the scent of roses, the golden light of the late afternoon sun filling the room, the white gown settling like snow over her abdomen, and the way her eyes held joy. His stomach tightened at the thought of a baby soon to be born and before she could say a word, he knelt in front of her and asked her to marry him.

He took her hand, the roses placed next to her. She started to cry. Nathaniel waited, her tears finally stopping. Dread flowered through him, his words bottlenecking in his throat. Isabel looked at him, and asked, "Will you dance with me, Nathaniel Keegan?"

He was stunned by the request, but then stood, saying, "Yes."

She smiled, her mouth only lifting a little at the edges. He took her hand and helped her up from the settee, turned to face her, holding her at the waist. They danced to her soft humming and then when the spirit rose in her, she sang. Nathaniel held her close to him and gently rubbed his hand over her back.

A breeze picked up and the scent of roses came through the open windows, filling the room and making him dizzy. He held her tighter to keep his balance and spoke into her hair. "I don't want you to worry, Isabel. It will be alright."

She pushed away from him and looked him in the eye and then turned and walked back to the settee. Her face again wet with tears, her eyes downcast. When she sat down, settling herself, she looked up at him, but didn't speak. Nathaniel shifted his feet under her intense gaze, but remained silent.

He flinched when she gasped and placed her hand on her stomach. She smiled and beckoned him to her. He knelt and she took his hand in hers and placed his palm on her belly. Nathaniel felt the steady movement of life beneath his hand and his heart lifted. He looked in her eyes while keeping his hand on the tight skin of her abdomen without embarrassment. Their eyes held each other, and she said, "If there is any doubt in your mind, the baby is yours."

Again, Nathaniel's heart rose, and he nearly whooped out loudly with joy. He reached for her and buried his face into the swell of her belly and wept.

Isabel

The house was dark save for an oil lamp in the bedroom lit hours ago. It cast a white square of light through the open door into the hall. Nathaniel was stretched out on the bed in a sound sleep. Isabel alongside him turned herself to watch him in the lamplight. The sheet covering him hid the ribbon of a scar running across his abdomen to his hip.

Before they were together, she had skimmed the tip of her finger over the healed wound from left to right as she had done that first time, and then held her hand there for a time, her palm pressed over it. While her eyes were shut, Nathaniel had pulled her hand away, startling her and when she looked at him, he had kissed her full on the mouth and had laughed.

Since he was afraid he would hurt her, she had led his hands and his body until he was sure of things. She had laid over him, the baby inside her resting against the flat of his stomach and she had smiled at his pleasure.

Afterward, she had settled on her right side next to him, marveling at his beauty for more than an hour, not able to keep herself from tracing her finger lightly down his forehead's center and over the long straight length of his nose. Nathaniel had shuddered, awakened by her touch, his eyes slowly adjusting to the light. He had smiled up at her when her face had come into his view. Few words had passed between them, Isabel accepting this as the true nature of their relationship.

Now Isabel sighed and brushed at his long black hair and watched it fall into place. He unabashedly rested his ear against her belly, listening, his eyes closed. The hours they spent together seemed to Isabel to be an unattainable dream, her perfect wish upon a thousand stars, come to fruition. Yet even as she lay beside him, her heart began to ache for her inevitable loss.

"I will not marry you."

It was only whispered, but she could tell Nathaniel heard her words when he lifted his eyes to hers and saw the hurt in them. She hurried to offer explanation. "You don't love me. I can't make you happy."

"That's not so, Isabel." Nathaniel raised himself up on his arm to see her better.

"It's the baby that makes you happy, that you love. It's not me. It may never be me."

Nathaniel lowered his head. "Give me a chance, Isabel, please."

Her words came out choked, a sob. "Great God, Nathaniel! You don't know how easy it would be for me to—but I can't do that to you."

"I want you and my child to have my name," Nathaniel said.

"The child will, Nathaniel, without any guilt or beholding to me. My father has left me with little worries."

Nathaniel raised his eyes and looked closely at her, outwardly surprised by what she had said.

"Guilt? There's no need to be weighed down by guilt. I'm a man grown and I chose to be with you that night like I choose to be with you now."

"I do thank you for that." She smiled and cupped her palm against his face and kissed him on the mouth. "Will you dance with me, Nathaniel Keegan?"

He was silent for a time and then he nodded his head in agreement. He rose from the bed and stood next to her, offering his hand. She took hold of his long fingers and smiled. The sight of him in the lamplight, unclothed, untamed, broke her heart.

337

They began to dance together while she hummed and sang when she knew the words. Nathaniel joined in, too, when the song was familiar to him. They danced for hours and when they were too tired and too sad to dance any longer, they dressed side by side in silence. After they finished dressing, Nathaniel held her and gave her a kiss in the centered part of her hair. They walked to the door holding hands, and then kissed goodbye.

John

Dulcet birdsong filled the courtyard and a blaze of sunshine shone down on the white Blackfoot daisies and purple asters bordering the porch. In that moment, John was taken off guard, harkening back to the haunting tones that had sprung from Nathaniel, one coal black night, while singing a Cheyenne death song for Two Crows. It had been a few days after Nathaniel had returned home, John hoped, for the final time. The doleful song had brought them all to tears, even James who seemingly overnight, all those months ago, became a changed man. Nathaniel and James had never spoken in detail of what had happened to them back then, but John sensed straightaway there had been killing.

A week after Caden had been felled by his mother and the Colonel murdered by Caden, a company of U.S. Army Mounted Infantry had arrived on their doorstep. His father had been hospitable, inviting the lieutenant inside the home, offering him a cup of coffee or a glass of bourbon. At the time, James had been off with Adair, away from the ranch. The officer had entered their home with a cursory glance at his surroundings and then sat, rigid and straight as a ramrod, his cavalry hat balanced on his knee, and drank the alcohol down soundly, while his father described what had occurred. The lieutenant had nodded his head, satisfied, and chose to not disturb them further, not wishing to cause more distress. John had gone to tell his mother all was well and quickly rejoined his father in the kitchen. The lieutenant had shaken his father's hand, donning his hat before heading out the door. Once mounted, he had saluted and rode off with his men behind him as if on a string.

A decent fellow which had pleased John and his father as they both had stood on the porch, lifting their hands in cordial farewell. While watching the procession of soldiers traverse under the huge iron arch embossed with the Keegan name, his father had mentioned that they had found all Caden's men dead, and an Indian bound in a blanket, buried and snugged tightly into the boughs of a large tree several miles from the fighting. They had looked at each other knowingly, and gradually shifted their gaze, each in deep thought.

In John's mind, Nathaniel had once more defended his brother and this time, *Praise God*, James a better man for it. But John hadn't been able to keep his thoughts to himself, as his head had filled with images conjured about what had ensued, hero-worship keen in him. "He smote them all," was the entirety of what he had said as goosebumps rose on his arms.

"Indeed," his father had replied, unable to suppress his satisfaction.

339

John heard his name being called, rousing him from his revelry. Guest would soon be arriving for the nuptials of James and Adair and John still mystified by it all. The courtship had been very quick, perhaps James too old for sparking or both having seen too much of life's travails to abide by frivolous formalities. They heeded to their own notions and choices.

Many had thought he would be Adair's beau, closer in age, but truth be told, he wasn't ready for such things, finally finding his way with running the ranch and all it entailed with James' interests elsewhere. Namely, Jane and Nathaniel's old homestead, building more rooms and a fine dining area with a large brick fireplace. Nathaniel never cared much about all the trappings, the finer things, only for Jane, although he would have fulfilled her every wish, her heart's desire.

During that time, James had confided in John he had caught sight of Nathaniel one morning on a distant knoll, watching the goings-on, and uncertain if he approved, even though it was all for Adair. A few days later, his concerns had been put to rest when Nathaniel, hammer in hand, had joined James with the carpentry without a word spoken. He had come each day after and helped with the bricklaying, and when it had been completed, placed a tintype of Jane and the baby on the wooden mantel with Adair and James' silent nod of assurance. John had been there at the time and his emotions had ratcheted when Adair began to weep, James hugging her close. Throughout the weeks, John had been privy to the reawakening of the great bond between his brothers, a bond his father declared had originated at Nathaniel's first breath.

On the evening James and Adair had announced their engagement and the wedding was to be in three weeks' time, Nathaniel had slipped out of the room, returned and unfurled a large parchment paper on the cherry wood tabletop. Nathaniel's signature had been visible on the document to all there, signing over the homestead to James. Stunned by Nathaniel's generosity, James had embraced his brother with such sentiment everyone had been overcome, which seemed an everyday occurrence with his family of late.

Of course, his mother had been overjoyed with the news, but the turning point for her had begun with Nathaniel's return home as well as James' revelation from Two Crows that Nathaniel was in fact of Keegan blood, a thing explained to John in alarming detail one evening by Nathaniel. They had moseyed their way to Two Crow's lodge and once there had smoked a pipe together. He had listened intently to Nathaniel with great respect and watched as his brother had lifted the pipe to the West, then the North, the East and the South, explaining each of the powers and then to Mother Earth, touching the pipe to the ground and next holding it up to the sky. After a time, he had again lifted the pipe straight up to the Great Spirit, to God, Nathaniel had said, the unexplainable source of all life and had told him everything as they smoked.

It had been a bitter pill to swallow learning of Two Crows' perfidy and the suffering endured by James and his mother, especially his mother which had brought him to sickness, vomiting in the nearby brush upon hearing it, but understanding them far better. At least, Nathaniel

341

had been spared, but then thinking it had all come at once to his brother, a fusillade. *Had that been worse?* John wondered. He couldn't say, deciding not to dwell too much on it.

"John Keegan!" His mother called out the screen door at him. "Please, come help your father. We need room for the guests."

"Coming, Ma! Be right there!" He smiled and pulled open the screen door. The weather was perfect, and he was certain the nuptials would be as well.

After the house had been put in his mother's envisioned order, the abundance of flowers meticulously arranged, and the assortment of chairs placed in rows on each side of the room forming a center aisle, had John been allowed to get cleaned up posthaste as the guest, he had been told, would be arriving at any moment. And they soon did arrive, John barely able to get on his waistcoat as he opened the door in greeting.

Shortly after all the guests had entered the house, the Reverend summoned everyone to the sizable dining room and the musicians began to play and all stood, turning their gazes toward the grand staircase. James, with Nathaniel beside him, smiled broadly, his eyes shining, strong emotions visible on his face. Isabel Langford appeared first, although fuller of face remained as beautiful as the day John had first met her and had commenced to stumble over himself and his words. She had given him an expensive leather-bound book of blank pages to write down his stories she had said, thinking him to be a great talent at storytelling. Of course, the gift had been given much later when he had come to know her as a friend and able to summon his tongue to make sense when speaking to her. Though being of a delicate condition, all had been concealed well beneath cascades of silk satin, hoops and lace.

John glanced at Nathaniel watching his brother's face, a play of emotions so swiftly wrought and then hidden. But John could see a hint of longing remain in his brother's blue eyes, his gaze only upon Isabel as she assuredly and splendidly took each step. She stopped a moment on the third stair from the bottom and looked over at Nathaniel, and John saw a moment of hesitation, a slip of resolve in her demeanor.

Nathaniel walked over to her and extended his arm and John did see then a thousand words spoken between them without a word said, and what sprung up in his thoughts, in his mind: *they are in love*. This made John happy as he looked around the room, and saw the softening of his mother's face, a genuine release of recrimination, an epiphany, that perhaps she had not done wrongly by either son and God's plans, His will, would always have precedence, no matter man's machinations or desires. He knew he would write this all down in Isabel's gift of the leather-bound book come nightfall when his imaginings and questions stole their way into his thoughts, even as a child unable to hold them at bay.

When Adair appeared at the upstairs' landing, John heard discernible gasps around him and he immediately understood their response, remembering that Jane had worn the selfsame gown on her wedding day to Nathaniel. John supposed it had been Nathaniel's wish and sensibly made due to the haste of the nuptials. Sensibly made and yet of great sentiment as the entire room of wedding guests appeared as though they were seeing a magnificent apparition, a beautiful reawakening of Jane McPherson Keegan. Near him he heard whispers of Adair's beauty, as if surprised by it and she, a butterfly newly emerged, taking flight around them.

Quickly, John turned his gaze to Nathaniel. His brother stood with eyes lifted, his gullet working with jowl clenched, seeming to be overcome with every emotion thinkable, a few John could not identify, not having yet experienced a depth of love or loss that acutely. He watched Isabel take hold of his brother's hand while Nathaniel looked down at her graceful gloved fingers curled around his and then into her eyes.

When the musicians began to play Pachelbel's Canon in D, Adair descended the stairs to where John's father stood waiting to escort her to James' side. She reached the bottom step with a swirl of silk taffeta and candlelight satin and near to sixty-five inches of lace for her veil. He had only been aware of the details upon hearing the women speak of such things late into the night.

She held a bouquet of the asters and daisies, John had clipped that morning at his mother's request. He had furled a ribbon of white securely around the stems, pleased by his mother's sweetly voiced approval when he presented the bouquet to her. It felt quite good to have a small part in James' happiness, but then surprised to discover an oppressive weight fall on him of shame and sorrow. He had been hateful to James during the years Nathaniel had been away at war.

Deservedly so, he told himself, as he caught a quick glimpse of his older brother's broad smile before turning to face the Reverend. *But understandable*, he countered.

He nodded and recalled that all had been forgiven several nights earlier when all three brothers came together and drank bottles of Tennessee whiskey and talked of their boyhood days, with John mostly quiet being younger than both, James by ten years. It had been a good night, thinking this while half-listening to the Reverend speak and the vows exchanged. He allowed his gaze to circuit the room, pausing on a beautiful young woman in the gathering of guests. He muffled a cough in his fist to hide his discomfort when she looked over at him and then smiled. He was floored by the strangest sensation coursing through his body as she continued to watch him. His heart ramped up double-quick and his palms began to sweat. She was a stranger to him, new to Burnet County. But one thing, John knew for a certainty, he had to meet her, talk to her.

He started visibly at the hoorays and clapping, but soon joined in, still watching the young woman. As the guests moved to congratulate the couple, John made his way over to the woman and thrust out his hand. "Hello," he said.

She smiled up at him, reaching mid-chest. "Hello." Her small hand cupped his briefly and then slipped from his gentle hold.

"You're a Keegan brother, are you not?" She looked toward James and Adair. "You look quite like the groom."

"My brother, James," John said. "Are you acquainted with the bride's family? I can't say I've seen you in town. Though, I don't often get into town with the ranching, but they say it's grown by leaps and bounds."

"No," she said abruptly, "I must apologize to you and confess my societal impropriety. You see, while only in town a few short days, I overheard the excitement and anticipation of the Keegan nuptials. It was said to be the grandest social event in years. I had arrived in search of an old family acquaintance, Isabel Langford after reading of the Colonel's death while back home in Connecticut. Such a terrible loss of an influential and well-respected man, a hero. You see, my brother, Lieutenant Quinton V. Cullen, was a dear friend of Miss Langford's, close to betrothed really, until he was prematurely felled at the battle of Bethel Church. The loss of my brother was painful, but more so, not having achieved the honor and glory he so thoroughly deserved, having graduated nearly at the top of his West Point class. But I do go on far too long."

John gave himself an internal poke, having fallen under a spell, mesmerized by her voice, her blue eyes. He regained his wits and said, "Stay then. I'm sure Isabel will be happy to see you. I didn't know she had a serious beau. She never mentioned him, your brother, Quinton. Did I get it right?"

"Yes," she said and lowered her eyes.

"But you haven't told me your name, yet. Miss…" John waited for her response, fearful she would say, missus, and that she was married.

She lifted her head and smiled up at him. "Miss Rebecca Cullen, but you may call me Becky if it pleases you."

"It pleases me just fine," John said, laughing. "I'm John. John Keegan. If you'd like, I can take you to Isabel."

Becky Cullen looked over to where Isabel and Nathaniel stood surrounded by guests, her eyes hooded, considering. "Perhaps later when she's not so busy. I'd so love a glass of lemonade and air. A few moments on the portico would be lovely."

"Of course," John said, a bit too eagerly. She smiled. *A kind of smile that holds a thousand secrets*, he thought. It gave him an odd feeling to think such things and wondered why the notion sprung up in his mind.

As he stood a moment to watch her walk out the door to the porch, he decided he wanted to know them all. He shook his head, chortling at himself, as he searched for a time and finally acquired a crystal pitcher of lemonade and two crystal cups, setting it all on a silver-plated tray. As he made his way outside, he was stopped by long-winded guests, attempting to excuse himself civilly, with his thoughts on Becky.

Once outside, he was greeted by friendly conversations of women sitting in rockers scattered on the porch while their children milled about them, and as he looked around his heart almost quit him when he saw Becky Cullen was nowhere in sight.

After inquiring of her whereabouts and an hour of searching with no luck, John eventually gave up and though disappointed, he chose to believe he would see her again. *With Isabel's help,* he mused, *I might soon give my pledge of engagement to Miss Rebecca Cullen from Connecticut.*

As it turned out, Isabel refused to talk about Rebecca Cullen or her brother Lieutenant Quinton Cullen and Nathaniel had warned John off from discussing it further. John chose not to leave it at that going into town early the next morning but had been told he was several hours late and Miss Cullen had already traveled on to Louisiana and from there they did not know, perhaps back to Connecticut as the south was still in disarray and a pretty young woman such as she shan't be traveling alone in such worrisome times. Thinking about her, John felt his throat tighten and his eyes mist over but remained resolute to one day see her again.

Isabel

December 21, 1866

The winter season was on them and Isabel was nearing her time. She had come to love the hill country's more clement days with its colder nights akin to her beloved New England. Her lying-in had begun a week before, refusing to be confined any earlier. Nathaniel had returned to help each day with whatever chores he saw needed doing, one morning arriving with a finely crafted cradle hewn by his own hand. It had delighted her, and she found herself wrapping him in her arms and Nathaniel smiling with pleasure down at her. Perhaps that had been the moment when she had embraced possibilities.

This night, wrapped in a knitted throw, a fire roaring in the hearth, curled on the settee with Nathaniel beside her, he had with great care taken a letter from the inside of his shirt, opening the envelope as though something sacred, as though handed down from God. His hands trembled a moment and he took a breath and without looking at her, he began to read the letter aloud:

December 22, 1862

My Dearest Beloved, my only Love,

I have not kept well our promise to abide as I am skirting on the edge of worlds and our babe, I fear, will follow soon after to our eternal rest. I ask you to promise to abide even after our earthly parting. My Love, wish not each night for our return as we will not find ease in the next life knowing you are sorrowed. Abide, my love, abide, it is my final request, be well & live heartily. I need for you to know, while you were at war, I came to understand the world's turnings and that God sees and understands all things, the heartbeat of each living creature, great & small. We must, My Dearest, accept Life's proper order of seasons.

And it is for you, my beautiful Nathaniel, your time to heal, to laugh, to dance, to embrace, to love again. With my heart forever beating in yours, with my kisses forever touching your lips, my last thoughts are of you and I fight, still fight to Abide with you. Know this well, my fight continues, as I raise a fist to the angels, yet still they come, a slip of light in the darkness. I am at ease, my heart is at peace, knowing you love me, have loved me well and I have you. Oh, how I loathe leaving you, my Darling. I must know you will not mourn far too long. I must know this to put my soul at ease. And then I know as I write that you would do all things for me, make all wishes come true if able. I wish for you to love again. I wish for you to marry again. My covetous heart will become that of an angel, the sainted. One day, my Love, we shall laugh about this unexpected Virtuousness. I cannot seem to bring myself to bid you farewell. My tears are bitter. Pray for us, my love and I will look after you, pray for you with every breath you breathe. Farewell, farewell. I wish my hand was in yours. Yes, I feel you now against me, a kiss against my cheek, my lips. Farewell, my most Precious. Farewell, my heart, my one true love.

Your loving & most faithful wife even in death,

Jane McPherson Keegan

When he had finished the letter, folding it, and placing it back in the envelope and then into his shirt front close to his heart for safekeeping, he looked at her. Isabel wiped her face of her tears and snuffled, unable to speak. Jane's generosity of spirit, her powerful and abiding love for him in every word she had written, eviscerated her, cut her to the quick.

How could she prevail over a love of such depth and devotion? Who would be favored by Nathaniel at their eternal rest? What odd thoughts she had been having lately as she neared her time.

She shook her head as if to physically rid herself of the notion, but then suddenly amused by the absurdity of it, envisioning a heavenly mêlée over Nathaniel and she smiled. Nathaniel smiled at her in return.

She watched him as he lowered to the ground on to his bended knee.

"I fought what I should have accepted all those months ago. You'd been right," he said softly.

"I may have appeared certain, but I was no more than you were, Nathaniel," she said to him. "In truth there was a fissure, a weakening in me afterward. I was lost and frightened."

"I'm sorry I caused you affliction. I hurt you."

"No, you did nothing wrong," she said. "I came to understand my decision, the reasoning sound, and deemed it right for myself and for you, my blessed Nathaniel. I required banishing old ghosts and you required to hold tightly to yours, perhaps even now. But this I did not know for certitude until later and after much derision. And although it seemed *I* had chosen James, it was not *my* choice, but that of my father's, pleasing him, pleasing everyone, really. But my heart, my love was only for you."

"I have chosen you," said Nathaniel. "Is that plain enough? I love you."

"Yes, it is plain enough," Isabel smiled. Tears sat in her eyes.

"I will devote my life to you from this day to our death," said Nathaniel.

Unable to stop herself, unable to keep from spoiling her happiness, her wish come true, she heard her voice, full and sorrowful, saying, "But what of Jane?"

"Jane had the right of it, to everything there is a season," said Nathaniel. "A time to mourn and a time to dance..."

He stood then, asking her, "Will you dance with me, Isabel

Langford?"

Her eyes filled, her heart full, a ringing so loudly in her ears like a heavenly bell pealing its exultation, and then a sudden cold rushing as her water broke, embraced in his arms.

Isabel

So, in this season of winter on the day of December 22, 1866 came to them a son born of Isabel, plump and hungry, bellowing out his discontent at the world and all those around him, as he was snatched away from the safety and comfort of his mother's womb.

Isabel saw the boy and loved him even more at first sighting, having loved him fiercely all through her confinement. She called to mind Jane's words from her letter, her generosity of spirit, her deep and abiding love for Nathaniel. She prayed in that moment Jane would approve of her as Adair so graciously had done, now both the best of companions, sisters. *How happy she was for Adair finding love and comfort in James, soon to beget their first child in the season of late summer!*

Even Mary's spells were not as virulent with Caden buried and long forgotten, but her father still in the forefront of their thoughts, the bloodstains a lingering reminder. Isabel had deduced Mary had been the one her father had dreamed about and had wanted to tell Isabel that morning in Nathaniel's bedroom. It was an unrequited love, never to be his. He had tried to save Mary, gave his life for her, no truer or greater love. He had died hero and savior, and all remembered him with utmost respect, a deserved honor. Perhaps, Isabel thought, the sins of Caden would no longer be on her father's hands and she prayed for this to be so.

She and Nathaniel had married the evening before in the seventh hour of her laboring, John riding to get the Reverend before the babe came into the world. After her initial refusal to Nathaniel's proposal, she had needed reassurance, her pride having want of love and not obligation. She was a wealthy woman, independent and strong, able to rear her child alone.

At those thoughts, she turned her gaze to see Nathaniel watching her with such love, her heart filled, and tears rolled down her face. She had so much joy beyond her greatest wishes. But then, she thought of the other. She had not named her son and felt a pang of regret, choosing to believe he was in God's keeping and, perhaps Jane and her father had before long taken him to their bosom, giving their love to him as she had not been able to do. She declared in that moment, if he had lived, she would have come to love him.

Nathaniel wiped her cheeks with the side of his thumb, tender. "What are you thinking, my wife?"

Isabel smiled and held the baby closer. "About the other."

Nathaniel nodded and kissed her on the mouth. "He is in God's care."

Isabel nodded to him. "Yes," she said with certainty, "I trust he is contented."

"I do as well," Nathaniel said and then, gently, "Should we ask them in? Are you up for it?"

At his query, they both looked to the midwife who smiled her assent, excusing herself from the room and into the large hallway which sprang to life, voices rising with excitement.

Nathaniel helped her ready herself and the babe, asking again, "Are you sure?"

"Yes," she said to him, smiling.

Nathaniel stood then, kissing her again, this time on the crown of her head and went to the closed bedroom door of her father's home, now their home.

He grinned and gave her a wink as he opened the door.

"Come see our son!" he called out to his family, her family.

Isabel laughed when a hurrah was shouted out, recognizing it to be James, and all at once the Keegan clan entered the room and clustered around her bed, Mary there at her side and Nathaniel on the other.

"This is truly a glorious day," Joseph announced. "Our first grandson, mother," he said looking at Mary, "carrying our name, our blood."

Mary smiled and gripped Joseph's hand. Isabel so pleased with it all wore a full smile as well. She looked at Mary and asked, "Would you like to hold your grandson?"

Mary's face was alight, and she reached out for the child without hesitation and then held him close to her, pressing her lips to his head of full black hair. Mary looked up from the baby slowly, as though a difficult task to take her eyes from him, asking, "What will be his name?"

Nathaniel put his arm around Isabel and smiled. "He will be called Raphael."

Mary lowered her head a moment, tears filling her eyes. Joseph stepped closer and placed his hand on her shoulder. Isabel became worried and Nathaniel shook his head and smiled at her.

"A fine and most fitting name," Mary said after composing herself.

John stepped forward from where he stood next to James and Adair, and as a shaft of light shone on the baby, he asked, "What does it mean, Ma?"

But Nathaniel answered first, his voice hopeful, at peace, as Isabel clutched his hand, smiling at him and he, staring into her eyes, saying it as if just for her, "God has healed."

---

epilogue. spring 1867

Isabel could not remember a happier time in her life. This day she stood on the porch with the baby on her hip, now heavier than a twenty-pound sack of flour and nearly twenty-six inches tall. Everyone who saw him couldn't help but stop and comment on the boy's remarkable good looks. Nathaniel's blue eyes shone from his perfectly shaped head and tufts of black hair sprung up thick and full. His fair skin was striking against the dark mop and he smiled easily, never fussy and sleeping well throughout the night. He was an exact copy of his father, an easy, sweet soul, a blessing.

She looked to the west, marking the time by the sun and smiled to know Nathaniel would soon be home. As she turned to go inside, she was surprised to hear the clacking of shod hooves on the macadam road which ran on the lee side of the large house. It was a new trace, running from the TML to the Keegan Ranch and onward to James and Adair's cottage. Isabel lifted the baby in the air above her head and she threw back her head in laughter at his happy coos.

"I wonder who has come to visit?" Isabel hugged the baby close and kissed his pink cheeks as she moved along the long porch.

She smiled again when she recognized the rider as John Keegan but couldn't quite make out who was riding beside him. A woman. She put a hand to her mouth, suppressing giggles in her excitement. *John is courting? What a wonderful surprise!*

Isabel waved and John waved in return. "Hello!" she called out to the riders. "Hello there, John!"

"Hello, Isabel!" John called back.

When John and his companion stopped in the courtyard, dismounting and tethering off the horses, Isabel invited them inside for a cool glass of lemonade and hoped they would stay for dinner. On the cookstove, potatoes, corn on the cob and string beans boiled in the cast iron pots, and beef roasted in the fire pit outside which was far more food than Nathaniel and she could eat.

"Come in, come in!" She smiled as she opened the door and stepped into the home. The sunlight filtered softly through the sheer curtains and a light cross breeze riffled the loose hair around her face. Isabel left John to take care of his female companion as she placed the baby in his cradle and checked the pots, preoccupied. She stirred the potatoes and string beans with a wooden spoon and then placed it down away from the heat.

"Now, that's done. So, sorry," she said and turned to see John and the woman over by the cradle.

"He is very beautiful," the woman said and turned to look at Isabel. "John has written me all about his nephew."

"He has, has he? And yet he has been quite tightlipped on other matters." There was something familiar about this woman and foreboding rose in her, Isabel's heart thumping in her ears.

John lowered his eyes, embarrassed. "I couldn't help, but boast about Rafe, Isabel." He took the young woman's hand and they moved across the kitchen toward her.

She was a pretty thing, blonde and blue-eyed, and John clearly smitten. Isabel smiled at John and said, "I do know you love him well. You're a good uncle."

"I hope you don't mind us just showing up like this without warning. Becky and I have been writing each other since Adair and James' wedding. Well, to be exact a few months after when Becky arrived back in Connecticut and decided to write me."

Isabel nodded mutely, barely breathing. "Rebecca Cullen?"

"Yes, Isabel. Do you remember who I am?" Blue eyes were trained on her evenly. "Do you remember my brother?"

"It feels like a lifetime ago, but I do remember you and your brother." Isabel fisted her hands and looked out the window, hoping Nathaniel would arrive home early. "I do recall John asking about you and how you had come to Burnet County after reading of my father's death. Which was so very kind of you, but rather curious as to why you had traveled so far to offer your condolences, but then disappeared so abruptly. I know John was dismayed by your leaving."

"Were you as well, Isabel?" Becky asked.

"Dismayed by your leaving?" Isabel's temper rose. "I do remember you as a very lovely girl and your brother cherished you. I certainly hoped you were well. There had been abductions in the county, but John had gone to town to find you and was told you were on your way to Louisiana."

John stepped forward and Isabel sensed his apprehension. She

358

wondered, *why hadn't he listened to Nathaniel?*

"We can come back another day, Isabel. Becky mentioned you were nearly betrothed to her brother and his death must have been quite a blow to you as it was to Becky. The last thing, Becky and I would want is to cause you any distress. Isn't that true, Beck?" John said, reaching for the young woman's hand.

"John is correct. I hadn't even given thought to how hard this would be for you. Please forgive me. The loss of your father is enough to overcome without dredging up old sorrows," said Becky. "Perhaps another day before I return home to Connecticut. A picnic, possibly? Wouldn't that be lovely?"

"Certainly," said Isabel. Raphael began to cry then. It was unusual for him, but she was grateful for it, allowing her an excuse to usher them from her home. With a quick goodbye, she then hastened to her baby.

After he settled, Isabel decided she would wait on the porch for Nathaniel to come home, sitting in the rocker with Raphael in her arms, and again remembered how happy she was, while giving no more thought to Lieutenant Quinton Cullen or the dread rising in her or the worry for John, uncertain of Rebecca Cullen's intentions.

But still she could not keep her concerns at bay, feeling her throat closing and the pinch of tears at her eyes, and just as she was about to cry, Nathaniel rode into view toward her, his hand lifted, smiling. Entranced by him and certain he would be forever her saving grace, her blessed Nathaniel, she shut her eyes in prayer, thanking God for him and Raphael, and before she opened them, she felt herself being lifted to her feet while still holding the baby in her arms. He hugged them both while he kissed them, her on the lips with such intent, she was at once unburdened, caring only about what they had then and there, together.

She remembered the potatoes and corn and string beans as well as the beef roasting in the fire pit and she handed Raphael to Nathaniel and kissed her husband hard on the mouth for a very long time, loving him so much she could barely breathe, and she stood a moment at the threshold and took in the image of him holding his son as he rocked and sang a Cheyenne lullaby.

Twilight was near, and the stars and moon would soon circle the earth and the days and months would pass as well and they would love each other always and would live life as Jane had bidden in accordance with the proper order of seasons. Isabel blew out the last candle lamp and climbed the stairs. Smiling when she heard Nathaniel calling out to her.

About the Author:

Kimberly Baker Jacovich lives in Connecticut with her husband, son and daughter. This is her first published novel. Her other novels and writings can be found at her website: www.brookdalepark.blogspot.com and www.thewingedflight.blogspot.com You can follow her on Instagram @kimberly_seasonsina1916home and @thewingedflight and on Facebook – Kimberly Baker Jacovich.

Made in the USA
Middletown, DE
22 April 2022